GU01018516

Christina Wieland was born in Cyprus but spent most of her adult years in London. She is a practising psychoanalyst and psychotherapist and the author of two books on psychoanalysis and society. This is her first novel.

For my parents and grandparents

Christina Wieland

UNDER THE CAROB TREE

AUSTIN MACAULEY PUBLISHERS™

LONDON * CAMBRIDGE * NEW YORK * SHARJAH

Copyright © Christina Wieland 2024

The right of Christina Wieland to be identified as author of this work has been asserted by the author in accordance with sections 77 and 78 of the Copyright, Designs and Patents Act 1988.

All rights reserved. No part of this publication may be reproduced, stored in a retrieval system, or transmitted in any form or by any means, electronic, mechanical, photocopying, recording, or otherwise, without the prior permission of the publishers.

Any person who commits any unauthorised act in relation to this publication may be liable to criminal prosecution and civil claims for damages.

This is a work of fiction. Names, characters, businesses, places, events, locales, and incidents are either the products of the author's imagination or used in a fictitious manner. Any resemblance to actual persons, living or dead, or actual events is purely coincidental.

A CIP catalogue record for this title is available from the British Library.

ISBN 9781398498044 (Paperback)
ISBN 9781398498051 (ePub e-book)

www.austinmacauley.com

First Published 2024
Austin Macauley Publishers Ltd®
1 Canada Square
Canary Wharf
London
E14 5AA

Table of Contents

Chapter 1
Limassol 2010

The silence of the evening enveloped Marina like a good old friend. Sitting on Nellie's bed, in Nellie's room in June 2010, the evening after Nellie's funeral, after all the guests left and the last kiss was given and returned and the last promise to come and visit again faded away, Marina felt the silence of the house embracing her and the presence of so many loved dead hovering in the empty rooms. The house that appeared so many times in her dreams and memories all those years that she spent abroad was enveloped in silence.

The house was only 100 yards from the seafront—a mere two minutes' walk. On stormy nights, you could hear the waves thrashing the old walls of the promenade, splashing on the tarmac, where they formed small pools of sea water that dried in the sun the next day leaving behind salt crystals that sparkled in the sunlight. On calm nights, you could just about hear the gentle lapping of the water on the rocks that lulled the senses into a dream drenched sleep.

The house on Aristotelous Street belonged to Marina's grandparents. That's where her mother was born and where she had spent her childhood. For Marina this was her second home, often more of a home than her own home. Here she spent long afternoons and weekends and summers with grandparents, and auntie Nellie and Anna. Strictly speaking, Anna was also an "auntie" like auntie Nellie, her mother's sister. But Anna could not be an "auntie", Anna was a child, she felt, just like her, a child looked after by grandmother all day long.

The house was on Aristotelous street, number 11 Aristotelous street. The name kept the four-year-old Marina awake on endless lunchtime siestas when everybody was asleep and the house was like a 'morgue'. The name intrigued her. Why Aristotelous? Why not Aristoteles? She had been told by her father that Aristoteles was a great philosopher in ancient Greece, one of "our hallowed ancestors". But Aristotelous? Who was Aristotelous? And what or who was "our hallowed ancestors"?

The house was silent. Marina sitting on Nellie's bed in June 2010 became aware of the intense silence that embraced her. Despite the sounds coming from outside, a neighbour singing, a car passing, a distant dog barking, the silence was intense. *All gone*, Marina thought, *all gone*.

Nellie was the last of the family to depart at the age of ninety-five and three quarters. *She didn't make it to ninety-six*, Marina thought, *she could have lived to be hundred, if only she had used the zebra crossing.*

Suddenly the silence and the stillness were gone and the house was full of ghosts—benign, loving, garrulous ghosts, arguing, gesticulating, pushing for space, reading, writing, cooking, explaining, always explaining themselves, as if that was a matter of life and death. And now death had arrived and they were all gone. But still talking, talking, talking, words, words, words, unintelligible words. It was all too fast for Marina to catch. All too familiar, like a dream. She understood everything but it would be impossible to put it into words—bodies, laughter and tears.

Nellie's ninety-five years in this house, surrounded by these walls with the same scent of jasmine and amaryllis wafting through the window, and fried aubergines and the brewing of coffee, Marina thought. The same splash of blinding red blossoms on the pomegranate tree, the same palm tree swinging in the wind. Above all the same light, the same pale, blinding Mediterranean light that transformed objects into works of beauty to fascinate and seduce generations. And now she was back to this light, to this house, and Nellie was dead.

She was back to the endless siesta afternoons when she was imprisoned in her room on Aristotelous street in case she woke up the grown-ups who wanted their siesta sleep. And the puzzle of the name persisted. Aristoteles, Aristotelous. What did Aristotelous mean? Was he another philosopher? And what did philosopher mean? Why is everybody asleep at 2 in the afternoon and the house is like a morgue? And what did 'morgue' mean? She had heard it from grown-ups, "like a morgue", but she was not sure what it meant. "Silent as a morgue", she felt like a grown up just saying the word to herself. Why is everybody asleep at two in the afternoon and what is she supposed to do with herself as she was not allowed out? Aristoteles, Aristotelous—a real puzzle.

She wished the ice cream man would pass by on his bicycle. Then she could spend her two grosha to buy an ice cream through the window to the street. She had seen Alexandros doing this once. But no ice cream man was to be seen or heard. Aristoteles, Aristotelous, a real enigma. And her parents a long way away in the mythical land of England.

She was four years old and she had many questions not just about Aristoteles/Aristotelous, but about her parents and England, how far this England was and her parents choosing to leave her and her brother and go there. It's only for two months, they told her, it's a holiday. Another strange word—holiday. What was this? She was four years and two months old and the word meant nothing to her. She knew no other parents who had a 'holiday' in England. What did it all mean?

These were the questions she never asked but which swam in her little brain as she tried to entertain herself through the endless siesta hours when everybody was asleep and Alexandros was out with friends on the beach.

'Why can't I go with Alexandros?' she would ask repeatedly.

'You are too young,' grandmother said.

'You are too little,' Nellie said.

What sort of explanation is this, she thought but did not insist. Instead she waited patiently for the ice cream man to pass by and shorten the endless siesta hours.

All this was in 1948. When a couple of years later she asked again her father about Aristoteles/Aristotelous, he gave her an explanation that was even more peculiar. It's the same name, he had said, the same philosopher, there is only one Aristoteles, but Aristotelous was the genitive and Aristoteles was the nominative. Another puzzle—nominative, genitive. To make things even more incomprehensible her father had added that this was the archaic language, something called "katharevousa", and that in everyday language they used something called "demotiki". It would be different in "demotiki", he had added. She had to wait for another few years to understand all this, the archaic language and the everyday language and where England was. But why her parents chose to go to England for a holiday and leave their two children behind, this she could never understand.

And now it was 2010 and the last member of the family to die was Nellie. No more close relatives from that generation. She missed her chance to ask more questions, to clarify matters. She was away, living abroad in this distant land of

England, where her parents had disappeared for two months in 1948. She had missed her chance to find out more about everything.

But she had Nellie's diaries, all thirty of them, lying on the bed in three piles each one held together with a red ribbon. Nellie loved red, it was her favourite colour. She had red dresses, red skirts, red blouses, red shoes, red sunglasses, red scarves, red handbags.

'It's the colour of life,' she often told Olga, Marina's mother, who never wore red as far as Marina could remember. 'You should wear red and come alive.' Nellie often told her serious, subdued sister who preferred grey and blue and sometimes ochre. But mother died twenty years before Nellie, and Marina's memory of her was fading.

And characteristically, her mother's diaries, that she had entrusted to Nellie, were held together by a blue ribbon. Only one pile of them, just five volumes compared to the thirty of Nellie's. It was the way she remembered her mother—self-effacing, few words and no nonsense.

With auntie Nellie dead Marina had nobody to direct her questions to, or to listen to old stories. That was it, that was the end of the Aristophanous family. Now she had to read the diaries to find answers to so many questions and secrets and half told stories and hidden truths.

Her father in his last two years when he lay in bed half blind he used to tell her stories from his childhood and teenage years, stories he never told her before. She could now piece together a whole life. Her father's early life, her mother's early life—two so different lives coming together to create her and Alexandros.

She stopped her ruminations and looked around the room. The sun coming through the prism at the corner of the top window spread a rainbow on the wall. Nellie's room was tidy and quaint, as she had always known it. Strange to know that she will never see her again sitting on the bed and examining one of her dresses, trying to decide whether it was the right one to wear on that particular day, for that particular occasion. At ninety-five Nellie was still meticulous about her appearance, the right dress with the right shoes and the matching bag and the matching sunglasses. 'Only peasants do not care to match their accessories' she often said, or implied. All this care and meticulousness, Marina thought, and now she was gone.

They are all gone, Marina thought. First grandfather, 50 odd years ago. Then Anna, dear, dear disabled, child-like, always present Anna. Then grandmother. People said that she could not live long without Anna, they were together in a symbiotic love/torture life sentence. In fact she lived a few years after Anna's death always tortured by guilt that she had to send Anna to an institution for the last year of her life, when grandmother was already ninety years old. Then her own mother was taken away suddenly, unexpectedly. Then father who never quite started a new life after his wife's death, and continued to protest that he depended on nobody, that he was sufficient to himself and so on. And finally, finally Nellie, the last to go. The house would now be silent for ever.

There were distant sounds—birds fighting, cars passing by, people singing, arguing, talking. But the room was silent, even if it was full of sounds. That's how she remembered the evenings with grandmother, a little four-year-old, six-year-old, and ten-year-old Marina. She and grandmother sitting together on the veranda, absorbing the scent of jasmine and amaryllis and above all the silence. It could not have been for very long, as the house was always alive with arguments, demands, singing or crying or piano playing or mere petulant misunderstandings. But there were those moments between noise and noise, those moments on the veranda, the moments of silence. Perhaps everybody was out, perhaps Anna was with the nuns, perhaps Aristos was with his unlikely friend the Jehovah witness.

Marina looked at the picture that was hanging between the twin beds: Jesus the Shepherd carrying a lamb wrapped around his shoulders. Nellie insisted, until the end of her life at the age of ninety-five to sleep in her twin bedroom, complete with two single beds, two wardrobes, two side tables, two side lamps and two armchairs all matching. As if she had been always waiting for the man of her life to come and take his place next to her. Marina thought that she had never given up. She always waited. In her nineties, she still waited.

On the other wall, at a right angle to Nellie's bed, a reproduction of Titian's painting of Aktaion and Diana, with its mixture of voluptuous nude women and primitive male terror and desire, hung in a heavy frame dominating the room.

The painting showed young Aktaion standing in amazement at the entrance to Diana's cave, gazing awestruck at all the naked nymphs who in all their innocence and isolation were bathing by a pool, ignorant of male desire. Aktaion's body language shows him simultaneously moving forward and moving backward. The desire and the terror seem to mix in this young man trying to stop himself from entering Diana's sacred forbidden place, but finding it was already too late as he found himself already there, already a trespasser. The tragedy had already been written. What was done could not be undone.

Marina took a moment to recall the tragic death of Aktaion who, hunting with his dogs, had strayed into Diana's sacred cave and saw what no mortal male had ever set sight on: Diana's and her nymphs' nakedness.

Diana's revenge when it came was hideous. The fierce virgin goddess transformed Aktaion into a stag. Marina remembered her reading of Ovid as a teenager, the amazement and the terror as she read the tragic transformation of Aktaion by the virgin goddess: 'She lengthened his neck, brought the tips of his ears to a point, changed his hands to feet, his arms to long legs and covered his body with a dappled skin. Then she put panic and fear in his heart as well.'

Marina sat motionless looking at the moment before the transformation as Aktaion was at the entrance of the cave and no return was now possible. And then the cruel fate of Aktaion as his own faithful hounds tore him to pieces and he tried to say to them 'I am Aktaion don't you know your master?' but the words would not come and the hounds sank their teeth into his body 'till there was no place left for tearing.'

Marina thought of her grandfather, Nellie's father, the stern, upright male tyrant of the family, her fear of him, the fear of the whole family of women, their submission to him, their lies and subterfuges that enabled them to get away with subversion. She thought, as she was gazing at Titian's painting, of the big secret at the heart of males, the terror of dismemberment, the terror of disintegration in the hands of a woman. Nellie, sweet, vulnerable, unreal Nellie with her head full of romantic heroines and patriotic slogans, myths and lies, with her fighting spirit still intact at the age of ninety five, never dented by reality, formidable Nellie who somehow guessed the secret at the heart of this Greek myth—guessed but was never able to articulate it as she continued to fight battles with windmills and phantom armies.

Nellie never talked about the painting. It seemed to have been a remnant of her series of trips to London in the '50s with her sister and her brother-in-law and her regular visits to the National Gallery. For a few moments, Marina found herself contemplating Nellie's contradictory nature, her rebellious yet submissive nature, eccentric and utterly conventional, man-hating and man-idealising. Somehow it all made sense now.

Nellie's appearance had always struck everybody as exuding both eccentricity, conventionality, and vulnerability. She dressed with taste and always within the latest fashion but she would use some ornament, a scarf, a pendant, eccentric shoes or eccentric sunglasses that made her mark. There was always something that would distinguish her from the rest of her friends. And there was a steely determination to go on fighting, even when this made her appear like some neurotic female spinster. Yet very few people took her seriously and there were many jokes at her expense among the extended family as Marina knew very well.

Marina had always been very fond of auntie Nellie while at the same time feeling exasperated by her, her absolute beliefs, her inability to see another person's point of view, her being imprisoned in her own manufactured world of dreams, beliefs and patriotism. She existed in a world of absolute good and absolute evil. Nellie took it upon herself to defend single-handedly this world as if she were on some divine mission that had been entrusted onto her. This world being so abstract and so ossified, never changed. It was the same in 1938, when Nellie wrote her famous article published in the local paper on the rights of women, as in 1962 when Marina left the island to go to university, as it was in 2010 when Nellie died. Fired by this sense of mission she seemed to ignore the rest of humanity.

Not that she was asocial or anti-social. On the contrary, she had scores of friends and had an unquenchable thirst for fun—music, dancing, cinema, tea parties, theatre (if there was anything at all going on which at times there wasn't), opera (when foreign companies toured the island), ballet (again relying on foreign input). It was incumbent that she should go out every single day, meet friends, do something exciting. She had not developed the ability to miss things or allow herself to be disappointed and was therefore always dissatisfied.

Marina looked at the lemon tree outside Nellie's room. 'It's getting old,' she thought. Some of the branches had died already and were left untrimmed, side by side, with the lush green branches that bore fruit and blossoms at the same time. The scent of the blossoms wafted through the open window and took her back, a long way back to childhood's mythical times. Grandma distilling orange and lemon blossoms.

'Go and pick the orange blossoms that have fallen to the ground Marinoulla. Here is a bag to put them in. It would be a shame to go to waste. Go.'

Marina loved grandma's blossom water. Grandma would wash her face and hands with it, every morning and every evening before she went to bed. Blossom water smelled of grandmother. Together with the scent of amaryllis, jasmine and gardenias it was part of Marina's memory of grandmother.

The lemon and orange orchard, the pomegranate trees and the generous vine, providing ample shade and juicy grapes (not to mention the vine leaves for cooking) were imprinted in Marina's brain long after the fruit orchard had been sold to developers and had been transformed into a five-storey building of twenty flats and an underground parking space. The house itself however lived on in its original incarnation, bearing its decline and anachronism with pride and dignity, reminding the world of another, more leisurely time.

Marina forgot about the tragic fate of Aktaion and listened again to the silence of the house and the sounds that invaded the room through the silent decades—grandmother helping Anna to wash and Anna getting angry with grandmother's haste. Anna's protests which consisted of incoherent sounds sometimes culminating in a word "sssstop" or "ennnnnough". Grandmother would stop and say something like "we can't be here all day". Olga would intervene and say something like 'can I help Anna?' and Anna would panic in case her mother would give up and allow Olga to do it. Anna accepted only grandmother as a carer which put an enormous burden on grandmother's shoulders.

Nellie was in front of the mirror combing her thick hair and trying different ways of arranging it. It was a daily ritual that the 4-year-old Marina knew very well. She would sit on the small sofa at the end of the bedroom and watch Nellie in her self-absorbed activity, fascinated by the lazy, leisurely act and the gestures that accompany it that seemed never to end. So different from mother, so fascinating and self-indulgent.

At times, Nellie would let her dig her hands into her treasure box, the box with the elaborate carvings that contained Nellie's colourful necklaces and earrings and pendants. Nellie would let her try them on and Marina pretended to be a princess getting ready for the royal ball.

In those early days, her life was divided between two houses—the house on the hill and the house near the sea. The house on the hill was the house with the carob tree that dominated the back garden. The "carob tree" of her childhood was actually four carob trees, four trees emanating from one root forming a square. The space in the middle was "her house". This was her kingdom, her territory. Adults and everybody else had to knock first to be let in. But Alexandros was for ever threatening invasion. Trespassing was not unusual as far as her older brother was concerned. He used to tease her about the sanctity of her "house" and how it was all nonsense. Thinking of it later in her teens, she wished she had possessed Diana's powers to guard her territory.

The carob tree was her house only when she and her babies were there. It was then that an empty space between four carob trees (which were in fact one carob tree) was her home, her sacrosanct space. At any other time, people were "allowed" to walk or stand or sit there. But when she and her dolls and teddies and animals—a lion, a toucan and a terrier were there, the magic was working, and the transformation was complete—the transformation of an ordinary carob tree into a magic place. What mysterious incantations, what secret formulas were pronounced to achieve this transformation? The mystery of the place did not allow these questions. It just was.

At lunchtime in the summer, Kyriakou would bring her lunch there. She would have her lunch at 12 noon, long before her dad would be back for lunch at 1.15 precisely. Dad had one of the first cars in the town and he would go and come back in the car. But 3-year old Marina was hungry long before this time. So Kyriakou would bring the food—moussaka, macaroni, bean ragout, rice and meatballs or red mullet fish (her favourite) with freshly fried chips—and after knocking at the door and being formally admitted she would sit down on a stool beside Marina and feed her like a baby. 'This one for mummy,' 'this one for daddy,' 'this one for grandma.' Grandfather, the scary, distant grandfather was never mentioned. 'One for auntie Nellie,' 'one for brother Alexandros,' 'one for auntie Anna.'

The carob tree was teeming with cicadas singing themselves to death. The carob fruit in the summer heat hanging like long earrings from a big lady. She and her brother used to eat them. Mother told them again and again that they were pig food but they ate them all the same, the honey spurting out as soon as you broke one into two was delicious they insisted. Time extended for ever. Hot June mornings. The acacias in decline, their dead white flowers still hanging from the trees. The yellow grass and the harvested fields that heralded summer.

She would wander in the big garden that seemed to extend for ever—one third of it turned into a kitchen garden, one third into flower beds with marigolds and zinnias and hibiscus and oleanders splashing their colours in the blinding light. The last third was left wild, nobody having the time or the will to turn it into something civilised. The cats wondered there catching insects and geckos, sometimes snakes.

The house was situated at the end of the town on top of a hill. Only wheat fields and olive trees and of course the ever-present carob trees extended from there on to the next village 20 minutes away. From the upstairs window, you could see the dark blue ribbon of the sea extending into the horizon. And the wind was always singing or howling. Yet it was only 10 minutes' walk to the house on Aristotelous Street, ten minutes which her mother, Kyriakou, Alexandros and Marina walked every single afternoon. The mornings belonged to the house on the hill, the afternoons to the house on Aristotelous street, grandmother's house as they called it. The two houses summarised Marina's early years.

Thirty years later she took her husband on his first trip to the island to show him the house of her childhood, the house of her waking dreams. They had brought their little baby girl with them to meet her grandparents. Marina was so eager to reminisce, to share with Alan her early days, her early magic. When they arrived at the spot where the house ought to be, she felt quite confused. For a moment, she thought she was at the wrong place. She thought she got confused and took her husband to the wrong spot. Where was the house? Where were the fields, the olive trees, the acacias? Where was the carob tree?

A huge roundabout spanning five streets took most of the space with cars and motorbikes zooming at alarming speeds, creating a haze of emissions and smells and a jungle of noise, revving, hooting, breaking, shouting, swearing, cursing. And where the house once stood, there was now a new, official looking imposing building. When she went closer, she could read: Courts of Justice. You could still see the blue ribbon of the sea from the top of the hill through cars and lorries and the blue haze of the exhausts.

Marina was trying to cross the road with little Anita on the sling and Alan holding her hand. Cars zoomed by in a cruel, unconcerned way, unregulated, totally oblivious to their little, vulnerable family. Pedestrians were totally unwanted in this part of the city.

Later on, lying in auntie Nellie's house, the whole house silent during the siesta time, with Alan and Anita out on the beach, she lay awake. Images, fantasies, real episodes and vague memories crowded her mind. Mornings in June. Alexandros at school. She had mother to herself. She must have been three, she thought. Bits of life, bits of colour, bits of words. Mother pushing the buggy downhill—towards the sea, the sun burning on her skin. Getting up from the buggy—no, no, I want to walk. I am not a baby anymore. Walking and pushing the empty buggy. She was big. She was big. Nobody on the road. Only she and mother.

The sea was restless. Foam and spray on her face. The fishermen had laid out their nets on the pebbles to dry. Strong smell of fish. She could not swim then. She played and paddled in the shallow water, her skin full of salt and sun, mother beside her. Then to the Municipal Gardens—an oasis of pine trees, palm trees and eucalyptus. Water in small artificial ponds, colourful fish and exotic birds in the aviary.

Marina was brought back by the church bells that announced the evening mass. Time had slipped through her fingers and she realised that the sun had gone and there was a chill in the air and the sky had turned yellow and pink. She realised that she was holding the box where Nellie had kept her numerous diaries and she thought that her job had just begun.

She now turned her attention to the third picture on Nellie's wall, the one opposite her bed. It was a print of a well-known painting, present in every classroom, in every school on the island (at least in all the schools Marina had attended, which were of course Greek schools) declaring the island's Greek roots. It was a picture of Palaion Patron Germanos (the archbishop of Old Patras) raising the Greek flag and in this way declaring the beginning of the Greek Revolution in 1821. The picture was so well known that Marina had never really looked at it carefully. She now turned her attention to it and for the first time scrutinised it. The picture showed an elderly Clergyman, dressed in the black clerical robes of the Greek Orthodox Church and surrounded by a dozen men all dressed in the traditional Greek "foustanella" and saluting the flag which was raised by the Clergyman, a flag that Marina did not recognise as Greek. The body language was one of fervour, elation and deep emotion. Next to it there was another print that Marina was not well acquainted with although it had been hanging on Nellie's wall for decades. *It was a less well-known painting depicting the same archbishop blessing the* flag. Next to him on his right is a figure recognisable as Jesus and on his left was what could only be the Virgin Mary blessing the flag. These three figures were surrounded by the well-known heroes of the Greek revolution. They had all raised their thumb and the two fingers touching in a symbolic gesture of the Trinity. The picture put the painting securely into a Nationalist/Christian framework. This was a revolution for freedom and for Christianity blessed by the archbishop and by Jesus and Mary against the oppression and slavery by the Muslim Turks.

It suddenly occurred to Marina that in all her early years nobody ever mentioned the fact that there was a substantial Turkish minority on the island. The certainty with which the island was "Greek" was absolute.

The picture expressed another one of Nellie's striking characteristics—her fervent nationalism, her passionate feelings about classical Greece and about the new order that was to come one day that would include the island as part of this great nation—Greece. The times of Homer, the times of Pericles, the times of Byzantium. and the times of the declaration of the Greek Revolution merged into one with the island's perpetual struggle for *enosis*—union with the motherland. Poetic expressions like the re-unification of Greece's "last child" with the motherland were abundant in Marina's childhood, as well as the labelling of people as "traitors" if they had any doubts about the possibility of this.

The three pictures expressed Nellie's three sides that exposed the many contradictions in Nellie's personality—her naïve Christian beliefs, her love for European Art but also her ruthless feminism that was reflected in the fate of Aktaion, and her fervent nationalism, her passion for union with mother Greece. Marina contemplated this as she looked from one picture to the other.

The island lived under the Ottomans for 300 odd years until it was eventually leased to the British in 1878 who finally annexed it in 1914. Its fate was therefore different from the fate of other islands which joined the "motherland" at different times. The fate of this "abandoned child" of the Eastern Mediterranean was the cause of much conflict, violence and tragic events that developed during Marina's lifetime.

As Marina sat on Nellie's bed undoing the red ribbons that kept the diaries together, she thought about the last hundred or so years since the house was built.

Built in 1907 (the date proudly exhibited above the tall front door), the house was, like most family houses in that part of the city, a bungalow. It benefited (as any estate agent would have told you) from a large hall that could be used, but rarely was, as a sitting room, a living room of ample dimensions used only for grand family occasions and for receiving guests, but also used as a music room where the grand piano was proudly exhibited. There were 5 bedrooms, a dining room, a kitchen and a room next to the kitchen which could be described as "food preparation" room, or a larder, or both. One of the bedrooms was used as grandfather's study, complete with a heavily carved huge desk that dominated the room, a heavily carved armchair and a couple of less haughty armchairs. There were three big free-standing bookshelves with glass protecting the leather-bound volumes. The two huge windows were protected by iron bars apart from the heavy wooden shutters. The house was a physical manifestation of the standing of the family of Aristos Aristophanous, a family that extended back a few generations of educated upright citizens, but which by the time Marina was 6 years old in 1950 had neither wealth nor a particularly high status apart from its own self-esteem and the many family stories told and retold. Marina's great grandfather had been a judge at the time of Ottoman rule and family legend had it that the Turkish governor in the 1870s was so pleased with his lack of corruption and his fair rulings that he offered him as a special gift a mountain in the region of the Troodos mountains. The story goes that the judge Aristides thanked the governor but declined the gift saying that it would be useless to him, how on earth was he ever going to get from Limassol to this mountain and in any case what use was a mountain to him? The story had been circulated among the family of grandchildren and great grandchildren as they were sitting under the pine trees in the mountain of Troodos for their summer holiday in 1951, and wished that the great grandfather had accepted the mountain and wondered what it would be like to own a whole mountain to themselves.

The Aristos children were brought up with stories like this about their illustrious grandfather who was called according to another ancient story the "just Aristides" evoking the ancient Athenian statesman famous for his just rulings. The rest of the ancient story was not told however and Marina learnt it later at school, how for instance the ancient Athenian judge fell victim to his own good name and uncorrupted mind and to the envy of those who could not tolerate it. And how the Athenian citizens voted to ostracise him because they were too fed up of his "just" rulings.

Surrounded by illustrious Greeks from all ages and tragic mythological heroes and Nellie's red dresses and, shoes and sunglasses and Nellie's diaries and red ribbons, Marina fell into a reverie as the dusk began to fall and Nellie's bedroom was full of shadows and phantasms and past and present merged into one.

Chapter 2
Limassol 1935

A Game of Tennis

In 1935, Nellie was 22 years old and her illustrious grandfather had been dead for 32 years. Her father, the stern and fearful Aristos, had in no way the reputation or the salary of his father. The family had to be content with the salary and the status of "Deputy Director" of the Bank of Greece, a position that sounded grander than the salary that went with it. With two marriageable daughters and not much dowry apart from a few pieces of land and a third disabled daughter, Aristos' nights were full of anxious thoughts. Having had such an illustrious person as his father, Aristos felt always inadequate and never quite reaching the real or imaginary expectations that he was brought up with. His sense of responsibility was endless and crippling. His manner, at best formal and remote, at worst intimidating or straightforward frightening, alienated his whole family. His children were afraid of him and his wife connived with the children to avoid his fury. A conspiracy of women was at work in this household, on the surface an obedient wife and obedient children, but scratch the surface and a whole secret society was at work.

At 22, Nellie was a dreamy young woman steeped in English, French and Russian romantic novels and in the new ideas about the emancipation of women arriving on the island via some educated graduates returning to the island after some years abroad, and some enlightened members of the press writing articles about what was happening in Europe at the time. Spending a great deal of her time fighting an autocratic father Nellie had no idea what the world around her was like. Her main ideals came from romantic novels written in faraway lands and cultures. At 22, her world was populated by heroes and heroines from these books—Prince Andrei, Mr Darcy, Emma Bovary, Elizabeth Bennett, Anna Karenina.—a mish mash of foreign women. Educated at the convent school that brought up eligible middle-class young women to speak at least three languages and play at least one instrument, she thought she was more educated than she was. In fact, education was the banner under which the family, like any other middle-class family, lived.

Nellie was strikingly beautiful. Her blonde hair, unusual for the island, and her white, almost translucent, skin made her stick out among her brunette sisters and friends. She was given to devising elaborate hairstyles that imitated engravings of 19th century women seen in old books. Her sensitive, if technically imperfect, rendition of Chopin's Nocturnes made her piano playing one more of her assets as an eligible young woman. Next to her rather plain and mundane, some would say "realist", older sister, Olga, she shined like a diamond on a heap of coal.

That Saturday afternoon in April 1935 Nellie and her sister Olga were due at the tennis club in the Municipal Gardens at 3 in the afternoon. There was however one major obstacle to this enterprise and this was Aristos. Aristos was guarding his daughters like a jailer guards his prisoners. For instance, there were bars in the windows that opened onto to the street. These were apparently there to keep burglars out, but the girls joked that this was for them not to escape at night and go and find their beloved. And this joke contained more truth than they knew.

Going out in the evening, apart from visiting relatives with their mother, was out of the question. Exceptions could be made if Thalia would take them, say to a concert at the Rialto theatre, or at the Town Hall, and collect them afterwards. At times, an aunt or uncle would perform this function. But these were rare occasions. Evenings were spent either at home, reading, playing the piano – that was especially Nellie and Thalia – and listening to news as the family gathered around the wireless. However, despite all the restrictions, a great deal went on behind Aristos' back. A pact between mother and daughters to deceive Aristos made life more bearable for the two girls and for their mother as well. A game of tennis was one of these occasions where mother and daughters devised complicated manoeuvres to avoid being detected by Aristos' ever watching eyes.

Tennis was coming into fashion in Limassol in the 1930s as a middle-class sport, mainly played by men. However, a number of progressive women were joining timidly, or sometimes ostentatiously, proclaiming their independence. Watching highlights of the doubles at Wimbledon on the cinema screen had become a talking subject for well-informed people to show off their knowledge of what went on far away from these shores.

Tennis courts were of course a meeting point between young men and women and, for both Olga and Nellie, the pinnacle of the week. The Aristos girls, fuelled by a rebellious nature possibly inherited through their mother, were among the first few women to embrace the sport. And for this pleasure a whole charade began on Saturday afternoon at 2.30 at home. Dressed in their demure midi skirts that hid the shorter tennis skirts underneath and accompanied by their mother, Nellie and Olga left the house apparently to visit their relatives at the other side of the town. At the end of the road, they turned left apparently to go the cousin's house, but once out of sight they turned into a side street and through a maze of narrow streets they turned towards the opposite direction which eventually led to the municipal park. Mother and daughters being very excited by the conspiracy and the deceit of Aristos and, slightly frightened with the idea that this deceit could one day be discovered, giggled and chatted endlessly, and hurried through the narrow, old streets.

At the gates of the park, they said goodbye to their mother and agreed to meet her at the same spot again in one and half hours inside those gates. Thalia proceeded towards the playground where women sat and watched their children play and run and scream and shout and quarrel and found her usual place on a bench at the edge of the playground. Her distant cousin Calliope was already there knitting as usual. The bench had the benefit of having a good view of the tennis courts which were about 20 metres away. Women, mothers and aunts and grandmothers, sat and watched over the children, doing their knitting or embroidery or simply chatting to each other and exchanging the latest gossip.

The two young women hurried through the eucalyptus lined path to the ladies' toilets where, having got rid of their skirts and having put them safely in the big bags they carried with them, they proceeded to take off their black shoes and to replace them with the white tennis shoes. In their white short skirts, their white tops and their white tennis shoes they headed towards the tennis courts. On arriving at the tennis courts, the usual exchange of welcoming greetings, smiles and handshakes followed. The two young men, who were their tennis partners, handed them their tennis racquets which completed the Aristos girls' transformation. They were now among friends, men and women, all dressed in white shorts and skirts chatting and laughing and ready to begin the game.

There were two tennis courts side by side and eight players, four men and four women playing side by side. This was Nellie's idea of freedom. She could have been anywhere in the world—Paris, London, Vienna. She could pretend to be there, in these famous faraway places. This was freedom and culture— freedom to move, be and do whatever you liked. Away from Aristos' straightjacketed upbringing, Nellie could live out the novels she was steeped in.

To be fair she knew she was not that good at tennis. The whole thing was a bit of a charade for boys and girls to meet, flirt and perhaps fall in love and get married. Although Nellie never quite put it into words, she considered herself a cross between Emma Bovary and Georges Sand. The Georges Sand in herself was crystallised in the idea of an article, a revolutionary article, that she was going to write for the local newspaper one day. This article would revolutionise the relations between men and women and would elevate Nellie to a writer. Fired by ideas of freedom known only in the literary circles of Paris and London, Nellie confused the world of romance with the limited clandestine freedom obtained by the conspiracy of women in the Aristos household.

In 1935, the ideas about a girl's honour were unchallenged on the island. The loss of "honour" was a euphemism for the loss of virginity and the loss of a girl's honour was of course extended to the whole family. It was not unheard of that fathers and brothers, mainly in the small isolated villages in the mountains, would "do their duty" that is would kill the girl's lover, the man who disgraced and dishonoured the whole family. This was not only revenge but an attempt to take back the lost honour. The fight was between men, and often seducing somebody's daughter was a revenge against a father or brother who had injured in some way the pride of another man. However, more often than not there was no blood shed, and despite the hatred that raged between men, the "bastard" who had disgraced her was not killed, but on the contrary was forced to marry the girl to save the family's honour.

There was a story circulating in the family in the 1960s, when Olga and Nellie were in their fifties and Marina was 20 years old. The story concerned Olga as a sixteen-year-old girl in the late 1920s—when the word teenager had not yet been invented. Sixteen-year-old girls were supposed to behave with dignity and purity and not let themselves be touched by men. The story goes that 16-year-old Olga had apparently one day swum too far into the sea and found herself being carried further and further away from the shore by strong currents. She began to panic and fearing for her life she began to scream for help. A young fisherman hearing Olga's cries for help jumped into the sea and dragged Olga to his boat. The story however does not stop there. Apparently when the young fisherman brought Olga home at last, drenched, weak and in a state of confusion, Aristos was furious. 'You let that man touch you,' he screamed at the shivering girl. 'You'd better be dead.' In the '60s, when the story was repeated as an anecdote, the whole family would laugh in disbelief at Aristos' moral cruelty and Olga would say 'yes, that was how it was.' The story reaching Marina's innocent teenage ears in the '60s sounded absurd, funny and horrific all in equal measure. The story was usually told with humour and disbelief—'that's what your grandfather was like' the caption went. 'Can you believe it?'

To be sure the late 1950s and '60s were years of change and confusion. Unlike the 1930s, in the '60s nobody was quite sure what was allowed for young girls and what was not—at least the liberal middle-class citizens educated in Europe and reading European literature felt more liberal. They wanted to be liberal and be seen to be liberal. At the same time, who would marry their daughters or their sisters if they were too liberal? Educated middle class felt divided inside themselves and utterly confused. They did not really believe in the archaic morality of their parents, but the social price for being seen to be too liberal was to be reckoned with.

Marina reading Nellie's diaries in 2010, sitting on Nellie's bed, in Nellie's room which had been unchanged for 40 years, thought of her own upbringing and her own confusion growing up in the '50s and '60s. But the '30s were not a time of confusion. In 1935, Nellie and Olga knew exactly what was expected of them. At the same time, they had read enough French, English and Russian novels to know that theoretically at least life could be different. Inside each of them there was a rebel in waiting.

Olga was the older sister, serious, reserved and realistic about her chances in life. Olga let go only when she played tennis, or when she swam in the sea, or gone for long, adventurous walks in the mountains with a group of aunts and cousins. And now the game had begun. The girls excited by the sunburnt, sweaty, muscular young men excelled themselves running, intercepting, volleying and letting small feminine cries escape their lips as they returned a particularly forceful ball. This was the peak of the week, Saturday afternoon in the winter, spring and autumn months when the heat was bearable they could escape the constraints of home and Aristos and the boredom of it all and get to know the excitement of sport, competition and a vague strange feeling that they did not feel anywhere else and which they could name much later as sexual attraction.

The word sex had of course no place in their vocabulary. It was not clear whether they knew its exact meaning. Love, passion, even seduction was known to them through the romantic novels they had read and continued to read. Their own sexual awakenings were vague and confusing. They did not know what they wanted, or what they were seeking. They wanted love, affection, warmth, admiration, affirmation. Like any of Jane Austen's heroines, they wanted a husband who would love them and give them a new home away from the stern, joyless Aristos. A home of their own, their own household, their own children. Yet it was all hazy and confused. They were 22 and 24 and they were treated like children. Obedience and modesty were the prime virtues.

Yet it was not all doom and gloom. Thalia, their mother, was a blithe spirit that filled their lives with love and hope. Coming from a less haughty, less educated and more artistic, family she was much more easy-going and cared more about being happy rather than being upright. Thalia's father was an importer of "good food and good wine". Among his imports was caviar from Russia, port wine from Spain, red wine from Italy and foie gras from France. The family could be classified as middle, middle class (to be distinguished from the upper middle class where the Aristos family thought they belonged to) and as such was keen to prove their credentials by education and a suitable marriage for their children. Education in music and foreign languages plus a generous dowry were the girls' equipment for a suitable marriage to an eligible man from the upper middle class. And who would be better eligible than Aristos, the son of the judge.

To be sure Aristos did not do as well as expected. Not because of any fault of his, but because his father died suddenly, prematurely of a heart attack. Aristos was at Athens University at that time, a second-year student of Law. The tragedy of this event is difficult to understand from Marina's vantage point in 2010, but in 1895 when Aristos was 21 years old this personal trauma was at the same time a serious social, economic and educational setback. For it really meant the end of Aristos' studies at the university as the family's savings and the meagre widow's pension were just not enough to ensure his sister's dowry and his mother a modest life.

It is difficult to appreciate Aristos' predicament in its full impact. A young man of superior intelligence, aspiring to reach his father's juridical heights, is

27

suddenly called back to the island by a panicky and needy mother and a sister of marriageable age. He was now asked to take his father's role and be the head of the family. There was nothing he could do but obey. In any case, he had no independent means with which to finance his studies. All his dreams were in tatters, and his career too. Maybe also his hopes to marry a girl of equal social status.

Aristos' anger about the overturning of his fortunes and his feeling that life had treated him cruelly and unfairly could not find an outlet in real life. He felt bitter and cynical. The old man had snuffed it just in time to ruin my life, he thought. His anger for the old judge, his hatred about his austere, joyless life with its strict moral code that permitted no personal feelings of love or hate, all his convoluted feelings for the old dead man turned into depression.

Back on the island with his life in ruins, he had to attend to his mother's grief and his sister's need for a husband and most of all to the financial needs of the two women. Notwithstanding his depression he accepted a job offered by the Director of the Bank of Greece, an old friend of his deceased father. His dreams of becoming a renowned lawyer and, following in the steps of his father, maybe one day a judge, were for ever dead. The long path of re-adjusting his life and his ambitions had begun.

Thalia on the other hand had grown up in a happier and more joyful environment. The youngest daughter of Elengo and Anaxagoras, she grew up in a household where good food, good wine and appreciation of good life, was taken for granted. Money was not a problem as Anaxagoras did very well in his import/export business and the household was full of laughter, music and good things. Thalia was sent to the convent school where she learnt to speak fluent French and play the piano to quite an advanced level.

By the time she had reached 18, she was quite an accomplished pianist and by the time she met Aristos at 22 she was an elegant and well-presented young lady that could have come from any well-established upper middle-class family. She was small and delicate, full of "French finesse", as the person who introduced her to Aristos had previously told him. Having finished the Catholic Convent School she was fluent in French and straddled the gap between Europe, Greece and the Middle East, between the finesse of the French language and the harshness of the local dialect which no person from Greece could understand. In this sense, she spoke, like so many middle-class girls, at least three languages, the local dialect, the official Greek, and French.

It was probable her musical talent as well as her beauty, not to mention the considerable dowry that came with her, made this improbable marriage between Aristos and Thalia possible. By this time Aristos was 32 years old, handsome with a dark, depressed personality, morally upright, truly reminiscent of Mr Darcy in Pride and Prejudice which was a novel that Thalia and other girls of her age had read avidly. Only his Greek moustache and his dark chestnut hair put him definitively into the Mediterranean spectrum.

The depressed and pessimistic Aristos saw a ray of light as he was introduced to the talented and lively 22-year-old Thalia. Whether he was in love with her it was not something he had asked himself. What was true was that he was fascinated by this torrent of life that emanated from her and immersed himself in it, emerging out of his chronic depression and his pessimistic view of life.

Engagement followed and the house on Aristotelous street was built financed by Thalia's parents as part of Thalia's dowry. One could excuse the 22-year-old inexperienced and naïve Thalia for confusing this stern and dark man for the hero of her favourite book and falling madly in love with him. The couple married in 1907 and moved to the new house.

As Thalia made her way to the playground that was some 20 metres from the tennis courts and settled down to do her embroidery, her thoughts about Aristos, their initial meeting, the wedding and her abysmal disappointment that followed it, jostled in her mind. She was determined not to let Aristos ruin the girls' life and their chance to being happy the way he had ruined hers. She raised her eyes from her embroidery and followed the girls as they were approaching the tennis courts.

The initial greetings and chit chat were soon followed by the game itself. The players apart from Nellie and Olga were Evripides and Stavros. Evripides was the young scion of a very old and wealthy Limassol family which had begun the first industrial production of wine a few generations before. He was charming and comfortable in his skin and in his family wealth and in his new convertible car. He was in fact the quintessential playboy. Winning hearts, if not minds, was his speciality, especially women's hearts. But neither Thalia, nor the girls were aware of this special talent of his. All they knew was that he was the elder son of an established Limassol family and as such they were suitably impressed.

Looking good in his expensive casual clothes, or his tennis shorts, or his office shoes and silk tie was his constant preoccupation. Thalia was not aware of the subtleties of his personality and the name of his father was enough to reassure her of his good character. 'He comes from a good family' was the best recommendation one could have on the island.

And Stavros, the fourth player? Thalia did not know much about him except that he was a civil servant in the Public Works Department and that he was, as her cousin had eagerly informed her, of humble origins but nevertheless educated in London. The rumours that were circulating about him had him as a "rising star". Thalia did not exactly know what that meant but she had heard only good things about him, including from her cousin's husband, Sotiris, who was the owner and editor of the local newspaper. So, she concluded, it was all right for the girls to play tennis with him (under her discrete eyes of course). After all, he was a friend of Evripides, what more recommendation did one need?

Nellie and Olga exerted themselves on the tennis court. They were transformed, Thalia thought, from delicate young ladies that they were, to fearful amazons, full of pride and energy, full of competitive aggression. Thalia was trying to distinguish the features of the two young men but she could not, so she resigned herself to doing her embroidery and watching the action from a distance.

The two sisters, fascinated by both men were nevertheless pretending, like any well-bred young girls, to be totally unaware of the testosterone that flew towards them with every tennis ball and every cry of triumph or disappointment and electrified the atmosphere. Nellie was completely smitten by Evripides. Although fascinated by the attention Stavros paid to both sisters, her heart already belonged to Evripides. At night, she stayed awake in her room that she shared with her sister and, which in September was enveloped in the scent of jasmine coming through the open shutters, thinking of Evripides. Like a lover drowned in the scent of her beloved, Nellie absorbed the strong scent coming through the shutters at night and became full of the presence of Evripides—his suave smile, his eyes fixing her and pinning her like a collector pins a beautiful butterfly on a velvet background. Drunk with the scent of jasmine and her hormone-saturated dreams and fantasies Nellie tossed and turned in her bed and imagined a future full of love and bliss.

As the game progressed and it became clear that Olga and Stavros were winning Nellie looked yearningly at Evripides for a sign. He knitted his brows and pursed his lips in a childish expression which for Nellie was full of charm and secret love and, she thought, sent her a secret kiss.

At the end of the game, Thalia made her presence known by coughing aloud. Sitting under the eucalyptus trees she had waited patiently doing her elaborate embroidery which like Penelope's stitching never ended. Guarding the girls' honour was as much her job as her husband's. Livelier and more liberal than Aristos she had compromised with the girls. They can play tennis once a week, but she was going to sit a few yards away and watch over them discreetly, silently. Next to her Mrs Calliope, a distant cousin of hers, knitting a yellow pullover for her son, who was a student of Law at Athens university, was watching over her daughters playing at the next court. The secrecy from their husbands was essential. The women went on stitching and knitting, and exchanged news about their common acquaintances, friends, relatives, swapped recipes and complained mildly about their husbands' habits and peculiarities. Calliope was talking about her son's last letter from Athens and how much she missed him and how cold the winters in Athens were, 'nothing like here' she said, 'they are real continental winters and snow was not unknown either.' He needs a thick pullover, she added, I will finish it by next month and he can have it for the winter.

Waiting patiently for the girls to say their goodbyes and then change into their ordinary clothes in the women's toilets, they exchanged their last bits of news and got up slowly and reluctantly to go. Thalia treasured these leisurely afternoons under the eucalyptus trees and Mrs Calliope's company who, unlike many of her other cousins, was a discreet and gentle woman.

The sun was heading decisively towards the horizon and the few scattered clouds had turned pink and yellow. The playground was now silent and empty. Mothers and children had gone some time ago and Thalia and the girls headed for home getting prepared to tell Aristos an elaborate story about having been to some aunt or other at the end of the town.

Chapter 3
Marathasa 1907

Despite his meteoric career at the top of the civil service, despite his fame as an incorruptible and very competent servant of the British Empire and later of the new Republic, despite his popularity as a member of the Civil Servants Club, as the president of the Chess Society and twice champion of the whole island, despite being loved and admired by his whole family and friends—despite all the good fortune that surrounded him—Stavros thought of himself always as an orphan boy, abandoned by his father, taken in by his very poor grandmother, going to school without shoes and often going to bed hungry. Beneath the comfortable and pleasant manner, the benevolent attitude towards everybody, the liberal thinking and the philosophical mind, the happy and slightly superior attitude towards the world, the abandoned little boy was only skin deep.

In 1907, the year when the house in Limassol was built, the house that was the object of envy and admiration of the whole town at the time, and the house that was to be the residence of the Aristophanous family, another drama was unfolding in the distant mountain region of Marathasa. The region of Marathasa, in the mountains of Troodos, although in terms of actual distance was only some 45 miles away it was nevertheless light years away from Limassol and its comforts. Life here was at its most basic and raw. Here in the small villages dependent on the soil to give them enough to see them through the long, harsh winters, life was about survival. It was cruel and basic and governed by strong traditions and a strict moral code. Digress from these and you were better dead.

In this region, lost in the valleys of cascading hills and mountains, somewhere in the range of the Troodos mountains, forgotten by God and government, was the small village which Stavros called home. One evening in the summer of 1907, as the sun dropped behind the mountain range and the birds fell silent and a purple colour enveloped everything, and as a light breeze began to soften the heat of the day, the small family comprised of Christos, Eleni and the18-month-old Stavros were installed under the grapevine for their evening meal. A grapevine in the back or front garden was an indispensable necessity for a household. Grapevines were blessed by God to provide shade and coolness all through the hot summer months, as they formed a canopy of thick foliage under which the family could sit and enjoy a cool shade at noon and a soft breeze in the evening. Heavy grapes hang from it throughout the summer which, when they ripened in autumn, they would be served as fruit, used to make wine, and juice and make *soushouko,* the long sweets of grape juice and flour filled with almonds or walnuts that hang like sausages from hooks to dry in the sun. And, of course, vine leaves were available in generous supply to be used for cooking the delicious stuffed vine leaves that Eleni made once a week. Filled with rice and chopped onions and cooked in a rich tomato, lemon and cinnamon sauce, they provided a cheap and delicious meal.

The family had just finished their evening meal of beans, potato and celery casserole cooked in tomato sauce. Eleni served it with a generous portion of bread she made a couple of days before, a couple of raw onions, a huge tomato, the size of which was only known in the villages around, a cucumber and some olives accompanied by a carafe of spring water. They had already fed the few chickens they possessed, and they saw that they were locked securely into the chicken coop to protect them from the forays of foxes. They checked on the two pigs and the three goats and made sure the sheds were shut and secure. The two cats were asleep next to the baby cot and the shaggy mongrel breathed heavily in the evening heat, raising his ears and opening one eye every time a noise from the village below reached them, but falling back into a kind of lethargy immediately after.

It was a moment of peace. The day's work done, the animals fed, secure and asleep, their own belly full and content. Their baby asleep in the crib next to them, breathing quietly, peacefully, an angel sent from God himself. The rest of the village quiet, the busy-body, nosy women were at last silent, or almost silent, the cantankerous old men of the village already asleep. The silence of the mountains surrounded them like God's blessing. They did not talk. They felt quietly happy and content. Things were going well for them. The wheat did well this year and the walnuts and almonds were in abundance. They had smoked pork, sausages, potatoes and beans to last them through the winter. The aubergine and courgette plants kept producing more and more fruit. The onions were lying on a mat to dry for winter and they had already dried some of the tomatoes and some of the cherries. Dried cherries were a delicacy that one could sell in the various fairs in the mountains together with olives, almonds, walnuts, hazelnuts, raisins, sesame cakes and other delicacies.

Their peaceful evening was however full of anticipation. Eleni was in her ninth month of pregnancy and it was a matter of days now. Not that this anticipation stopped them from their ordinary activities. Eleni still worked, like any other woman in the village, in the fields all day, under a cruel temperature of 34C. This was a time when a great deal was needed to be done in the fields and on the slopes of the mountain where the vineyards were. Vegetables needed to be watered and constantly weeded, potatoes and onions needed to be picked and packed away, fruit like apples, peaches and figs needed to be picked, sorted out and sold to the people in the village who then sold them further away in the towns or bigger villages, grapes needed to be sprayed. Costas and Eleni worked side by side methodically without speaking apart from the most essential things to do with the work. Little Stavros was playing and exploring around them and every now and then Eleni would stop to pick him up, breast feed him and let him go again.

Around midday Eleni's mother, Elengo (or Elengou as she was known in the village), would sometimes arrive with some freshly cooked beans, bread and olives and they would stop for their lunch. She would feel Eleni's belly and add something about how many weeks or days were to go. Like an old hand—she had had eight pregnancies and five live children—she wanted to show off her wisdom on the subject. At other times, when Eleni's mother did not come, they had to content themselves with the food they brought with them which consisted of bread, olives, perhaps an onion and fresh water from the spring on the slope of the mountain which provided generously for all.

Eleni's mother owned one of the two small coffee shops in the village. In the summer, old men spent most of their day under the huge vine at the front of the shop drinking coffee, playing cards and gossiping, swearing or getting into endless rows with other old men. They cursed their wives, they complained about their sons, daughters and relatives and they thanked God for their good fortune all in one. Eleni's mother, used as she was to these contradictions, listened and smiled and served coffee and ouzo and sometimes when she felt generous accompanied them with some almonds and olives. She listened to the old men's stories and added some details or asked some questions. What went on in the village was exposed here in every detail.

Elengou was a widow; her husband having died prematurely in the asbestos mines of Amiantos where so many men from the village sought employment. The mines of Amiantos, some 20 miles from the village, were a mixed blessing for the people of the neighbouring villages. The mines provided employment to the villages starved of any other income apart from their own produce. On the other hand, the mines were the cause of death for so many. As the dangerous qualities of asbestos remained undiscovered in 1907 people considered the mines their saviour. So many men from the village would seek to supplement their income by working in the mines in winter when not much went on in the fields. They would leave their wives to look after children and animals and they would move to the snow-capped mountains of Troodos where the mines were.

With the mines, some sophistication entered the villages as they were situated not far from the main resort of Troodos and the miners came more and more in contact with people from the towns making their way to the top of the mountain. They also came in touch with the engineers who ran the company and heard stories about other places and other countries.

For instance, in 1907 it was not unusual for a person, man or woman, who grew up in the remote villages of Marathasa to die without seeing the sea. Although living on an island, the sea seemed light years away from the consciousness of these people in these remote regions in the mountains. Some of the villagers would of course travel to the towns, mainly for business, or because a relative may have moved there to try and make their fortune there. But this big undertaking lasted days on end relying on the donkeys to take them the 45 miles to Limassol.

For most of the villagers, the sea was something they knew from rumours and descriptions by people who had been there. The sea was this blue, endless lake which had no visible end. They tried to imagine it as they heard stories about fishermen and their boats, about voyages to foreign countries, about shipwrecks and marine tragedies. But it was as if these were happening in another country at another time. At the mines, people could talk to people who were from the coast, who had travelled by boat, who would even have swum in the sea and enjoyed its pleasures. This mythical entity of the sea began to become a reality. Elengou would come home with endless stories she heard at the coffee shop by men who had talked to other men who had talked to people from the cities near the sea. The mythical entity of this blue fluid element, this mysterious domain of a limitless expanse of water surrounded the little family like a miracle. Christos had already secretly decided that one day he would make the journey, he would see this miracle with his own eyes and touch it with his own body, he would perhaps move the family to one of the sea-side towns and change their whole soil-dependent life. People in the towns had "jobs" he heard, defined and clear-cut jobs, and they could go home in the evening with their wages and relax, go home to their clean, white painted houses with the green shutters, heavy front doors, indoor toilets and kitchens and a separate room where one could wash and shower.

Christos was a progressive man. He had spent a few winters in the mines where he came into contact with all kinds of people—people from the mountains, people from the seaside towns, people from the villages around the towns, English people, Turkish people, people from the motherland, rich people, poor people, educated people and people who could not write their own name and put a cross instead whenever they had to deal with any administrative issues. Christos had finished primary school thanks to his uncle's benevolent offer to pay his father 10 shillings a year to allow his son to finish school. Uncle Panayiotis had been to Egypt for years working there and meeting people from all walks of life. He made some money there, nobody knew how, and came back "to die in his village". He encouraged Christos to finish primary school and widen his horizons. 'The world does not end in Marathasa, he used to say, or the Troodos mountains, or this island. The world is big and wide and needs people with open minds.'

Christos' mind boggled as he contemplated the diversity of the world and of the human beings and strengthened his determination that one day he would take his whole family and head for the sea. When this day would come, he was not sure. Now they were expecting a second child, just days to go. Nothing else mattered just now, but the future was open to him and his family. Open to all possibilities. As he quickly sussed it out that people from the towns treated their wives and their children differently, talked to them differently and listened to them differently he promised himself to be different from his father and from the other men in the village. He wanted to be gentle and fair and sound like a "civilised" man. Listening to conversations between townies he realised that this was a different world, an open world where the horizon shifted all the time as he heard stories of fishermen and seamen talking about the sea. One day, he thought as he bit hard into the raw onion and gulped down the rest of the zivania that remained in his glass, one day he would.

Christos did not drink much. He had hated his father coming back from the coffee shop late at night drunk on wine and zivania and collapsing on the bed— sometimes on the bench outside the house, sometimes on the floor—his mother hysterically accusing him of neglecting the family and his children, 'just look at them they look like orphans, they have no shoes and no proper clothes. And you are wasting your life drinking your money away, you, useless wreck of a man. God is punishing us all for your sins.' And on and on. A huge exaggeration, Christos thought as he gulped down his zivania, as his father earned enough from the work at Amiantos and the fields and vineyards he owned to keep them all well clothed and fed.

When Christos' father died at the age of 45, Christos was 17 at the time and took over from his father as the main breadwinner. His 19-year-old sister was already married with two children, and his youngest sister was 8. So it fell onto Christos to take the responsibility of looking after his mother and his brother and sister. He began to spend more time at the mines to earn more money and in the summer he would work in the fields and vineyards, helped of course by his mother and his 15-year-old brother. His 13-year-old sister looked after his eight-year-old sister, as mother went out to the fields more and more. Now, ten years later, with all the daughters married and with his mother joining Elengou to run the coffee shop together, and as the grandchildren kept coming, the world looked a much friendlier place.

The silence in the mountains was deep and intense and was paradoxically enhanced by the distant sounds that came from the village. The distant conversation of two women—the cadences and melodic lines of their voices could be distinguished but no words could be deciphered. A child was crying. A donkey raised an agonising and triumphant braying which was repeated a few times before finally falling silent. Some disagreement between two men was too far away to tell whether it was an everyday event or something more serious.

The silence of the mountains dominated the evening. Christos held his breath and listened. This was his way of being religious. Embracing this silence and the beauty of the fallen sun was his kind of prayer. If he could put it into words he would have said silence, this silence after the sun had fallen behind the mountains and the world was at peace, this silence was God. But his mind remained, like the mountains around him, still. No words disturbed it. He embraced his young family with his eyes and thought that he and Eleni will be a different couple, a different family.

Suddenly, without any warning, the peace of the falling dusk was broken by an avalanche of human activity, human pain and human hysteria. Screams, cries and wailings broke the silence. Eleni's sister, Penelope, was suddenly there, very much there, screaming and throwing herself around.

'The animal, the beast, the bastard—he beat me again,' she was screaming, 'this time in front of the children who got so scared they first tried to help me and when he turned against them, they ran off to their grandmother's. Look at this.' She screamed, 'look at what this animal did to me,' and she exposed the bruises on her arms that they were turning red and blue and black as they were looking. 'He hit me on the head as well the bastard. He wants to kill me. I feel dizzy, I will faint.'

She collapsed on a chair and Eleni rushed to bring some rose water to spray on her face to revive her frail sister. 'There won't be any baby if he goes on like this! Penelope was wailing. It will be like last time. The bastard. He is not human this guy, he is a monster.'

Penelope was three months pregnant and the "last time" was a reference to a previous miscarriage she had which she attributed to her husband's violence.

'Calm down Penelope,' Eleni was saying in a soothing voice. 'Shhh, shhh. It's all right now. It's OK.'

She was rubbing her sister's forehead and was trying to soothe her as if she was soothing a child with a lullaby.

In the meantime, Eleni's mother Elengou, had arrived out of breath, shouting and gesticulating. 'Somebody has to teach this savage a lesson. He's gone too far this time. Yiota is going to fetch Manolis. He should go and teach this beast a lesson.'

Manolis was Eleni's and Penelope's brother and what grandmother Elengou was saying meant that her sister Yiota was going to fetch Manolis, who was going to go and beat up Penelope's husband.

'No, No,' Penelope was screaming 'No don't let Manolis do this. It will make things worse.'

'Somebody has to teach him a lesson. He is an animal, he is worse than your father,' Penelope's mother screamed out of breath. 'Panayia mou, panayia mou (oh mother of god),' she wailed suddenly as she clasped at her heart 'my heart. This animal is going to kill us all.'

She collapsed in a chair next to Penelope and Christos went into the house to get some surgical spirit which they always kept in the house as an antiseptic. She gave it to Eleni who rubbed her mother's chest with it until Elengo relaxed and fell quiet. In the meantime, the children had arrived and were sitting on the steps of the veranda looking sheepishly at what was going on. They were used to scenes like this and waited for things to calm down.

'I am not going back home,' Penelope declared suddenly. 'I am not going back to this beast tonight. I'll stay here Eleni and the children can sleep on the floor. I want to teach him a lesson. We are all staying here and Manolis can go and tell him. If the beast does not change his ways, we are not going back at all.'

These lines were pronounced with the same conviction every time something like this happened and both Eleni and Christos were used to them. They said nothing and tried instead to calm things down by trying to make Elengo more comfortable taking her to the bed inside the house and offering her a glass of water. The children were left to their own devices as they sat on the steps and whispered to each other.

In the meantime, little Stavros had woken up and he was now crying abundantly, tottering towards his mother with open arms. Eleni picked him up and kissed his wet face. 'It's OK Stavro,' she said gently 'It's OK, it's only yiayia (grandmother) and auntie Penelope, go back to sleep.'

But Stavros was in no mood to go back to sleep. He rubbed his face with his hands and looked around a bit more re-assured. A moment of silence followed, and Christos took a deep breath feeling a sense of relief. Maybe the worst was over. At this same moment, Sofia's screams were heard before they could see her making her way up the hill towards the house. Sofia was Manolis' wife and Penelope's sister in Law.

'Christo! Christo! Come immediately, for God sake somebody must stop them. They are going to kill each other.'

She was running up the hill, screaming and gesticulating, her two little boys running behind her.

She reached the house out of breath screaming hysterically.

'Christo you have to stop them.' Manolis took the kitchen knife and left saying that he was going to butcher the bastard. 'Panayia mou, panayia mou, this time he might do it. Mother of God help us all.' She crossed herself, took a deep breath and began again. 'Christo you have to come immediately.'

'I am coming,' Christos said and looked at his wife who was holding Stavros on her knees seeking a way out. But she only said, 'You have to go Christo.'

Penelope who had now felt reassured enough to open her eyes said, 'Yes Christo you have to go. Manolis should teach him a lesson but see that they don't kill each other. You are the only one Manolis will listen to.'

Christos began to descend the slope followed by Sofia and the children. The noise from the village reached them as they were approaching the first houses. They went around the church and the big square around it and entered the inner village with its narrow streets and the houses almost touching each other across the street. Then they saw them all—a crowd of about twenty people, men women and children shouting, swearing, crossing themselves, appealing to the virgin, cursing. In the middle Costas, Penelope's husband, and Manolis were exchanging insults. There was no danger of "killing each other". There were no knives and no sticks, forks or spades. There was no punch-up either but there was the threat of one. The two men were standing a foot from each other exchanging threats and insults, trying to prove that they were *men* and that they had "honour" and everybody in the village should witness this.

'If you touch my sister ever again, I swear to God I'll kill you,' Manolis was shouting.

'Your sister is a whore,' Costas was saying. 'She should do what I say and stop talking to people I had forbidden her to talk to.'

'You bastard, you are going to kill my sister.'

'I'll do what I want,' Costas said provocatively 'I am her husband.'

'You are a beast, not a man,' Manolis shouted.

Reading between the lines Christos gathered that this latest eruption of violence between husband and wife was a matter of jealousy. Penelope was the beauty of the village and Costas never quite got used to having married this beauty who was the secret, and sometimes not so secret, object of desire of all the men in the village. Costas and Penelope had married through love—a passionate and frustrated love which had to wait for years for her older sister to marry first. In the meantime, the courting went on exchanging glances and words as they met for a few seconds outside the church on Sundays, or at the big festivals, or as they sat side by side at the feasts at christenings, weddings and wakes, or danced in somebody else's wedding always exchanging glances and touching as if by chance. During the year before their engagement they began to meet secretly in a cave above the vineyards and distant goat pastures on the hills. Penelope would steal half hour when she was sent for an errand by her mother or when she was sent with food and water to the fields where her father and brothers worked. She would then make sure she passed as if by chance from the fields or vineyards where Costas was working and throw him a glance full of meaning. He knew what this meant and a few minutes later he made an excuse and left for the cave. The few moments of bliss and lust they spent in the cave sealed their love and the waiting became unbearable as sister and brother took their time to find their husband and wife. But the day came after her older sister and his older brother got married. By then, they had been waiting for four years. Penelope was nineteen and Costas twenty-one when one Sunday freshly shaved and washed, dressed in his best Sunday clothes and his best shoes, he went to Penelope's house and asked her father, Odysseas, for her hand. The father who was not surprised in the least and who was waiting for this occasion pretended he was taken by surprise. He said he had to consult with his wife and ask his daughter. He also mentioned what his daughter's dowry was going to be "to avoid any misunderstandings".

Some toing and froing went on the next few weeks. Penelope's father pretended he was hesitating. They were others, he said vaguely, others who wanted his daughter. He wouldn't just give her off as easily as that. He had to be sure that Costas was the right person, that he would treat her properly, that he had enough land and stock to provide for his daughter. Costas was taken in by the older man's manoeuvres and began to despair whether he would ever say yes. He knew that all this had to do with Penelope not having a big dowry, no house of her own and not enough cash. On his side, his father was also nagging and haggling. 'You have to ask for a house,' he insisted. 'Where are you going to live? The stingy man can afford it. He is just mean and spends all his cash on booze. He can start building the house now and then we can believe that he is serious. Don't be so naïve and don't make yourself so available. I'll go and see the old miser myself.'

After a few weeks of negotiations mainly between the two fathers, nothing specific emerged. Both fathers dug their heels in and wouldn't move. They exchanged niceties, they exchanged abuse, and they nearly exchanged blows. Penelope's father threatened. 'I am not giving my daughter to your son and that's that,' he said in the end. 'My daughter is not for sale.'

Costas was desperate. All he wanted was Penelope. After that, they could work together and build the house together. They could live in one room to start with. What was the problem? The two wives tried to negotiate. Costas' mother supported her husband but in a gentler, more diplomatic way. 'We can find a way,' she kept saying. 'Where there is a will there is way.' Penelope's mother supported her daughter and thought her husband unreasonable. 'The children are in love, he kept reminding him. They want to get married. What's wrong with you?'

Penelope for her side became hysterical, wailing and threatening in equal measure. She tried fainting, she tried screaming, she tried shutting herself in her room for days and refusing food, she tried leaving the house and taking refuge in her auntie Antigone's house.

Auntie Antigone came around one day to add her voice to the cacophonous orchestra that constituted the so-called negotiations.

'You are killing this girl,' she begged. 'What has come over you both?'

'It's a matter of honour,' Penelope's father said solemnly.

'Honour!' she sniggered, 'Don't give me this bullshit! It's a matter of spite and stubbornness and meanness and competition between men. Your poor daughter's happiness doesn't enter into this.'

'You women,' Odysseas growled 'You have no idea about serious business.'

Aunt Antigone sprang into action. She went to see Odysseas' father, the grumpy old man of seventy-two and father of ten and asked him to talk to his son and bring him to his senses. She talked to Odysseas' mother who was revered in the village as a saint for her deep devotion to the church and to the poor and not only in her village but in all the villages around. She went to see Odysseas' older brother, a sensible and hardworking man who considered his brother a bit of a waste of space, stubborn and useless in equal measure. She mobilised the regiment of Odysseas' sisters who were loud and opinionated and had as much spite as Odysseas himself. Endless conversations between family members ended nowhere. Sometimes members of one family would disagree with each other as to who was right, Odysseas or Costas' father, Auntie Antigone or Costas' mother. Seen from the outside one would be forgiven to assume that families were threatened with splintering and irrevocable damage so high ran the passions. Yet there was nothing unusual in all these. The older people had seen it all before and they rather enjoyed the excitement and the fuss.

Costas himself tried to keep in the background so as not to make things worse. At the beginning, he threatened that he and Penelope would elope and go away, far away from this cursed place where common sense was so scarce. Then he wanted to go and beat up, or threatened to go and beat up his aspired father-in-law, but he soon realised that this would seal his fate. In the end, he was persuaded by his mother and other relatives, mainly female, to sit it out. The old man was going to come to his senses. (The old man was hardly fifty but anybody above forty-five was an "old man" or woman.) In the end he did, but not before he extracted a major concession from his future son-in-law's family. He would give a piece of land to his daughter and some money to contribute to the building of the house but no house, and that was that. The men shook hands and drank ouzo and zivania and got drunk and shed tears before it occurred to them to let their wives and children know about this.

The wedding followed in a year during which Costas with the help of all the brothers on both sides managed to build a couple of rooms which constituted the "new house". The wedding itself was, like all weddings, a village affair. People from nearby villages were also invited. Celebrations lasted for two whole days, and lamb, pork, sausages, all kinds of local dishes, cheese and olives were abundant. Local wine and zivania were also abundant. People ate and drank and danced and flirted and gossiped and got sentimental and cried and laughed and sang. Old men exhibited their skills in devising rhymed verses and competed in this. One would start a two-line verse and somebody else would finish it in a humorous and often pungent way. People would laugh and clap and encourage them to continue. Young people looked around for a future husband or wife exhibiting their manly or womanly skills in dancing and singing.

As he was approaching the scuffle Christos remembered with a sudden flash of longing that he first noticed Eleni at Penelope's wedding. She was seventeen at the time, a shy and modest girl, not particularly beautiful but with the sweetest, sparkling, chestnut eyes he had ever seen. When she smiled, her eyes became a "pool of heaven", he thought, as he was formally introduced to her and found it difficult to take his eyes from hers. He knew her since he was a child but never paid any attention to her and never saw her at any proximity. But now her eyes became a centre of mysterious energy, a magnetic field that got him captive ever since.

She was four years younger than him and always lived under the shadow of her sister who "broke many hearts" as everybody referred to her. She didn't have the beauty of her sister but had a slender, supple, tall body and long velvet hair and those two magnets for eyes. Stavros knew immediately where he had seen this face. It was the face he loved since he was a kid and went with his father to the fair at the Church of Archangelos on the 15th of August, the day of Mary's assumption to heaven. This was one of the holiest days on the island, equivalent to Easter Sunday. The face of Mary in the old frescoes of the Church of Archangelos never left his mind. The deep humanity of her eyes and the dignified sadness of her face stayed with him forever as the ideal of womanhood. And here she was, staring at him smiling shyly and warmly and with the same unmistakable sadness in her eyes.

'If you touch my sister ever again, do you hear, ever again I'll come and kill you. I swear to God I'll come and kill you,' Manolis was shouting no.

'Manoli cut it! Entaxi? This is none of your business, this is between Penelope and myself. She knows exactly what she did wrong and I'd do it again if she doesn't listen to me. Maybe your wife does what she likes, and you have no control over her. Maybe you are not enough of a man to show her how to behave properly.'

This was too much for Manolis who however much he tried to keep the whole thing to exchanging insults he just lost it.

'You bastard,' he shouted as he landed a punch on Costas' chin. 'I'll show you who is a man. You chicken beating up a woman. Take this from a man.'

In a few seconds, the whole atmosphere changed from a half-hearted exchange of insults to a full-blown fight as each man tried to defend his honour and prove his manhood to everybody who was there to watch and judge. Violence erupted suddenly and rather unpredictably as each man tried and failed to push the other to the ground. Manoli's nose was now bleeding profusely and Manolis' wife who had just arrived screamed and tried to interfere, but was held back by a few men.

'Go home Calliope,' they said gently 'This is no place for a woman.'

The children began to cry and shout 'papa, papa will die.'

Some men tried to interfere to break up the fight, but the two men held tied to each other as they struggled to push each other to the ground. Some men shouted at them to stop, others cheered or tried to support the one or the other.

Suddenly the crowd gave way to a man in his fifties with a generous moustache, a generous belly and a dignified stature. He had an air of authority. It was Nestor, the Muhtar of the village and next to him Father Ieronymos the priest. The two men constituted what every person recognized as authority in the village.

'That's enough,' Nestor said with a distinct authority in his voice. 'If you go on like this, your wives won't have a husband to return home to, and your children will be fatherless.'

The crowd fell silent and the two men stopped suddenly. To be sure this is the moment they were both hoping for—a way out of this lunatic fight—a way out without losing face. They could now stop without their honour or their masculinity in question.

'He nearly killed my sister.' Manolis turned to Nestor offering an explanation for his behaviour.

'I gave her a good hiding, so what?' Costas shrugged. 'Because she talked to people I forbade her to have anything to do with.'

'OK,' Nestor pronounced in his official authoritative voice. 'Time to go home, both of you, and we shall all do the same,' he added.

It was getting dark now. Dusk was falling rapidly. The crowd began to disperse. Christos wiped the sweat from his forehead and began to walk back to the cottage wondering how Eleni was.

He was aware that he had not intervened in the fight as Penelope had urged him not to. He could not quite understand these fights between men. He was a peace-loving person and since he had worked at the asbestos mines became more and more of a "townie" without ever having been in a town. At least, he aspired to be one. He had talked to engineers from Nicosia. He had exchanged jokes with managers from Limassol. He had lunch or a glass of ouzo with advisers and lawyers from all over the island. He couldn't imagine them having street fights or beating up their wives. They looked and sounded more…Christos could not find the word and hesitated in his mind as he began the ascend towards the cottage, they sounded more civilised, he concluded.

It was almost dark now and he had to guess the path that led to it. Stavros should be fast asleep now, he thought, and a rush of affection enveloped him as he thought of his son asleep and his pregnant wife dosing off next to him. His mind went to the baby they were expecting. It could be any day now, or night, for that matter. It will be a girl everybody had predicted. Some said it was the shape of the belly. Others said it was the kind of food Eleni craved for—sweet things instead of savoury things. It was also the fact that the baby kicked less. It's a girl, all the old wise women pronounced with certainty. The midwife of the village who had delivered all the babies in the village for the last thirty years had also pronounced: a girl. They had already given her grandmother's name: Panayiota.

The last time the midwife had examined Eleni's belly she looked worried. It's bridge now, she explained, I hope she will turn in time. It might be a bit tricky. Christos arrived at the cottage and as he had predicted Eleni was asleep next to Stavros. He lit a candle and sat at the chair watching them with deep affection. *I am the luckiest man on earth*, he thought and crossed himself. He fetched a glass from next room that served as a kitchen, dining room, living room and work room all in one, and poured himself some zivania. All this nonsense with Costas and Manolis passed him by. The truth was that Penelope, the beauty of the village, couldn't stop flirting with her admirers, even at twenty-nine, and Costas was going mad with jealousy. That was all, simple and stupid, he thought, the whole, complicated truth. Very simple really. One day he will make it to Limassol, he thought, and he and Eleni and the kids will live another life.

The silence that surrounded him gave him a deep feeling of peace. He could hear his wife's breathing gentle and regular. Stavros seemed to be dreaming something as he made some strange sounds as if he was trying to say something. He then resumed his regular breathing as well.

Nothing, he thought nothing was worth more than this—to be surrounded by love, to be surrounded by innocent sleep, to be surrounded by peace. The fools in the village can fight and posture, but this is happiness.

He contemplated their life together from the moment he and Eleni began their courtship, their exchange of glances, their "accidental" touching of hands, their first kiss after they got engaged. Eleni's father had died by then so the torture that Penelope went through was not repeated. Eleni's mother gave them her blessing and a piece of land and Costas understood that they had to build their own house and that was that. Poor or not poor they were wildly happy. His family owned enough land to be able to earn a living and support a family. And his few months at the mine supplemented their income.

Christos finished his zivania, contemplated whether he was going to pour himself another one, decided against it and began slowly to take his clothes off and prepare for bed. He threw a last glance at his little sleeping family, blew out the candle and fumbled his way to the bed to join Eleni and Stavros.

This was Christos' last happy day before disaster struck.

***

That morning Christos would remember to the end of his life. It was the day when everything would change for ever and the world would never be the same again either for him or for his 18-month-old son. It was the day when death would show its dark face and its reality would rupture the very essence of their life.

After Christos had blown the candle out that night, he lay next to his wife and listened for a while to her gentle, regular breathing and he could hear his own breathing and his son breathing all co-existing side by side in counterpoint contributing to the music of the night. Peace and gratitude filled his mind. He could hear the resident owl hooting in regular intervals. Every now and then a fox emitted his wild cries. Between the sounds silence prevailed.

He woke up around 5 in the morning by his wife shaking his arm. 'Wake up Christo. The time has come.'

He jumped out of the bed and put on his clothes in great hurry.

'I'll fetch Aglaia and your mum,' he said, 'Lie down and wait.'

Aglaia was the village midwife. She had delivered Stavros eighteen months earlier as she had delivered all the village children for the last thirty years. There was no hospital or doctor in the village or in the nearby villages. The nearest hospital was 25 miles away and it took several hours on donkey to reach it. So, most children were delivered by Aglaia who did a marvellous job if there were no complications.

By the time Aglaia and two other women helpers, followed by Eleni's mother and accompanied by Christos, arrived at the cottage dawn was already breaking and Stavros was crying pulling at his mother's skirt. Eleni was sitting on a chair and looked white as a sheet, her face distorted in pain.

'Something is wrong,' she managed to say. 'This is not the same as with Stavros.'

Aglaia took control of the situation immediately ordering Eleni to lie down and the two women to boil some water and get some sheets. Christos was ordered out of the room and he and Stavros went to the kitchen. Stavros sensing that something was wrong began to howl and wanted to get back to his mother. Christos had a real time trying to restrain him and keep calm himself as an iron hand had gripped his heart and stomach and would not let go. Stories of birth disasters stormed his mind and family stories of his great aunt dying in childbirth together with the baby clouded his judgment. Should he rush and get the doctor? Should he wait for Aglaia to tell him what to do?

'It's all right Stavro,' he heard himself saying to his son in a quiet voice 'Everything is all right. Your mum will give you a little sister to play with. It will be a tiny little thing like you were once, like a little doll. You will see. You will see.'

As Stavros stopped screaming Eleni's screams rose from the other room more and more desperate and Stavros began to howl again and tried to get free from his father's strong clutch. Eleni's mother came out the room and took Stavros outside talking to him constantly. Christos buried his nails in his cheeks and drew blood out of them.

Aglaia came running out of the room.

'Christo, you've got to get the doctor. This is difficult. The baby will tear her insides. Quick! Go!'

'Oh God,' he whispered, 'this can't be happening.'

In the village, his brother Hektor joined him and both men set out on donkeys for the small country hospital at Platres, which had one resident doctor and two nurses.

They took the various shortcuts over the mountains they knew and in three hours they arrived at the hospital. The doctor was out trying to save the life of a man from the nearby village who had fallen thirty meres down a cliff and was unconscious. The nurse informed them that people said he might have been drunk but that others had said that the man had often had dizzy spells and that perhaps this happened during one of his dizzy spells.

The village was 45 minutes away and the doctor was not expected back before noon. There was nothing for Stavros and Hector to do but wait. The nurse chatted a bit about the man in question, that he was a widower that was why he took to drinking and that he had five children the eldest a girl of fifteen was looking after the children. Seeing that Stavros and Hector were not in a mood to listen to stories she left them and went to change the bandage of a man who had just arrived with a badly bandaged leg soaked in blood.

After two hours the doctor arrived, dishevelled and tired, his face pale and depressed. On hearing about Eleni, he seized his mule and went back the same way they came.

By the time they arrived back at the village, it was 5 o'clock in the evening and Eleni was dead. Next to her lay the dead baby washed and dressed. It was a girl. Half the village were in the room, wailing, chanting and lamenting. Eleni was laid out on her bed which had now new clean sheets, her eyes shut, her hands folded in front of her, with a crucifix on her chest.

Christos threw himself on his dead wife and howled like a baby.

Chapter 4
Marathasa 1918

It was May and the green carpet of the valley was slowly being dappled with golden splashes. The mountains turned from a mixture of grey and purple into a soft green as the vineyards came alive and began to grow and spread. The swifts crowded the village and the crows occupied the valley. Birds of prey occupied the mountains.

Harvest will be early this year, everybody kept saying. Early and poor. The rain had been scarce, and it was as if summer came in May. The world is upside down, people were commenting, crossing themselves. God help us. All these new inventions, electricity, motor cars, radios. Nothing is natural anymore. Night turning into day, people driving a carriage without horses or mules, people listening to other people miles away. The villagers listened to the stories about the miracles that were taking place in the towns and admired and were filled with awe and dark premonitions. The older ones crossed themselves just in case, as if the devil might be involved in this trickery. The younger ones talked about science—a new word that began to circulate among them. Science, progress, town life. And there was the war that was raging for years a long, long way from here.

A couple of young people from the village had volunteered and their families were both proud and anxious, always hungry for news and accounts of the battles. Every now and then a letter would arrive from the front and it would be read aloud at the caffeneion and it would be passed from hand to hand to be examined as if it were a work of art or a strange object.

On this Sunday morning, as the sun was rising behind the mountains, Stavros went to milk the two goats his grandmother kept in the shed at the back of the house. The air was still cool and the light gentle. The mountains looked pristine. But Stavros could not rejoice in this glorious morning. His heart was heavy, full of worry and premonition. Life as he had known it for the last 10 years was about to change. His stable, if not exactly happy life, his predictable little life, was going to be interrupted. Feeding the animals in the morning, milking the goats, lighting the fire in winter then off to school until noon. Back at 12.05 doing all the menial jobs in the house as his grandmother was getting old and very busy with looking after the small vegetable plot she possessed. They lived on the small income she made from making baskets which she tried to sell at various fairs and from selling the produce of her olive trees and walnut trees which was harvested by her children. Regular handouts from her children also helped. Since the return of Stavros' father, she also received money for Stavros' upkeep. She had given up looking after the Caffeneion for some time now and her eldest son had taken it over. It was enough looking after her aging cantankerous father who was getting frail and was slowly losing his sight.

Watering the vegetables at the back of the house was also one of Stavros' jobs at this time of the year. The last rains had fallen about a month ago and the soil had begun to crack. Deep holes appeared between the cracks and ants began to make their appearance in thousands always running frantically as if they were on an emergency mission. A snake sometimes appeared out of one of the holes and this was much less amusing. Stavros learnt to differentiate between the big black snakes that were protectors of vegetable plots and the grey small vipers and adders which were lethal. Picking fruit, collecting eggs from the chickens, helping in the picking of grapes from the vineyards in late summer and harvesting the almond and olive trees were all jobs that Stavros routinely carried out.

In the evening, it was homework. In winter, after he had finished his school work, he would sit with a single candle on the table and read all kinds of books borrowed from Mr Socrates, the teacher. But Stavros very rarely did homework as he learnt almost everything at first hand from the teacher's mouth at school. He had a phenomenal memory and he could retain everything the teacher said including his answers to pupils' questions.

Stavros had always been top of the class in an effortless, natural way. More than this he was ahead of everybody of his age in every way. His teacher was so impressed with him that he took a personal interest in him. It wasn't just his ability which was above anything and anybody the teacher had met in his teaching career. It was Stavros' thirst for knowledge that he felt was so extraordinary and refreshing at the same time in a place where people overall did not have much curiosity. "Don't ask" or "curiosity killed the cat" were often answers that Stavros' got to his questions at home. But the teacher, so appropriately named Socrates, was delighted to have a pupil so hungry for knowledge.

It was almost like physical hunger, the teacher thought. It was impulsive. It was compulsive. But unlike physical hunger this hunger had no satiation point. The more Stavros read, the more he wanted to read. The more he learnt, the more he wanted to learn, to ask for more, to follow the teacher around the school. Often after he finished his chores in the evening he would go to the teacher's house to ask more questions and borrow some books.

The teacher was the third most important person in the village after the Muhtar and the priest. The three of them represented Authority, Religion and Education. Mr Socrates had taken Stavros under his wing. 'This orphan will achieve great things,' he told people at the caffeneion and told the priest and told the Muhtar as well. By the time Stavros was 10 years old, he had already become a regular visitor to the teacher's house. The teacher, the son of a rich farmer from another village a few miles away, felt proud for his protégé and asked his wife to prepare food and sweets for him. For his side, Stavros used the teacher's house like a library. Mr Socrates lent him books that he himself had been given as a boy by his uncle who lived in Limassol.

One of these books was Oliver Twist in translation and in a simplified form for young readers. Stavros read the book again and again and knew it almost by heart. He dreamt of this unknown noble woman who was really his mother and who would come to rescue him from the shame and rejection of being an orphan. He dreamt of a house where there were things like a teapot and porcelain teacups and saucers and servants dressed in white aprons (the book was full of illustrations). He had told himself many times that his father was not really his father. His dead mother was far away from here living in London, a lady, an educated daughter of a gentleman, beautiful beyond imagination. Maybe she had a face like the virgin in the various icons seen in different churches and monasteries. There was a fresco in the local church that looked so different to the rest of the church frescoes and icons. Mr Socrates told him that it bore the influence of the Venetians who conquered the island in the 15th century and kept it until it fell into the hands of the Ottomans in 1541. 'Look at what the men are wearing,' Mr Socrates would say pointing to the fresco in the church of Panayia Kardiovastazousa. 'They are western clothes. And look at what the lady is wearing. Look at the intricacy of the dress and the subtle nobility in the woman's face. It's amazing. It's a masterpiece.' That's perhaps how his mother was, like this woman who was so different, Stavros thought. One day he will find her, he thought. One day.

Maybe one day his father would come from London, his real father, his gentleman father with a gold watch chain and a whole house full of books, leather bound and wise. He could smell the leather as he was lying in his bed in the dark, hot and humid night listening to the silence of the mountains. His gentleman father would come to claim him one day. My wife died in childbirth, he would say, died here on this island when I was the governor here a few years ago. A wicked nurse swapped the children, he would say, and told everybody that his son died together with his mother. They buried the dead mother and the baby 11 years ago. Heartbroken he went back to London and never left his study again mourning the loss of his wife and son. But now the wicked nurse had confessed. Just before she died she confessed so that God would forgive her. There had been a plot. Things were difficult to explain in detail but now everything has been sorted out and he came to take his son back to London with him.

'Stavro! Stavro!' His grandmother was calling him. 'You are taking your time out there. What is Aglaia telling you? A secret?'

Aglaia was the older of the two goats grandmother kept, and she was her favourite.

'Coming yaya,' he replied, 'I was just giving her a hug.'

'If you go on like this we will be late for church. Grandpa wants his milk and bread. And you can boil some water for me. I'll have some sage tea.'

Stavros came in carrying the milk he had just milked from the two goats. Grandma had already put a new clean embroidered tablecloth on the table as she did every Sunday morning.

'My stomach is upset,' she said as she was continuing a conversation. 'Sage tea will be good.'

The tablecloth, reserved for Sundays and other holidays, had elaborate stitching in the middle and in all four corners. It was one of many that had constituted grandma's dowry that she brought into her marriage together with this house some 45 odd years ago. She had spent evenings on end in her teens doing the elaborate stitching passed down to her by her mother who had passed away blind and deaf a few years ago "God bless her soul". She crossed herself as she thought of her mother and her tortured soul. Living with a tyrannical, cantankerous and mean husband had been enough purgatory for her. Maybe she rests in the arms of Archangel Michael, she thought now with tears in her eyes.

'What is it stete?' Stavros asked as he saw her crossing herself. Stavros used the colloquial term stete instead of yaya as he wanted to get a bit closer to her.

'Nothing Stavro, just thinking about your great-grandmother Theodora.'

'What about her?' Stavros asked.

'Nothing, just nothing.'

'I didn't like her much yaya.' Stavros was now pursing his lips as if he was offering an apology. 'She wasn't very nice to me.'

'I know Stavro. She was really not herself for the last few years of her life.'

'She was cruel,' Stavros insisted.

Grandma opened her mouth to defend her mother when Penelope burst through the door suddenly.

'Good morning,' Penelope's face was smiling a big, open smile. 'I brought you some halloumi and some eggs—we had too many eggs this week. And some sausages. You said you liked them last time I brought them, so I brought you some more. I know Stavros likes them, don't you Stavraki.'

Stavros ran to auntie Penelope and she embraced him warmly.

'I love your sausages auntie,' he said. 'But I like it even more when you come to visit us.'

Penelope hugged him and then took a seat at the table.

'I'll make you some sage tea,' Stavros said and poured some more water into the copper saucepan and put it on the stove that grandma had lit in the meantime.

'Can you make me a coffee instead Stavro. I am dying for one. I almost forgot,' she added 'I got you some coffee.' She delved into the depths of her bag. 'I know grandad loves a cup of coffee in the morning and the price of coffee has gone up so much. I wish we could grow it,' she said and laughed at her own joke.

Stavros set out to make the coffee exactly as auntie Penelope wanted it—one heaped spoon of coffee and one spoon of sugar, i.e. "metrio". At the same time, he was preparing yaya's sage tea. He was painfully aware that his grandmother and great-grandfather lived from handouts from their children. The basket making and other small enterprises that grandma pursued brought in some cash but not enough to feed herself and Stavros. Stavros' father gave her also a bit of money, but he seemed to be so afraid of his wife that it was all secretive and irregular.

'I nearly forgot the olive bread,' Penelope cried and searched in her big canvas bag. 'I made it yesterday,' she said as she got a big loaf out of the bag. 'Antonis and Elias loved it,' she said, 'and Calliope tried to nick the part I saved for you. They are all so greedy. And Costas always complains, about me, about the children, about the food, about everything. I hear nothing but complains.'

Penelope sat at the table and began to nibble at the olive bread. The aroma of strong Greek coffee filled the room as Stavros poured it into a coffee cup and put it in front of Penelope.

'Mmmm!' Penelope made a sound of contentment and appreciation. 'Stavro you should open a Coffee Shop in Limassol one day. You will become rich.'

'Don't put ideas into his mind,' grandma said. 'He is finishing school in a few weeks. He needs to get used to working in the fields with his father. He can also work at Amiantos. He's got to make a living.'

'The teacher says he must go to the Gymnasium (grammar school),' Penelope said.

'Well the teacher can say what he wants,' Elengo said, 'but where is the money going to come from?'

There was an uneasy silence.

'His father probably has the money,' Elengo continued, 'but he won't pay, will he?'

Penelope sipped at her coffee. 'We'll see,' she said in a reconciliatory manner. 'Nevertheless Stavro, you make a first-class coffee,' she added cheerfully.

Stavros smiled at his aunt feeling her warmth enveloping him. She was his substitute mother—a warm presence that emanated love and did not demand anything from him. Yet he was very worried, very anxious. What will happen to him? He wanted so much to go to the Gymnasium, but how? He didn't dare ask this question aloud?

Penelope read the worry in his face. She dug her fingers into his hair and ruffled it affectionately.

'It will be OK,' she said. 'Stavro you will be fine, won't you Stavro?'

He nodded and once again he felt enveloped in warmth.

'He needs a haircut,' grandma said.

At that moment Nestor appeared, hugging his moustache. He looked at Penelope and said good morning under his breath. He eyed everybody as if he was a general inspecting his troops. Was there a rebellion? Was there a riot? Was there a revolution? Did order prevail?

'Grandad,' Stavros said, 'are you ready for your coffee?'

***

The Church was the hub of the village. On Sundays everybody, apart from the very old and the bedridden were there, including mothers with babies, mothers to be and old people like Elengo. Nestor was too old and too far from the world to make the five minutes' walk to the church, so he was one of those exempt without social or religious repercussions. Stavros put on a clean shirt, the one kept for Sundays and holidays, and his good pair of shoes, again the one he wore only on Sundays. it was the last few years, since his father came back that Stavros wore shoes to go to school. Before that he went, like many other children, barefoot to school.

He had washed his feet, his hands and arms and under his arms (as auntie Penelope had showed him when he was little), his face and his teeth and combed his hair. Elengo examined him, letting her eyes wander from head to feet and back again and announced her approval. 'OK Stavro, that's good.'

She had also already changed into her best black skirt and shoes and her best black mantilla.

They set off through the narrow shady streets exchanging good-mornings and other small talk with neighbours and other faithful who were making the short walk to the church. The sun was already hot and walking through the shady streets was a blessing.

The service had already been going on for a few hours when they entered the church. Most people went to church around ten, for who could manage getting up at six in the morning on a Sunday and attending 5 hours of liturgy? People arrived at any time and only very few people were there at 6am when it all started—usually widows and old people. Who else would have the time?

This was a ritual of belonging, of participating, of being there to see and be seen and see others who also wanted to be seen. Penelope was there with Costas and the children. Manolis was there with Sofia and the children. Andreas was there with Maroulla. Stavros sought to locate his father the moment he entered the church knowing that he would also be there. Sure enough he was there, a few rows to the front with his wife Marilena and their son Alexandros.

It didn't matter how often Stavros saw his father with his wife and their son. It always hurt. It was now more than four years since his father came back but he always felt a knife entering his chest and his breathing stopped for a moment and the pain in his chest became very sharp. Then his heart would race, and his head would spin. He could think of nothing but how to lull the pain.

It was now almost five years since they had heard news about his father returning from Egypt and getting married in a village near Limassol. He had sent invitations to the whole village, but nobody made it to their wedding. It would have been 2 days journey to get there and two days to come back. In any case, people had no sympathy with him. His own brothers turned against him and accused him of abandoning his son. Eleni's relatives were even stronger in their condemnation of him. So, returning to the village with a new bride from a village near Limassol was a very controversial subject for the inhabitants of this village, something they endlessly discussed at the caffeneion in the evening as men relaxed and played cards and discussed politics and above all gossiped and condemned. But the subject was also discussed in the fields as they were tending the crops and the vegetables and in the kitchens, and back gardens as women cooked, tended the animals and cleaned and scrubbed and mended and embroidered, and in the churchyard after church on Sundays when the faithful lingered and talked and gossiped.

So, returning to the village was no simple affair for Christos, but bringing a bride 10 years older than him and from a faraway village who was reported to have money was almost provocative. The day he and Marilena arrived became a day to remember as the word spread around, and people gathered in the main square to see the new bride. That was almost five years ago, and Stavros remembered it like yesterday—the day he had waited and longed for and so often dreamt of in waking dreams. A father who would come back and claim him, lift him from poverty, give him a real home, make him a normal boy again—a boy with a father.

An objective observer would say that without exaggeration this was Stavros' most painful and most disappointing day of his life. Yet for Stavros it was the day when he began to think of only one thing: how to impress his father and make him love him. On this, he never gave up even when he later rejected his father and never went back to the village to see him. The wish to impress and to be loved by everybody, by family, relatives, friends, acquaintances, guests, strangers, employees, employers, strangers never left him.

Hidden by a crowd of people who gathered in the square out of sheer curiosity rather than to welcome the newlywed couple Stavros was able to observe his father and his step-mother who were quite unaware of his presence. Only after all the questions have been answered and the various degrees of relations have been acknowledged—father, mother, brothers, sisters, nephews, nieces, uncles, aunts and all their families and friends addressed—only then did Christos asked about Stavros. Lost in the crowd Stavros had remained hidden and silent, not sure about his own importance in all this. And when Christos asked at last 'but where is Stavros? Is he not here?' did Stavros dare to shout blushing all over 'I am here. I am here.' People pushed him to the front and his father embraced him for a moment and then had a good look at him. 'You are a big lad now,' he pronounced. And then, 'we have to do something about these bare feet.'

Needless to say, Stavros' dreams never came true. His father was in thrall to his older, richer and bossy wife who took a glance at Stavros and declared that she did not want this barefoot, uncouth boy at home with her. She wanted her own children thank you very much. They could pay some money to his grandmother to look after him, they could contribute with food and clothes but taking him in was out of the question. Anyway, he was now used to living with his grandmother, why disturb his life and his routine?

So, the couple established themselves in a newly built house which they paid for with Marilena's money and Stavros reclaimed his old field and trees and vineyards from his brothers. The couple soon established themselves and the locals slowly accepted this bossy and snobbish woman from Limassol who slowly became one of them. So, when, after a few months, she became pregnant she was treated like any of the villagers, if only a "difficult" one. Of course, difficult also meant "special" and "superior" so many women courted her attention and her advice. She was after all from the town, or very close to one.

Stavros had now shoes to wear every day, not only on Sundays and holidays, and owned a good, warm coat that Christos bought for him from one of his trips to Platres. He saw his father irregularly when he popped in to give Elengo some money. Christos found the boy's shy and defensive attitude very difficult to handle. He saw endless accusations in it and started avoiding seeing him alone. He felt uncomfortable with him and did not know what to talk to him about. So this new relationship with his father was a very difficult one for Stavros who returned father's uncomfortable presence with an uncomfortable silence. But in his innermost thoughts he dreamt of doing big things to impress him.

'Kyrie eleyson, Kyrie eleyson, Kyrie eleyson,' the priest was chanting as he waved the incense towards the congregation in all directions. 'Lord have mercy on us.'

The incense filled the church merging with the strong scent of beeswax from the candles and the warm body smell from the faithful. Stavros stayed close to his grandmother. They found a place to sit at the back of the church which was now filling up very rapidly. The newcomers had to stand at the rear of the church close to the door.

Gone were the days when he would leave his grandmother and go outside to join his friends at the churchyard. He was now at the threshold of adult life. He felt he was entering another stage in his life and he was scared. He felt not quite a grown up and certainly not a child anymore. He was about to complete his 12th year and his primary school days were coming to an end. Contradictory voices within him and within the family and the community made him feel very confused.

'The boy must go to the gymnasium,' the teacher repeated.

'Education will not feed you,' grandfather said. 'You need to work in the fields or learn a trade if you want. Work will make a man out of you.'

'This boy should be educated,' Manolis joined in. And Penelope agreed.

'All this is hot air,' Grandad said.

Stavros' head was full of voices. His own, weak voice wanted to scream 'NO! I am not going to work in the fields.'

His father had been open to both sides, listening weighing the arguments. He had insisted that his son completed primary school. He gave money to his grandmother to keep him at school. Stavros looked at his father who was a few rows in front of him and next to him his wife. Their son was not with them. He must be with his grandparents, he thought. Maybe Marilena's parents were here visiting.

Stavros' head was bursting now. His father was so far away from him and his concerns. In two weeks, it was the end of the year, his last year at school, the end of his life as he knew it. And his father seemed oblivious to all this.

After his wife's death, and the death of his new born daughter, Christos fell into depression and took to drink for a while. He neglected his son, whom he seemed to resent for living while his wife was dead. Stavros went to live with his grandmother, Eleni's mother, who looked after him waiting for Christos to recover and perhaps re-marry so that Stavros would have a home again.

But Christos had other things in mind. One day, a year after his wife's death, As Elengo began to hope that her son-in-law was finally emerging from the depths of depression, he announced that he was going to Egypt, to Alexandria, to work. He received a letter, he said, from a friend of his distant cousin Sophocles. There was work there, he said. People get rich there. There are different people there, different conditions. 'Your life will change,' The friend of the cousin said, 'you will see, you will see.'

'I shall come back rich and give Stavros a different life,' he said.

For a year, he went to work in the mines and saved enough money for his ticket and then he was off. Stavros was then hardly 4 years old.

Letters arrived at irregular intervals from which Elengo deduced that all was not well with the ambitious Christos. The big city did not suit him well. Life was fast and impersonal. The women, free and provocative, would take his mind and his money and would disappear. Friends were scarce and relationships not quite clear. He could not decipher the meaning of all this. He fell into depression once again and took once again to drink. That was when he decided to go back to the island. That's when he married Marilena. That's when he came back, married and aloof, not exactly what Stavros had dreamt of in his endless dreams about his father. Stavros was seven years old.

Father had been a word, a person he longed for but could put no face to, a person who was not there. Father was for Stavros a physical craving, a hunger that was never satisfied. His mother had faded from his memory. She was like a fairy presence, perhaps an angel, perhaps the Virgin Mary herself as she appeared in the frescoes of different churches, sad, wise and all embracing, solemn and gentle at the same time. But father was different. Stavros had kept his father's image in his mind all those years. He was four when his father left, and he remembered walking with him and his grandmother to the end of the village where Christos' brother lived. His father kissed him good-bye and said he would write to him from this distant land he called Egypt. He was going to cross the mountains and get on a ship and cross the waters and go to this magical place across the waters.

Stavros watched the two men mount the donkeys and disappear behind the mountains. His mind was full of endless water—endless blue water as people described it—separating him from his father. He had seen photographs of it, cards that people got in Limassol, and the big ships that travelled a long way, further than the horizon. He stayed awake all night thinking of this endless water and his dad disappearing in it.

But now the year was 1918, eight years after his father left, four years after he returned. He was now there, in front of him, both a father and a stranger, standing with his wife a few rows in front of him. The pain was unbearable.

Chapter 5
Limassol 1936

Nellie's Story

Nellie had big plans in her mind. She would become a great writer and a great musician. There was no contradiction to this. She would write great books and she would be the best pianist in Limassol. She would challenge all the small-minded, narrow-minded people around her. She would marry the most desirable, the most sensitive and the richest man in Limassol. She was to be Georges Sand, Anna Karenina (not withstanding her tragic end) and Elizabeth Bennet all in one. Perhaps somewhere there was Emmeline Pankhurst and the suffragettes, and also somewhere there in her mind, was also Aspasia, the great hetaerae from Miletus and wife of the great Athenian leader Pericles. And then there was the great poet Sappho, and the *nearly* Byzantine empress Kassiani. Romantic heroines, freedom fighters, poets and saints all got mixed up in her mind as well as the woman who lost the throne by a whisker, Kassiani. She proved too clever for the Byzantine emperor, Nellie thought. She, Nellie, would have to change singlehandedly this feudal relationship between men and women. She would have to avenge Kassiani's fate—the woman who nearly became the empress of Byzantium.

Kassiani's fate had been a warning for every Greek woman for centuries, a warning for women not to challenge men, not to be "too intelligent", and not to abandon their place in society and be seduced by ambitions and illusions. Nellie considered Kasiani's fate as she was sitting on the patio slicing an orange and sipping at her coffee. The morning was glorious and the March sun enveloped her like a warm mother's embrace. Yet her thoughts were far from being comfortable as she considered Kassiani's predicament.

Kassiani had been a well-known poet of the 9th century A.D. The story went that emperor Theophilos who had heard about her beauty and her talent and intelligence decided to set up a contest to choose his bride. Like Paris in the mythical time of two millennia before, he had a golden apple to be given to the one he chose. The contest was between Kassiani and Theodora. The women lined up in front of him surrounded by courtiers and clergymen. The emperor, so the legend goes, who had already heard a great deal about Kassiani's intelligence wanted to test her obedience and her modesty and said glibly to her "from woman emanate all evils" in this way implying Eve. And the great poet looked at him in the eye and answered with the assertiveness that was not expected of her sex "But from woman emanates also all that is good" implying the virgin Mary. The emperor defeated in his own game could not take this quick answer from a woman. He told Kassiani that she was too clever for a woman and gave the golden apple to Theodora in this way choosing Theodora as his wife and the empress of Byzantium. Disappointed beyond belief the intelligent lonely woman devoted the rest of her life to the church. She became a nun and wrote beautiful hymns. The best well known is the hymn that is recited during the Holy Week on the Tuesday before Easter. The hymn is about the penitential woman who anoints Jesus's feet with costly ointment, in this way demonstrating her own penitence for her own hubris. What a humiliation, what a sell-out Nellie thought. *I will never compromise!*

Nellie heard this story from her teachers at the all-girls school where the main moral to be drawn from it was 'you are a woman, don't be too clever as nobody would want to marry you.' Nellie however heard something very different. 'You are a woman you must fight for freedom. You must fight for all the women. And you must avenge Kassiani.'

In 1936, Nellie was 22 and full of herself. She was beautiful, blonde (a big asset among all the brunette majority even if she enhanced the colour of her hair by using chamomile to lighten it). She had lovely honey colour eyes and a slim figure. She was intelligent, sensitive, she read avidly, could play the piano, she spoke three languages, she played tennis and swam like a dolphin. What else would anybody want from a woman?

Many eligible, and well to do young men, wanted to ask for her hand some willing to wait until her sister Olga was married first as the custom was. Although her parents always said Olga, the elder, had to marry first, it was Nellie who would not hear anything about prospective young men. For by now, she was absolutely infatuated by her tennis partner Evripides, the rich, good looking, fast driving playboy who flirted with her and let her know how fascinating he thought she was. It was a matter of time, a matter of time, she thought. He would one day take her in his arms and kiss her passionately and pronounce his hungry love and beg her, yes beg her, to accept his marriage proposal.

Nellie played this scenario many times in her mind, in fact it became an obsession. That moment, that unique moment when their eyes would meet and they would know beyond any doubt that they were in love with each other. It was early evening, the sky was on fire and the sea turned pale—a huge sheet of pale blue, motionless and silent. Only the gentle sound of the waves lapping the shore. Their eyes would meet. For one moment, they would both be helpless and clueless as to what to do. Nellie could feel his passion in her body, burning like hot iron. Then he would suddenly seize her by the waist and drew her towards him. 'I love you,' he would say, 'I loved you from the first time I set my eyes on you,' and his burning lips would touch hers. 'There is only you,' he would say, 'There has always been you even before I met you.'

They would stay like this in each other's arms for an eternity, the sea lapping the shore and the light fading in the west. Then he would release her and would look searchingly in her eyes. 'Will you marry me?' he would say. 'Please don't say anything. Please think about it. Don't reject me out of hand,' he would say. 'Please say that I am not deluding myself. Please say that you have some feelings for me.' And she would fall once again in his arms and she would say 'I love you. I've always loved you.'

After that, the story deteriorated. She was not quite sure how it was going to go. He would have to come and ask for her hand of course. Her father might have reservations as Evripides had a reputation of a womaniser. But this was gossip from people who did not know him. They did not know him the way she did. They did not know that all the other stuff was a cover-up story to hide their secret love until the time was ripe. Her father could be easily won over. After all, Evripides was the son of one of the most prominent families in Limassol, the scion of an old, respectable family. They had old money as well as respectability. Aristos would certainly be won over.

By this time, Nellie had rejected a couple of suitors who came to ask for her hand, respectable men in their early thirties from a good family and with a good job. She was terrified that anybody would think that they were good enough to win her hand. Anybody, that is, except for Evripides. She kept herself for him. She knew, like nobody else did, that she was to be his. She was to be the gift that made his life worth living.

She would confide to her sister bits and pieces about this secret relationship that was going on in her mind. She would ask her sister what she thought about that particular day's exchange of words and glances after the tennis match. The shaking of hands, the lingering of his hand into hers. The compliments he paid her. It was a foregone conclusion that he was in love with her. Olga was much more realistic and reserved about this. 'But he *is* like this,' she would say timidly and with a great deal of uncertainty in her voice. 'It's his character.'

'You've never been imaginative Olga,' Nellie would say. 'You are not romantic. There are things that never enter your mind.'

There was a great deal of condescension in Nellie's voice as she pronounced the words. 'You are more like our father,' she would continue in a ruthless way. 'You are dead to real passion. You will never fall in love.'

Olga would shake her head and say nothing. What was there to say? Nellie was deluded. Everybody who knew Evripides would know this. But Nellie lived in a world of poetry and romantic passion and was not only oblivious to the real world but deeply despised it.

As the year of 1935 came to an end and the tennis games became more infrequent because of the unreliability of the weather Nellie began to feel impatient and somehow depressed. The reality did not match her expectations and felt completely helpless as to what to do. She would meet Evripides when she went for a stroll on the promenade with her sister and her friends on Sundays. This was the best moment of the week, Sunday early evening. Dressed in her best Sunday dress, with her hair done in an elaborate coiffure above her head, exposing her long, aristocratic neck, her face carefully made up so that it did not look made up at all (as Aristos forbade his daughters to look like "loose women" who used make up and talked and laughed with men). Nellie and Olga and three other friends would take each other's arm and walk arm in arm along the promenade—to the end of it and back and all over again. Together with many other young girls, young men, mothers and young children and elderly couples, the girls walked. And of course they watched and were watched. They were there to see and be seen. They met people they knew well, old friends from school, family friends, aunts, uncles and relatives of aunts and uncles, friends of friends, acquaintances, people they knew about from others, people they barely knew and many others they didn't know.

There were small stalls along the promenade selling pumpkin seeds, roasted chick peas, freshly roasted peanuts that spread their aroma inviting everybody to buy, sweet almonds coated in sugar and small, sugary sweets for children. Corn on the cob was roasted over charcoal and spread its pungent smell everywhere.

'Hello Olga, hello Nellie.' An elderly woman stopped to talk to them. Olga recognised her as the mother of her second cousin's brother-in-law. She was accompanied by her husband, a small man who looked permanently in a sulk and who also whispered a reluctant "good afternoon". Mrs Castoriadis was dressed in black and Olga remembered that her mother had died a few months ago. Her mother had gone to the funeral.

'Good afternoon Mrs Castoriadis,' Olga said taking Mrs Castoriadis' offered hand. 'I am sorry about your mother.'

'God giveth God taketh,' Mrs Castoriadis said in a solemn manner. 'Blessed be God,' she said and crossed herself.

It seemed to Olga that the husband looked even more bad tempered as his wife crossed herself, but it might have been just an impression of hers.

'How is your lovely mother?' Mrs Castoriadis enquired immediately after. 'I couldn't go to church last Sunday, so I missed her. My gout was so bad I had to stay in bed. And today my daughter needed me to look after her daughter. I hope your lovely mother is well. She had this neuralgia in her left arm last time I saw her. How is she?'

'She still has the pain,' Olga replied. 'The doctor said there is nothing he could do. He said she should take aspirin.'

'We are all getting older,' Mrs Castoriadis said. 'God help us all. Doctors are useless anyway. Only God can help us.'

Olga uttered somewhat reluctantly something which sounded like "yes, I guess so". She hated it when women of Mrs Castoriadis age assumed that she and everybody else would or should think the way they did. But she was too polite and too submissive to say anything else.

'And this is your lovely sister?' She enquired as if she were seeing Nellie for the first time. 'I remember you as a little child,' she told Nellie. 'You were so cute and so clever.'

Nellie smiled and said, 'How are you Mrs Castoriadis?'

'Not too bad, blessed be God,' she replied. 'Only my gout torments me every now and then and my digestion is not so good. But blessed be God I am not too bad.'

'And the family, children, grandchildren?' Nellie asked politely.

'They are well Blessed be God.'

The husband and the friends waited patiently for this conversation to finish.

'Give your mother my regards,' Mrs Castoriadis said. 'Hope to see her in church next Sunday.'

They said their goodbyes and continued their walk in the warm afternoon. It was now February and the sun was friendly and welcome. They stopped to buy hot roasted peanuts in their shells and began straight away the ritual of shelling them, sucking all the salt from the shells and eating the kernels. Talking and laughing and munching they walked and exchanged hellos and small talk with friends and acquaintances.

But Nellie's eyes were wandering, deciphering all clues from a distance. A tall young man talking to a friend over there. No, it wasn't Evripides. Another young man with an elderly couple—their son perhaps? But no, it wasn't Evripides. Why was he not here? Didn't he want to see her? Didn't he know that she was here every Sunday with her sister and her friends?

Last Sunday it was one of those stormy days that nobody dared to go outside. The streets of the city became rivers for a few hours and the sea rose angrily over the barrier. But the Sunday before he was there. Wearing a hat and a very elegantly cut new suit he looked like she imagined Mr Darcy to be. Walking with his friends and stopping to say hello to her and her friends—it was all like a dream.

'So good to see you,' he had said looking mellifluously into her eyes and keeping her hand in his hand for an infinitesimally longer time than the usual formal handshake. So that nobody would notice but she, she thought. *It is our secret*, she thought. *Nobody should know. Not yet. But one day it will be public. This secret passion will be public. We will get married for everybody to see. He can't come and ask for my hand*, she told herself. As long as Olga remained unmarried they were barred from marrying. And Evripides was such a sensitive young man. He wouldn't want to put her in a difficult place.

'We should resume our tennis playing,' he said, 'The weather is improving.'

'Yes, that would be lovely,' she said. 'Nothing I would like better.'

'Stavros is keen,' he said turning to Olga.

This seemed to have a double meaning. Whether Olga understood the double meaning she showed no sign.

'Good,' Olga said. 'It would be very good.'

Then he turned to Nellie, 'See you soon,' he said looking deep into her eyes.

He didn't say much more but for Nellie this was enough. This was paradise on earth. This was a secret message delivered to her personally and nobody else had access to it. So, when Olga tried to reason with her she called her heartless, unimaginative, severe and prosaic.

And so the story continued in Nellie's mind full of secrets, innuendos and images of love and bliss.

But winter was long that year, long and difficult. It had rained more than usual and the sea was so angry that it jumped over the barrier and onto the promenade, so that walks on the promenade had to be cancelled. Nobody dared to walk there anymore, and the girls felt imprisoned in their house.

As day succeeded day and nothing earth shattering happened Nellie craved to rise above the boring, everyday limitations of being a woman. She became a regular visitor to her cousin Maroulla's house where her husband Sotiris kept his well-stocked library. Sotiris was the owner and editor-in-chief of the local newspaper The Observer. A very intelligent and well-educated young man, he was willing to lend books to Nellie and to share with her some of his ideas. So Nellie took to reading more and more romantic literature and more and more books about the suffragettes.

But now it was almost spring, February coming slowly to an end, and the weather was warm and friendly and the sea calm inviting young and old back onto the promenade. The small stalls opened again and the kiosks selling newspapers, magazines, cigarettes and children's toys were thriving as the new season began. The possibility of love was smiling at Nellie once again.

She continued to look around. Why is he not there? Does he not love her anymore? That's impossible. She loses her faith so quickly. She is weak and feeble minded. Perhaps he was ill? How would she know if anything happened to him? Would anybody tell her? Her parents were not friends with his parents and they had no friends in common. Nellie's mind was deeply preoccupied. Dark thoughts clouded her mind.

Some girls from their old school came from the opposite direction.

Screeches and laughter and embraces. How are you? And you? What are you doing? Congratulations about your sister. Now it's your turn.

The girls exchanged information and good wishes.

'I had a marriage proposal,' one of the girls said suddenly. They all turned towards her. This was so personal they all went silent. 'But he is so old and ugly. I know this shouldn't matter. He is from a good family and he is a solicitor and earns well. But can I love him? My mother said love comes later, when you live together, she said. But she is of another generation you know. We are different. Our generation is different.'

'That's what I say,' Nellie said with passion. 'We don't have to marry whom our parents want. We have our own life to live.'

The girls became excited.

'I want to marry and have children,' one of the girls said, 'If I wait for Prince Charming I might miss my chance.'

'For God's sake,' Nellie almost shouted 'Would you marry anybody who would give you children?'

'Well not *anybody*,' the girl continued taken aback by Nellie's aggressive tone. 'It has to be the right person. But he doesn't have to be prince Charming.'

'So,' Nellie continued provocatively 'So you are not so different from us then!'

Toulla went silent. 'Well maybe not,' she said after a pause feeling however shut up by Nellie and resenting it very much.

'Do you still play tennis?' a girl named Agatha asked.

'Oh yes,' Nellie said. 'We stopped for winter, but we are about to resume.'

'My parents wouldn't hear of it,' Agatha said. 'They think that women get corrupted through things like this. They are so old fashioned my parents.'

'Rubbish,' said Nellie. 'We have fun and meet young men. What's wrong with this?'

'My mother wouldn't hear of it,' Agatha continued 'so I stopped asking.'

'Our mother is so good,' Nellie said. 'She keeps it from father. It's our secret.'

'Ah,' Agatha said. 'You are so lucky having such an understanding mother.'

'She is open minded our mother,' Nellie continued 'and she feels so restricted by my father that she is determined not to do this to her children.'

'You are so lucky,' Agatha said again.

'You know Toulla got married,' Agatha continued. 'Do you remember Toulla, the girl who wouldn't talk to anybody at school. We were all too inferior for her.'

'Oh yes,' Nellie said. 'Who did she marry? Tell us,' one the other girls jumped in.

'Oh, it's a long story,' Agatha said. 'The man, who seems to have made a lot of money in Africa, asked for her cousin's hand and she declined despite the pressure from her parents. But her parents insisted so in the end she gave in. They got engaged and at that moment this other man she loved secretly declared his love for her and asked her to dissolve her engagement which she did as she secretly loved this man all along. Anyway, the groom was now without a bride and thereupon he went to Toulla's parents and asked for her hand. They accepted instantly, and she also was delighted.'

'What you would expect from Toulla,' one of the girls said.

'Well all this is so disgusting,' Nellie was almost shouting. 'Parents deciding for their daughters.'

'No, she was happy about it,' Agatha continued. 'I know all this from my brother-in law's cousin who is a cousin of Toulla's mother.'

'So what?' Nellie continued. 'And how could Toulla's cousin get engaged to a man she didn't love just because her parents wanted her to?'

'She couldn't wait for Yiorgo to make up his mind,' Agatha said. 'Anyway, it all ended well. Yiorgo made up his mind and they are now happily married.'

'I would never get engaged to somebody I don't love,' Nellie said with passion again.

They all looked at her.

'Sure,' one of the girls said. 'It's so much better if one loves the person before one marries. But this cannot be guaranteed.'

'Then one shouldn't marry,' Nellie declared. 'Under these circumstances marriage is not different from prostitution.'

Nellie had read this phrase somewhere, she could not remember where, but she agreed with it, agreed wholeheartedly. The vehemence of this took everybody by surprise.

'You don't mean that!' Agatha said.

'Yes, I do,' Nellie said. 'Giving oneself for security, good salary, good position, and children, is like selling oneself.'

'Come on Nellie.' They were all talking together. 'You don't mean this. But this is nonsense. This is crazy what you are saying.'

'What you are saying,' Nellie was now shouting, 'is completely, utterly, totally unacceptable. It's giving up everything one believes in.'

'Speak for yourself,' one of the girls said. 'I don't believe in what you believe.'

'Girls, girls,' one of them said. 'Stop it. We are out to have a good time. And maybe find a man,' she added giggling. 'Let's have a good time and forget the arguments.'

'We are not merchandise,' Nellie began again but nobody was in any mood to argue.

They parted giggling and kissing and sending regards to mothers and sisters and brothers.

But Nellie was now in a foul mood. All this talk about arranged marriages and wanting children and wanting a good secure marriage made her feel like an alien. She objected to all this, she *knew* in her heart that this was all wrong, but nobody wanted to listen, Not even her own sister.

Olga had remained silent throughout this discussion. She could see both sides of the debate and could not put into words any convincing argument for either.

They walked in silence Nellie looking around for Evripides, the man who would save her from all this mean life, these sordid marriage arrangements, these old-fashioned ideas. She, Nellie, would show them, would show them what was true, pure and worth pursuing.

But however hard Nellie scoured the promenade and the people who came and went, she could not see Evripides. But another well-known person appeared suddenly. It was Stavros with his friend Spyros. They were deep in discussion and they nearly passed the girls by without seeing them.

'What a lovely surprise,' Stavros said as he suddenly stopped in his tracks. He took his hat off in an exaggerated gesture of cordiality. If Olga blushed, nobody saw it as it was imperceptible. But Stavros directed his attention to her.

'How lovely to see you,' he said. 'By the way, this is my dearest friend Spyros.' Handshakes all around.

'How are you?' Stavros said suddenly turning towards Nellie as if he had suddenly remembered her.

'Very well Stavro. We were wondering when the tennis season is due to start.' Nellie said.

'I hope soon.' Stavros was again directing his attention towards Olga.

Olga visibly blushed now but only Stavros noticed.

'The weather has improved so much,' he said, 'we should resume soon.'

He stopped for a minute, not sure whether to continue. Then he said looking a bit uncomfortable 'but I am not sure about Evripides,' he added.

'What about Evripides,' Nellie asked, 'Is he not well?'

'He is fine,' Stavros was again sounding vague.

'What's wrong then?' Nellie's heart was racing sensing a disaster approaching.

'Nothing,' Stavros said. 'He is otherwise engaged.'

Nellie's heart went from racing to stopping. She was sure her heart missed a few beats and was soon going to stop altogether.

'What sort of "otherwise engaged"?' She sounded matter of fact, almost sarcastic but her heart was threatening to abandon her. She had gone white but again only Stavros noticed.

'Oh, I don't know,' Stavros said. 'I don't really know.' He seemed to regret mentioning Evripides. 'He might come who knows.'

He seemed embarrassed. Olga intervened.

'We'd love to start again,' she said. 'When do you think we can do it?'

'I hope in a couple of weeks,' Stavros said. 'I went to see the tennis courts, they are still full of puddles but in a couple of weeks they will be ready, waiting for us.'

'Good,' Olga said.

Olga used always understatement, but Stavros liked this reserved, focused woman. She made up for her sister's "being in the clouds", a bit superior, a bit arrogant, exaggerated manner.

Stavros made his excuses shortly after this. He seemed to be regretting opening the whole subject of Evripides as he could see that Nellie was clearly affected by what he said.

'See you soon,' he said. 'I'll send you a message when we are ready to resume,' and touching his hat and directing a last glance towards Olga he walked away followed by Spyros.

'Send a message' was a complicated manoeuvre whereby Stavros would tell his friend Antonis who would tell his sister Fotini who knew Olga from school to go and tell Olga the date and the time when they could resume their tennis practice.

'Good,' Olga said and gave him one of her rare warm smiles.

'I like his friend,' Olga's friend Elena said suddenly. 'Do you know anything about him?' She was addressing her question towards Olga as if anything to do with Stavros was Olga's domain. Olga noticed this and wondered whether her friend assumed there was something going on between her and Stavros. But there was something, wasn't there? Or had she imagined it all?

'I don't know anything about him,' she said. 'It's the only time I met him.'

'Is it possible to find out?' Elena went on.

'I'll see what I can do,' Olga continued.

'Oooh!' Lina mocked. 'Falling in love?'

'He looks like an interesting guy,' Elena went on disregarding Lina's sarcastic remark. 'And if he is a friend of Stavros he must be a good guy.'

Stavros had a reputation of an earnest, hardworking man of strict morals but full of fun at the same time.

Olga blushed again but as her friend was looking at the sea she did not notice.

Nellie was in her own world hardly hearing a word of what was said. She did not know what to make out of what Stavros had said, but her body was reacting before she had any time to decipher the enigmatic words. She felt faint and sick as if she were going to throw up.

The sun was slowly sinking below the horizon and the whole sky went into a riot of colours. The sea put on a purple mantle that gave an unreal feel to the promenade and its occupants.

'Time to head for home,' the sensible Olga said. 'Dad will already be waiting by the door counting the seconds.'

The girls were supposed to be home by sunset and if they were late by a few minutes Aristos got very upset, angry and displayed all the signs of an absolute monarch in charge of his vassals.

The girls headed for home in a hurry.

Chapter 6
Marathasa August 1918

The Need for a Pound

It was now August. Another Sunday in church. Another Sunday when Stavros had to endure his father being more interested in his other son, much more than in him—his father with his perfect family, his new house and the obvious good life he was having (with his wife's money, as people gossiped).

Stavros was extremely sensitive to gossip and to the whole relationship between his father and his wife, strictly speaking his step-mother but Stavros would never allow himself to think or pronounce this word. When his father came back with his new pregnant wife, it was clear to Stavros who the boss was in this new household.

Marilena—even her name sounded exotic and foreign to village ears—knew exactly what she wanted and if there was one thing she didn't want was for Stavros to come and live with them. She considered herself much more sophisticated than the people in the village. Coming from a village near Limassol and being in touch with the sophisticated Limassol people these mountain villagers looked primitive to her. This barefoot boy, dirty and unkempt was not coming to her house. Not as long as she was there. And she was there to stay, everybody should be sure of this.

Stavros looking at his father and his wife felt ashamed and bitter at the same time. His only chance to get out of this situation he found himself in was to go to the gymnasium, to educate himself, to show everybody what he could do. But this gift was denied him. He had no money.

On this August morning, four years after his father returned to the village with Marilena on his right arm, with the temperature rising to the mid-thirties and the faithful dispersing from the church, Christos approached Stavros and his grandmother.

'Hi Stavro,' he said giving him a pat on the shoulder 'we need to talk about your future.'

This remark referred to the backstage talks with the teacher and with Penelope and Manolis who were pressurising Christo to find the money to send his son to the gymnasium. There had been a great deal of meetings and negotiations behind the scenes. The teacher had gone to see Manolis, Penelope's brother and Stavros' uncle, who was very much of the opinion that his nephew should go to the gymnasium. Manolis then went to see Christos who said that yes, he wanted Stavros to go to the gymnasium, but he didn't have the money to pay the fees. Penelope was also recruited in this campaign. She went to see Marilena, but she did not get very far as Marilena was of the opinion that her step-son would be better off working in the fields and in the mines and should not be encouraged to have all these illusions that he was different from the rest of the village. Penelope could sense the intense jealousy and envy that emanated from her as her son seemed to be rather dull and people inevitably made comparisons with Stavros' abilities, but said nothing.

Marilena went to see Charalambos, Christos' uncle, who was known to be against the idea of Stavros going to the gymnasium. The two agreed on this and Charalambos ranted quite a bit about "this boy's mind being inflated by all this useless education which cut people from their roots and destroyed their lives."

'All is hot air,' he bellowed 'hot air that turns children against their parents.' Marilena agreed and left promising to do what she could to prevent this scandalous thing from happening.

Christos, who wanted Stavros to go to the gymnasium but did not dare to say this aloud in front of his wife, went to see his other uncle who had a bit of savings and asked him whether he could help. Philippos listened in silence and promised to think about it. But the days went by and Christos did not hear from him.

So the negotiations went on and time was running out. The new school for boys had opened a few years before and was 10 miles away from the village. It was a private school founded by a rich benefactor who was born in a nearby village and made a lot of money abroad. The lessons were all in English and the pupils were offered weekly board.

There was a great deal of excitement in the village that such a school was built so close to their village. 'This village will gain in importance,' some people said making gestures of appreciation and exaggeration. We might get a new road and even electricity like in the towns. 'You will see! You will see. This village will gain in importance. The government won't be able to ignore us anymore.' Others were totally indifferent to it as if it did not concern them. A gymnasium in English! Who would benefit from it?

Stavros was the first pupil from the village seriously considering of attending secondary school and the gossip in the village was spreading. Discussions about it were taking place at the caffeneion among men, in the fields as both men and women harvested the crops or attended to the vineyards. And at home where women tended babies and children and cooked and washed and gossiped with each other.

It was now August and Stavros was getting impatient. He had finished the primary school wiping out all the prizes. But the prize he treasured most, and the prize that got him closer to his goal to go to the gymnasium was the prize for overall excellence. With it came the big sum of £1 sterling. It had been given every year to the most outstanding pupil and it was based on a local benefactor's will. Everybody knew about the fact that this year it had gone to Stavros. And not only that. The teacher announced in his speech that this was the most intelligent, the most talented pupil he had ever encountered in his teaching career and that he hoped that his education would not stop there. Everybody was there to hear this, his father, his grandmother, Penelope, Manolis (Marilena had excused herself claiming a minor illness of her son).

The great news was however that now Stavros had one pound—a great deal of money that is. The fees for the first year at the gymnasium were two pounds. How to get this missing pound? This was the big conundrum that Christos, Penelope, Manolis, and to a lesser extent Stavros' uncle were trying to solve. The meeting today was to see whether they could get together one pound from relatives and friends.

Christos looked at his son and felt pride and pity as he stood there facing his father with eyes like an abandoned dog.

'I will see to it that you go to the gymnasium,' he promised knowing very well that there was not much he could do. 'I'll do everything I can.'

The people were now dispersing going home for lunch and siesta.

'We shall all meet this afternoon at my house,' Christos continued 'after siesta at 5 o'clock. Entaxi?'

'Entaxi,' Stavros said.

His heart was pounding. His fate was going to be decided today, this afternoon. To go or not to go the gymnasium. To have his dreams fulfilled, or to have his dreams smashed for ever.

'If they ask me,' his great grandfather said as they were having lunch that day 'If they ask me I would say leave the boy alone. He doesn't need all that poppycock! He is a hard worker. He will do well in the village and in the mines. Why confuse him with all these foreign ideas? But nobody wants the opinion of an old man,' he said bitterly. 'They think I passed it. My ideas are not fashionable anymore. Nobody asks me about anything anymore.'

Stavros' heart froze at these words. Not that it was anything new. He knew his great grandfather's opinions and ideas. But nevertheless, every time he heard him speaking he felt an iron hand gripping his heart and stomach.

Elengo said nothing. She had very conflicting feelings about Stavros' going to the gymnasium. What could he do with all this education? Perhaps become a teacher? Well that was not bad was it? But The village had a teacher already. He might be sent miles away, God knows to which corner of the island? Would she lose him for ever?

She remained silent and they continued to eat in silence.

In the afternoon, they all gathered at Stavros' and Marilena's house— Marilena, Penelope, Manolis, Nearchos who was Christos' brother, Charalambos, Christos' uncle, and Christos himself.

Marilena was taking orders for coffee—2 sweets, 3 metrious. Stavro I'll bring you some lemonade.

Stavros managed a thank you.

By now, he was beside himself with anxiety, overwhelmed with the seriousness of the situation and with his own powerlessness. What he did not realise was that some of them at least were there to help, to find a way for Stavros to go to the Gymnasium. He saw everybody, apart from Penelope, as an enemy who would find excuses not to help him. His own father he did not trust as he was so much under the thumb of his wife. And his wife was against him getting on with his education.

The men were now exchanging small bits of information about their families trying to lighten the atmosphere. Penelope's youngest boy had chicken pox and he was quite ill with high temperature. Everybody gave advice—'keep him warm,' 'he needs to cool down,' 'give him lots of chamomile tea, it will help him sleep,' 'give him a series of "ventusas" (cupping) they will reduce the fever,' 'he needs to sweat it all out.'

'I remember when my children had chicken pox,' Manolis told everybody. 'Sotiris got so ill I went to bring Dr Theodoracopoulos from Platres. It took so long that by the time he arrived Sotiris was well and Yiannis was now ill, so he saw Yiannis.'

Everybody commented how the government did not care much about this village, lost in the mountains.

'They don't give a damn about us' Manolis said. They forget we exist. No proper roads, no doctor, no transport. You know in the towns the government has brought electricity to people's homes. People have electric light at home. Imagine no candles, no paraffin lamps anymore. Can you imagine?

They all shook their heads. 'The government has forgotten us here. This thriving village, the pride of Marathasa, is totally forgotten.'

'The English think only of themselves' Manolis interrupted. 'They don't have our good in mind. They have theirs. That's what imperialism is.'

Everybody nodded and made noises of agreement. Stavros began to feel that everybody had forgotten him and forgotten why they were there.

Marilena appeared with a big tray that contained the coffees, the lemonade and some Greek Cakes—baklava, kadeifi, bourekia. Noises of approval and appreciation accompanied this.

'Marilena's coffee is the best,' Christos' uncle pronounced.

'Is iyian,' (to health) everybody said and they drank their coffee.

Marilena who caught the end of Manolis' sentence spoke as she distributed the coffees and the cakes continuing the conversation.

'Of course they don't care,' she said. 'More than this. They want us to be slaves and shut our eyes. They don't want us to thrive and know about progress. Then we might rebel.'

Everybody agreed.

'The English are much better than the Turks' Penelope intervened, 'but they are still our masters. Greeks are not born to be slaves.'

The voices of agreement became louder. Somebody mentioned the Greek Revolution and Lord Byron who came to fight on the side of the Greeks during the revolution against the Turks and who died of typhoid fever at Messolonghi in West Greece.

'The English were on our side then,' somebody said. It might have been Christos.

'Times have changed though. We need another revolution, our own revolution. We need *enosis (*union with Greece*)*.'

They all agreed in a noisy and enthusiastic way.

'But we missed our chance.'

It was Christos again referring to the hesitation of the Greek government to enter the First World War and Britain's promise to Greece that if she had entered the war in 1915 the island would be returned to Greece.

'We've been cheated,' Charalambos, intervened. 'As always we have been betrayed. We are small and weak, and nobody takes us seriously. But we must show them. We must show them what being Greek means.'

'The blame is with the Greek government,' Penelope argued. 'They hesitated and hesitated.'

Penelope was referring here to the Greek government's prevarication in entering the war. The British had promised Greece that if she entered the war in support of the allies they would allow the island to unite with Greece and the long-awaited enosis would be accomplished. In the end, Greece entered the war in 1917, after protracted discussions and disagreements between the King and Parliament. In the end, the king abdicated and Greece entered the war, but this was considered too late for Britain and as a result the island remained under British rule.

'No,' Charalambos bellowed. 'How dare you suggest such a thing? Mother Greece did everything she could. We were betrayed. Once again, we were betrayed, but not by Greece. The English look after their own interests not ours.'

'Penelope has a point,' Manolis rushed to the defence of his sister. 'Greece did not have our best interest in mind.'

'You are not only a traitor,' Nearchos bellowed. 'You are also stupid.'

'Can't you see,' Manolis tried again 'can't you see that Greece thinks of her interest not ours? If it was in her interest to go to war she would—If it is not in her interest she will let us down.'

Now Charalambos was beside himself. Red in the face and hyper-ventilating he went on frontal attack. 'You are a traitor,' he repeated and again. 'You are a traitor, how dare you say things like this?'

Marilena seemed to be relishing the possibility that this political discussion will end up in a physical fight and then Stavros and his problem would be forgotten. While everybody else tried to calm things down, she stepped in.

'Charalambos is right,' she said defending her husband's aging uncle. 'You are a traitor Manolis. How dare you speak like this about Mother Greece. How dare you, you a little, uneducated peasant in the depths of Marathasa, question the decisions of well-educated people in Greece.'

Marilena was trading here on her origins in a village near Limassol. She hinted by what she said about the fact that she considered people in this village a bit thick, a bit primitive and certainly uneducated.

'You keep out of this Marilena and let the men fight this one out.'

Manolis was angry and slammed his fist on the table. The coffee cups rattled and some of the lemonade in Stavros' glass overflowed and stained the beautifully embroidered tablecloth. 'Charalambos is not only stupid but also naïve.' It was now his turn to shout at the top of his voice. 'He thinks that Mother Greece has no other problems but to look after her baby island.'

A pandemonium broke out here. People talked all at the same time trying to be heard.

Marilena who was told to shut up and leave this serious debate to the men stepped in the middle and shouted. 'Manoli you are a traitor.'

Penelope had not said a word. She could see Stavros' face from where she sat, and she was sure he was trying to hold back his tears.

Charalambos got up and challenged Manolis. 'If you are a man come and fight like a man.'

'I don't fight with men who are twice my age,' Manolis answered referring to the fact that Charalambos was at least 35 years older than he.

Penelope got up and tried to calm down the situation. 'We've come here,' she said to find a solution to Stavros' problem not to have political discussions.

Nobody was listening however. Penelope tried again. 'Let's calm down,' she said 'and think about Stavros.'

By then, Charalambos was already at the door. 'I am not going to sit here with traitors and morons,' he said, 'who are also cowards. You will not fight. In my time, men could fight for what they believed in.'

Marilena was now talking to Charalambos. 'Calm down uncle' She was saying. 'You know how stupid some people can be. Stupid and coward. A lethal combination.'

Manolis got up as well and in one leap she was next to Marilena. 'Shut your stupid mouth,' he screamed. 'You have no right to pass judgment on any of us. You are a stranger here.' He raised his hand, but Christos was there in a split second and held Manolis' hand.

'Coward,' he screamed 'you want to hit a woman. You are not a man'

Manolis was now beside himself with rage but it was obvious that he tried to calm himself down. 'I would hit her,' he said a bit calmer, 'because she is stupid and wants to stir up trouble here. But we are family,' he added in a more conciliatory tone. 'She is family and families must stick together.'

'Now you thought about it,' Marilena chuckled. 'Look at this lovely family specimen here. The personification of loyalty,' she said pointing to Manolis.

Manolis hesitated for a moment and then walked out of the door saying, 'we'll sort this out some other time.'

Penelope made a last effort to bring the rest of the group back to the original task. 'We gathered here,' she began, 'to talk about Stavros' education.'

But nobody was listening. Marilena was screaming now saying that Manolis was not only a traitor but he let the family down. He talks about family, but he doesn't give a damn. He doesn't care about Stavros. He only cares about himself.

This was so obviously not true that Penelope got up as well. 'I don't think you have any right to talk about my brother in this way,' she said. 'He cares about Stavros in a way that you cannot even begin to imagine as your little head is full only of yourself and your own interests and your own son.'

Marilena was now ready to hit Penelope. 'You come to my house,' she screeched and shook uncontrollably 'you come here in my house to insult me. Out, out,' she screamed.

'I am going,' Penelope shouted. 'Come Stavro let's go.'

Stavros was now crying without trying to hide his tears.

'What about my school?' he sobbed. 'What will happen?'

'We'll talk again Stavro,' Christos now said. 'Don't worry,' he said putting his hand on his son's shoulder. 'Don't worry, we'll talk again.'

Out in the blazing sun Stavros sobbed and Penelope put her arm around him and they walked together until they arrived at Stavros' home.

Chapter 7
Marathasa September 1918

It was now the beginning of September and the vineyards on the hills exhibited proudly the ripe red grapes ready to be harvested. The olive trees, the almond and the walnut trees yielded to the violent thrashing and shaking which constituted the native way of harvesting them. The souzouko sticks hung, like sausages, from the ceiling of the sheds ready for the next fair on September the 14th, the day of the Cross. Mary's Assumption on the 15th August, and the big fair that accompanied it, came and went. Stavros' grandmother had made some money in the big fair at the monastery of Trodhidissa selling baskets, walking sticks and olives, dried cherries and walnuts. She was now preparing together with the rest of the village for the 14th September.

Stavros' fate was still hanging in the balance. Nobody was willing, or nobody could afford, to pay the one pound that he needed to go to the Gymnasium. But Penelope kept re-assuring him.

'We'll find a way Stavro, don't worry. I am working on it.'

But it was now the beginning of September. The intense heat had given way to a gentler sun and a cool breeze. The evenings began to feel chilly and the days shortened. Even at midday the shadows were longer and the colours more vivid.

Charalambos, who acted as Christos' father, became more and more impatient with Stavros.

'You've got to learn a trade,' he kept repeating to Stavros like a mantra. 'If you don't want to work in the fields or in the mines you can become a cobbler, or a smith. You need to stop fooling around with school and education. These things are not for us. We are hard workers, not idle dandies. Maybe people in the towns can make a living from education but here we are hard workers. This is us.'

Stavros never said anything to his cantankerous grandfather, but he was always close to tears when he spoke to him.

'Are you a man?' Charalambos would scold him when he detected tears in his eyes. 'What sort of man are you? A sissy? You've got to toughen up my lad. Toughen up. I always said schools make sissies out of boys look at me, Stavro, nobody taught me how to read or write but I am a man Stavro, a real man who is not afraid of the hard work in the fields and in the mines,' and without waiting for Stavros to say anything he would turn around and walk away.

Stavros would often go and visit his teacher after such a dressing down. Arriving there in tears, his teacher would take him in and give him a glass of lemonade and a sesame sweet.

'Don't worry Stavro,' he would say in a gentle voice. 'There are a few of us working on this. We'll find a way.'

But the days and the weeks passed by and no way was found. It was now September. The school was due to start on the 1st October as all Gymnasiums. Time was running out and Stavros' anxiety increased.

'I would like you to go to the Gymnasium,' Christos told Stavros, 'but I don't have this damn pound and I don't know how to go about getting it.'

Stavros knew, as everybody else knew and some even talked about it, that Marilena had the money, in some bank in Limassol. But Christos could not, would not, humiliate himself by asking her for the "damned pound". She was bound to say no anyway. She was bound to deny that she had it. She would invoke her parents who might need the money for doctors from Limassol, they were not getting any younger were they? She would refer to their son who would need the money for *his* education.

Christos was well aware of Marilena's feelings towards Stavros, as everybody else in the village also was. It was the unmentionable truth that Marilena did not want Stavros to get more education, or to thrive at all. And Marilena had powerful allies like Charalambos and Elengou's father as well. Stavros himself was aware of this and his grandmother did not mince her words.

'Marilena,' she would say with a disdainful expression in her face and with the raising of her right hand in a gesture that spoke volumes about how she felt about this foreigner in their village, 'Marilena has only one interest in mind Stavro. She doesn't want you to progress. She is green with envy that you are so clever, and you have won all the prizes in your school and if you go to the

Gymnasium you will win all the prizes there and by comparison her son will be proved to be like her—thick and dumb.'

So the days dragged on and Stavros became more and more depressed.

But then came the day that Stavros would remember for the rest of his life as the day in which his fate was finally decided.

It was an evening in mid-September, just after the festival of the Cross when Penelope burst into her mother's kitchen waving a letter. Elengou was cooking lentils with olive oil, onions and rice and Stavros had just come in after he had fed the goats and the chickens and had watered the vegetables.

'Look, look!' Penelope was still waving the letter and was so out of breath that for a moment she could say nothing. 'Look mum, Stavro, look! It's a letter from Vassilis from Alexandria.'

Letters arrived in the village once a week brought by the only coach that reached the village. Penelope had gone especially to meet the coach master that evening as she did for the last few Thursdays but without any success so far. But this evening there it was: a letter addressed to her. Penelope snatched the letter and opened it in a hurry tearing the envelope but being very careful not to erase the address. In front of some idle villagers, she screamed with joy. 'I knew it, I knew it,' she cried and without explaining anything to the amazed and very curious villagers she ran to her mother's house.

'Listen! Listen!' she was shouting almost. 'It's from Vassili. I wrote to him in despair and look he has answered. He says he can pay the pound for Stavros' school. He will send the money with a friend who works on a ship. The ship will be arriving in Limassol next week and somebody needs to be there to meet him and collect the pound. Maybe Manolis will do it.'

Vassilis was Penelope's youngest brother and Elengo's fifth child who chose to leave the village and go and work in Egypt. They heard from him every now and then when a letter would arrive with news of this wonderful city, Alexandria, and how different it all was from the village and how much people earned and how houses were modern with running water and indoor toilets and electricity.

Penelope was waving the letter and Elengo and Stavros were hanging on Penelope's every word. 'I told you it will be all right Stavraki,' she said embracing him. 'I promised. And when auntie Penelope promises she doesn't lie.'

Stavros snatched the letter from her fingers.

'Read it Stavro,' she said. 'Read it aloud so that your grandma will also hear.'

By now, Nearchos was out of his room and was standing at the kitchen door silent, listening.

'Your grandpa as well,' Penelope added. 'He needs to hear.'

Stavros began to read.

"Dear Penelope,

I was very happy to hear from you. You and mum and Manolis and Maroulla and Evridiki and Androulla and Vassos and everybody in the village are very dear to me. One day I shall come back and embrace you all. At the moment, I have to earn my living and save some money before I return home to see you all. When I left, Stavros was only seven years old and now you are talking about Gymnasium. I am very happy to learn that he is very intelligent and that his teacher thinks that he must continue his education and that the new Gymnasium is only 10 miles away. I am also happy that he won the Sophronion prize of £1. We should all be grateful for our benefactor Nicos Sophroniou who left the money for this prize. Now it is time for me to contribute to Stavros' education and I shall do this with great pleasure. Listen to how this can be done. I shall give the pound to my friend Antonis who works on the ship Poseidon. He is a dear friend and a person I trust absolutely for his honesty. He is like a brother. The ship will be in Limassol on the 22nd September. If somebody (maybe Manolis?) can come to Limassol and meet Antonis the transaction will be accomplished, and Stavros can go to the Gymnasium. I am not sure whether there is time for you to answer this letter. Just come, one of you, to the Limassol port on the 22nd September in the afternoon and ask for Antonis who works on Poseidon. He will be waiting for you with the much-needed pound.

I kiss you and your mum and all brothers, sisters, cousins, nephews, nieces, uncles, aunts and friends and the whole village. I miss you all.

With all my love, Vassilis"

Penelope's face muscles were fighting the tears which insisted on appearing. And she kept wiping them with her old handkerchief.

'You see Stavraki, you see. We have won. You are going to the Gymnasium.'

'It's true. It's true, auntie Penelope, it is true,' he repeated embracing Penelope. 'It's true grandma. It's true.'

'I am so glad my boy,' Elengou said wiping her eyes with her apron.

Grandfather framed by the kitchen door had said nothing up to now. No sound. No comment. Suddenly he cleared his throat noisily and everybody looked at him suddenly remembering that he was there.

'This is bad news,' he said solemnly as if he was announcing a death, 'bad news,' he repeated. 'They distort young people's minds. They fill them with hot air. Education! Nobody taught *me* anything. I didn't go to school and I am none the worse for it. Had to go and work in the fields and earn my living with my own two hands. I had to work my way through life not sit in a chair and read books. My eight children are all doing well and my grandchildren also. All married here and in the neighbouring villages—apart from Vassilis who chose to go to Egypt and make money and now wants to give us lectures about education. Everybody else is happy and fulfilled. They want to drive this boy out of the village. He will be stranger among strangers. Never one of us again, but never one of them, either. He will be all alone in the world. They want to fill his head with dreams and hot air. They want to ruin him.'

Silence fell like a shroud after grandpa's speech. A donkey brayed. A dog barked. The wind blew. The wailing of the child was audible somewhere in the distance.

'Times have changed granddad,' Penelope said after what seemed to Stavros like an eternity. 'We don't live in the 19th century anymore.'

'Then God help you all,' granddad said and turned abruptly and went back to his room.

Chapter 8
Limassol 1936

Nellie Has Some Bad News

It was now April and Nellie and Olga had not heard from either Evripides or Stavros. This deafening silence would have made any other young lady suspicious and worried. But not Nellie. She did not cease to dream her dreams of being swept off her feet by Evripides, of being kissed in the moonlight while the sea was lapping the shore and Chopin's piano music came out of a window somewhere in the distance. The dreams of being with him in his open car and her hair loose on her shoulders being blown away as they sped into the future leaving behind all the dreary world of her parents, the prison called home.

But as time went on and no news about resuming tennis came she manufactured another explanation. She thought about Elizabeth Bennett and how she had to wait and wait for Mr Darcy to come, how she had been disappointed and full of prejudice and anger and how at last her heart was ready to receive him. She told herself that perhaps she hadn't been ready. This disappearance of Evripides was a test for her. He was testing her. She had to bear his absence and wait. Wait patiently.

She now spent more and more time at home reading English and French novels borrowed from Sotiris' library and finding out more about the suffragettes. Instead of embracing any kind of reality Nellie got more and more enveloped into the dream world of distant lands and distant heroines.

And then one day disaster struck. And it was so final that it left no room for doubt.

It was a Thursday morning in April, a few weeks after Nellie and Olga met Stavros at the promenade. Nellie had just finished her breakfast which she took, as every day, together with her mother, Anna and Olga. Aristos took his breakfast much earlier as his work at the bank began at 8 o'clock. She was now sitting in the sun, in the small courtyard at the back of the house, under the pomegranate tree that offered some shade and read her book. It was a novel by Virginia Woolf and Nellie was instantly transported into another world, away from the small town of Limassol, from her imprisoning parents and disabled sister. Thalia and Kyriakou worked side by side in the kitchen washing up the breakfast things, cleaning and sorting out lunch. Olga was sorting out the bedrooms, making the beds, sweeping the floor, tidying up.

Anna was sitting on the patio composing a poem to Mother Madeleine with whom she was madly in love. She wouldn't of course use these particular words, but it was obvious to everybody else that Anna worshipped Mother Madeleine and wrote endless poems to her. When the first crop of violets from the garden came she asked her mother to pick them and took them to Mother Madeleine together with her latest poem.

Mother Madeleine was the Mother Superior at the convent of St Michael, and the director of the convent school which Anna, Olga and Nellie had attended. Mother Madeleine was like a mother, a lover and a saviour for Anna. She was this special human being who had saved her from a life of meaninglessness. She had recognised Anna's ability to learn and her unique type of intelligence, her aptitude for foreign languages and her talent for poetry. And she encouraged her to stay at school until she was 16 years old, just like her sisters. She had recognised Anna's intelligence when everybody else including the doctors shook their heads and said that she would never learn anything. She was a "cripple" and an "idiot". This child was incapable of learning.

Anna thrived under mother Madeleine's protection and attention. Slowly a special relationship developed between her and Mother Superior. On Sunday afternoons for instance Mother Madeleine, accompanied by one of the senior nuns, would drop in at Anna's house and take her with them either to the convent when some lecture or some concert took place, or simply for an outing—a walk on the promenade, or a walk to the municipal park. Anna slowly became a kind of honorary member of the convent taking part in many activities.

There was however one obstacle to all this. The nuns were both Catholic and foreigners. Mother Madeleine was French, sister Maria was Italian, sister Gloria was English and so on. None of the nuns were born on the island. But Anna felt at home with them, more at home than with anybody else apart from her mother.

The nuns treated her as equal and respected and admired her determination to make the best of her restricted life. Quite early, at the age of nine or ten, Anna became deeply religious and said to everybody that she wanted to become a nun. She was not aware at this time of the deep gap that separated the Catholic nuns from her Orthodox parents, sisters, relatives, friends. After all, her parents chose to send all their children to the convent school, so what was the problem?

As she entered her teens however she began to understand that things were not as simple as she had imagined them to be. She could not just become a nun like the other nuns. She began to ask the nuns to come and collect her and take her to church—the Catholic church—the church where the priest and the nuns were her friends and treated her as a friend. She began to prefer the Catholic liturgy and the personal attention that children received in the Catholic church.

When she was fifteen, she announced to Mother Superior that she wanted to become Catholic and then a nun. It was now well understood that her parents would never consent to such a conversion, so it would have to be a secret one. Mother Madeleine said that she had to wait until she was eighteen and could make this decision independently of her parents.

And the secret continued. The nuns treated her as one of them and Anna experienced herself as one of them. But she still had to wait in silence and in secrecy. Thalia and Aristos saw this friendship between the nuns and their disabled daughter as a good thing, something that brought a great deal of happiness to Anna. But in no way did they imagine, not even in their worst nightmares, a conversion to Catholicism!

And the years went by and Anna became more and more Catholic if not in name. She began to attend the Catholic church and participate to its rituals. Every Sunday Thalia would get her ready, wash her face in rosewater and put Eau de Cologne on it, comb her hair and put on her nicest hair clip, and dress her in her best Sunday clothes. She would then wait by the door for the nuns to come and collect her and she would then walk with them the five minutes that separated the house from the Catholic church.

Anna was now nineteen and had been Catholic for a year and the family came to accept the unacceptable—that she had converted to Catholicism. For a while, the whole thing had remained a secret between Anna and the nuns until one Wednesday morning, an ordinary Wednesday morning, when Thalia had gone, like every Wednesday morning, to the market at the centre of the town and bought the fish she was going to fry that lunchtime, the olives and the cheese for the whole week and herbs, walnuts and raisins for the whole month. As she was about to pay, her distant cousin Aspasia approached her. As they were both paying for their purchases Aspasia made small talk—how was the family? Has Thalia heard about so and so that he lost all his money gambling, or, so and so who had a mistress and his wife beat him up the other night and the whole neighbourhood had been kept awake all night.

Thalia listened silently making small sounds to show her attentiveness. She had never liked Aspasia and her gleeful gossip. Aspasia never got married and in her early '50s she was envious of most ordinary couples, so Thalia kept well away from her if she could, which was impossible at the moment as they both queued to pay for their purchases. Suddenly Aphasia's voice became more provocative as she turned towards Thalia and tried to catch her eye.

'And you never told me,' she said stressing every syllable 'you never told me that Anna converted to Catholicism. I had to learn it from Ero, Egli's cousin. You kept it a secret, even from your relatives, and we all had to hear it from total strangers. Well, in a way I understand it is difficult for you. But not telling me, your cousin, or my mother, your auntie!'

Aspasia spoke with an exaggerated tone of wounded pride.

Thalia's head began to spin. Has she heard well? Was it true, or malicious gossip? This woman thought nothing about spreading false rumours and telling straight forward lies.

'What?' she managed after a moment of utter shock 'who said that? It is a complete lie.'

'You mean you didn't know about it? It seems the whole town is talking about it and you didn't know?'

'The whole town is lying,' Thalia said. 'Lies and malicious gossip.'

'I don't think so,' Aspasia went on relentlessly. 'It's absolutely true. Either you have no control over your daughter, or you don't care about it.'

Thalia's mind was now racing. She remembered small innuendos by friends during the last few months. She remembered how Anna and the nuns would stop speaking when she approached bringing them a coffee and cake and suddenly seemed to have run out of something to say. They would change the subject and praise her home, or the sweets or her good coffee. She remembered Anna's secrecy and guilty face. She always thought it was just her imagination because Anna was too attached to the nuns and to Mother Madeleine and in a way it was embarrassing, but Anna was Anna and Thalia was very grateful to the nuns for taking such good care of her. On the other hand, it was nobody's business and Anna was so happy with the nuns. It would have been so cruel to forbid her to see them or not to let her go to church with them. But convert to Catholicism!—surely that was a lie.

Yet it all suddenly made sense.

'You had no idea,' Aspasia exclaimed. 'I can't believe it. You had no idea. You can't control your daughters it seems, neither the older ones nor Anna.'

These innuendos about Olga and Nellie were obviously referring to their tennis playing and the rumours circulating. She was furious but felt also vaguely afraid of this woman who could, if she chose, cause a great deal of damage to the girls with her malicious gossip.

'Thank you for telling me Aspasia,' she said in a formal and composed way. 'I shall find out.'

'No need to find out,' Aspasia continued with glee. 'I am telling you this is the naked, unpleasant truth. I am really sorry for you and your family.'

"Sorry" is a euphemism for "glee" Thalia thought but said nothing, and left in a hurry.

At home, there were interrogations, hysterics, shouting, screaming, crying, accusations and counter-accusations but in the end there was nothing that either Aristos or Thalia could do. Their daughter was now Catholic, in fact she had been Catholic for a whole year and they knew nothing.

For Aristos, who was an atheist and thought that religion was for women and weak, ignorant men, being converted to Catholicism meant really nothing much except exchanging one set of illusions for another. But the fact that this was done secretly, without his permission, that a daughter could so blatantly show disrespect for her father and for the whole society, that was the main issue.

For Thalia, it was different. She was deeply religious, especially since Anna was born disabled and felt that God was now the only one who could help since the doctors shook their heads and said there was nothing to be done. In fact, when Anna began to walk at the age of seven, after everybody had given up hope that she would ever walk, and after years of Thalia's praying to various saints and to the Virgin Mary, Anna's first walk was pronounced a miracle. This happened on the day of St Nicolaos, when suddenly Anna simply got out of her chair and made a few uncertain steps. From then on that day was Anna's second birthday, and second name day. She was now Anna-Nicoletta. For all this, Thalia prayed and gave thanks to the Orthodox Madonna and it was the Orthodox Madonna that made Anna walk. For this, she was absolutely sure. She could see in front of her eyes the big, beautiful fresco at the Church or Archangelos, A fresco of the

Virgin dated from the 15th century, an icon full of the worship and love that inspired generations. Thalia was absolutely convinced that it was this virgin Mary, the one she prayed to, the big, beautiful icon in the middle of the church, the one who looked at humanity with such compassion and empathy, the one who said to her 'I know what it feels like'. And this Mary, the source of hope, love and human understanding, the icon in the Church of Archangelos, was Orthodox. And how could Anna betray Mary, the Orthodox Mary, who made her walk? Not of course the way other people walked, with secure and certain strides, but tentatively, insecurely, shaking with every step, but still walking. Oh the miracle of it! Anna walking!'

For Nellie, there was a very different problem—that of nationalism and Hellenism. Orthodoxy was synonymous with Hellenism, with being Greek. It was an act of treason to become a Catholic. How could Anna ever betray her country like this?

Olga was the only one not to make much fuss about it. She knew how happy Anna was to be with the nuns and especially with Mother Madeleine and how happy she was to go to church with them. So, what was the big problem? They were Christians, weren't they?

Slowly, painfully the rest of the family came to terms with it and stopped protesting, stopped accusing the nuns and the Catholic priest, stopped arguing and crying and shouting. And even Nellie slowly came to accept Anna's Catholicism as something that helped Anna in her everyday life and therefore as something good. Not as good as Orthodoxy, of course not, but then Anna was not a normal person, was she? And now, on a sunny April day, Anna was sitting on the patio with the sun on her head, which was protected by a straw hat, and typing away a new poem to Mother Madeleine.

'You have the heart of an angel,' it began and for each letter an elaborate assortment of spasmodic movements had to be mastered to press the right key. It took her about 5 or 6 seconds for each letter. But then time is what she had. Plenty of time. 'An angel is a thing of beauty,' she wrote and continued to type. She was writing in French as it was Mother Madeleine's language and Anna had mastered the language and its poetry out of this burning love for Mother Madeleine. '…a-t-h-i-n-g-o-f-b-e-a-u-t-y,' she typed, painfully slow.

Thalia was in the kitchen helping Kyriakou to prepare the elaborate stuffed vine leaves in tomato sauce and whole fried potatoes. Olga was tidying up the room she shared with Nellie.

Nellie herself was sitting under the pomegranate tree reading her book and steeped in the beauty of an afternoon in London spreading out of the words of Virginia Woolf, the soft colours, the magic of a woman planning a party, with flowers everywhere and servants and friends, dear, cultivated friends. She was deeply engrossed into her book hearing nothing of the everyday familiar sounds of the birds and the chickens and the neighbours and Thalia's and Kyriakou's voices coming from the kitchen as they were preparing lunch, or even Anna's typewriter. Nellie was deeply immersed in her imaginary world.

A loud knock on the door interrupted the peaceful morning and Nellie's dreams. It announced the delivery of the local newspaper, The Observer, that arrived every Thursday morning around this time. Kyriakou rushed to the door and came back with a copy of the newspaper which she handed to Nellie.

Nellie reconstructed the sequence of events many times in her mind the next few months as she lay mute and uncommunicative on top of her bed all day. How Kyriakou handed her the paper and how she put it aside and continued to read her book. The planned party was taking shape in Mrs Dalloway's mind, the friends, the magic. Nellie was deeply absorbed in the dream, in this other world.

Thalia came out of the kitchen and asked.

'Was that the newspaper Nellie?'

'Yes mamma,' Nellie said without lifting her eyes form the book.

'Any news?' Thalia asked.

'I don't know. I haven't looked at it yet.'

'Aahhh,' Thalia said and went back to the kitchen.

After a while, Nellie got up and poured herself a glass of lemonade. The heat of the April sun was getting to her. Bringing the lemonade back to where she was sitting she placed the glass carefully on the ground beside her and took up the newspaper. She looked uninterested at the first page and then turned it to the "social events" page—births, deaths, engagements and weddings. For a moment, she was absorbed in it.

Then the world went mad. It spun and went round and round and it looked weird and unrecognisable. She gave a shriek so wild that her mother and Kyriakou ran towards her and Olga came running out of her room to see what was happening. Nellie looked wild. She looked mad.

'What's the matter?' Thalia asked, 'what's wrong?'

Nellie could utter nothing recognisable as language. She kept uttering shrieks. Olga picked up the newspaper. It was open at what was called "Social

Corner" where all births, engagements, marriages and deaths were announced. In one corner, it read:

'Mr and Mrs S. Anastasiadis announce with great pleasure the engagement of their son Evripides to Miss Toulla Joanidou. Telegrams of congratulations to be addressed to…' and the address was mentioned.

That was all. A few words in a newspaper. And the whole world collapsed. And Olga could not recognise her sister anymore. She tried to talk to her. Thalia tried to talk to her. Anna was calling trying to articulate a question but, like Nellie, had lost the capacity, limited as it was, to articulate anything. Thalia had to rush to see to Anna's needs. Anna was calling her as she needed to go to the toilet. Thalia took her down the steps and into the toilet at the end of the patio.

'Whaaaatttt's wrong?' Anna finally managed to ask.

'Nellie has just read that Evripides got engaged,' Thalia said.

'Aaah!' Anna said. 'It ssssounds ssssserrrrious.'

After Thalia finished with Anna, she went to bring some methylated spirit and rubbed Nellie's temples in it. Olga kept talking to her sister but to no avail.

Then suddenly, unpredictably Nellie was on the floor shaking uncontrollably with foam coming out of her mouth. Her eyes had become one huge white space as if the irises had disappeared inside her head. Not to see. Not to feel. And she kept shaking and shaking.

Olga was now shouting to her mother and to Kyriakou to come there urgently and to bring a towel. Panic invaded everybody.

'Put it in her mouth!' Olga was shouting to her mother to put the towel in Nellie's mouth to prevent her from biting her tongue. She had read it in a book and remembered exactly what one was supposed to do in this case.

Thalia went down on the floor and placed the end of the towel between Nellie's shaking jaws and tried to hold Nellie together as she was shaking and writhing for a duration that felt like eternity. It was as if time had slowed down, as it does during earthquakes, or other unexpected disasters, when a few seconds look like they would never come to an end.

Then it all stopped and Nellie lay limp in Thalia's arms.

'We must call the doctor,' Thalia said. 'Maybe he can give her an injection.'

They carried Nellie into the house and put her in her bed. For a while, she lay on her bed like a dead person, limb and lifeless and white as a sheet. But it was obvious that she was breathing so the first panic was now replaced by a deep concern as to what to do to make her better. Kyriakou rushed to bring the doctor and Thalia did the only thing she knew, which was to rub some surgical spirit onto her forehead and speak to her. 'Come Nellie talk to us' she repeated, 'wake up Nellie, wake up, we are all here, talk to us.'

And Anna sat at a chair next to the door and made noises every now and then and kept asking the same question 'what is wrong with Nellie' in the same tortured way of formulating words and sounds.

Dr Nicolaides came and went without having enlightened the women as to what was happening. After he examined Nellie, he pronounced her OK. 'Nothing really wrong with her,' he pronounced. 'It's nerves. Young women's minds are unfathomable,' he added.

And that's how the word entered the Aristos household. When Aristos came back at lunchtime and heard the word that was repeated by Thalia and Olga "nerves", he became irritated. Any concern for Nellie that might have been there was instantly transformed into irritation.

'You have spoiled the girls,' he said, 'spoiled, nothing else. She is all right.' And declined to enter Nellie's room.

When Nellie came round later that evening, she opened her eyes and saw a dead, meaningless world. Her sister was reading by her bedside. Otherwise everything else was unknown. Dead.

Olga sensing that life was returning to Nellie raised her eyes from her book and looked at her sister.

'You have woken up,' she said. 'How are you feeling?'

Nellie said nothing. It was not clear whether she could not or would not talk.

'You gave us such a fright,' Olga said. 'I am so glad you are feeling better. I'll call mum.'

No reaction came from Nellie. Olga was not sure whether Nellie heard her, or whether she was not interested in what she said.

'Shall I call mum?' Olga insisted.

As no reaction came from Nellie Olga made her own decision.

'O.K.' she decided 'I'll get mum.'

Thalia came bringing with her a great deal of emotion, tears, anxiety and relief all in one.

'Nellie you are well again. You gave us a shock. What's wrong with you? Maybe you can tell us now. Are you feeling better? What are you feeling? Dr Nicolaides said there is nothing wrong with you. He said you are fine. But he seemed puzzled. He was not sure at all.'

As no answer came from Nellie not even a sound Thalia and Olga exchanged glances and were silent.

Nellie didn't speak for many weeks. Olga and Thalia made many attempts to involve her in conversation but to no avail. She refused to eat for several days and would take only water. Slowly, however, she began to take some soup prepared by Thalia herself. She would take small spoonfuls and have long pauses between them.

Olga would sit by her bedside and see that she had finished the small bowl that Thalia had prepared.

Dr Nicolaides came and went several times in the next few days but he always repeated the same thing: there was nothing wrong with her. It was just "nerves".

The very word irritated Aristos. As he had no idea about the origin of this mysterious "illness", his worry and his irritation fought with each other. "Nerves" to him meant selfishness, women's self-absorption and meaningless emotionality. But there was nothing he could do to change the situation, so he had to keep quiet. He could have easily flown into one of his rages, but he somehow knew that the situation was beyond anybody's control, least of all his. He had to bear his own powerlessness with dignity. For Nellie, he had no sympathy whatsoever. She was a huge and shameful embarrassment and her selfishness was immense. She was endangering hers and her sister's chances of getting married. She was worrying everybody and driving her mother to despair. She was driving the family into disrepute. For, however one could try and keep this strange and inexplicable thing in the family, people would soon start to talk.

And people did talk. It started of course with Olga's and Nellie's friends and relatives. Is Nellie ill? Why can't she come with us to the promenade for a walk? Are you two not playing tennis anymore? Is this the reason Nellie is ill because your father had found out? And so it went. Some kind of believable illness had to be invented but what? Glandular fever perhaps?

The good society, the middle-class society of Limassol, which consisted of a handful of old families and their branches that extended into a few hundred people, began to gossip.

'I always thought that Thalia was very soft with the girls,' one distant cousin said. 'She hasn't done them any good. Nellie is really not from this world.'

'But what's wrong with her?' another of Nellie's distant cousins would ask.

'Dr Nicolaides says it's just "nerves", dear God, nerves is a byword for "being spoilt", and for having no sense of duty or respect for her parents. Nerves! A very modern disease. There were no nerves in my time!' one distant aunt said.

And this auntie distributed the information with all the spite and the malice that accompanied it to all those who wished to listen.

With Nellie's illness and the depression that descended on the whole family, Olga had to forget her own dreams and plans. Playing tennis was now out of the question. She felt ashamed and avoided people as she had no idea how to answer all these questions and comments. What could she possibly say to all those questions that were hurled at her as soon as she dared outside the house. So Olga confined herself to visiting close friends and close relatives in their own house mainly her aunts and cousins on her mother's side and her close friends Toulla and Irene who often came to visit her. The girls would sit out together on the veranda at the side of the house and would drink lemonade and eat Thalia's Greek sweets, crystallised melon peel, green crystallised walnuts and apricots, or Thalia's bureks and ravani cake.

Olga missed tennis and missed more than anything the contact with Stavros. She never quite dared to hope that anything between Stavros and herself would develop. But something in her did hope although she was not supposed to know about it. Her cousins were a great comfort to her always inviting her to their house or coming to visit her, never asking unnecessary questions, always discreet and loving, sometimes bringing a cake or home-made biscuits baked by their mother, Thalia's first cousin.

On the other hand, Thalia's sister was more remote, involved as she was with her own son who had just been engaged to a Greek woman from Alexandria, exotic and strange, with dozens of golden bungles dangling from her arms and golden necklaces hanging down her chest, and a shaggy dog called Fatou who entered the room in front of her and annoyed everybody.

Her son never got a "proper job", as all the cousins kept reminding her. He thought himself a "genius", a musician of unique talent, a pianist of rare endowment and capability. People could hear him through the open window play for hours on end Beethoven, Chopin and Liszt. He had a few pupils but was that enough to bring up a family? Was that a profession for a grown-up man? Was it the mother who maintained him and now his fiancé who had arrived from Alexandria? The good citizens of Limassol gossiped and wondered and Thalia worried how her sister who had been recently widowed would manage to keep her son and his eccentric wife. On the other hand, the few artists of Limassol took courage from the pianist's example and felt supported by his courage to do what his talent guided him to do.

Thalia's remaining two brothers were rather remote, living on the other side of the town and being involved with their children and their grandchildren.

As far as Nellie's problem went this side of the family offered no support steeped as they all were in Miltiades' "genius" and how to support him. So for the moment it was Olga's other cousins Deana and Fotini and their mother Arsinoe who were of real support. Maroulla the third sister was already married with two lovely children.

Maroulla, who was eleven years older than Olga and ten years younger than Thalia, formed a link between the generations. Although formally of Olga's and Nellie's generation, she was nevertheless more Thalia's friend and confidante. Being married with two lovely children Thalia often found refuge in her home, especially now that disaster had struck the Aristos' family and Thalia did not dare talk about the real cause to anybody outside the family.

Maroulla was married to Sotiris, the owner of The Observer, the local paper that was delivered to the Aristos' family that fatal Thursday morning. The Observer was published once a week, on Thursdays, and was full of news of local politics, local gossip, weddings, baptisms, births and deaths, funerals, local exhibitions of Arts and Crafts, There were some articles about cinema and theatre and some letters from readers. There were announcements about Charity dinners and Charity Teas and Charity activities by the "Women's Charity Association" and generally information about everybody who was somebody in this lively, tiny town on the Eastern Mediterranean.

The paper was also a vehicle for Sotiris to "educate the people", as he often told Aristos, in one of their discussions over dinner, accompanied by a glass of brandy and a fat cigar. It was a vehicle to express his own ideas and fight for a more liberal, more "Europeanised" island, but more often than not it was a vehicle to satisfy his own ideas about himself as a man of "higher intelligence" and "higher education". Sotiris was very proud of his paper although his main income came from his printing business where all invitations for weddings, baptisms and parties, all announcements of funerals and memorial services, all posters and leaflets for local businesses were printed. Notwithstanding Sotiris' self-importance he was nevertheless a very warm and congenial man, very supportive of his friends and relatives and, like his wife, a very loyal friend of the Aristos' family.

Olga loved going to visit Maroulla who lived with her husband and the two girls above the printing business in a house full of Greek Art, reproductions of ancient pottery and of Greek statuettes and old embroidered tablecloths and cushions and chair covers, artefacts from the mountain regions of the island. Ceramic pots and decorated gourds from mountain villages were all exhibited together with classical Greek art behind glass cabinets. The whole house looked like a museum. Olga loved it and now that walks on the promenade were not to be recommended she took to visiting Maroulla regularly. Her cousins, Maroulla's sisters, were also there regularly and Thalia was also a regular visitor there and found Maroulla a real support in these difficult days.

As spring changed into summer and the green fields became gold and the wild flowers disappeared and the temperature rose and rose to the late '30s, Nellie began to gain in strength. She got out of her bed and spent a lot of time sitting quietly in her room, sometimes reading, sometimes writing. She began to exchange a few words with Thalia and Olga but said nothing to her father who would visit from time to time asking always the same question 'are you feeling better?' And Nellie always nodded.

Dr Nicolaides paid regular visits every couple of weeks and never changed his diagnosis "nerves". One day however, after Nellie began to improve and began to eat solid food and sometimes eat a bit of Thalia's homemade cakes, he took Thalia aside after he examined Nellie and said to her that in his opinion the girl needed to get married. The faster the better. In his experience, young women often suffered from nerves which however disappear as soon as they got married and had children. Thalia nodded and thought that the doctor had a point but to convince Nellie to marry anybody apart from the man of her dreams would be a task that was beyond her power, or Aristos', or anybody else's for that matter.

The early days of summer arrived and the young women of Limassol began to attend the "municipal baths" where they went to swim. This was a part of the beach, five-six minutes' walk from the Aristos' family house, towards the end of the town, which the Municipality had assigned to public swimming. It was equipped with changing cubicles, showers and sun umbrellas. Men and women remained separate, entering from separate entrances but on the beach some inter-mixing took place. But as women went only in the morning it was mainly women and children and some students who attended them. Nevertheless, Thalia kept it secret from Aristos who could never entertain the idea that men could see exposed a woman's legs and still respect that woman. To Aristos' mind the whole thing was an assault on family values, on the dignity of women and on their virtue. The whole idea was absolutely abhorrent to him.

Nellie who used to be a regular attendant to the baths and a passionate swimmer showed no interest for it now. She mainly stayed at home in her room reading, writing or just sitting quietly. Olga for her part began to go swimming with her cousins and tried always to stay close to them as if seeking their protection from intrusive questions by friends and relatives whose hostile interrogations about Nellie frightened and embarrassed her.

A couple of times she met Stavros who was always friendly and seemed genuinely interested in Nellie's welfare. Once he commented how difficult it must be for her, Olga, and everybody at home, especially her parents. Stavros showed a great deal of understanding for her predicament, something she was grateful about. After these encounters, she found herself thinking about him more and more. At this time of her life, he was a beam of light in the darkness of her mind.

There was of course no question about playing tennis without Evripides and without Nellie. Olga couldn't even consider it and Stavros, who seemed to know much more than he was showing, seemed to tacitly agree with her. So, she relied on these casual meetings, which gave her life a vague hope which she could not even put into words.

Life continued as it had always been but without Nellie and tennis. The loss of both felt to Olga like a huge hole, an inexplicable lack which she tried but without much success to avoid thinking about.

As July arrived and the heat reached 37C and the talk in the town became more and more about the temperature and the humidity and the lack of a breeze and how unbearable it all was, the Aristos family began preparing for their annual summer holiday in the mountains of Troodos, in the village of Pera Pedi, about 35 miles from Limassol which could be reached by horse drawn carriage or by the newly established "bus" that travelled regularly once a week to the villages and to Platres, the big holiday resort north of Pera Pedi.

Thalia, Olga, Anna, Nellie and Kyriakou set off every year in the middle of July for Pera Pedi. Together with them their cousins, Deana, Fotini, their mother, and Maroulla with the two children would also make the same journey. The two families occupied two houses very close to each other. Aristos and Sotiris stayed behind and went to work every day as usual.

Aristos' clockwork life continued as always leaving at 7.50 every morning, returning home at 1.10 at lunch time when the food from the restaurant would be delivered. He would leave for the afternoon work at 1.50 and return at 4.10 for his coffee which he was obliged to make himself and he would rest until his evening meal which the restaurant would deliver at 7 every evening.

Aristos both loved and hated the month between the end of July and the end of August. He loved the peace and the silence, the expansiveness of his being, the freedom. The freedom from women. The silence. Bliss.

No women to cause problems. No women to have emotions and hysterical episodes. No women to try and control him, to tell him what to do—him the son of his father! No women to remind him how weak he was, how unable to solve their problems, or how unable he was to understand what went on in their minds.

A household full of women! He understood nothing of what went on. In a way, he wanted to know nothing although it was his duty to know everything. He just wanted things to run smoothly, predictably. But they never did. Even when he was first engaged to Thalia and he thought that the heavens had open the gates of happiness and bliss and had welcomed him in. Even then, when he thought that Thalia was the most beautiful and the most gifted creature on earth and he was the luckiest man alive, even then the clouds began to gather all around the clear blue skies of happiness. Even then he had to confront woman's moods and woman's otherness. For example, Thalia would suddenly go cold and withdraw all affection from him. She would turn away and would not look him in the eye. Her beautiful lips would purse and she would sulk for hours, sometimes days. He had no idea what he had done to deserve such a treatment. He was always puzzled, never quite getting it even when twenty-two-year-old Thalia would tell him after many tortuous interrogations the reason for her cold withdrawal. He could still not understand. Women were a mystery! Even after so many years living with women he had no idea how their labyrinthine mind worked.

And now they were all gone, for one whole month. The complicated, hysterical Nellie with a mind as mysterious as it ever was one, who would not stop causing problems, one after the other. The latest one, her "illness" was the talk of the town and his own shame. Anna and her disability were causing a different kind of problem. Not to mention her conversion to Catholicism which was the constant gossip of relatives and friends—the scandal, the shame, people whispering behind his back. The worst was when people tried ostensibly to be kind. One cousin said 'at least she is still a Christian. I know a woman from Nicosia who married a Turk and converted to Islam.' And another cousin: 'you will get used to it. It's not the end of the world.' He wanted to tell them to shut up. He didn't need their pity. Instead he smiled and agreed.

Of course it was not the end of the world. As a non-believer he could not justify one set of illusions over another. But people talked and condemned and saw him as an ineffectual kind of father. And this worried him and kept him awake for nights on end.

And Olga, well she was another mystery. Quiet and reserved, more like him than any of the others, he did not know how to judge her. She seemed to know more than any of the others what was right and what was wrong, what was allowed and what was forbidden. And yet sometimes she seemed more quietly rebellious than the others. He was puzzled. And so Aristos counted his blessings and felt free to be without worry, shame, fear of scandal and heavy responsibility for a whole month. As long as the women were in the mountains they were, and he were, out of trouble. One whole month of bliss and freedom.

But then there were the evenings, the long, lonely evenings when the house was silent as a morgue. No women to sing, whisper, quarrel, giggle demand, complain—of simply take refuge in endless talk, this talk that drove him crazy but which he was now craving, craving the life of it. No female presence—no warmth, no life.

Aristos, being the son of a judge, was the dream husband which parents dreamt for their daughters. He possessed all the so-called "negative virtues"— he did not drink, he did not gamble and he was not a womaniser. These "negative virtues" constituted the dream ticket to a good marriage. However, these very virtues made Aristos dependent on his wife and daughters for company, for love and affection, and for some very basic human communication. Aristos would not like to admit it but he was emotionally dependent on the women in his life. If he were to become aware of this, he would feel deeply ashamed. But such thoughts never entered his mind. The women were dependent on him for survival, protection and for the defence of their honour. And that was that.

But as the evenings stretched in front of him empty and silent he almost wished he was a drinker and a gambler. He would then have company all evening long in the clubs, and the caffeneia, he would be with men and talk about men's things. He could even be in one of those establishments that he could not even permit himself to know that they existed. He would then be in the company of women—but different women, more dangerous than his wife and daughters.

These thoughts existed only in Aristos' disturbed dreams about dangerous women, dangerous men, dangerous occupations. Aristos would wake up from these dreams and wonder what the hell was going on with him. And then he would get up, shave, go to work and forget all about it. After all, there was still Plato to keep him in line.

But the vague longing for the company of men continued. He wished that the endless responsibility of looking after women, of trying to shape their minds and their life, this endless impossible task that was entrusted to him by his dead father would come to an end. With Nellie's latest "illness", Aristos was close to despair. The wish to be in the company of men and in men's straightforward world of order and rationality—or its underside—the world of gambling and drinking and womanising—continued in a vague, unarticulated way.

In any case, the wish was an impossible wish. The only drink Aristos ever allowed himself was a glass of Commandaria at Christmas and perhaps, only rarely, a glass of brandy with Sotiris after dinner. As for gambling the truth was that he could not play cards. He was not sure what men did in clubs when they sat endlessly in front of a pack of cards and shuffled them and got very absorbed in the game. Rumours of people losing big sums of money circulated from time to time. For Aristos playing cards, even among friends, even without money just for the pleasure of it, was an evil act that carried the risk of getting on the slippery slope that ended with pawning one's watch, one's coat, one's wedding ring and ended with losing one's home.

The only male company he had ever had was the occasional visit from relatives—Anaxagoras for instance his brother-in-law and father of Miltiades the pianist. He was a lawyer of some standing with whom he could exchange ideas about politics and the state of the world. But Anaxagoras was a member of a club and he did spend his evenings there playing cards, something that Aristos strongly disapproved of. Sotiris was the other man with whom he had some contact. With Sotiris, he had some stimulating discussions about the role of religion in society, about nationalism and about books, especially about Plato's ideas. Sotiris was the owner and editor of *The Observer* and the husband of Maroulla's who was his daughters' cousin. A younger man by eighteen years, Sotiris represented the new generation, and Aristos was curious, despite himself, to find out how this new generation differed from his. He liked exchanging ideas with this younger man, even if he found some of his ideas a little too radical. Nevertheless such was Aristos' hunger for male company that he enjoyed this young man's radical ideas and the enthusiasm with which he carried out his job as the founder, the editor and the owner of *The Observer. He is trying*, Aristos thought, *trying to do something for this town. It's admirable, admirable.*

But it was the women who kept the relationship and the friendship going. It was Thalia and Maroulla (Sotiris' wife) who were dear friends, and Olga, and in the past Nellie, and Maroulla's sisters who chatted endlessly, a meaningless chit-chat that he could hear from his study in the afternoons and got on his nerves. But they kept the friendship going, they kept it alive and they nurtured this so necessary relationship between the two families. Aristos knew this but found it difficult to acknowledge it. And now they were away and he and Sotiris had no excuse to meet and chat and discuss and debate.

So, Aristos spent his lonely evenings on the veranda, listening to the sounds the neighbours made, their arguments, their quarrels and sometimes their lovemaking. He hated to admit to himself but he knew that he felt lonely. He tried to read Plato and for a while he would get engrossed in his ideal world of perfect order and perfect virtue, the philosophical rarefied atmosphere of absolute truth. At moments like this, he could leave behind his endless anxiety of everyday life—his own Xanthippi—and the endless demands of his daughters and the chaotic, unpredictable world of his household of women—the worries about their honour, the worry whether good, young men could be found to marry them. But Plato's world was light years away from his and moments after putting the book down he would return to his own anxious ruminations about the family, the trouble women were causing and his own loss of control over them.

At about eleven o'clock, Aristos would retire to his solitary bed, empty and morose, knowing that the next day would be an exact copy of this one.

Chapter 9
Marathasa 1918

Stavros at the Gymnasium

It was early December. The big walnut tree at the back of Elengou's house had turned rusty and the plane trees by the stream had lost their leaves. The air in the evenings had a bite. The days grew short and preparations for Christmas were under way. The women were half way through the 40-day fasting—no meat, no fish, no sausages nor ham, eggs, milk, yogurt, butter, or cheese, in short no animal products—only bread, beans, pulses, potatoes, olives, some tahini with carob juice and honey on bread for something sweet. Honey balls were a real treat very rarely to be had.

Preparations for the feast of Christmas were under way. The chickens and ducks were fattened and the legs of smoked pork and sausages hung from the ceiling to mature. Halloumi cheese which was kept in salt water in big tin pots was frequently disturbed by men at this time of the year claiming to be working so hard out in the cold that they needed something more substantial than bread and olives. They had to break their fast otherwise the cold would get them and what use would they be to anybody?

It was Saturday evening and Stavros was back in the village for the weekend. He had walked the shortcut of 8 miles from his school over the hills and valleys to his village. It took him three hours to get home but this was the sweetest time of the week. Walking alone on the hills, listening to the cries and songs and screeches of the birds, to the gurgling of the water in the streams, to the braying of some lonely donkey carrying a lone traveller across the mountains, to the bells of distant goats and sheep following the outline of a shepherd. The colours changing. Silence surrounding the sounds like an invisible blanket, everywhere silence, deep and indestructible. The silence of the mountains.

His mind was full of the wonderful things he had learnt at school. Every week new knowledge, new wonderful things. They had eight subjects in the first year—Modern Greek, English Language, English Literature, Maths, Science, History, Geography and Sport. It was all taught in English and the pupils, the moment they entered the school premises, were supposed to speak only English among themselves. His English had improved so much in the last few months that he was hoping to read Oliver Twist in the original very soon. What a treat! And as he walked down the slope that revealed his village in the distance, his mind was full of poetry, *lonely as a cloud*, he thought and he looked at the mountains as he had never seen them before, the changing colours and the fading of the light and felt the happiest boy on earth.

He would get home by 4 o'clock and Elengo would greet him with an embrace and a glass of warm milk and a piece of bread and olives. 'Never mind fasting,' she would say handing him the milk, 'you are young and you have walked for hours in the cold. Drink your milk. You need to keep your strength. God will understand and forgive you.' After this welcome, it was all work—feed the chickens and the goats, clean the house and help Elengo to cook.

Stavros did this journey twice during the weekend—each Saturday afternoon getting back to his village, and each Monday morning getting back to his school repeating the whole journey in reverse. The rest of the week he was boarding together with 50 other boys. In the rain, in the snow, in the blazing sun all through his 5 years at the school he repeated the journey through the hills and valleys around his village. But he got used to the routine very quickly. In fact, he loved it. At the beginning, it was difficult to believe that he was now going to secondary school, that an uncle living in Egypt, somebody he didn't know and never met, had paid the pound needed to pay the fees. What difference a pound can make, he wondered.

He had overheard once Penelope and grandmother talking about his father— 'he is useless,' Penelope said.

'He is under her thumb now,' grandma replied.

'He is useless,' Penelope repeated. He knew that they were talking about his father.

His father "useless"! He could not contemplate this. Yet the truth was that he could do nothing to help his son to get to secondary school.

'Useless.'

As he fed Aglaia the goat, the word echoed in his ears.

'Useless.'

He touched the elegant face of Aglaia and run his fingers over her nose. 'Beautiful girl,' he whispered, 'good, beautiful girl. You and I understand each other.'

Penelope would turn up without fail at about 5pm to say hello and bring Stavro some honey balls or some other delicacy she had just made.

'My boy,' she would say, 'my sweet boy, you are back.'

They would sit down and Elengo would make them a cup of hot sage tea and add some honey in it and Stavros would begin to tell Penelope what he had learnt at school that week. He already knew so much more than his father that Stavros began to see him more and more for what he was—an ordinary, weak and ineffectual man "under his wife's thumb" as his grandmother put it.

'He would start now telling Penelope about the periodic table he had just learnt about. 'All the elements are included there' he would say with excitement. 'Everything that exists on earth comes from these "elements". They are the building blocks of the world. Science has discovered all this.'

Penelope would drink her sage tea and listen to Stavros, her eyes full of wonder. Everything is made out of them, Stavros would continue, the gold crucifix that was hanging on his chest, a present from his father; the spade his grandmother and his uncle Manolis used to dig up the vegetable garden; the tin pots his grandmother used for cooking; the asbestos that his father and father's father had mined from the asbestos mines in Amiantos; the big distiller for zivania that lay in the centre of a big room in old Zinonas' house and around which the children gathered to keep warm and to listen to endless stories from Zinonas who had travelled as far as Lebanon and Egypt and could tell stories from the great war mixed up with old village stories and fairy tales from Grimm Brothers in equal measure. All these objects were part of an orderly world of primary elements and their combination. And they were all on this periodic table in order of their atomic weight. Even the air they breathed was made out of these elements—mainly oxygen and nitrogen. But it was only 21% oxygen, the stuff we breathe. So he could now tell his grandmother that if she left the oil lamp or the wood burner burning for a long time without ventilation they could all die of asphyxiation as the oxygen in the air would be burnt out. And grandmother would laugh and say 'fairy tales, my boy, I've done this my whole life and look how old I got, still alive!'

'Rubbish' thundered grandfather who had been listening all along through the open door of his room and who now chose to intervene. 'Rubbish, they teach you rubbish at school. Nobody has ever died of asphyxiation in this village because they burnt oil or wood.'

'That's because there is ventilation.' Stavros stuck to his guns. He had absolute trust in his teachers and in the truth of science. 'People have learnt this by experience. People are good scientists.'

'Rubbish!' Grandfather's thundery voice almost shook the frail wall of the house.

'OK grandad,' Stavros tried to be reconciliatory. 'We are not going to quarrel about what I learn at school.'

'That's not true granddad,' Penelope intervened. 'Maria, Chrisostomos' mother, for instance, people say that she slept all night with the wood burner burning and that's why she died.'

'Old wives' tales' shouted granddad. 'She was old that's why she died and that is that.' 'And you Stavro you believe these old wives' tales and all these women who have supported you,' he howled 'should be locked up. You should be working in the fields like a man.'

Penelope rolled her eyes and said nothing. Elengo smiled feebly and also said nothing. Deep silence enveloped the house. After some time of silence when they all seemed to be waiting for something, they heard grandad's snoring from the other room.

'OK Stavraki,' Penelope would say, 'you can start now.'

He had learnt about electricity that week—the flow of electrons, the transformation of energy, for instance kinetic energy into electrical energy, he would explain. And then this electrical energy would be harvested and transformed into light. Imagine light at the end of a switch! Can you imagine.

By now, everybody in the village knew about the miracles of electricity but only the few people who had been to places like Limassol and Nicosia had actually experienced it. But Stavros could explain the whole thing—how and why. And Penelope was full of questions. What is electricity? People say that electricity is dangerous, you can die if you touch an electric cable, is it true? And why?

Stavros would get his books out and show her the diagrams and the numbers and the symbols and the equations. She could not understand everything but she was nevertheless fascinated.

'Look,' he would say, 'this is hydrogen. It has one electron that circles around the nucleus. This is carbon. It has 6 electrons.'

Elengo would stop and look and marvel. 'What you learn,' she would say, 'nobody here knows it or understands it. You will become a great man one day.'

'It is too late for me', Penelope was thinking, 'and too late for my children. But perhaps my grandchildren.'

'The elements are simple structures' Stavros was saying now, 'but they combine to create complex structures. Like this bronze saucepan for instance. It is made out of copper and zinc, two pure elements that combine to create a third much more useful one, useful for us that is, human beings.'

Now Stavros was trying to explain to Penelope about electricity. 'The movements of electrons create electricity,' Stavros was saying, 'it is a form of energy,' he explained.

'Yes I know about it,' Penelope was showing off a bit. 'Uncle Neophytos who lives in Limassol came over last year and told us all about the miracles of electricity.'

'Electricity comes in many forms.' It was now Stavros' turn to show off. 'There is what we call "static" electricity for instance.' He stopped and picked up a notebook of his. 'Look he said. Let's make an experiment.'

He tore a piece of paper out of his notebook and tore it further into small bits.

He then conducted the experiment that all children have always conducted when they were first taught about static electricity.

'Look,' he said to Penelope as he rubbed the handle of a spoon on his hair. 'Just wait.' He then showed the astonished Penelope how the little bits of paper were attracted by the spoon which was now charged with static electricity.

'You can try it out too.' He added.

Penelope tried it out and marvelled as the bits of paper clung to the spoon she was holding.

'I must show Koko,' she said excited. 'You know it's fun, it's like playing this science of yours', she said.

Kokos was her youngest son one year younger than Stavros. He was finishing primary school this year. She had insisted that he finished school despite his father wanting to take him out of school after the fourth year. But he was certainly not going to secondary school. He did not want to anyway and he did not do brilliantly last year either. In any case his father was dead against 'things like this that fill the children's heads with hot air.'

'Kokos is always interested in what you are doing Stavro. You should talk to him about all this you are telling me.'

This was a bit of an invention of Penelope's and Stavros knew it. In fact, the competition between Kokos and Stavros was intense but unspoken. Stavros was nevertheless acutely aware of it. With only one year between them and with Stavros having done so well at school and now being the talk of the village that he was going to secondary school, and with Penelope treating him as one of her own children, Kokos was silently, and sometimes not so silently, enraged.

The fact that the whole village was talking about Stavros as a miracle child, the first one from the village to go to secondary school, made him wanting to shut his ears when his mother talked about him. He was certainly not in a mood to learn about periodic tables or electricity, static or otherwise. Stavros knew that and said nothing when Penelope mentioned Kokos' interest in science. In fact, it was Penelope herself who was interested in science. If she lived in another time, in another place she might have been a scientist, Stavros thought forty years later, when Penelope was dead for several decades and he was at the peak of his career.

Stavros himself was more fascinated by language, literature, poetry. He loved the English Literature lessons and could already recite several poems by Wordsworth and Keats. But it was no good reciting English poetry to Penelope who could not understand a word of English. So science was the best alternative.

Elengo appeared drying her hands on her apron.

'Trahanas is ready,' she said. 'You must be hungry.'

'Famished,' Stavros said and then turning apologetically to Penelope 'I am going to eat auntie Pilou,' he said.

'Of course my love, of course. Go on. I must go back anyway and finish the beans ragout I started earlier.'

'Stavros is allowed trahana,' Elengo said as an explanation since trahana had yogurt and halloumi in it and it was time for fasting. 'He needs to build up his strength. God will forgive a bit of halloumi in the soup,' she added.

'Of course.' Penelope was already getting up. 'Of course. My Andreas says the same. He works hard and needs his strength. God knows that and will forgive him.'

Penelope embraced Stavros.

'See you tomorrow in church,' she said and she was out into the village street where the chickens chased by a neighbour were running wild and the dusk was falling and another neighbour's donkey was braying. And it was as if a painter had suddenly decided to change the colours of this village scene turning the mountains into purple with hues of blue and grey and the sky into deep crimson. The houses took an orange hue, being transformed into strangely beautiful objects. She descended the steep, muddy, slippery street and headed for her house at the other side of the village, a few minutes' walk from Elengo's house.

Chapter 10
Pera Pedi 1936

Pera Pedi is a small village a few miles south of the more fashionable resort of Platres. It's about 800 metres from sea level and it is situated in a green, fertile valley where apple trees, pear trees, plum trees, peach trees, walnut and almond trees are in abundance. Plane trees line the streets and create shade for the caffeneion at the centre of the village. The sound of water flowing in the various man-made streams through the village and towards the orchards creates a background to every other sound. 'Where there is water there is life' Aristos once said when he saw the green oasis of Pera Pedi and experienced the gurgling ever present sound of water.

In this green oasis, the Aristos family and the Sotiris family together with Maroulla's sisters and mother took refuge from the heat and humidity of Limassol from the end of July to the end of August. Seeking the cool air of the mountains and of the village orchards the two families enjoyed a whole month away from Limassol and the stifling heat of August. Maroulla, and her two children, her two sisters, Deana and Fotini, and her mother Arsinoe were there as well. The two families occupied two big village houses and spent the days together like one family. Apart from meal times and siestas and nights, the rest of the time was spent together.

Olga, Nellie, Deana and Fotini would spend the mornings at the Cafeneion where many other young people from Limassol would gather to play backgammon, draughts and card games or simply to chat and gossip. They would eat glazed young walnuts, or almond sweet and drink lemonade or coffee. A few young men back from the university of Athens or Beirut would talk to them and sometimes flirt with them discreetly and politely. This year Nellie stayed mostly at home on the veranda reading or writing her diary. She constantly excused herself from any outdoors activity and the cousins stopped asking after a while.

But Olga and the cousins enjoyed this welcome freedom to come and go more or less as they pleased as a real blessing. The mountains created their own freedom and the constraints of Limassol did not seem to apply here. At noon, they would go home at Thalia's or Kyriakou's or Maroulla's, or Arsinoe's delicious cooking and this was usually followed by siesta. Late afternoon after a cup of coffee or tea and a piece of cake, they would set out for their long walk of the day, among the orchards or along the mountain tracks.

It was one of these afternoons when Olga, Deana, Fotini and Maroulla set out with Thalia and Anna trailing behind and Zoe and Alexis running forward and backward between the two groups giggling and giving out cries of excitement and delight. The girls were telling stories or jokes and enjoying the ever-changing view of the mountain. It was early evening, the sun still high in the sky but the cool breeze had begun to spread its benevolent presence everywhere. Nellie had stayed at home as she had done every single evening and the girls had stopped asking her to change her mind. They chatted and laughed and giggled and Maroulla divided her attention between her own children and Thalia and Anna who were trailing behind.

Maroulla suddenly spotted an old man selling figs by the roadside. She left the others and approached the man but the girls seeing her going towards the man followed. He was wearing the traditional "vraka" of the mountains and a long-sleeved shirt and the girls wondered how he was able to bear the heat under his heavy clothes. His face was like a landscape of lines and troughs and the girls thought he was hundred years old. But his eyes sparkled with life and his voice was steady and sonorous. They all gathered around him and watched with interest.

'Kalispera kyria,' he said respectfully.

'Kalispera,' Maroulla answered and took a fig between her index finger and her thumb and examined it carefully.

'How much?' Maroulla asked.

'Five grosha kyria,' he said with a pronounced tone of respect.

'Five?' Maroulla put on an exaggerated tone of surprise. 'Five? I get them for four in Limassol.'

'No kyria four is impossible. You can't get good figs like these ones for four grosha. I picked them up with my own hands this morning from the fig tree. They are fresh and juicy, the best figs you can get around here.'

'Four, Maroulla repeated and I shall buy an oke.'

'But kyria this leaves me with nothing. I have a wife to feed and my grandchildren need some new clothes.'

'Four,' Maroulla insisted, not being impressed by the old man's entreaties about his wife and grandchildren.

'Kyria,' he said, 'that's not possible. Four and a half.'

'Four,' she said, 'or I'll go.'

'Entaxi kyria. Four, just for you, but you must know that I lose money.'

He put a bronze weight on the scales and the figs on the other. The scales tilted towards the weight. The man took a few more figs and put them on the other side. The scales now tilted towards the figs.

'There,' the old man said. 'You can have a few more kyria. From me.'

'Evharisto (thank you),' Maroulla said as the man put the figs into a newspaper and into the cotton bag she was carrying with her.

'God bless you Kyria,' the man said.

Thalia who in the meantime had caught up with them and had listened to the conversation said suddenly.

'Give me an oke as well.'

'You are making a wise decision kyria. They are the best figs you can find.'

The same transaction followed and after they wished the old man a good evening they continued on their evening walk through the mountain track with Thalia and Anna trailing behind, Anna holding on to her mother's arm and walking slowly, shaking and performing some kind of strange choreography.

These afternoon walks took them all through the village main road and out into the orchards and the streams and onto the mountain tracks. On the way there, they would meet other young women and sometimes some young men who also sought the cool breeze of the evening. So laughing and chatting they carried on.

And then suddenly Olga's heartbeat changed its rhythm and her face blushed. It happened suddenly before she had the time to acknowledge the cause of this. It was what she least expected to find in Pera Pedi. For suddenly in front of them, coming from the opposite direction was Stavros accompanied by another young man.

'What a lovely surprise' Stavros said approaching the girls and looking straight into Olga's eyes. 'What a lovely surprise.'

Olga blushed even more.

'Nice to see you,' she said. 'Are you staying in the village?' she remembered to add.

'No, I am staying at Platres, at the Forest Hotel,' he added.

'Ah,' she said.

The Forest Hotel was the most fashionable and expensive hotel at Platres.

An awkward silence followed.

'By the way,' Olga remembered to say, 'these are my cousins, Deana and Fotini.'

'Pleased to meet you.' Stavros extended his hand. 'And this is Nicos, my friend,' he said introducing his friend. 'Nicos Papanicolaou,' he added.

Olga recognised the surname as one of the richest families on the island and offered her hand for a handshake. After the smiles and the handshakes and the small talk, Stavros addressed Olga once again.

'We shall be playing tennis on Saturday,' he said. 'Nicos here is one of the players and his sister will be the other.'

'We need another woman player,' Stavros continued. 'Antonis, your cousin, said we could find you here.'

'Yes' Olga said, 'Yes.'

Not knowing what else to say she fell silent.

Deana intervened rather quickly. 'Olga loves tennis' she said, 'but since Nellie…' she hesitated here and stopped for a moment. 'Well,' she said finally 'since Nellie stopped playing Olga had to miss tennis as well.'

'Yes, I know,' Stavros said. 'I understand.'

Again, an awkward silence followed. Everybody in town knew about Nellie's "nervous" illness and Stavros was probably one of the few people who knew, or guessed, the cause. But Stavros never said anything to anybody. About this Olga was sure.

'When are you playing?' Olga asked at last.

'On Saturday afternoon at 4.30.'

'I'd love to come,' Olga said, 'but I am not sure how to get there.'

'Nicos here is one of the few people on this island who possesses a motorcar. We can come and collect you.'

Olga now made a miserable sight. She went from red to pale and felt terribly uncomfortable. She felt terribly torn. This sounded like a unique opportunity, not only to play tennis, but to see Stavros and to be in a motorcar with him, to be with him for a whole afternoon at the beautiful Forest Hotel with fashionable, modern people, maybe have tea with them. For a moment, Olga's mind was racing.

But Olga was a very down to earth person, very much aware of the conventions of the time, of what people might say going alone, a young woman of a good and sound upbringing, with two young men in a motorcar.

'I am not sure,' she said. 'I'll have to think about it.'

Stavros looked disappointed.

'OK,' he said, 'we can come again tomorrow.'

A short silence followed.

'Now that I think about it,' Olga said and her voice was almost breaking 'now that I think about it, I don't think I can come.'

She sounded sad, if not depressed. This was an opportunity that would not be given to her again. Yet she knew that this would be short of a scandal. A woman from a good family travelling alone with two young men. The whole of the middle class of Limassol would be gossiping, condemning, frothing with envy and malice. What was more important, she didn't want to put her mother in the difficult position of either to say 'no' to her or to endure the malice that would be circulating after the event. Better if she took the responsibility herself and with it the disappointment.

'I am sorry,' she said. 'I am really sorry. I would love to, but I think I can't do it.'

'I understand,' Stavros said. 'I understand.'

He sounded disappointed even if he tried in vain to hide it.

'Maybe another time,' he said.

'Yes, maybe another time, maybe in Limassol,' Olga said. 'It's much easier.'

'Yes' he said and turned to his friend ready to go. 'Well, see you around.'

'Yes,' she said, 'yes.'

She felt like crying as the two men made their goodbyes and left.

Olga's cousins giggled as the two men disappeared.

'He is smitten with you,' Deana said.

Olga blushed. 'Don't talk nonsense,' she said, 'they just want a fourth player.'

'Yeeeees!' Fotini mocked, 'Yyyeeees! That's all. They just want a fourth player,' and they all giggled.

'There is nothing between us' Olga said blushing even deeper.

'Yeees, we can see that,' Fotini kept mocking ruthlessly. 'It's obvious.'

The cousins laughed.

'You just broke his heart,' Fotini said now following Deana's banter.

'I don't know what you are talking about,' Olga said.

The cousins giggled and Olga blushed even more.

'Look! Look!' Fotini giggled. 'She is blushing!'

'I am not,' Olga protested. She felt very depressed and uncomfortable.

'OK. OK,' Deana said, 'we should stop it. Olga is embarrassed.'

'OK,' Fotini said and they fell silent.

Olga suddenly remembered her mother and Anna and Maroulla and she looked around for them. They were some 20 metres behind sitting on a bench under a plane tree. It was obvious that they all had, and certainly her mother had, witnessed the whole scene from a distance but had chosen to stay there and let the girls get on with it. She had always hoped that Stavros would choose one of her daughters. From what she had heard, Stavros was a hardworking man with a university degree who had just become a civil servant. Her distant cousin seemed to know him and always spoke highly of him. So what else could she wish for her daughters? Olga was pleased that her mother was not closer to see her blushing and hear her cousins teasing her. She felt a deep sense of relief.

The girls continued their walk through the orchards and the vineyards telling stories and pulling each other's leg. Their laughter echoed across the valley and over the distant mountains.

As they returned home the moon was hanging orange and heavy above the mountains and the sky was turning purple. The girls tired from the long walk headed for home experiencing a healthy appetite for Kyriakou's and Arsinoe's stuffed vine leaves and aubergines that were left from lunch. It was time for dinner and for the games that followed after dinner.

Chapter 11
Limassol 1936

Olga's Loneliness

It was late September. The town dwellers had returned to their towns from the mountain villages and once again the villages belonged to the villagers. The Aristos family had been back to Limassol for the last three weeks and Olga went swimming with her cousins every morning. Auntie Maroulla's house continued to be a refuge for her for the afternoons and evenings, a place where she could feel free from people's inquisitive eyes and questions and feel less lonely. Nellie continued to improve eating better and talking more, mainly to Olga and mainly about a book or an article she had read. She spent the mornings in her room but after siesta she would take her chair under the pomegranate tree and read. She would not dare outside the house. By now, she had not been outside the house for almost five months, apart from travelling to Pera Pedi that is. She would often ask Olga to go to see Sotiris and borrow some books from his library and Olga was all too happy to be of some help to her sister.

For Olga, life began to feel lonely and without much meaning. It was as if she had caught Nellie's illness. Day came and day went and it felt all the same, a monotonous ongoing greyness that had no end. She met with friends and went to her cousins' house and to Maroulla's house and on Sunday afternoons she joined her friends for an ice cream at the new fashionable ice cream parlour on the sea front. At times, she would meet Stavros during these walks on the promenade and they would exchange a few words which always seemed to have a secret meaning which made her heart beat wildly. But then Stavros would disappear for weeks and she had no idea whether she would ever see him again, or whether she would one day, just like Nellie, read an announcement about his engagement in the local paper.

Every time she felt happy after she saw him she had to remind herself again and again of Nellie's predicament. So, she made herself have no thoughts and no hopes, no dreams and no fantasies. But then in the end this made for a meaningless life. All sparkle had gone. Nellie, her best friend, had lost all hope and as the months went by Olga could see that Nellie would never be the same again.

It slowly occurred to Olga that the stigma of Nellie's "illness" was having its effect on her as well, as Aristos so much feared. The small-minded people of Limassol had a lot to talk about and some thrived on gossip and on malice and on other people's unhappiness. She never wanted to think about things like this, but life had taken another turn and all of a sudden her innocence was gone. Her faith in life, her love of everyday little things, taking happiness and security for granted, her small protected life as a guarantee for a happy future, all this had gone. Life seemed humdrum and time extended indefinitely, utterly meaningless. Aristos' view of the world prevailed. Enemies were everywhere ready to pounce on the weak and on those who were different.

Until now Olga felt protected by Aristos and his hallowed parents and their standing in society. Their family was one of the oldest and most revered in the town. It might not have been one of the richest, it was true, but it was certainly one of the most respected ones. Aristos valued this status much more than any material goods which were not lacking either. The family was "comfortable" if not rich. But more than material goods, the family was a haven of security. It was this "security" and this respectability that Aristos could no longer provide and this realisation affected the whole family.

It was as if Nellie's "illness" with all the malicious gossip that accompanied it, threatened to de-stabilise an old securely established family. Aristos himself looked drawn and unhappy. As month succeeded month and Nellie refused to go out and show herself to the nosey citizens of Limassol, and as speculations about her "condition" increased, he felt totally helpless. All his assumed "power" as the head and protector of the family was gone. The patriarch whose duty was to protect his family and carry out the ancient law that was entrusted on him, felt totally powerless. Faced with woman's unknown, secret, labyrinthine thoughts and emotions and his daughter's utter refusal to conform with what was expected of her, he felt crashed. A kind of depression descended on him and with him on the whole family. Nobody could see a way out of this situation.

In the morning, after Aristos left for work, the family would linger a bit longer around the table, but conversation was scarce and the depressed mood prevailed. Kyriakou would get on with cleaning the breakfast things and sweeping and washing the floor of the dining room, the bedrooms and the hall, dusting all furniture, hanging out the sheets and bed covers to get "aired". In the meantime, lunch was being prepared. They had hardly finished breakfast and Thalia began the preparation of lunch. Looking up the ingredients, did they have enough flour, oil, butter, onions, tomatoes etc. to prepare whatever was going to be prepared. The menu was decided the evening before as Thalia, Kyriakou, Olga and Anna chatted after dinner while Aristos was reading the newspaper in his study and Nellie would withdraw to her room and her books.

After breakfast and cleaning, Kyriakou would go to the grocer carrying the big shopping bag and Olga would go and sit with Nellie and read her book or offer to help her mother with some house work but not with cooking as Thalia insisted that this was her job and yes Kyriakou can help but that's all. Kyriakou would come back with the groceries and the baklava or another delicacy and would help Thalia to start the cooking. Anna sitting on the patio in front of the typewriter would ask, 'Wwwhhhat are wwwe hhhaving fffor lunch tttoday?' And Thalia would answer 'I've already told you—okra with lamb, or moussaka, or stuffed vegetables or lentils, or beans in tomato sauce' and Anna would say 'ggggooood,' or 'I ddon't llllike this' and Thalia would say 'I'll fry an egg and make some chips for you.' Aristos would arrive for lunch at 1.10 exactly and lunch would be served soon after.

Olga had read somewhere that the philosopher Immanuel Kant had such exact habits, going to university and coming back every day at exactly the same time that the citizens of Koenigsberg set their clocks by him. Olga thought the same about her father. At 1.10 every day, he was at home expecting the table to have been set and the food to be ready. He would wash his hands and sit at the table and Olga, Thalia and Anna would sit down as well. Nobody expected Nellie to come to the table anymore. Kyriakou would go to the kitchen to get the food which had already been placed in big platters. Aristos would unfold his white linen napkin and wait for Thalia to serve him. He would then wait patiently for everybody else to be served and then would say 'kali orexi' (bon appetite) and thus would give the sign to everybody to start eating.

Olga realised that in other families the father would say a prayer or simply offer a "thank you" to God and ask him to bless the food they were about to eat, but her father was a professed atheist and anything to do with God he considered a childish illusion. Not that this prevented him from feeling utterly betrayed when Anna converted to Catholicism. It was as if Anna had declared that she was given the wrong thing by her parents. What her parents gave her was faulty and not working. Her conversion to Catholicism was felt unconsciously by the parents as a rebellion against them for having given her a disabled body. Aristos continued to preach atheism as a new religion and felt even more alone in his family where this was considered blasphemy. Only Olga secretly shared his views and he suspected that. But Olga was such a secretive person she never let anybody know what she was thinking and although Aristos respected this, he wished she would be more vocal and support him for a change.

At 1.50, Aristos would set out for the Bank and at 4.10pm he would be back for his "café au lait" and a piece of Thalia's cake. He would then spend the rest of the afternoon in his study reading. At 7pm, a light dinner was served. Aristos favoured tea and toasts accompanied by cold meat or salami, boiled eggs, olives and tomatoes. Or alternatively a soup with fried bread, cheese or fried halloumi. Sometimes Thalia would make fried courgettes and scrambled eggs and a salad. Sometimes Kyriakou would be out visiting her 'family', a few cousins at the other end of the town, and Thalia would do it all by herself.

Sometimes there was lively conversation and Thalia would tell everybody some news to do with her cousins or friends, some gossip or some news from *The Observer*. In such occasions, Aristos would allow himself to be drawn into the conversation and make some comments and even make a joke or two. Aristos' humour was sharp and dry, and he had a special irony in his voice as if he was at a distance from the part of himself that was telling the joke. Olga appreciated her father's humour but she was the only one in the household who did so. Thalia found it cruel and Nellie (when she was present and listening) just ignored it. Anna would sometimes violently disagree, especially if the joke had something to do with religion or with priests, or the Pope, something which often made her choke on her food as she tried to express her disagreement in a violent ways. Jokes about religion or the Pope could not be tolerated by Anna. Full of exploding anger which she could not express in words Anna would begin to shake uncontrollably and would put all effort into trying to formulate a few words which however remained unarticulated. She would utter some sounds like "yyyyooouuu arrrr bbbblll". Olga thought that perhaps she was trying to say 'you are blasphemous but nothing clearer than that came out of her mouth.' Thalia tried to pacify her and tried to say to Aristos that he should be more careful as to what he was saying, but Aristos would shake his head and smile one of his dry smiles. 'Women, what do you expect' seemed to be thinking. Perhaps this was his revenge for Anna's betrayal in converting into Catholicism, these dry jokes about the Pope or religion in general.

All this continued with frightening, and perhaps reassuring, familiarity while everybody was aware of the different circumstances that surrounded them, Nellie's depression and the uncertain future that hung over them all.

Olga's depression, like her father's, was palpable but imperceptible. She went through the everyday routine in the same way. She helped mother and Kyriakou in everyday tasks like she had always done, she talked to Anna, and went to visit her friends and cousins regularly, and went to get books for Nellie, but slowly a hopelessness began to descend on her. The vision of a future that would be an extension and an exact copy of the present, empty, shameful, lonely would sometimes overwhelm her and at night she cried quietly under her pillow.

She had not seen or heard from Stavros for some time now and her suspicion which she did not dare verbalise even to herself was that he was avoiding her perhaps because she was part of a family where girls fell prey to inexplicable illnesses or "nerves".

Then one day she heard from her cousins, who heard it from Sotiris who heard it from Antonis, that Stavros had been re-located to Paphos. Of course, as a civil servant Stavros had no choice where to work, she knew that. This was a promotion, it seemed, so he was happy, the cousins said at the same time watching Olga's face losing all its colour. Olga had never been to Paphos and although it was some 50 miles away from Limassol, it took four hours to reach as the road was very bad, and it felt like another country. Olga's mind was racing. Stavros was gone to this distant and unknown place which had the reputation of a backward place which the English were trying to develop. All her hopes were suddenly gone. In a split second, with a few words everything changed, all hope gone. Like with Nellie, when she read a couple of sentences in the newspaper, life seemed to change irrevocably. She would never see Stavros again. He would make his life in Paphos and perhaps marry there. This was the end of her dreams. She now wished she had gone to Platres to play tennis when he invited her. What sort of message did she give him when she refused his invitation, she wondered. Perhaps he thought that she was not interested in him at all. But there was no answer to this.

The days that followed were very dark for Olga. She had real trouble hiding her feelings from her mother who was by now stretched to the limit with Nellie's condition. Caring for Anna, trying to cope with Nellie's "illness" and with Aristos' accusations that it was all her fault, that she had spoilt the girls and now everybody was paying, Thalia found it difficult to have any time to think of Olga's emotional condition. Not that Olga gave her much opportunity for this, withdrawn as she was into herself.

So, Olga's hopelessness found no outlet. She could not talk to anyone about it. She had always been secretive and self-controlled and responsible, and she could not justify to herself this hopelessness and loneliness. She found some solace in her cousins but as she could not bring herself to talk to them about what she was feeling she received no real support. It was now October and the first rains had arrived spreading slowly a green stubble over the scorched earth. Olga and her cousins had given up swimming in the sea. She stayed more and more at home reading books on Byzantine culture, playing draughts with Anna who enjoyed the extra attention very much, or going to get some books for Nellie. Aristos had at last his wish—the girls did not go out. But now he wishes they did. The heavy atmosphere of his household was difficult to bear even for Aristos. And there was no sign that things would ever change. This heavy, depressed atmosphere was to continue for ever, he feared, and the women feared exactly the same.

Christmas arrived and the usual preparations were made. Two weeks before Christmas Thalia and Kyriakou began to clean the house thoroughly, particularly the big lounge that was rarely open unless visitors came, polish the silver, wash and starch the linen tablecloths and the linen napkins, get the Bavarian porcelain down from the cupboard where it was kept hidden and protected most of the time. The family was getting ready to receive aunts and cousins for the traditional Christmas lunch.

On Christmas day, the women got up early to prepare the goose, the chicken, the beef and the potatoes in two big tins to be sent to the baker for roasting. Simos, the young lad from next door, would take the two tins to the baker for four grosha. Then Thalia would get Anna ready to be collected by the nuns who would take her to the Catholic church and Kyriakou would prepare the soup which would be the first course—egg and lemon soup with rice and bits of chicken floating. Thalia, Olga, Kyriakou and Nellie would then go to mass at ten to receive the holy communion. Thalia was the only one to fast for two weeks before Christmas. Needless to say, Kyriakou had fasted all the 40 days before Christmas and Olga and Nellie fasted for three days. Nellie managed to make it to church on Christmas day to receive the holy communion. Aristos had not entered any church, apart for weddings and funerals, for the last twenty-five years and nobody questioned this anymore.

Despite the depression in the Aristos house, the Christmas lunch was organised with the same excitement and luxury as always. The big table was set for 12 people in the big lounge and another smaller table was set next to it for the children (Maroulla's two children). The linen tablecloth would be spread on the big table and the Bavarian porcelain, the crystal glasses and the silver knives, forks and spoons would be placed in exactly the right way according to etiquette that young middle-class girls were brought up with.

After that, Thalia and Kyriakou would prepare the trifle, a local variety that is, with sponge cake and blanched almonds, vanilla cream and rose water, for dessert. Anna, having received the holy communion at the Catholic Church, and beaming with pleasure, would be brought back at 12.30 by Mother Madeleine herself and another couple of nuns. Thalia would invite the nuns in and they would sit in the small parlour for 10 minutes as Kyriakou offered some Christmas biscuits and a lemonade. Thalia gave them paper napkins to wrap the biscuits in and take them with them. As they sipped the lemonade they chatted about Christmas and the Christmas customs in France where Mere Madeleine came from. Anna, sat there emanating pure happiness. The whole visit lasted less than ten minutes and, wishing the whole family Merry Christmas, they were soon gone.

At 12.45, Thalia and Kyriakou would prepare the big salad and the goose and the meat would arrive at 1pm and would be served into big platters. At 1.10pm, Maroulla and Sotiris and the children arrived and all of a sudden the house was full of life and love and kisses and laughter and jokes and stories and children running around opening their presents. Soon after Deana, Fotini and Arsinoe arrived.

At 1.30, Thalia's sister, Katina, and her husband, Anaxagoras, accompanied by their son Miltiades, arrived. Now this was a surprise which presented Thalia with a problem. She had not expected Miltos to come for the big Christmas lunch as she had wrongly assumed that he and his fiancée were going to spend Christmas at her family house. But the family had to leave unexpectedly for

Egypt, where they came from, to visit a dying relative and so Miltos accompanied his mother to auntie Thalia's.

Thalia's problem was twofold. Firstly the table was set for twelve and worse than this the Bavarian set was for only twelve people. To add another plate from a different set was to spoil the carefully planned table arrangement. Secondly, thirteen people at the table was considered bad luck and the last thing Thalia, or the Aristos family, needed at that moment was more bad luck. For a moment, Thalia felt defeated. But she solved the problem by attaching the children's table to the big table and putting another plate for Miltos at the children's table. Miltos was now seated next to Aristos, although at another table, and would now be able to participate in adult conversation while being part of the children's table. This solution gave Thalia great relief as her carefully arranged Christmas table would not be spoilt and more importantly there would still be twelve at the table, not thirteen!

In the kitchen, Kyriakou was transferring the avgolemono soup into a big soup bowl after Thalia had tasted it and pronounced it fit for consumption and told Kyriakou to bring it to the table and begin to serve. In the dining room, the atmosphere was jolly. Sotiris was telling the mayor's latest gaffe who after his trip to London he had been asked whether he had been to see "Carmen" at the Covent Garden and he answered looking very offended that he was not the sort of person who cheats on his wife. Everybody laughed loudly and with a certain glee.

As Thalia and Olga arrived back, Aristos handed them a glass of Commandaria, 'the wine of the gods,' he reminded them, and everybody they raised their glasses. 'Merry Christmas' Aristos said formally and they all replied 'Merry Christmas' and auntie Arsinoe added 'and God give us health and happiness' and everybody repeated the words apart from Aristos who felt very annoyed about this intrusion of God into his Christmas meal.

After this, they all took their places at the table as indicated by Thalia who sat at one end of the table facing Aristos at the other. Kyriakou, dressed in a white pinafore preserved only for formal occasions came in with the soup and began serving.

The family and their guests were now free to enjoy the meal, the lively conversation, the jokes, the laughter, the good atmosphere and the good food. The transformation of the Aristos household couldn't have been bigger on this Christmas day. Even Nellie managed some lively conversation with her cousins and as the soup was served and Commandaria, the local wine that Richard the Lionheart had allegedly called "wine for the gods", was also served and the toasts and goodwill wishes were expressed everybody felt for a while that this was the good old world, friendly, warm and loving and real fun. The goose and the chicken, and the beef, accompanied by roast potatoes and a freshly cut winter salad and freshly cut bread followed.

All this time Nellie kept a low profile talking to her cousin Fotini who was the bookworm of the family and who told Nellie about her studies on the habits of Eskimo. It was obvious that nobody wanted to draw attention to the fact that Nellie had not been out of the house for several months and that she had lost a lot of weight and she looked drawn and strained, but that today for the first time she managed to get to mass at the church of the Holy Trinity and had dared to show herself to the world. Everybody pretended that things were as usual and Nellie had no intention of contradicting this pretence.

Aristos and Sotiris were locked into a serious discussion about the possibility of war in Europe and about the future of democracy as the clouds of Fascism were spreading across Europe. They meandered into democracy in the 5th century Athens and into the demise of democracy in Rome. Then the question of the vote for women arose.

'It is bound to come to Greece,' Sotiris said, 'it has become law in the major European countries.'

'Women having the vote? You think this is progress?' Aristos chuckled 'I know this is the fashion in Europe but everybody knows that women can't think. They are governed by their emotions and their hysterias.'

'The question,' Sotiris added directing the discussion away from the vote of women, is whether Herr Hitler will allow anybody to vote, men or women. 'Democracy is dead in Germany.'

'Not to mention Italy and Mussolini,' added Aristos.

'Yet England and France are as democratic as ever,' Sotiris said. 'Democracy will win in the end and giving the vote to women is part of it.'

'Bravo Sotiri,' Nellie shouted drawing attention to herself. 'Bravo Sotitri, you must take up the rights of women. Of course women must have the vote in Greece and eventually, when we become part of Greece, here as well. But first we must become independent from the English and unite with mother Greece.'

Everybody stopped eating for a moment and their knives and forks remained suspended between the plates and their mouths. By now, the goose and the beef and the chicken had been served and everybody had already offered their comments of appreciation to the hostess. And as they were digging into the soft, succulent meat and the crusty potatoes and the green salad with feta and olives Nellie's triumphant voice rose above all conversations. There was a stunned silence for a moment.

'You will make a good member of parliament one day, Nellie, when this island becomes part of Greece,' Sotiris said after he recovered from his surprise.

'Nonsense,' Aristos said, 'don't put funny ideas into Nellie's mind. She's got enough funny ideas of her own already. Women should not interfere into the affairs of the state.'

'You have always been a tyrant and you will always remain one,' Nellie shouted.

The guests began to feel uncomfortable. This political family row threatened to destroy Christmas for everybody.

'You've proved my point Nellie,' Aristos said in a cool, measured way. 'You've proved my point.'

'The only point I've proved is that you don't want to listen to any other opinion that contradicts yours.'

Nellie was almost in tears.

'Nonsense,' Aristos said.

'You don't listen to anybody,' Nellie shouted.

'Calm down Nellie,' Thalia intervened. 'It's Christmas.'

'What do I care about your stupid Christmas.'

Nellie was now out of control.

'What do I care about your narrow, stupid world?'

She got up and without looking at anybody she left the room throwing her napkin violently on the table.

A deep awkward silence followed. Thalia felt defeated. Aristos was full of unexploded rage.

'What was that about?' Maroulla said at last after what felt like an eternity of silence.

'She hasn't been herself recently,' Thalia tried to explain.

'Yes it seems so,' Maroulla said.

'Dr Freud has something to say about hysterical women,' Aristos said mercilessly.

Nobody replied. Olga wondered what her father meant as she had no idea what Dr Freud has said.

Another long silence followed. The only sound in the room was the one of knives and forks hitting the plates.

But after a while conversation around the table began about different subjects and Nellie's outburst was slowly forgotten as the guests dug more into the duck and the potatoes and Commandaria flowed freely and the atmosphere became once again festive.

The trifle was served, and the guests praised once again Thalia's skills as a cook and as a cake maker. After lunch, the girls played games and chatted about the presents they were expecting to get from St Basil on the 1st January. This was a muddled state of affairs as St Basil was the equivalent of Father Christmas for the Greeks and brought the presents on the 1st January, but the island being under the British adopted Christmas as well as the time children got their presents. The result was that some children got presents twice, while others got them only on the 1st January, or only at Christmas. This was one of these cultural muddles that the middle-class islanders had got into.

'What do you want St Basil to bring you?' Alexis asked his sister.

'There is no St Basil,' Zoe answered with a voice full of importance. 'He doesn't exist.'

Zoe was seven and she was proud of her grown-up knowledge about these things, which her cousin Maria who was nine had transmitted to her in confidence having warned her not to tell her brother who was five.

'Yes he does,' Alexis said with conviction. 'He will bring me the big car I have asked. I asked him, I asked him, he knows' he insisted with a tone of desperation in his voice. 'Mum said he would bring me the big car and he will, he will, you will see.'

'It's mamma who will bring you the big car,' Zoe insisted, 'it's mamma and papa, not St Basil.'

'It is St basil, it's St Basil whatever you say,' Alexis shouted.

'You are just a little child,' Zoe said in a tone of grown-up importance, 'Just a little child, you believe whatever they tell you.'

'But St Basil exists. He is coming on New Year's day You will see.'

'Children, children just eat your trifle, it's delicious,' Maroulla said, ' and stop arguing. Otherwise St Basil won't bring you anything.'

'You see,' Alexis said, 'St Basil exists. Mamma said so.'

'Nonsense,' Zoe said and the whole thing started once again.

The adults laughed and they relaxed as they ate the trifle and exchanged comments and recipes and news about friends and relatives, leaving the episode with Nellie behind. Thalia was happy that everybody was enjoying themselves but at the back of her mind was always Nellie and her explosive rage. This raw rage was new. She had never seen her addressing her father like this especially in front of other people. This was a new chapter of her "illness" and God knows where it would lead to, Thalia thought to herself.

On New Year's Eve, the two families gathered once again in the house on Aristotelous Street and stayed up until 12 to welcome the new year, playing games and chatting endlessly. But Olga's heart was heavy, underneath all the merriment and the laughter and the love and the gossip. The hopelessness, she had felt for months, persisted just under the surface. She watched Nellie who remained subdued and hardly spoke, and Aristos, who would not be seen dead handling playing cards, and who talked all evening with Sotiris about politics, philosophy and the growing power of Herr Hitler. She watched her mother who did her best to provide food and drinks, but her drawn face was visible under the mask of congeniality she had put on. The women played cards and tombola putting have a penny on the table, something that was allowed only on New year's eve at Aristos' household, and screamed with delight every time one of them won and collected the few pennies from the table. Anna participated fully, winning a few times, and Olga could see that she was the only genuinely happy member of the family, being in her own simple world where she was fully loved and protected by God, Mother Madeleine and Thalia.

St Basil did come on the 1st January and brought the children their favourite toys. Alexis was triumphant and told his sister that he was proved right, St Basil did exist and whatever his sister might say was a lie, a wicked lie. The grown-ups were consoled with the coin in the New year's cake, which this year was won by Anna. Aristos family had been invited at Maroulla's and they had another, if smaller, festive meal, and good wishes and endless talk.

It was now end of January and Olga felt that life would be a repetition of the present for ever. There was no hope that anything new would ever happen. Day succeeded day and Olga felt that the days were absolutely identical despite the frequent walks on the promenade and the not infrequent invitations to friends and relatives. But all this activity was meaningless. It gave her some respite, but no meaning. Meaninglessness engulfed her like an illness and she had not the necessary defences to fight it. The only thing she could do was to endure it.

Nellie seemed more angry and more depressed. She became what people might call "difficult". Things were never right. If Thalia made a cake and Nellie condescended to eating a small piece, it was guaranteed that she would find some fault in it and leave half of it uneaten. If Olga brought a book that she thought might interest Nellie, she would denounce it as "rubbish" leaving poor Olga to wonder how she could ever please Nellie. She would read the daily paper that arrived every day at 11am and she would criticise every bit of it in an angry contemptuous voice. She had become an angry critic of others, of her family and of society. The fun-loving Nellie had disappeared. She had lost a great deal of weight and her cheeks had sunk a little. She was still very beautiful but she had lost the sparkle that used to be her characteristic. She spent no time on elaborate hairstyles anymore. She wore her hair in a bun on top of her head. Olga observed all these changes in silence and despair and thought that things would never return to normal i.e. to the carefree state they were before.

It was now February. Limassol was cold and windy, the sea angry and frothy rising above the sea defences and into the promenade. Troodos had shown its majestic presence, haughty and snow-capped spreading cold weather to the whole of the island. People talked about the weather endlessly, how cold, how windy, how unusual, how sudden. Would it snow here? That would be unheard of, but one never knows. This weather was a freak weather.

Olga who had never seen snow in her life, only on English Christmas cards, wished for it. It would be something to break the monotony of her life that extended to the end of time. But no, it didn't snow. And the weather improved after a few cold days and life continued as before.

***

It was a Saturday afternoon in early March. Aristos who had Saturday afternoons off was enjoying a café-au-lait sitting on the veranda, his skin enjoying the warm, protective sunshine that enveloped him. As usual he was engrossed in Plato—this time it was Timaios—and he was steeped in deep philosophical idealism, the life of the soul and the life of "ideas", far from the muddled reality of home and Nellie and family, when a knock on the front door made him stop and wait in anticipation. Who could the visitor, or visitors, be?

Cousins, aunts, uncles, friends? Would they bring good news, bad news, illnesses, deaths, concerns, tears? He looked up from his book. The pomegranate tree had begun to show splashes of bright red blossoms. Even Aristos, steeped as he was in the world of ideal forms could not fail noticing the exploding beauty of the pomegranate tree as it displayed itself in the afternoon sun. He blinked in the sun and a feeling of wonder overtook him, a feeling he hadn't felt for a long time.

The distinct voice of Thalia as she welcomed an unknown visitor could be heard from the other side of the house. 'Yes, he is in,' he could hear Thalia saying. 'He is sitting on the veranda.'

Aristos sighed with resignation. His splendid isolation was coming to an end. He would now have to face the world of the humans so full of problems and troubles. Why couldn't people leave him alone on a Saturday afternoon?

Thalia's voice became more distinct as she and the unknown visitor approached the veranda.

'No problem at all,' she was saying, 'it's nice to see you after such a long time.'

When Thalia and the man entered the veranda, Aristos recognised the son of a distant cousin of his whom he hadn't seen possibly for a couple of years.

Aristos got up from his reclining chair and offered his hand. The two men shook hands cordially.

'Dimitri,' he said, 'good to see you. How are your parents?'

'They are fine,' Dimitris said, 'they are sending you their greetings.'

'Good to hear,' Aristos said who was wondering now what really brought this young man here to visit the Aristos family.

'And your sister?'

'She is fine. She had a bad cold, but she is recovering.'

'Yes' Aristos said, 'the cold weather has affected everybody. And how are you? How is the new job?'

Aristos knew that Dimitris was now working in the Department of Public Works as he had learnt this from somebody who knew somebody who worked there.

'Oh, it's great,' Dimitris said, 'it feels good to have a secure job for life.'

Aristos sat down and at the same time pointed to the chair opposite him. Dimitris sat down opposite him and continued.

'It's good being a civil servant and work with the English. Everything is so well organised and civilised.'

'Yes I can understand this.' Aristos said.

Still suspicious about Dimitris' visit and fearing a sting in the tail Aristos kept his alertness, ready to fob off every possible disaster that could suddenly leap out on him and his family.

Thalia came in and asked Dimitri how he would like his coffee.

'Metrios,' he answered (that meant with a little sugar).

Thalia disappeared inside the house to make the coffee and Aristos waited.

'Uncle,' Dimitris was now adopting a formal tone, 'I am here for a purpose.'

Aristos waited saying nothing. (I thought so, he thought, let it all out son).

'Hm,' he said.

The silence was now intense.

'It's about Olga,' he said at last.

Aristos was still silent giving no encouragement to the young man to proceed. All his alarm bells began to go. *But he is still a relative, if only a distant one*, he thought, *he called me uncle. It's not right for him to ask for Olga's hand.*

Thalia returned with the coffee and pieces of her delicious "ravani" cake. Dimitri helped himself to a piece of cake and began to sip at his coffee.

'How is Despo and your father?' Thalia asked.

'They are both fine,' Dimitri said. Thalia picked up the tray which she put on the little table in front of Dimitri and left.

'I'll leave you to it,' she had said and it sounded to Aristos like a life sentence.

'As I was saying,' Dimitri began tentatively, 'as I was saying…'

Aristos remained silent betraying nothing of his complicated thoughts which went a bit like this 'it would be good if somebody wanted to marry Olga. A couple of years ago this very rich older man asked for her hand, but he could not blame his daughter for refusing him. He was old and a bit coarse, not exactly refined in his manners. But on the other hand a cousin? Is that right? He knew that the church accepted marriage between "third" cousins but still is this right?'

Dimitris seemed to gather his courage.

'Well,' he said, 'it's like this. A good friend of mine, a very good friend of mine, an educated young man with a very good job in the civil service wants to ask for Olga's hand. But, before he approaches you in person, he wants to know first whether she is interested, and whether you and auntie Thalia might consider giving your consent.'

The young man looked obviously relieved that he had let all this information come out of his mouth. He knew enough about uncle Aristos to be properly intimidated by him.

Aristos was also relieved. He drew a deep breath and let some time pass in silence.

'Well,' he said, 'well.'

There was another deep silence during which Aristos was thinking 'this is such a relief, but I must not look very eager.'

He remained silent, torturing the young man who did not know what to make out of the silence.

Thalia relieved the situation by coming back with a bowl full of "courabiethes" (a kind of biscuits).

'I made them yesterday,' she said, 'I thought you might want to try them.'

'They look delicious,' Dimitris said as he picked one and put it in his mouth.

'Mmmm,' he said, 'it's delicious. Your cakes have always been delicious auntie Thalia.'

He was in fact grateful for this interruption and for the sweet alternative to Aristos' silent torture.

'Well I shall leave them here and please help yourself to more,' she added and placed the plate on the table.

Thalia left, and Dimitris tried to use this opportunity of feeling more relaxed to break the ice.

'Sorry to bring you this so suddenly uncle,' he said.

'It's OK Dimitri,' Aristos was now speaking to the young man more directly. 'It's OK. Tell me a bit about this young man.'

'There is not much to say,' Dimitris said apologetically 'he has a degree from London university.'

He stopped waiting for Aristos' reaction.

Aristos seemed impressed and for a moment he was silent.

'A degree in what?' Aristos finally asked.

'In engineering.' Dimitris continued to sound apologetic. 'He is a civil engineer.'

If Aristos was disappointed, he did not show it. Engineering? Not his subject at all. What did engineers do anyway? He heard about railways and tunnels abroad. He heard about the London underground—"a triumph of engineering" they called it at the time. But here on the island? What did engineers do here?

'I see,' he said and silence reigned again.

'I am not very good in describing people,' Dimitris ventured, 'but I think he is a very exceptional man.'

'In what?' Aristos asked.

'He is extremely intelligent,' Dimitris said, 'very kind, cordial, good mannered, witty, well read. He will make your daughter very happy.'

'I see,' Aristos said again betraying nothing of his feelings.

Another silence followed.

'What family is it then?' Aristos asked at last.

Another awkward silence followed.

'Well you see he is not from Limassol.'

'Ah I see, from Nicosia then?' Aristos asked.

'No,' Dimitris said and again his apologetic voice came to the fore despite himself, 'he is from a small village in Marathasa.'

Deep silence followed and one could cut the atmosphere with a knife. It separated them like a wall. Dimitris looked deeply worried as if he had brought bad news to uncle Aristos not a marriage proposal.

'He is an exceptional individual,' Dimitris repeated himself.

He stopped abruptly as if he was scared to continue. But then he added, 'I am sure you will think the same when you meet him.'

'If I meet him,' Aristos said, 'if!'

'Uncle, I can vouch for this man. He is the most intelligent, the most responsible, the most kind and pleasant person I've ever met. He is exceptional. He impresses people wherever he goes. He impressed his professors at the university, he impressed his English superiors at the civil service who have already recommended him for promotion although he has been in the civil service for hardly a year. He will go far.'

Dimitris stopped, being out of breath, and was silent. He said what he had to say, now it was his uncle's turn.

'Mm,' Aristos said, 'Mm.' And then, after a short silence, 'I will have to think about this.'

'Of course,' Dimitris said, 'of course.'

'What is his name anyway? Has he got a name?'

'Stavros Georgiou,' Dimitris said.

'Never heard of him,' Aristos said and silence prevailed once again.

Aristos' thoughts were tortured. Just when he thought for a moment that there was somebody for Olga, it turned out to be a "nobody" from "nowhere". He had no family in Limassol rich or poor, good or bad. He had no family. Olga was not a beauty, but she was serious and reliable and kind and honest and caring. She would make a very good wife. And she wasn't ugly either, but maybe rather plain. She didn't take after her mother either her looks or her personality. She was more like him. When he married Thalia, he thought that she was the most beautiful creature he had ever seen. But, he had to shape Thalia when they got married. He had to reform her and shape her to his requirements, to be more domestic, less lively, less ambitious about her piano playing. The family was not rich and playing the piano was of course lovely, but they could not have any soirees or big parties anymore like when his father was alive. They could afford just one maid and that was all. Thalia would have to do with what was there. But money was not everything. Aristos carried the name of his family with pride. He came from one of the oldest and most respected families in Limassol, he reminded himself as he often did, when he was in front of a dilemma. Could he let his daughter marry a "nobody"? Even if he had a degree from London University, he was still a nobody.

Yet it might be an opportunity that Olga may not have again. They were an old family, that was true, and he was proud of his family and his name. But Olga was not going to have a big dowry. The house they lived in, she would, of course, inherit as the eldest, and possibly a piece of land from her mother's dowry. That was all. But the house was theoretical as they needed somewhere to live so they would stay there, although Olga's name would now be on the deeds. They would pay her a small rent of course but that was all. And this man, this "nobody", had a secure, respectable job in the civil service, a job for life, that would guarantee Olga's future. That was a big plus.

'I will have to think about it,' Aristos said finally and made a gesture as if the audience with the king was over. He got up with the dignity he inherited from his venerable father and offered Dimitri his hand. He had to save face, he thought. If a young man from "nowhere" would ask for his daughter's hand, what sort of family where they?

Dimitri got up to leave and as was getting up to go still saying his goodbyes to Aristos, Thalia suddenly appeared out of nowhere with a small parcel of courabiethes asking him to give her very warm greetings to his very dear parents and his lovely sister and thanking him for coming to see them. After Thalia escorted the young man to the front door with yet more greetings to his parents and urging him to come and visit them again, and after the front door had shut behind him the house fell into silence. Olga was out with her friends and Anna was at the convent for tea with Mother Madeleine, followed by prayers at the chapel. Nellie, as usual, spent the afternoon in her room. It made Thalia nervous not knowing what Nellie did in her room all these hours. It was true from time to time a friend would come to visit her, and they would have coffee and talk about books, but that was all. Thalia stood in the big dark hall and had a strong feeling of loneliness and helplessness as she waited for Aristos to call her—for she knew Aristos would call her. And she waited. She retired to the small parlour next to the hall and began her knitting and waited.

Aristos remained seated on his reclining chair on the veranda and absorbed the silence around him. It was Saturday afternoon and the workshops around the house had fallen silent preparing for the day of the Lord next day. A distant cry of a baby. A dog barking. The voice of the woman next door saying something urgent to somebody who remained silent. The cry of a seagull. Silence emerged as the background to life—golden, soothing, silence.

But Aristos' thoughts were turbulent. The news from Dimitri was both exciting and disconcerting, and despite his conviction that these things should be decided by the head of the household he called Thalia. For her part, Thalia was waiting patiently. She had an idea that Dimitri was bringing a proposal but for whom and from whom?

When she heard her name being called impatiently, urgently she jumped from her chair, put down her knitting and straightened her skirt. It was as if she was going to visit an important unknown person and she had to appear her best.

'Coming,' she called and hurried to the veranda.

As Thalia came out to the veranda Aristos' worried face disappeared. His lips pressed together gave him a look of a surgeon ready to begin an operation. His eyes had the cold piercing look of a scientist examining a piece of equipment.

'Sit down Thalia,' he said showing her a chair as if Thalia was one of his clients at the bank.

Thalia sat down feeling Aristos' deep worry and his wish to appear in control. She said nothing waiting for him to open the subject.

'You know,' he said, 'Dimitris was here with a proposal.'

He paused and looked at her. He expected her to express excitement, curiosity, worry, something to reduce his anxiety. But she remained silent so he continued.

'It's for Olga,' he said.

'I see, for Olga,' Thalia said. 'Well she is the eldest after all,' she added.

'Yes,' he said.

At that moment, hell broke loose from the next-door house. The three-year-old boy who lived there with his parents began to scream out of control and all they could hear was 'no, no, I don't want to.' Mother's entreaties and father's threats were soon added to this and pandemonium filled the air. Aristos was almost grateful that somebody was expressing the utter frustration of the situation in very urgent terms.

Aristos and Thalia remained silent while all this was going on. It was obvious to Thalia that Aristos was not pleased with the proposal, but neither could he turn it down out of hand. So, she waited patiently.

After a while, the toddler's screams became less urgent and were soon transformed into a whimpering. Mother's consoling voice was heard, and father seemed to have disappeared.

'The trouble is,' Aristos said, 'I am not sure whether the man is suitable.'

He paused.

'What do you mean?' she said.

'He has no family,' he said.

'He must have some family,' she said.

'That's not what I mean.' Aristos sounded angry now. 'You deliberately distort my words.'

'Explain to me then.' Thalia pretended not to hear the anger in Aristos voice.

'He comes from a village in the region of Marathasa,' he said, 'I've never even heard of the village.'

'Why is Dimitris bothering then, has he got money this man?'

'No, not money. He has a degree from London University.'

'But that's worth a lot,' Thalia said spontaneously.

'Mm,' Aristos said.

'Has he got a good job?' Thalia now asked.

'He is in the civil service. He is a civil engineer.'

'That sounds good,' Thalia said.

'Yes, but no family,' Aristos said.

'Mm,' Thalia said.

The bells from the nearby Catholic church began to chime. It was time for the vespers. They sat quietly listening to the bells and taking in the evening breeze. Thalia thought that Anna and the nuns were preparing to go to church. She also thought that Olga would be back soon.

Suddenly strong scent of jasmine wafted onto the veranda. Thalia took a deep breath and shut her eyes. The evening was descending cool and scented and she suddenly felt a feeling of wellbeing. Life was moving on. Whoever this suitor was it was good news even if they did reject him.

'Dimitris seems to think the world of him,' Aristos said suddenly breaking the silence.

'That's a good sign,' Thalia said. 'Dimitris is a very serious young man and a good judge of character. Remember when he advised his cousin Sofia not to marry this young man who although he came from a very good family he was quite unstable. Sofia didn't listen to him and look at the state of their marriage now! Money and a good family is not all that there is.'

Thalia stopped and they both immersed themselves in their thoughts about Sofia's failed marriage with her alcoholic, gambler husband and the scandalous separation.

'Yes,' Aristos said at last as if he was continuing a conversation, 'Dimitris is a good judge of people.'

'And what is the name of this young man who wants to marry Olga?' Thalia asked at last.

'I think he said that it was Stavros Georgiou,' Aristos said. 'I am sure this was the name. Never heard it before.'

Thalia's mind began to buzz. Could it be the same Stavros? Olga's Stavros? It looked like it. It was as if she was struggling to hold ten different thoughts in her mind. What could she possibly say to Aristos? That she probably knew who Stavros was and Olga was already in love with him and he possibly in love with her? That things were happening behind his back?

'Ah,' she said finally, 'I could make some enquiries about him. I can ask Maroulla who can ask Sotiris. Sotiris knows almost everybody in Limassol. But Olga must also know.'

'No, not yet,' Aristos said. 'Don't tell Olga anything. Let's make our enquiries first.'

'What if Olga wants to marry him anyway? Thalia dared to say.'

Aristos face was screwed into a knot.

'Since when a young woman does what she wants?' he asked provocatively.

'But this is about her life,' Thalia continued ignoring the clouds that were gathering on Aristos' face.

'This is about all our lives,' Aristos thumped his fist on the small garden table that nearly gave way.

Thalia could now see the storm gathering.

'Well, let's make some inquiries,' she said.

Olga and Kyriakou came back soon after, and Thalia went to the kitchen to prepare the evening meal.

That evening at supper Thalia and Aristos were unusually silent, even by their own standards. The dining room was like a morgue. Olga wondered whether her parents had heard some kind of bad news but what about she could not imagine. A close relative ill? A cousin in financial crisis? A brother's or sister's daughter "in trouble"? (a euphemism for losing her honour, or being pregnant outside wedlock).

Nellie who had begun to attend the dinner table was in any case absorbed into her world. The only sounds came from Anna's lips, protesting that her mother forgot to help her with the soup which could not manage on her own.

On Monday afternoon, Thalia said to the girls that she had to go and see cousin Lenia to discuss "a family matter". This mysterious excuse given to the girls made Olga more suspicious that something serious was going on in her family, but as usual she kept her suspicions to herself and got ready to go and visit her cousins, Deana and Fotini.

Chapter 12
Amiantos 1924

Stavros spent the summer of 1924 at Amiantos working in the administration of the asbestos mine, the first person from his village to have an administrative job at the mine. He did some desk work, some ledger work, some errands and a great deal of socialising with the British engineers and managers who, when they realised that he could speak perfect English, treated him with great cordiality.

Now that he knew he was going to Nicosia in September he began to relax and look forward to his unknown new life. He began to detach himself from the village and its life, its smallness, its small-mindedness and its human warmth. There was a painful realisation that his vision of life did not include this village and these people however much he loved them.

His graduation from secondary school had been a triumph. He had swept away all the prizes but most importantly he was granted the £10 prize for the best performance during all five years. He now knew he could go to Nicosia to study at the prestigious English School to take his matriculation. His father was beaming with pride while Stavros felt vindicated.

Apart from his father the graduation ceremony was attended by Elengo, Penelope, Manolis and his old teacher Socrates who also beamed with pride as if Stavros was his own son. Marilena did not attend claiming that the 4-month old Yiannis was not quite himself and she would better stay at home. Alexandros stayed with her.

And now he was among the pines of Amiantos, 1400 metres above sea level, on the slopes of the Troodos mountains, sitting with his English friend Keith on the veranda of the cottage, which was Keith's home, overlooking the deep ravine and the asbestos mine that dominated the mountain. The view was a mixture of the deep green of the pine forest surrounded by a lunar landscape, a devastated, wounded slope exposing its nakedness to the world.

Keith was asking Stavros whether he was going to go to university.

'I'd love to,' Stavros was saying, 'but I can't see how.'

'Why are you saying this?' Keith asked rather fervently.

'Because it's the truth,' Stavros said. 'I can only go to the English School in Nicosia because I got some prize money from school.'

Stavros felt the enormous gap that separated him from Keith and the other British people. How can he explain his circumstances? They treated him as equal, they treated him as if he were the same as them, and yet the chasm was unbridgeable. For a moment, he felt despair welling up in him.

'There are grants, scholarships,' Keith was saying encouragingly. 'Somebody like you should go to university. You should find a way. You will find a way.'

'Yes,' Stavros said. 'Yes.'

The light was getting faint. The mountains loomed like dark, huge, silent creatures all around them. Darkness was slowly spreading.

Keith got up and went inside the office that also served as his house and came out with a hurricane lamp which he put on the table. He then brought a bottle of brandy and two glasses and put them carefully on the little table in front of them.

The pool of light that came out of the lamp circled and embraced them and turned the mountains and the ravines into a distant dark presence that was more guessed than seen.

All around them was the silence of the mountains that Stavros knew so well and loved like a mother. This embracing silence was the closest Stavros had to a mother. He bathed in it and felt embraced by it.

The workers, some from Stavros' village, had gone home to their communal cottages and were probably already asleep. The managers had gone to their cottages they called home and were probably relaxing on their loungers with a glass of brandy and a book.

'What about you?' Stavros broke the silence. 'Did you go to university?'

'Yes,' Keith said. 'Yes, of course. Civil engineering,' he added.

Stavros looked puzzled.

'Ah,' he said.

'I am a civil engineer,' Keith said. 'You didn't know?'

'Yes, yes, of course.'

Stavros didn't want to tell Keith that he had no idea what "civil engineering" was or what civil engineers did and that he had heard the word for the first time.

'I loved the years at university,' Keith continued completely unaware of the terror that Stavros was experiencing in case Keith discovered that he was so ignorant, so terribly, shamefully ignorant.

'Being away from home, from my god-fearing, disciplinarian parents,' Keith was now saying, being so obviously in his own world, 'finding my freedom to read, talk and think what I wanted—well that was a new world for me. That was freedom.'

Stavros was now very interested.

'Tell me more,' he said.

'You know I grew up on a farm,' Keith was now saying. 'Away from people. Our closest neighbours were a few miles away. So my first years of life I played only with my brothers and sister. But then they sent me to boarding school, a very religious catholic boarding school. I got a good education, but I was even more lonely than at home.'

Stavros didn't know what to say. Keith's experience was so different to his. What could he say?

'Oh,' he said. 'Oh.'

'But then came university and London and the freedom of being hundreds of miles away from home. And then the Arts music and the theatre, not to mention women,' he added rather boastfully.

'It sounds like another world.'

Stavros found himself blushing in the glow of the lamp at the mention of women.

'Yes,' Keith said. 'Yes. It opened all kinds of new worlds for me. It was like a miracle. The big city, people who questioned things, people who put a great deal of importance in questioning things. Now that was new. Very new to me.'

Keith stopped and took a sip at his brandy.

'Mm,' He said. 'This stuff is good. It's worth being here just for this stuff. And for talking to you,' he added.

'Tell me more, Keith, tell me more,' Stavros was now looking at Keith with eyes full of curiosity.

'You know,' Keith said, 'it was the cultural life I loved most. Art, theatre, music, oh music, concerts, big orchestras echoing in my ears, as I went to bed at night bathed in sublime sounds and melodies. Beethoven's music, Mozart's music, Tchaikovsky's music—another world.'

'Oh,' Stavros said. 'Oh.'

An owl hooted and they stopped talking for a while as the silence that followed felt deeper and more pervasive. Keith was once again the one to break the silence.

'I would have liked to study English Literature or Art History or Classics. But my parents wouldn't have any of it.'

'Tell me more,' Stavros said eyes full of hungry curiosity.

'Where can I start?' Keith said looking as eager to talk as Stavros to listen. 'Seeing Shakespeare on stage performed by a first-class company, well, now this is an experience I shall never forget. Macbeth's hallucinatory madness, Hamlet's noble doubt, Othello's murderous jealousy. The whole humanity on stage. And modern theatre too—Ibsen and Chekhov and Bernard Shaw. And then Art— seeing the old Masters Rembrandt and Vermeer and Velasquez and the modern masters too—Van Gogh and Cezanne and Renoir and more and more. And the music, the music is of another world. A big orchestra playing Beethoven or Brahms, or Wagner. It was another world for me who had grown up on a farm in the North of England. You must go there Stavros, you must go to London.'

'Don't you miss it?' Stavros asked. 'How can you be here after London?'

'I shall go back one day,' Keith said. 'I am just beginning my career.'

The word "career" echoed strangely in Stavros' ears. What exactly did it mean? It's not that he never heard the word, or that he did not know the formal meaning of it, but it was out of his scope of things, his expectations, his experience. It had connotations of freedom and adventure and breaking loose. Of leaving one's family and country behind. Of pursuing one's own path.

'Yes' he said. 'Yes.'

'One day,' Keith said prophetically, 'one day we shall meet in London. Then I shall take you around and show you the city and the people and the museums and the galleries and you will have the same feeling as I did when I first went there.'

'Yes,' Stavros said, 'Yes.'

The moon had crept unnoticed on top of the mountain and spread a silver light everywhere. To Stavros it felt like a dream. Sitting there, at the edge of the ravine, with the mountains looming like huge dark phantoms in the silver light of the moon, and the silence enveloping them, speaking about London, the London he knew only from his school books and his history books.

'I am getting hungry,' Keith said after a while and got up to go indoors. He came back with some bread, halloumi, tomatoes and olives and some beer. The moon was now high in the sky and the huge ravine was illuminated by its silvery light. The stars, half extinguished by the light of the moon, were nevertheless visible, bearing witness to the two young men so deeply involved in conversation about the wonders of a city two thousand miles away. An owl hooted. A dog barked.

'Still I love these mountains,' Keith said. 'I am here only for a short while but, I shall never forget these mountains, this silence, this air. And you Stavros. You must come and find me in London. I shall show you London.'

'Yes' Stavros said seeping his beer and biting at the red, juicy tomato. 'Yes, I will.'

Chapter 13
Limassol 1937

Thalia Makes Enquiries

Thalia left the house at about 3.30 in the afternoon. She left instructions with Kyriakou to make Aristos' cafe au lait when he came back at 4.10 and gave her detailed information as to which cake he liked best. Making Aristos' coffee was Thalia's speciality and Kyriakou was involved only in a case of emergency. And today it was such an emergency. Her purpose was to visit her cousin, Lenia, who lived a fair distance from the Aristos' house and extract some information from her, if possible, about Stavros.

It was now the second week in March and spring showed its face everywhere. The almond trees were in full bloom, the pomegranate trees splashed their explosive red flowers and the yellow wild flowers that lined the streets were already announcing the advent of Easter. The scent of blossoms of the orange and lemon trees was overwhelming. Maybe, just maybe, Thalia thought feeling a surge of optimism, maybe there was a future. Maybe, just maybe, there was a way out of this dreary, depressing, monotonous life that they had all sunk into.

Thalia arrived at her cousin's house just before 4 o'clock on this Monday afternoon dressed in her Sunday best. She had recently felt intimidated by cousin Lenia who had married a rich wine producer 20 years older than her and lived in affluence and style in a newly built villa at the edge of the town. Aristos, every now and then, unleashed his acerbic humour on the pretentious couple who wanted to create Vienna in the suburbs of Limassol, as he often joked. Thalia however was in awe of cousin Lenia's parties with music and poetry and a very refined menu. As she went through the front gate this afternoon she looked around her. The substantial Viennese style house was surrounded by a well-designed formal garden with geometrical borders. A couple of Greco Roman statues of Apollo and Venus hidden behind hedges and lemon trees emerged to greet her as she was approaching the porch which was supported by Corinthian columns. At the side of the house, a citrus tree orchard could be distinguished behind some eucalyptus trees. Thalia felt slightly intimidated as she knocked at the door. She waited for a few seconds that felt to her like a very long time. She felt very much like the poor relative, badly dressed and her hair badly arranged in a "boring" bun behind her face. As she was waiting for someone to open the door she tidied her hair and licked her lips to moisten them and felt very uncomfortable.

A maid dressed in a white pinafore over a black dress opened the door and led Thalia to the big living room at the end of the small parlour.

'Is Mrs Eleni expecting you?' she asked.

Thalia said. 'No, just tell her it's her cousin Thalia.'

Thalia was left alone for a while and she had time to look around. She had not been here before, as her cousin and her husband had moved to their new house only a few months ago. The building of the house had lasted three years and the furnishing of it and the gardens took another 12 months. Their previous house was big and comfortable but this one was grand, there was no other word for it, grand. Thalia thought of Aristos' acerbic humour about the nouveaux riches, or the "neo-Viennese bourgeoisie" of Limassol, as he called them, and she had to smile. 'Are they building the Belvedere Palace?' he had said in his dry deadpan way, as rumours of the construction of the house proliferated in the last four years.

But Thalia *was* impressed in an unpleasant sort of way. A feeling of competitiveness was stirred up in her. This was cousin Lenia, the daughter of auntie Sofia, her mother's first cousin. This was the Lenia that everybody thought would never marry and would never do well. This was "poor" Lenia, 'she is not exactly a beauty is she?' everybody would say in a pitying, if not malicious, sort of way. This was the Lenia whom as a teenager Thalia had taken under her wings to protect her from the unfair comments at school and outside school, the awkward and plain Lenia with very few friends if any.

When Lenia's father died leaving behind only debts, everybody felt pity for Lenia and her mother. Everybody was predicting a life of loneliness and poverty. Poor and socially awkward, not exactly ugly but bordering on it, and so shy that she became invisible. And without any money or dowry who would want this awkward creature?

Thalia looked around in more detail. The living room was huge. Next to it Thalia's living room, which she was so proud of, seemed to dwarf. This was of another league—bigger, heavier and, of course, much more expensive. The grand piano at one end of it—a brand new concert size Steinway—dominated one side of the room and was in stark contrast to the fact that neither Lenia nor her husband could play it. Thalia remembered Lenia's painful piano lessons as she waited patiently sitting on the sofa in Mrs Louisa's music room for her turn. Lenia was invariably in tears as Mrs Louisa would berate her time after time, humiliate her and at times hit her on the knuckles.

'You haven't practised again Lenia. I can't teach you unless you practise.' Or at times it would be worse 'you are the most unmusical child I have ever taught, Lenia' as if this was something Lenia was responsible for.

And Lenia would swallow her tears and promise to make an effort, but come next Wednesday the same scene would be repeated, because auntie Sofia would not hear anything about Lenia's lack of talent or lack of "an ear for music" and would insist that her daughter be put through all the humiliations that Mrs Louisa submitted her to. Auntie Sofia's competition with her cousin was such that no reason prevailed. Her daughter, she insisted, was at least as good as Thalia.

The competition between Thalia and Lenia was no competition at all. Thalia was beautiful, graceful, sociable, had many friends and many admirers and above all was musically gifted. She was the star pupil of Mrs Louisa and appeared regularly at the annual concert at the Rialto, the main theatre and music hall of Limassol, as her star pupil. But Thalia did not despise Lenia. On the contrary, she felt Lenia's pain and isolation deeply and made it her duty to introduce her to her friends and help her in her awkwardness.

Lenia was 41 years old when she announced her engagement to the 62-year-old Girogos Yiassemidis, a widower and a father of 5. Yiorgos was some kind of businessman dealing with the production of carob honey and had made a great deal of money. He came from a small village near Limassol but he became a well-known name in the Limassol society due to his entrepreneurial spirit.

The malicious gossip that this announcement triggered went on for months. 'She is marrying him for his money,' the bored middle aged, middle class housewives declared as if this was a big discovery. 'Poor girl nobody wanted her now that her father left her all these debts, what was she to do, she is not a beauty either is she now?' Thalia was incandescent with anger. Why can't they leave her alone, she told her mother she is not committing a crime is she? Lenia seems at last happy.

But now seeing all the redundant furniture from Paris and Vienna and the grand piano and the heavy curtains and the sparkling chandeliers she had an urgent temptation to join the chattering classes and push Lenia a few notches down. She was deep in her inner struggle between a wish to criticise Lenia and a wish to let go and be more generous in her judgement when Lenia appeared with open arms and a big smile.

'Thalia how nice of you to come and see me, I am so, so pleased.'

Dressed in an expensive French suit, high heels and hair as if she had just walked out of a hairdresser's salon, Lenia exuded money. But her kind, awkward face was still there, the old Lenia was there despite the careful makeup and the sophisticated coiffure. She was still the old, plain Lenia, Thalia thought with relief.

'And to what do I owe this pleasure?'

Lenia asked after she kissed Thalia with a great deal of warmth. And before she had an answer she continued, 'And how is the family, uncle Aristos, Olga, Nellie, Anna? I miss you all, it's a long way out of the town this house.'

'I came to ask for your opinion on a very important matter dear Lenia. But first let's catch up a little.'

Thalia paused for a moment and seemed to hesitate.

'This is quite a place you have created here,' she said finally, 'it's a masterpiece of good taste,' Thalia lied. She really wanted to say "expensive" taste but she thought this would be too cruel.

'Thank you Thalia,' Lenia said, 'coming from you I appreciate it so much. You have such good taste yourself. You come from such an artistic family.' Lenia was referring to Thalia's piano playing, to Nellie's piano playing, to her cousin Miltiades who was a musician, and Thalia's cousin, Egli, who was an artist, a painter.

'Yes.' Thalia laughed. 'Our family has more than its share of artists.'

She stopped as the maid came in with an elegant trolley carrying a tray with a chocolate cake on it as well as a three-layered porcelain cake stand with an assortment of what looked like fairy cakes with chocolate and vanilla icing. In addition, there was a tea pot and tea cups and saucers and small cake plates. She put everything carefully on the mahogany table.

'Thank you, Maria,' Lenia said, 'we'll call you if we need anything else.'

Maria left and Lenia poured the tea into the expensive porcelain cups and offered Thalia a piece of the chocolate cake.

'The cake looks delicious,' Thalia said.

'The new Viennese patisserie is so good,' Lenia said, 'the one that opened last year near the Town Hall. Have you tried it?'

'No, actually not,' Thalia felt like the poor unsophisticated relative once again.

'Well, try its creations,' Lenia added, 'there is nothing like it in the whole of Limassol.'

Thalia bit into the chocolate cake and expressed her appreciation profusely.

'It's absolutely delicious,' she said. 'You'd think a chocolate cake is a chocolate cake, but you are right I've never eaten anything so delicious.'

'It's Sacher Torte,' Lenia said proudly, 'the famous Viennese cake. When we went to Vienna, I had it every afternoon with that lovely Viennese coffee.'

Thalia felt again like the poor relative but tried to relax and to reassure herself that Lenia was the same old Lenia, her dear awkward cousin.

'And how are the children?' Lenia asked 'Olga and Nellie and Anna?'

'Well,' Thalia hesitated for a moment. 'Actually, this is the reason I came to see you.'

'Yes?' Lenia waited.

A silence descended between them.

'I know,' Lenia said after a while, 'I heard about Nellie.' She hesitated. 'Is she better?'

'It's not Nellie I came to see you about,' Thalia said, 'no it's about Olga I am concerned.'

'Olga?' Lenia sounded surprised. 'Olga?'

Olga was well known within the family as the sensible, stable personality who never caused any trouble.

'Is Olga not well?'

'No, that's not it.' Thalia was now impatient to come to the subject. 'I wanted to ask your opinion about somebody.'

Thalia's voice petered out. Aristos' voice invaded her. 'This "nobody",' he had said, 'This "nobody" had asked for our daughter's hand. Is that the best she can do?'

Feelings of inferiority took over Thalia.

'Somebody?' Thalia asked, 'who?'

Thalia remained silent. Lenia helped her to another piece of cake and poured a second cup of tea for her and for herself. In these surroundings talking about a "nobody" seemed humiliating.

'Well,' she began tentatively, 'well somebody asked for Olga's hand. Somebody we are not sure about.' She stopped again and took a sip of tea and a bite of cake. 'I think your cousin Dimitris knows him, you might have heard about him. You know so many people Lenia I thought you might have heard about him.'

She paused and Lenia waited. Thalia sipped at her tea and was in no hurry to continue. After a few moments, Lenia intervened.

'You are making me very curious Thalia,' she said. '*Who* is it? Get it out Thalia, come on.'

Lenia was really curious and a bit annoyed, as if Thalia was playing games with her.

Thalia picked up one of the petit fours covered with chocolate and almonds in the middle and took a bite. She was certainly taking her time. 'Mm,' she said, 'this is delicious.'

'Come on Thalia don't play games with me, who is it?'

'It's somebody called Stavros Georgiou,' she said finally taking a deep breath. 'He is not from Limassol that's why we are making enquiries. He has a university degree from London, though,' she said as this would make everything OK. 'And he has a good job in the civil service.'

'I have not met him but I heard about him. Yes, he is a friend of Dimitris, my cousin, well our cousin. I heard very good things about him. Dimitris thinks the world of him. She made a proposal for Olga? I think she is very lucky,' she added.

Thalia took another deep breath, one of relief this time. At the same time, she remembered Aristos' words and thought 'is Olga lucky because nobody else would have her but this "nobody"?'

'But he has no family Lenia. We really don't know who his family are, nobody knows. He is from Marathasa.'

'I know what you are saying,' Lenia interrupted 'You mean he is not the son of a well-established, educated, old family, a "good" family.' Thalia nodded feeling awkward, really ashamed of herself and her thoughts especially as Lenia herself married a man who did not come from a "good" family.

'Come on Thalia,' Lenia was now saying, 'my Odysseas doesn't come from such a family either. He was born in a village and they had no running water and no electricity and his parents could not read or write. He himself went only to primary school. So what? I didn't marry the family who are dead anyway. I married Odysseas a very intelligent, capable man who made his own fortune, who created himself.'

'Very true,' Thalia said and did not know what else to say.

There had been a great deal of gossip in the town about Lenia's marriage. Not just the age difference but the fact that Odysseas did not belong to an old, established family. People talked with malice and vitriol but eventually everybody accepted it as a fact and now Lenia and Odysseas are part of an established elite, if only a new type of elite, an elite of money. Of course the money helped, she thought, and the soirees helped, and the new house helped.

'Come on Thalia,' Lenia was now saying, 'times have changed. He is an educated gentle and sociable young man, from what I hear. He would make any woman happy. She would make your Olga very happy.'

Thalia knew all this. She knew that Olga was secretly in love with Stavros. She knew that the tennis matches and the "chance" promenade meetings, and the "chance" Pera Pedi meeting made her very happy and very worried about the future. And that since Stavros had moved to Paphos she was deeply, and very secretly, unhappy. But it was one thing playing tennis and another marrying somebody. Nevertheless Thalia felt happy about Lenia's support of Stavros and of the match.

'You lifted a weight off my chest Lenia,' Thalia said. 'You are absolutely right. From what I hear, I also think that he will make Olga happy.'

'That's done then,' Lenia said clapping her hands enthusiastically. 'It would be lovely to have a wedding in our family soon.'

'Well,' Thalia said, 'it's Aristos we have to persuade.'

'Ah, Aristos, yes. I forgot.'

The maid came in. She brought some fresh tea and asked whether they needed anything else—more petits fours or more profiteroles. Lenia said no they had everything they needed and the maid withdrew carrying the old teapot. Thalia remained silent. She helped herself to a couple of profiteroles and some fresh tea and became absorbed in eating and drinking.

'I'll tell you what,' Lenia said after the maid had disappeared. 'I know that Aristos values Sotiris' opinion. I also happen to know that Sotiris is very well disposed towards Stavros. He has met him through Dimitris and thinks very highly of him. I know that. So, why don't you say to Aristos something like "why don't you ask Sotiris' opinion? Why don't you say to him go and talk to Sotiris? He is family after all."'

'That's not a bad idea,' Thalia said and stopped for a moment with the petit four in her hand thinking. 'In fact, I think it is a brilliant idea,' she said at last.

A whole plan flashed through her mind. She would go and talk to Maroulla and then Maroulla would talk to Sotiris and prepare him for Aristos' visit. Then Thalia would suggest the visit to Aristos and then the two men would meet. She would gently "encourage" Aristos to go and see Sotiris and ask for his opinion as Sotiris knew so many people because he was the editor of the local newspaper. His opinion did matter. What a brilliant idea Lenia had, she thought. She had underestimated her cousin's intelligence and knowledge of the way the world worked.

'Lenia you are a genius,' she said to her cousin and the two women laughed conspiratorially.

Next day Thalia went to see Maroulla. Leaving the responsibility for Aristos' café au lait once again to Kyriakou's capable hands, she let the house at 3.50 and headed for Maroulla's house. She felt lighter than she had felt for months as she walked through the maze of streets that made the few minutes' walk to Maroulla's house.

On arriving at Maroulla's place that afternoon, Thalia encountered a scene of affectionate and exciting chaos as Zoe and Alexis were busy piling up all their toys in one corner of the living room and throwing them at each other. Maroulla's mother, Arsinoe, was making a cake in the kitchen and the vanilla aroma wafted into the living room. Maroulla was trying helplessly to control the children.

'Thalia how lovely!' Maroulla embraced her and Thalia entered into the scene of chaos with trepidation.

'Children, children,' Maroulla shouted 'go to the garden, go and play in the garden for a while.'

Maroulla's house was a two-storey house 5 minutes' walk from Thalia's house. On the ground floor, it housed the printing company and the offices of *The Observer*, while the first floor was the home for Maroulla, Sotiris and their two children.

Thalia liked the house with the big palm tree in the front garden where once a year Maroulla would hire a man to climb up the twelve-metre tree and pick the dates. A huge fig tree on the other side of the garden provided the family and their friends, including Thalia's family, with delicious black figs which ripened in late August.

The flat on the first floor was unlike any other flat Thalia had seen. Full of antiquities and other works of Art it housed Dimitris' "collection": Little Neolithic figurines standing facing the millennia with dignity were mixed-up with pots decorated with birds and octopuses from the Mycenaean age, some 5th century classical figures and some Roman figurines, all behind glass cabinets. Thalia was never sure which were genuine and which were copies but it all looked impressive and she never dared ask. Perhaps they were all copies, how could she know? Some local pots from the mountain region were also there among the antiquities. Some colourful weaves from various villages hang on the walls or covered the table and the sideboard giving the room a very joyful feeling. Some decorated gourds were also hanging on the walls. This was certainly very different house from the Lenia's "Viennese" house and also different from her own house which was a vague mixture of Viennese and Athenian style mixed with some local colour. Here everything was local. Here was a pride in "our island" which went back 6,000 years, written all over the flat. So many peoples, so many cultures, so many beautiful artefacts, Thalia thought. She felt good here with Maroulla and the children and with the aroma of the cake wafting through the kitchen into the living room. For the first time in months, she felt relaxed and happy.

Arsinoe, who had obviously heard Thalia's voice, was now calling from the kitchen.

'Come in Thalia, I am making the ravani. Come in, come in, it's almost finished.'

In a white pinafore and with her hands dipped in a bowl full of ingredients, Arsinoe stretched her cheek for Thalia to kiss.

'How nice to see you Thalia. The kids love ravani,' she added. 'I've just baked an apricot tart, you must have with the coffee. The ravani will take some time to finish though, so next time!'

She stirred the ingredients and poured everything into a baking tin. Maroulla was making coffee. 'It's sweet isn't it?' Maroulla asked Thalia, referring to how Thalia took her coffee.

'Yes sweet,' Thalia said.

The strong aroma of Greek coffee invaded Thalia's nostrils. She closed her eyes to take in the aroma. Here the world was in order and Thalia felt safe for the first time for a long time.

'What would we do without coffee?' she added.

'Life wouldn't be worth living,' Arsinoe offered as she was stooped over the cake tin.

'Well,' Maroulla laughed 'I wouldn't go as far as that, but life would be greatly impoverished,' she added.

'But just listen to them,' Maroulla added as voices of wild excitement about something unknown to the women reached the kitchen.

'My little angels,' Arsinoe was saying, 'my adorable little devils.' She laughed profusely.

She washed her hands clean from the cake ingredients and prepared the tray with the baked cake and the coffee that Maroulla had already made and the women returned to the living room. Maroulla rearranged the cushions and the throw on the sofa which the children had drugged onto the floor. She picked up the toys from the floor and carried them to the children's rooms and Arsinoe began to cut the apricot tart. In a few minutes, order was restored.

Thalia liked Maroulla's flat as it was so different from everything she knew. Take the living room for instance. It was what it said—it was a room for life and for living. In her house, and in everybody else's house, the living room, usually called the "salon", was opened only when guests came to visit. The family, and least of all the children, were not "allowed" in it otherwise. It remained closed and clean to receive the occasional "guests". It was a mummified, perfectly ordered and obsessively clean room, usually with a big chandelier hanging in the middle, velvet upholstered furniture, heavy curtains and expensive paintings in carved heavy frames. But in Maroulla's flat the living room was used by everybody everyday as well as by the guests. Books lined every bit of the walls and a couple of original paintings in ordinary wooden frames came out of the book shelves. The many figurines from different ages from the history of the island stared out of the glass cabinet. The room was steeped in intellectuality. These are the "new" people, Thalia thought, free from etiquette, more free to be themselves. I am already thinking like Nellie, she thought and laughed secretly and with some glee.

Aristos had said once that Sotiris was "over-reaching" himself, but then Thalia knew that there was a silent competition between the two men and that

Aristos was secretly envious of Sotiris' freedom to pursue the career and the job he wanted. Although Aristos was 18 years older than Sotiris, there was nevertheless a mutual respect between them, but also a not so secret competition. Sotiris wanted to impress the older man, who with a bit of a stretch of imagination could be his father. He had lost his own father when he was 13 years old and had since strived to impress everybody around him but especially older men, with his brilliant, precocious intellect. Aristos, on his side, who had also lost his father, but at an older age, put his own wish for a son on this young man who loved him as a man would love his father. But beyond this emotional link, Aristos admired Sotiris' sharp humour, his incisive and informed political satire and his knowledge of the Arts and sciences. His newspaper was an endeavour to educate the public, Aristos always thought. They did not always agree in their debates and sometimes Thalia and Maroulla would listen with alarm to their rising voices which often culminated into aggressive shouting as the debate got heated. But it was always good hearted and always ended with a warm handshake.

And now Thalia, after having eaten her apricot cake and praised Arsinoe who made it and after she drank her "sweet" coffee and felt surrounded by two warm and loving women, she came to the point.

'You know Maroulla,' she said slowly 'I need yours and Sotiris' help.' She stopped and Arsinoe put another piece of cake in her plate before she had the time to refuse.

'Thank you Arsinoe, I really shouldn't, but it's so delicious.'

'Anything Thalia,' Maroulla was now saying, 'anything we can do. You know we are here for you. You can ask me anything, we are like sisters really.'

'Yes dear Maroulla, I know, I know and this is so important to me.'

'And for us,' Maroulla said warmly. 'What is it Thalia? You look worried, is everything all right? Is Nellie not well?'

'Nellie is fine,' Thalia said, 'as fine as she can be at the moment,' she added. 'Nellie is more settled than she has been for a long time, but of course she worries me as she is so isolated, but not unwell. No, Nellie is fine.'

'So?' Maroulla hesitated 'Is Aristos all right?'

'Yes he is fine. No Maroulla the trouble is something else. You remember Stavros, the young man who came to Pera Pedi and talked to the girls?' She stopped there not knowing how to continue.

'Yes,' Maroulla said, 'Sotiris knows him.'

'Well this same person, Stavros Georgiou has asked for Olga's hand.'

'How marvellous,' Maroulla said, 'I think they are in love Thalia.'

'Well, I must explain,' Thalia said, 'he has not yet asked for her hand but he has sent Dimitris to enquire whether we would consider it before he makes a formal proposal.'

'Marvellous, marvellous, I am so pleased for Olga.' Maroulla was beaming.

Arsinoe coming out of the kitchen paused for a moment. 'What's so marvellous?' she asked. 'Is Thalia bringing some good news for one of her daughters?'

'Something like that,' Maroulla said.

'Wedding bells?' Arsinoe enquired.

'Slowly,' Thalia said, 'we are not there yet. There are many obstacles.'

'Like what?' Maroulla asked 'I am sure Olga is in love with him I could see it in her eyes in Pera Pedi. And the girls think the same,' Maroulla added meaning her two sisters.

'Aristos is the problem,' Thalia said.

'Ah.'

Maroulla seemed to comprehend without much of an explanation.

'Aristos. Yes, I see,' she whispered.

A silence followed.

'I'll send Sotiris to him,' she said. 'I am sure he will come around.'

Maroulla's mind seemed to be moving in the same direction as Lenia's and Thalia's. 'Sotiris will persuade him.'

'That's exactly what I thought,' Thalia said, 'but I thought maybe Aristos could be persuaded to come to Sotiris. Otherwise he will think this is a conspiracy to persuade him.'

'Yes you are right Thalia, yes you are definitely right. You know him so well. Yes I am sure you are right.'

They helped themselves to another piece of cake when the door opened and Sotiris followed by Zoe and carrying a howling Alexis covered in mud followed, 'Here we are,' Sotiris smiled 'we fell into the old muddy flower bed. Nothing to cry about Alexi. Everything is all right.'

'She pushed me, she pushed me,' Alexis yelled, 'she is a witch, a real witch,' he was howling.

'We were playing Hansel and Gretel,' Zoe began hesitantly looking very guilty. 'I was the witch, but I didn't push him, he fell.'

'You pushed me, you pushed me,' Alexis yelled again, 'you are a witch.'

'I didn't mean to.'

Alexis began to howl again as if he sensed that Zoe was winning the argument.

'She pushed me. She pushed me,' he repeated.

'OK darling come here, it's OK.' Maroulla opened her arms and Alexis disappeared in her arms and continued to sob quietly.

'It will be all right Alexi,' Sotiris said.

Alexis stopped sobbing for a moment and then, not sure whether he was losing ground, began again to howl, not convincing anybody anymore.

Zoe looked forlorn, ready to start crying. At that moment, Sotiris picked her up and put her on his shoulders.

'OK,' he said, 'let's go down to see the printers at work, shall we?'

'Yah,' she cried loudly.

Sotiris with a triumphant Zoe on his shoulders headed for the door.

'Sorry Thalia,' he called, 'sorry I can't stay and talk to you. Nice to see you and regards to Aristos.'

'Thank you Sotiri.'

Alexis had now stopped crying and Arsinoe took him by the hand.

'Come on Alexi, you need a good wash.'

Alexis took Arsinoe's hand and gave her a smile and they both disappeared down the corridor.

Maroulla looked at her clothes which were now full of bits of mud.

'Children!' she said, 'children! They are so full of energy and emotions. But I must go and change, sorry Thalia I won't be a minute.'

'I must go anyway,' Thalia said getting up.

'I won't be a minute Thalia, stay I'll be back in a minute.'

'It's time to go Maroulla, Aristos will be waiting for me.'

'OK Thalia but we haven't decided, is Sotiris to come and see Aristos?'

'No, no, Maroulla, this won't work at all. I shall persuade Aristos to come and see Sotiris. Just for another voice, Aristo, I shall say, you trust the man. Go and discuss this with him.'

'That sounds good,' Maroulla was now heading for the door. 'I am sure it will all end well and Olga will be happy.'

'I do hope so,' Thalia said.

Arsinoe was back with a clean and smiling Alexis.

'You are going already Thalia?' She asked and then to Maroulla 'why so early?'

'Aristos will be waiting for her,' Thalia explained, 'and you have to cook for the evening anyway,' she added.

Maroulla and Sotiris did not have a maid as it was the custom in all middle-class families. Young girls came to the towns from the mountain villages seeking to earn some money and send to their families back home and became almost exclusively maids in well to do households. But Maroulla and Sotiris either because of conviction (Sotiris was a socialist after all), or because they could not afford it, or because Arsinoe lived very close and did a great deal of the work for them, they did not have a maid. Thalia never knew why and she never asked either.

'The cooking is already done,' Arsinoe said.

'Oh what have you cooked?'

Thalia was genuinely interested as if it was a matter of great importance.

'Okra with lamb,' Arsinoe responded. 'And you know Thalia I don't fry the onions or the meat first, as most people do. I put everything together, the onions, the tomatoes, the meat, the oil. It's so much easier and so much lighter for the stomach.'

'I think Kyriakou does the same,' Thalia said referring to their maid who was not a young girl anymore but who came to the family when she was a young girl of sixteen when Thalia was still a baby.

'Kyriakou is a treasure,' Arsinoe said. 'You are so lucky to have her.'

'I know, of course I know, she brought me and Katina and Nikodemos up, and then she brought Olga and Nellie and Anna up. She is part of the family now.'

'I know,' Arsinoe said, 'she thinks of you as her family as well.'

'Yes I know,' Thalia said, 'her family back in the village are so distant to her now. She got used to the life in Limassol and it would be very difficult for her to go back. But I must go,' she suddenly added with urgency. 'Aristos doesn't like waiting alone at home.'

Thalia knew that Aristos should have been back for some time now and he must have had his café au lait already and he was probably having an afternoon nap sitting in his chair in his study with the newspaper in his lap. But around 6 he would look for Thalia and would be quite annoyed if she was not at home to prepare his evening meal.

'Oh Thalia, I must let you go but come again soon. We are all so happy to see you.'

'I will Arsinoe, I will. I love coming here and being with you all.'

As she was walking back home and the sun was slanting towards the horizon spreading long shadows around, and the sky was turning yellow and orange and the light breeze stroked her face Thalia had a feeling of well-being she had not had for months. Walking towards home she could feel the sea breeze on her skin and the sea smell permeating her nostrils. Spring was almost there, she thought, and maybe, just maybe (she should not let herself get too excited, she thought) maybe happiness was just around the corner.

Chapter 14
Platres 1934

The early light penetrated through the shutters in striped patterns and fell on the blanket that covered Stavros' bed. It was 6.30 in the morning and the nightingales had fallen silent. Stavros who was an early riser stirred in his bed and opened his eyes. It took him some time to establish where he was. He lay motionless for a while listening to the silence. He had not experienced such silence for a few years. The silence of the mountains used to be all around him and inside him as he grew up. He could tell the time fairly accurately listening to the sounds that disturbed it. The cockcrow at dawn followed by the braying of donkeys, the barking of dogs and eventually human voices. Crows at mid-day up at the highest peak of the village when he was sent with a basket of beans, bread, olives and a big onion to reach his uncles and aunts who were working in the vineyards. And he would linger for a while after delivery walking to the highest peaks, looking at a rare butterfly or a dragon fly or a gecko frozen, immobilised as he lay staring at him through glass eyes—if I don't move you won't attack me was the message—and Stavros would freeze his movements in response, observing this tiny descendent of the distant dinosaurs and, not wanting to disturb the universe, he stayed immobilised, fascinated by this world that existed without him and without his will and without requiring his existence at all.

And the silence around him embraced him like a mother. He fitted exactly in this sea of silence and movement and stillness, immersed in a sea of well-being. Only the crows above, the braying of the donkey below, a distant voice sinking into silence. And the immobilised geckos to remind him of animal terror and silence and time.

He lay in bed with eyes half closed, feeling the sun on his eyelids and thousands of colours and patterns dancing in front of him. He now knew where he was. He was not in his village, in his grandmother's house having an extra hour of sleep on a Sunday morning. He was not in Nicosia, waking up early in the morning in his rented room at Mr Anastasiadis' house, with Mrs Anastasiadis calling him for breakfast. He was not in his rented accommodation in London, on the busy street behind the university where silence was never one of its attributes. The always noisy, always busy always foggy street, at least that's how Stavros remembered it with a great deal of affection, as if the noise and the fog and the smog were endearing characteristics of this great metropolis. He lay motionless evoking in his mind the first paragraphs of Bleak House the indescribable description of 19th century London. He lay motionless and the awareness where he was began to emerge slowly and with it a creeping anxiety.

He was at Platres, the fashionable summer resort in the Troodos mountains. But it was not summer. It was now autumn and all the guests from Nicosia and Limassol were gone. The summer resort was now a deserted place with the few locals left behind feeling abandoned and bereaved. Images of his own village in autumn flooded his mind. The leaves of the oak trees turning rusty, the almond trees losing their leaves, the vineyards bearing the last of the year's grapes, the last of the year's wine. A chill in the air—it was not yet cold but there was an unmistakable chill in the air, the days getting shorter, the slanting sun giving little warmth, disappearing early behind the mountains. His conversation with the goats and the sheep and the wise, sad looking donkeys. Grandmother waiting for him every Saturday afternoon when he returned from his weekly board at the gymnasium, waiting with a cup of warm milk.

With a shock, he realised that he was not there. He was not in his village. He was in Platres, at a reasonably expensive, reasonably fashionable hotel at the end of the holiday season. He was there because he had nowhere to go. This was the bitter, cruel truth that invaded his mind. The first of his village to go to university anywhere, let alone London, the first of the island to graduate in civil engineering. In fact, when he told people that he studied civil engineering they looked puzzled—civil? engineering? What did it mean? He remembered when a few years back he was equally puzzled when Keith told him that he had studied civil engineering. It now looked like a century ago although it was only ten years ago.

And now he, the exceptionally gifted young man, was back on the island, fully qualified having graduated with "distinction" and having done a further year of practice which won him a membership to the profession and some excellent references from famous professors. He had caught the boat at

Southampton and travelled together with Nicos, his very dear friend, who graduated in architecture from the same university. They had "great expectations" the two of them to open an office together in Limassol, and through Nikolaos' family's connections, to make their name as new professionals in the expanding economy of the island. The year was 1934. The island hit by the 1929 crash was slowly recovering. The good citizens with higher than average income succumbed to their vanity driven wishes to build a bigger, more modern house to declare to the rest of the good citizens *who* they were and how much above everybody they were. Nicolaos, whose family was involved in the well-established wine industry of Limassol, had been optimistic about their chances.

'We can start with my family,' he said to Stavros. 'They want a big, modern house with a big indoor bathroom and, a modern kitchen with all the amenities and a huge living room for all their parties. Their house was built in 1910 and although it was a state of the Art then, it's really out of date now. There are many people like them, people with money but also people with taste and ambition. We can show them what we can do for them.'

And so Nikos spoke and Stavros listened and felt excited. The future, full of promise and hope and ambition was opened to him. He joined Nikos in his contagious optimism and was certain that things would be as he described. Nikolaos was a very dear friend. Although he was rich from an established Limassol family and he, Stavros, was a "nobody" from "nowhere", the two struck a strong friendship that defied social divisions. They declared themselves "brothers".

They were two exceedingly optimistic young men, steeped in the world of modern literature, Art, theatre, and the newly discovered art of the cinema. They both loved the Greek classics, which Stavros had made it his task to read in the original, and they spent hours in front of the Elgin marbles at the British museum discussing Pericles' speech about the glory of Athens, Plato, Socrates and the Greek dramatists. Yet they were both steeped in their studies always achieving the best grades and surprising their professors with their ingenuity. Stavros was more of a mathematical brain and Nikolaos more of an artist but they "complemented each other" they told themselves, and so went the 5 years of studying and doing their post qualification practice. 'If we lived in another time we would be blood brothers,' Nikolaos said one evening laughing as they drank their third pint and felt a bit under the influence. They laughed and laughed.

But it was not meant to be. When the boat anchored at Piraeus for a few hours, Nikos was taken violently ill and died a few days later from typhoid. Stavros did not only lose a very dear friend, he also lost a business partner, his only link to Limassol and to professional life, one that had the key to his new life. And now? What could Stavros do now? When the boat arrived in Limassol Stavros was the loneliest man on earth.

Nikos was dead and with him all the plans and hopes and ambitions. The void in Stavros mind was threatening to take over. He missed Nikolaos, he missed his lively spirit, his optimism, his creative mind. But most of all Stavros had no idea what to do. He arrived at Limassol heartbroken and nobody was there to welcome him. Nobody expected him, nobody knew he was coming. Nobody. He was all alone.

Leaving his village ten years ago felt final. After secondary school, he gained a scholarship to study at the English School in Nicosia and to take his matriculation. Then he worked three years at Amiantos being the founder, the director and at the beginning the only teacher of a new school for the miners' children and for the children of Cato Amiantos, a small village near the mine. Although his own village was a few hours away on donkey, he never made that journey. He even had at his disposal some of the company's cars but he never expressed any wish to go back to his village. His father and his family were not only strangers, but worse he felt a strong anger and aversion towards them. He wanted, of course, to see his grandma and Penelope and Manolis but there was no way he could go to the village and not see his father whom he now detested. So he put the whole memory of his village at the back of his mind and told himself that one day he would go to see his grandmother and Penelope and bring them many, many presents and thank them wholeheartedly, but he was not ready yet, not yet.

He felt like an exile in his own land—a gentrified, educated villager who felt a stranger among his own people. The mental distance between him and his village was slowly becoming unbridgeable. His grandmother had died in the meantime and he felt he had no home in the village. His auntie Penelope sent him her love and some village sausages, some walnuts and some almonds every time Elias, a cousin, came to work in the mines for the winter months. He had always been fond of auntie Penelope but now in his early twenties Stavros felt a long way from everybody in his village, even her. He was now a new person, somebody who shared much more with the English engineers at Amiantos than with his fellow villagers. A person who was now an island—completely alone.

Still in bed day-dreaming of his village and of his years at Amiantos and of London's foggy and noisy streets Stavros tried to consider his options which were grim. He had enough savings to last him for six months, especially if he stayed in Platres in winter where he could lodge for very little money, and only if he limited his food to beans, bread, onion and tea, maybe some eggs and occasionally a sausage. He had gone through these calculations many times and always came to the same conclusion: he could last for six months, maybe a little longer, under these conditions. But then?

He thought of Penelope's homemade sausages and a pain pierced his brain. He felt like a traitor. He had never contacted her in his five years in London. He was too busy creating a new life and a new self—an anglicised intellectual identity complete with a pipe, a raincoat and a perennial book in his hand. He didn't contact her when he returned to the island alone and lost. He was too proud for that. Dear, dear Penelope who told him so much about his dead mother and whose love for knowledge and new things lived in him. Dear Penelope who made it possible for him to go to the Gymnasium and get educated.

The voice of the hotel owner brought Stavros out of his reverie.

'Kyrie Stavro, are you awake? Come and have some breakfast with me.'

Stavros brought himself back to the present.

'Evharisto Kyrie Yiorgo, I shall be with you in a moment.'

This was an everyday routine. The breakfast that Stavros shared with the hotel owner was in fact a present. Yiorgos who knew Stavros' situation did not want to embarrass him but instead invited him to share his own breakfast. In any case, the hotel was empty of guests. Only at weekends people came mostly for one night arriving on Saturday afternoon and leaving on Sunday evening. These were the rich people from Limassol who could afford a car and a weekend in the mountains. Yiorgos' hotel was the only one open all through the year, mainly because Yiorgos chose to live there. The hotel was also his home.

Yiorgos valued Stavros' company and his breakfast with him over tea, bread, a hard-boiled egg, halloumi and tomato. It was an opportunity for companionship which he valued in his lonely, withdrawn existence. Yiorgos was a widower, his wife having died five years ago. His sons were away—one in Canada doing well, and writing enthusiastic letters every six months about the miracles of this new country. The other one was married n Limassol and Yiorgos saw him very rarely as his wives' family had an ancient feud with Yiorgos' family over some property. Yiorgos could not remember the exact problem but the feud was alive and well and poisoned past and future generations.

'My son choosing a woman from this family,' Yiorgos complained to Stavros. 'It's like a slap in the face. It's worse than going to Canada or Australia, I hardly see him at all, or the children.'

Only his daughter was regularly in touch visiting with the children every now and then and never stopping telling her father that he should retire, he should close the hotel and come and live with them in Larnaca, where she lived with her husband and children. 'But what would I do in Larnaca?' he asked Stavros. 'I am a Limassol guy, born and bred, Larnaca is a foreign land for me, Stavro. I might as well go to Canada and join my second son. There are many Greeks there, he tells me. It's like a little Greece where he lives. But you know Stavro these mountain do something for my soul. In the summer, this place is the closest place to heaven. There is a purity here, the air is like medicine, you breathe it in and it heals your body and soul. Your health and your faith in life are restored. It's strange Stavro, the more I retire to the mountains and live with the trees, and the silence of the mountains, the more I can let go and forgive and find peace. But Stavro I will never forgive the warmongers who took my Evagora—never, never.'

This referred to his eldest son Evagoras who had died in the Great War. Yiorgos never got over this loss, neither did his wife, who went to her death five years ago heartbroken and inconsolable. It was now sixteen years but the pain was as acute as the first moment he heard it. He was a real "leventis", he would say and his face would be lit up with pride and almost always followed with a mixture of pain and anger. He could not stop telling Stavros about his son— handsome, manly, brave, intelligent, the apple of his parents' eyes. Evagoras died at the age of eighteen after he had volunteered to go and fight on the side of the British, in a country he did not know, for a cause he did not understand, Yiorgos told him again and again.

'They inflate the young men's minds,' Yiorgos told Stavros with a voice that trembled with anger and pain the very first afternoon that Stavros arrived.

Over a cup of coffee and some Turkish delights Stavros heard about the tragedy of his eldest son. 'For what, Stavro, tell me for what? for Helen?' he asked rhetorically referring to the most futile of all wars some 3,000 years ago.

'One million people died in France alone,' Yiorgos continued. 'For what? What did this small, peaceful island have to do with these big powers of Europe fighting each other? But young men are impressionable, their minds full of heroic stories and fairy tales about the past which cloud their minds about the present. He volunteered, my Evagoras, thinking he was going to fight for freedom, for civilisation, for peace—and to prove his manhood.'

Stavros nodded as he allowed himself a second Turkish delight. It was a story he would hear many, many times during these three weeks. Now over a breakfast of tea, bread, halloumi, tomato and Turkish delights as a dessert Yiorgos was talking once again about Evagoras' pre-mature death and how meaningless this had been.

'It's criminal,' Yiorgos was saying, 'to inflate young men's minds and lead them to their death.'

Stavros nodded.

'You remember Achilles,' Yiorgos continued as if he was talking about a mutual acquaintance. 'His mother, Thetis, a goddess, hid him among the girls trying to protect him from the madness that was spreading at the time, the conscription that was to become the ten-year carnage of the Trojan war. She dressed him in girl's clothes and hid him among the girls, in the Court of the King of Skyros. You probably know the story. In this way she thought, wretched mother of a future hero, that he was safe from the likes of Agamemnon and his gang.'

Yiorgos talked about this 3,000-year-old story, told by Homer in the Iliad, as if it had happened in his village last year or even yesterday. As if these legendary names were people he knew and talked to, or talked about, with his friends at the coffee shop.

'I know,' Stavros was saying, 'I know.'

'However,' Yiorgos was now saying helping himself to more tea out of the big tea pot, 'however, she did not reckon with the cunningness of the most Machiavellian of the heroes of the Iliad—Odysseus. You surely remember how he went about to find out where young Achilles was hiding!'

He stopped and looked at Stavros who nodded again. 'Yes,' Stavros said, 'Homer knew young men well.'

Yiorgos laughed aloud, unexpectedly.

'The devil take him,' he said in a voice that bordered between anger, pleasure and amusement as the laughter overcame him.

'The devil take him, Odysseas, the man full of tricks and machinations.' He stopped and cut another slice of halloumi and another piece of bread. For a while, he was busy chewing and drinking. 'Homer says that he came to the house where the girls were, among them was young Achilles dressed as a girl. But who was Achilles among the girls? Odysseus pretended to be a wandering trader dealing with women's dresses and adornments and accessories and the girls streamed out of the house to look at all the wonderful things he was offering. But among his artefacts Odysseus had also a beautifully carved bow and arrow and a beautifully forged sword and guess to which artefacts young Achilles was attracted to!'

He laughed aloud.

'From there on, it was all the way to Troy and finally to his death—glorious death I should say, that's how they seduce these young minds. To fall for your country! What a sweet death! But my boy did not even fall for his country. He went to his death for countries he did not know, or did not care about.'

Yiorgos stopped again and spread some butter on his bread. He looked at Stavros. Stavros agreed eagerly as he was a pacifist himself and thought all wars were follies.

'Ingenious isn't it?' Yiorgos continues 'The old tricks of mature men towards younger men as if they are so envious of their innocence and their wish to live and not to die. But I am sure you know the story anyway,' he said, ' but I like telling it anyway. The madness of young men and their love affair with weapons and with death and how older men manipulate this passion to their own ends.'

He ate his piece of bread with the halloumi on top.

'Have you read the Iliad?' Yiorgos was now asking.

Stavros nodded again.

'It's a beautiful book about men's follies and men's intrigues and manipulations of other men. I used to teach it to young men of Achilles' age and I used to add my comments to the story, but nobody listened. They were seduced by the heroic deeds of these ancient men.'

Yiorgos was a grammar school teacher before he decided to take an early retirement and take over his father's hotel as he was approaching fifty-five. He had by now been on the job for ten years and he loved it. But once a teacher always a teacher, he used to say and he never lost the wish to teach, to tell stories from Antiquity, to show off his knowledge. This characteristic he shared with Stavros who loved quoting from the classics and impressing people with his knowledge of ancient history. But here Stavros deferred to the older man and his benefactor as he felt absolutely indebted to him for his hospitality and his warmth which reminded Stavros of his grandmother and of Penelope.

Yiorgos became very fond of Stavros who was roughly his youngest son's age but so much more mature and wise and humble, he thought, and he had first class education from a London university. So much more understanding than any of my children, Yiorgos was thinking lying in his single bed and watching the moon going in and out of passing clouds, sending messages of good will to insomniac humans like himself. So much more understanding of people than my own children, Yiorgos thought again. Why was life always the wrong way round, always the wrong thing at the wrong time?

It was now sixteen years since his son died, just a few weeks before the war ended—just a few weeks! He never came to terms with it and he never would. The story of Achilles came to his mind again and again, three thousand years ago—the Trojan war, the prototype of all wars—the seduction of young men to join the warriors, the betrayal of a mother and daughter by the commander in Chief—young Iphigenia's sacrifice—for nothing, for an adulterous wife! Or was it for greed and power, He wondered. The pompous chiefs of the various Achaean tribes. At school, he learnt the sanitised version of it, the poetry of war, and of killing and of men's vanities and men's pride and exhibition of power— men's hubris. The poetry of it! For this is life described for the first time in all its petty glory. For honour, for the Greek honour. All of a sudden a French word popped into his mind – merde – he thought, merde. Achilles, the most heroic and the most beloved of the Greek fighters died a hero's death, they learnt at school. Like my son, he thought. The lies that we are all told. For what?'

The moon disappeared behind some thick clouds leaving Yiorgos alone and inconsolable. Stavros next door was snoring, softly inspiring confidence in life despite everything.

Next day he told Stavros over breakfast that his nephew got involved in the 1931 "troubles" on the island and that he was deported to Greece. 'My sister, his mother, was inconsolable,' he continued. 'What a folly that uprising was,' Yiorgos said. 'They get these ideas into young men's minds Stavro,' he continued while sipping his tea. 'These young men have no idea what they are getting into. They think going to war, or getting involved in an uprising, however badly organised it might be, will make them men. If you are a man choose the weapons, otherwise you are a woman. What utter trash is this, going back three thousand years!'

Stavros agreed willingly. He had witnessed his fellow villagers falling for this argument when he was only a boy and he later read about the war, the trenches and the inhumanity and the millions who perished.

'It's true,' he said, 'it's time for people to rethink war and the violence of man against man.'

'But we are in the minority Stavro,' Yiorgos said mournfully. 'People want violence, revenge, blood. And men want to be men in case they are told they are like a woman.'

At that moment, the sun rose above the mountains and a warmth enveloped the two men giving them a sense of well-being. 'There are always the mountains and the silence of the mountains,' Stavros said suddenly. 'I was born in the mountains and this silence makes me happy despite life being so difficult and cruel.'

'It's very difficult for you just now my son,' Yiorgos said in a sudden surge of intimacy and affection. 'But you will see better days, I am sure of this. You are intelligent and confident and you will succeed, I know it.'

Stavros took in the words like food from a good parent. However confident he had been in the past, these last few weeks were a real trial for him.

It was mid-October and they were at a height of 1,200 metres and evenings and early mornings were cold but the two men insisted on having their breakfast on the veranda underneath the pine trees and the blue sky, listening to the water cascading down the mountain and to the crows circulating above screeching and swooping. As the day advanced the warmth of the sun enveloped them.

Katina came out to collect the leftovers and exchanged a few words with Yiorgos about lunch and what she was preparing.

'I am cooking the green beans I bought yesterday at the market,' she told Yiorgos 'but without meat. You can have it with rice and yogurt.'

'That's fine Katina,' Yiorgos said gently, 'you are right, I know. Too much meat is not good at my age. You are looking after our health. As for Stavros he has to adjust to old people's diet,' he said smiling.

'That's fine by me,' Stavros said, 'I am not used to too much meat anyway.'

Katina went back to the kitchen carrying a dangerous amount of plates and cutlery in her frail hands. She was approaching eighty but she was still active and strong and reliable and was the bulwark that kept Yiorgos alive and well.

'She is my rock,' Yiorgos was now saying to Stavros. 'In a way, we are like a couple, an odd couple. She used to be my nanny, you know, and now she is like a wife/mother. She had been in my family ever since I remember. Now she is like my own mother, or like an estranged but loved wife, or like a good friend, or like a sister. I guess all these together. Since my wife died, I've been relying on her more and more. I couldn't be here in the mountains without her. And I couldn't be anywhere else but in these mountains. I feel at home here. This is my home.'

Katina was back to collect the rest of the breakfast things.

'Two families are arriving for the weekend Katina,' Yiorgos was now saying. 'arriving on Saturday afternoon and leaving on Sunday evening. It's a husband and wife and their two children and the wife's sister and her family, not quite sure whether they have one or two kids.'

'Everything will be ready,' Katina replied as she was removing the rest of the bread and the tomatoes. 'Would be good to have some life here.'

Soon after, Stavros went to his room and began to write several letters to well-known architects offering his services as a graduate civil engineer. After the death of his friend, Stavros had been deeply pessimistic about his chances. In Limassol and in Nicosia, he was a complete outsider. Most people relied on connections—family, relations and friends, friends of relatives and friends of friends of relatives, or friends of relatives' relatives, or on childhood friends, neighbourhood ties, or school ties. Stavros came from nowhere—from the mountain region where the "peasants" lived. What chance did he have in Limassol or Nicosia? His only hope had been his dear friend from university but his death plunged Stavros into desolation.

On the other hand, Stavros was by nature optimistic and slightly over-confident so that his realistic pessimism did not get the better of him. He knew that he was an exceptional person, highly intelligent and blessed with a charismatic personality that won over friends and strangers, professors and ordinary people, men and women. Yiorgos was the latest person to fall under Stavros' unassuming charm that made every person who met him to feel lucky to be noticed by him and to be in his company. He had endless jokes to tell, a joke for each occasion, and countless stories from London, this mythical, cosmopolitan city, and from his village, this obscure, primitive place hidden in the deep valleys of Troodos mountains, not to mention the stories from Greek mythology, history, philosophy, Socrates, Plato, Thucydides, Sophocles. He would recite poetry ancient and modern, Shakespeare and Homer. He had always a suitable quotation for every debate or discussion. What a strange combination of cultures, what a fascinating man.

But now alone in his room, faced with an uncertain future and the unthinkable possibility of running out of money Stavros felt a pang of acute anxiety. Sitting at the table in front of his bed in his small room at the back of the hotel he began to write a letter to Nikos' father.

'Dear Mr Hadgipavlou,' he wrote. 'You may not remember me, but we met under extremely sad and shocking circumstances at your son's funeral. Your son and I were very close friends. If we lived in another time, we would have been blood brothers. Nikolaos and I were planning, as you might know, to open an office together combining the two twin disciplines of architecture and civil engineering. Alas, God seemed to be against our plans and took your son away so suddenly, so cruelly. I am a stranger in Limassol and have no family or friends here. I am in the difficult position of having to ask you whether you might have a suitable employment for me or whether you might know somebody who has.'

Stavros went on to recount his qualifications and experience in detail and offer to provide "excellent" references. He finished the letter feeling like the poor relative from the country begging for a job at a distant uncle's company. Years later he would be in the place of the rich uncle helping his nephews and nieces from the village to find suitable employment. But for now he was near to being desperate. He put the letter in the envelope and licked it to seal it. He then wrote the address on the envelope carefully and clearly. He told Yiorgo that he was going to the post office and he strolled down the slope towards the village.

After he posted the letter at the village's small post office, he lingered for a while talking to Vassos, the post office master, and to Yiannis, the head of the small police force of the village, and with Kyria Lito, the fruit shop owner. He bought some grapes and some apples and wandered a little at the central square that was deserted except for a couple of old men sitting on a bench deep in conversation. He then headed back uphill through the forest and towards the hotel when he heard his name being called loud and clear.

'Stavro! Stavraki! Oh my God it's you!'

He turned around and saw an old man in the traditional vraka and high leather boots leading a donkey laden with fruit and vegetables down the hill. For a moment, Stavros did not recognise the man and stood there surprised that the man seemed to know him. Then a sudden recognition occurred.

'Uncle Manoli, it's you!'

They embraced and Stavros realised that his eyes welled up without warning. He felt the warmth emanating from Manolis, and felt a feeling of belonging. Uncle Manolis was Penelope's, and his dead mother's, brother. This was home, this man, this smell, this village, the village accent, the intonation in his voice. He was "family", the only family he ever had—grandmother, Penelope and Manolis. But now looking at him he could hardly recognise the sturdy, handsome man he knew. Manolis had aged beyond belief in the eight years he had not seen him.

'Uncle Manolis, you here? Selling fruit and veg?'

'It's hard times Stavro,' he said, 'hard times.'

Manolis took a step back and said. 'My God Stavro, let me look at you, let me look at you. You are a real gentleman now, "sostos kyrios" now. You look good, real good. I am so proud of you and Penelope will be proud of you,' when I tell her.

'How is auntie Penelope, Manolis? Tell me all about the village and the news. How is my grandmother, how is everybody?'

'They are all well Stavraki. Your grandmother has left us though, god bless her. Quite suddenly, heart said the doctor. We didn't have an address to let you know. God knows she loved you very much and was so proud of you. God bless her soul.'

'God bless her soul.' Stavros crossed himself, something he hadn't done for years. He was stunned. Grandma was gone and nobody knew where he was to let him know. 'I loved her very much Manoli,' he said and felt deeply ashamed and deeply bereft.

'I know Stavraki. I know.' Manolis said, not even a hint of blame in his voice.

'These are my people,' Stavros was thinking, 'my people. What am I doing being a "gentleman"?'

'But how are things with you?' Manolis was now saying. 'Tell me. Nobody in the village has heard anything about you. We heard the news about you getting a scholarship to go to London University from people who worked in Amiantos but since you left for London not a word.'

Again Stavros felt a deep sense of shame and regret and a sadness beyond anything he ever felt before. He could see and feel the immense distance that separated him from Manolis and "the village" and yet he could feel the immediate connection with him, the warmth, the feeling of belonging. He also felt ashamed about his present situation. He hated the idea of the whole village

171

getting to know that after years of studying in London he was now without a job and without any secure future, alone and forlorn. Instead he told Manolis that he was waiting to hear from a friend in Limassol who would probably offer him a job.

'I am sure you will be good at whatever you do Stavro,' Manolis said with fervour and embraced Stavros once again. 'But don't forget your family back in the village. They would love to hear from you.'

'I shall come and visit as soon as I settle down,' he said and he knew he was lying. The love he felt for Manolis and for Penelope battled with the aversion he felt for his father and his wife and sons and for "the village" and its narrow minded, fixed ways. Love and hate clashed violently inside him and a strong pang of pain hit him. Lying didn't come easy to him and neither did hurting the people he loved. This violent conflict inside himself never subsided but he had learnt to push it aside and not to feel it. Life, learning, progressing, surviving took priority. But the pain of being homeless, being an orphan, without parents, without a real home, the absolute necessity of leaving his village and everybody who loved him behind—that pain never subsided.

'Can I give you some walnuts?' Manolis was now saying. 'They are from grandmother's walnut trees, strictly speaking you own a share in them.' Manolis laughed and Stavros joined in.

'These are the best walnuts you will find.' Manolis handed him half an oke of walnuts wrapped in brown paper. They embraced and parted and Stavros walked the few hundred metres to the hotel.

The rest of the story was well known within Stavros' family as he repeated it again and again to his wife and children for many decades and Marina had heard it dozens of times. How one morning when he went as usual to the Post Office in Platres to ask whether there were any letters for him there was indeed one letter addressed to him. It was from Mr Hadjipavlou, Nicos' father. The story that Marina and her brother heard so many times referred to this letter that changed Stavros' life. The letter from Mr Hadjipavlou concerned the Church of Holy Trinity in Limassol which had been left unfinished for many years for the lack of funds. But now the Church Authorities have decided to put some money and finish the church and Mr Hadjipavlou was very happy to recommend the newly qualified engineer from London, Mr Stavros Georgiou. The letter went on that the Church Authorities and the local Council were very interested in arranging a meeting in Limassol to discuss the design of the dome, with this young engineer that Mr Hadjipavlou was recommending.

He walked through the forest buried in his thoughts. He had imagined this moment many times—a letter that would change his life. He had imagined himself overwhelmed with happiness, running through the slopes of Platres to the Forest Hotel to tell Yiorgos about it all. But now he was numb, disbelieving what he had read. It sounded a bit like a joke, as if somebody was playing a trick on him. Designing a dome? for a church? It sounded like a huge project for a beginner like him. Yet the confidence in himself was immense. He was sure he could do it.

The smell of the forest woke him up. The pungent smell of resin mixed with wild sage made him feel alive. A feeling of vigour returned and began to circulate in his veins. This was only the beginning. His future lay in front of him.

For some reason, the face of his mother came to his mind. Not that he knew what his mother looked like. There were no cameras in the village and absolutely no images of her. But he had always had an image in his mind—a combination of the Madonna in the village church and Penelope's face—a composite secret face that he saw in his dreams and in his waking reverie. And now she was there among the wild sage and the pine resin and the proud tall pines and the birdsong and the distant braying of a donkey.

The moment broke abruptly with Yiorgos' voice. He looked up and saw Yiorgos in the distance, standing on the veranda of his hotel, shouting and gesticulating. Stavros could not understand what he was saying. He began to walk faster and when he came within a hearing distance, he distinguished the word 'telephone for you, Stavro, from Limassol.'

The events that followed were well known in the Stavros' family as he told the story again and again to his wife and children. How he went to Limassol to meet Mr Hadjipavlou who welcomed him like a son and introduced him to the Bishop and the mayor of Limassol; how Stavros undertook to design and oversaw the building of the dome of Saint Trinity's Church; how he adopted a rather revolutionary design that had no columns on which the dome would rest, and how the workers were afraid to stand underneath it for the fear that it would collapse. And how Stavros was the first to stand under it once it was finished and tell everybody that whatever he designed would stand fast for many, many years and centuries.

Chapter 15
Limassol 1937

Olga's Engagement

On the day when Stavros came to ask formally for Olga's hand Nellie had another fit, the second one since that terrible day when she read the announcement of Evripides' engagement in the local paper.

It was a Saturday morning in late April two weeks after Easter Sunday. All of Thalia's discreet enquiries about Stavros had had a positive outcome including "rumours" and "gossip" and "talk of the town". The combined view was of an educated, intelligent, charming and responsible young man who "would go a long way". But what clinched the whole thing was Aristos' meeting with Sotiris which Thalia and Maroulla had prepared behind the scenes. For, of course, it was Aristos' word that mattered in the end not Thalia's. It was not in her power to say yes or no to this proposal (which was not yet a proposal but a suggestion, but a suggestion which could become a proposal if Aristos let Dimitris know that he was prepared to consider it.) The only power Thalia had was that of persuasion, manipulation, planning and scheming behind the scenes. And this power was considerable. Some would say it was the decisive one.

However despite Sotiris' positive comments about Stavros, Aristos spent a few sleepless nights considering the issue, taking everything apart, looking at it from one side and then form another. Was he giving his daughter away to a "nobody"? Had his family descended so low that a "nobody" could ask for his daughter's hand? Could he, Stavros, guarantee that his daughter would have the life style and the standard of living she had been accustomed to? Was he cultured, this young man from Marathasa, did he have manners, did he know who Aristoteles was?

He knew that he had a degree from London University, something not many people had, in fact he couldn't name anybody when it came to it. His friends'

174

sons went to Athens to study Law, or to Beirut to study Economics. Dimitris studied engineering in Munich, it's true and that was the closest he could get to it. But London University sounded grand. Of course his degree was in engineering, something called "civil engineering" and nobody on the island knew what this "civil" engineering was.

But Thalia was very persuasive. 'I know she has seen him in church,' she said, 'and she liked him. I know she will be able to love him.' (This despite the fact that Stavros never went to church, but she could hardly have said, 'they met at tennis and they are in love with each other,' could she?) 'I think he will make her happy,' she added.

Thalia had secret wishes about Olga. She "knew" about Stavros' and Olga's secret "love affair". Well, to call it love affair was going too far. Stavros never said anything to Olga and Olga never said anything to her. But Thalia "knew", the way mothers know, with their hearts, with their guts. She could see Olga's despair since she had heard that Stavros had moved to Paphos. And she had seen the glint in Stavros' eyes when they played tennis, although she sat 20 metres away and she pretended to mind her knitting and take care of the wool that was unravelling and the eucalyptus leaves that got entangled with the wool as the wind blew them into her lap, she could see the way mothers see.

So one Sunday morning, a week after Easter, Aristos woke up and for the first time in a few weeks he felt lighter and a bit happier.

'I think you are right,' he said to Thalia 'we need to give this Stavros a chance.'

'I'm glad you think so,' Thalia said. 'He is a brilliant young man. Everybody I talked to thinks so.'

'O.K.' Aristos said, 'I shall tell Dimitris to arrange a meeting.'

The "meeting" was arranged for next Saturday at Dimitris' house, and that was where Aristos first met Stavros. He was surprised how young he looked and after the first introduction Aristos said with all the added politeness he could put in his voice and manner,

'I hope you don't mind me asking but how old are you?'

'Thirty-two,' Stavros replied.

'My goodness,' Aristos said, 'you look so much younger.'

'It's not the looks that matter,' came Stavros' answer, 'but what is in here,' and pointed with his index finger at his forehead.

'I absolutely agree,' Aristos said, 'and you don't find many young men these days with anything significant in there.'

'You will have to decide for yourself whether there is anything in there in this young man here,' Stavros answered.

They both laughed. Aristos instantly liked this young man. This was somebody he could talk to. Looking younger than his age but speaking like being older than his age and not being intimidated at all by Aristos' rather superior manner. And he had humour! This was worth a lot in his books. In fact, after a few rounds of random conversation about the ancient Greeks, the local elections, the situation in Germany, and "the English" on the island, Aristos, like so many people before and after him, was captured by this young man's knowledge, maturity and charm.

So, the meeting at Aristos' house was arranged for next Saturday. The plan was that Stavros would come to the house and meet Thalia first and then Olga, but only if Olga gave her consent to meet with him.

Olga was stunned. She knew nothing about Dimitris' approaching Aristos and about Aristos' sleepless nights and the agonising questions he asked himself endlessly, and Thalia's attempts to find out about Stavros from cousin Lenia and from Maroulla, and her attempts to persuade Aristos to meet up with Stavros. Nothing of the agony that Stavros and Thalia went through waiting for Aristos' answer. And now it was all arranged between Aristos and Stavros for next Saturday and she had to be at home waiting.

But now it was all decided. Stavros was to arrive after dinner at 8pm and ask formally for Olga's hand. If everything went well, Thalia would then be called to meet him and then Olga would be called in. Although both Olga and Thalia had already said yes, and had they not said yes this meeting would not be taking place at all, Aristos did not want to appear as if he was under the women's thumb—wife and daughter. Everything in its right place, he thought.

Olga blushed deeply as her mother gave her the news early on Saturday after lunch. Her heart was racing but she just said, 'what do you think mamma?'

'I think you will be very happy,' Thalia said.

'What about papa?' Olga persisted.

'He thinks the same,' Thalia said and she did believe it.

Olga went straight to tell Nellie who was sitting on her bed reading *The Man in the Iron Mask* by Alexander Dumas. Nellie looked up from her book as Olga blurted out about Stavros coming to ask for her hand. Nellie said simply 'I knew it. I knew it,' and then almost immediately 'what will you wear Olga? Let's have a look at your wardrobe.'

Thalia who had the same thought at the same time came into the girls' bedroom.

'What will you wear tonight?' she asked Olga.

'My new white red blouse?' Olga said tentatively. 'What do you think?'

At that moment, Anna tottered in. 'I hhhheard thhhe nnnews,' she blurted out, 'whhhhat exxxxactly will hhappen tttonight?'

'Well,' Thalia said, 'Stavros will arrive at around 8pm. Kyriakou will take him to the living room and your father will meet him there. If the two of them agree, I shall join them and then I shall call Olga. If everything goes well, we shall ask Stavros to join us tomorrow for lunch to meet everybody.'

'Oooooh,' Anna made an enthusiastic gesture that could be taken for dancing by somebody who did not know about her affliction and her whole body shook spasmodically, 'Oooooh!'

'On Monday, we shall put an announcement of the engagement in the paper, and the official engagement party will be in two weeks.' Thalia stopped abruptly, 'if everything goes well of course,' she added.

'Of course everything will go well,' Nellie said, 'we know that.'

Anna was the only one to show extravagant enthusiasm. Olga was too overwhelmed with everything to know what she was feeling and Nellie's feelings were too complex, too inexpressible that she concentrated on helping Olga to choose a dress, a pair of shoes and the jewellery she wanted to wear. Thalia's feelings were also dampened down by Nellie's plight.

'We are ggggoing to hhave a wwwedding,' Anna was saying, 'oooooh.'

'Yes I hope so,' Thalia said, 'our Olga will be a bride.'

Nellie was now choosing a dusty pink dress for Olga. 'This suits you so much,' Nellie was saying. 'It makes your cheeks glow and the pearls will go so well with it.'

'Yes,' Thalia said, 'I agree with Nellie. The colour suits your complexion.'
Anna joined in.

'YYYes Ollllga. Thhhat dress.'

Kyriakou, who had just heard the news, came in and embraced Olga.

'Olga, dear Olga, this is marvellous news.' Kyriakou could hardly speak as the tears were running down her cheeks. 'God bless,' she said in the end, 'God bless.'

As if Kyriakou's tears were contagious, Thalia's eyes welled up. 'God bless,' she repeated as nothing else came to her mind.

The atmosphere was in danger of becoming very emotional and Olga rushed back to talk to Nellie about the dress. She was glad about the fuss with the dress. She could bury her feelings in this senseless activity. But all of a sudden she wanted to cry—to cry and cry. All these months of silent suffering have come to an end so suddenly that she felt shaken and unable to speak. Tears began to roll down her cheeks and she buried herself more and more in the search for suitable shoes to match the dress. Nellie was also searching frantically as if her life depended on it.

Then all of a sudden Nellie stopped and the creamy shoes she was holding fell off her hands. All three looked at her. She was white as a sheet and her eyes looked far away.

'Are you all right Nellie?' Thalia asked but she suddenly knew what was happening—the same deadly look, the same rigidity on Nellie's face as before.

Nellie tried to speak but nothing but raw sounds came out of her throat. Then suddenly she fell on the floor shaking uncontrollably. The pupils of her eyes had disappeared and only the white of her eyes was to be seen and froth came out of her mouth.

'Quick,' Thalia shouted 'quick, put something in her mouth or she will bite her tongue.'

As Olga was holding her satin pink dress in her hands she gathered it together and stuck part of it in Nellie's mouth.

'Hold her head,' Thalia was shouting and handed Olga a pillow. Olga placed the pillow under Nellie's head and tried to keep her head still by holding it but without much success.

Aristos who heard the commotion was now standing at the door looking frozen as an ice sculpture. He never dared to cross the door and enter into the girls' room. Since Olga reached her teens this self-imposed taboo was held, like any taboo, with absolute conviction.

'I shall go and fetch Dr Nicolaides,' he said trying to keep his voice calm and authoritative, but fear had already gripped his body like an iron hand.

He had not been present when Nellie's first fit took place completely out of the blue as Thalia told him later, leaving out a few vital details. But now nothing could be hidden from him. He stood there frightened and clueless as a child who was witnessing an awful, incomprehensible event.

'I'll go and fetch Dr Nicolaides,' he repeated.

'Yes please go Aristo, please go. Now,' Thalia added urgently.

He put on his jacket in a hurry and he was gone in a few seconds, fleeing the panic from the dreadful sight of a daughter he could not recognise and an event he could not comprehend.

Like the first time Nellie eventually stopped shaking and fell into a stupor. With Anna's constant accompaniment of 'OOOOhh' Thalia and Olga transferred Nellie onto the bed. Thalia went to fetch a moist towel to wipe Nellie's face. Olga looked at Nellie's face as she lay unconscious and then looked at her ruined dress. The lace collar was chewed up and the elaborate embroidered bodice was torn and soiled. Olga felt a feeling of relief. *At last, she was punished for making Nellie so unhappy. She can now have Stavros as she has paid a price, however small—just a dress*, she thought. Who cares about a dress? That was justice done.

When Dr Nicolaides had gone, after he had examined Nellie and said that she would be all right, she needed to rest, the small family gathered around the dining table to discuss possible action.

'Should we cancel the meeting?' Thalia was saying.

She looked drawn and terribly pale. She could guess the cause of Nellie's sudden "illness" but said nothing. Her heart was torn in two: one daughter's happiness was the other daughter's illness. What to do?

'No,' said Aristos, 'No.'

Although it was Saturday morning and he had not gone to work Aristos was wearing a tie and his work jacket and looked very distinguished.

'No,' he repeated. 'It took us so long to agree to this meeting. Now we are going to keep it. In any case, what can we say if we cancel it? No, the meeting has to go ahead.'

He stopped for a moment.

'If you ask me,' he added after a while, 'it's hysteria, it's women's nerves,' he added exhibiting his knowledge of Professor Freud's theories that were just reaching the island.'

Thalia and Olga kept quiet.

'Stavros Georgiou is coming at 8pm,' Aristos said, 'and that's that.'

Olga sighed a sigh of relief. Her father spoke with a voice that admitted no objection. Things would take their course. For her part, Thalia was relieved that Aristos had not asked for her opinion. She felt so torn that she would have been unable to make up her mind. And she knew that Aristos knew that.

'Well, that's that,' Aristos said. 'We can now get on with the day.'

For Olga, the day consisted of trying to choose an alternative dress and a matching pair of shoes and a necklace that would match both. As Nellie slept and Thalia looked after Anna, Olga searched through her wardrobe. She was left alone to decide for herself as everybody was anxious and nervous and pretended that everything was fine. Kyriakou began the cooking of the Saturday meal of meatballs and bulgur cooked in tomato sauce.

Olga went through a number of dresses—a very formal blue dress with a white lace collar, a bright red satin blouse that could be worn with a black satin skirt and finally settled on an emerald green silk dress that looked both formal and "jolly". It was a dress that made her feel comfortable and natural and not dressed up although it was a dress for special occasions. Olga was glad that nobody was there to give her advice and she set out to choose the shoes and the jewellery that would go with the dress.

Nellie, sedated by Dr Nicolaides' medication, slept peacefully despite her white, stony face.

***

Stavros knocked at the door, as the clock in the hall struck eight and for the first hour he was received by Aristos and Thalia alone. They sat in the big living room, the *saloni,* with the grand piano and the huge crystal chandelier, and the heavily carved furniture and the Persian rugs.

Kyriakou brought refreshments and some home-made cake by Thalia and after some chit chat they came to the point. Stavros asked formally for Olga's hand in marriage and Aristos asked about his income, his position in the civil service, his future career, his education.

Stavros came across as a serious young man with a bright future in front of him. What was unexpected was Stavros' ability to "hold" a conversation, which Aristos, knowing about Stavros' humble origins, was so anxious about. In fact, he was a brilliant conversationist, knowing when to go on and when to stop, being able to listen carefully, sometimes answer with humour, sometimes show his considerable knowledge of literature and politics, sometimes remaining silent.

Aristos was completely won over by this engaging young man—if he had not already been so in his previous meeting with Stavros. But what pleased

Aristos most was Stavros' knowledge of the classical Greek authors, Plato and Aristotle, Sophocles and Evripides, for whom Aristos held a deep love and had very few people to share this with.

That evening, Aristos and Stavros were in danger of forgetting the reason of Stavros' visit as they got engaged in talking about Socrates' Apology and Pericles' famous speech. Stavros quoted some passages in the original which delighted Aristos. He had now absolutely no reservation handing his beloved daughter to this fascinating young man. He knew that she would be in good hands and he would also gain a friend to talk to about culture and the Greek classics.

'Is it time to call Olga?' Thalia said an hour after they had begun a debate whether Sophocles was a greater playwright than Evripides. 'Yes, yes,' Aristos said interrupting his highbrow speech about Sophocles, 'yes go and fetch Olga.' Thalia, relieved that Aristos at last remembered the reason of Stavros' visit, went to fetch Olga.

Olga had been waiting by Nellie's bed, apparently reading a book by her sleeping sister's bed, but she could understand nothing of the black signs on the white paper and the longer she waited the more anxious she got, having all kinds of thoughts about her father maybe becoming "difficult" and Stavros taking offence and leaving. When some laughter reached her ears every now and then, she was reassured that things were progressing well and she just had to be patient. But would her father turn around the last minute and say 'thank you for the offer Mr Stavro but I don't think you are suitable for my daughter?' She did not dare exactly think this thought but she felt it rather in her body that had begun to feel sick. As Olga's state of mind began to deteriorate into a frozen, frightened one, her mother's beaming face appeared through the door.

'Time to come Olga.'

It was all over in a few minutes. Olga followed her mother as if in a dream, her heart pounding, her face drained of blood. In a dream, she saw Stavros talking in a relaxed and friendly manner with her father and saw them both turning towards her as she entered the room. She said 'good evening' to Stavros and heard Aristos saying.

'Come closer Olga. It's your answer we need now.'

He paused.

Olga thought the light in the living room became dimmer and her father's voice more distant.

'Mr Stavros Georgiou is asking for your hand in marriage. Do you want to marry this man? You don't have to answer immediately, you might want to think about it.'

'I do, I do,' Olga blurted out without any conscious control. 'I know I do.'

It came out too quickly, she thought, perhaps too eagerly? But did it matter now? Now they were engaged to get married.

Aristos' voice was full of emotion as he took Stavros' hand and Olga's hand and brought them together.

'I give you my blessing,' he said trying to sound solemn but his voice was breaking. 'I hope you will be happy together.'

Thalia was in tears. She embraced her daughter and then embraced Stavros.

'With God's blessing,' she said.

'We must open a bottle of Commandaria,' Aristos said.

'Ah, the wine for kings!' Stavros said, referring to Richard the Lionheart's exclamation when he was served Commandaria. Stavros continued to show off his knowledge of the island's history by adding that contrary to the legend that the wine was made at the time of Richard the Lionheart for his wedding to his fiancée Berengaria, the wine, in fact dated back to 800 B.C. and was apparently known to Hesiod. Its name however, Stavros added, originates much later in medieval Cyprus when the Knights Templar finally gave it its name. And of course, legend had it, that Commandaria was drunk by Richard the Lion Heart at his wedding with Berengaria of Navarre which took place on the island in this very town of Limassol in 1191 and that it was then that when the king had tasted it he apparently said the famous phrase 'this is a wine for kings and it is the king of wines.'

Aristos knew some of these facts, or rather legends, but he had never heard that Hesiod had already known about this wine which was so particular to their island. He was pleased to hear Stavros, being so interested in the history of the island.

'Well, Stavro,' he said, 'I can now call you Stavro, can't I? Well, let's enjoy this king of all wines!'

As Aristos was opening the bottle of Commandaria, Thalia was saying almost apologetically, 'we would have called Nellie and Anna, but Nellie is unwell and Anna is already asleep.'

'We shall celebrate properly on another day,' Aristos said.

They raised their glasses.

'To Stavros and Olga,' Aristos said ceremonially.

'We must think about the engagement party,' Thalia said as they were sipping their wine.

'We can talk about it later,' Aristos said.

Chapter 16
Paphos 1938

It was now late September, twelve months after Olga's and Stavros' wedding. Olga was now seven months pregnant and living with Stavros in Paphos. Although some fifty miles from Limassol, Paphos was a totally unknown place for her. She had never been there before and now she realised how different it was from the lively, "cosmopolitan" Limassol. She felt with some disappointment, as if it was "the end of the world", a place without friends or relatives and without the lively, cultural world of her native town. Stavros was hoping that in a couple of years he would be transferred to Limassol, so Olga lived in hope, trying in the meantime to create a good home for Stavros and herself. At the moment though, the big event that was looming was the birth of her child and this overshadowed everything. And for the last two months Kyriakou had joined them, as Thalia thought that Olga would need some help with her pregnancy and asked Kyriakou whether she was willing to move in with Olga and Stavros. Kyriakou, who loved Olga as if she was her own child, agreed immediately and with great enthusiasm. The addition of Kyriakou to their small household made Olga happy. It was, as if part of her old family joined her in this strange place that was her new home.

For the last couple of months, Olga had taken to wandering on the beaches of Paphos collecting shells and pebbles and reading religiously a book about how to prepare for childbirth and for the first few months of the baby's life.

'Nothing prepares you for that,' Thalia had said to her. 'I shall come and be with you when the time has come.' And at another time she said, 'I didn't read anything. It just happens to you.'

But Olga continued to read religiously trying to control her fear for this unknown event that everybody was so enthusiastic about and about which she had no idea how she felt.

She looked at the sea, blue and calm and sparkling in the mellow September light. She let her eyes rest on the horizon where big boats were travelling to unknown destinations, and clouds were gathering. She relished this moment of peace, so full of the sea spray and the warmth of the sun. She was going to go home, in a couple of minutes, to help Kyriakou cook and wait for Stavros to come for lunch. Then Nellie was to arrive from Limassol with the afternoon coach at about 5pm. This was Nellie's first visit to Olga's new home and Olga was very excited. But for now, these few minutes were hers and hers alone.

Stavros came back for lunch at 1.10 every single day, just like her father had done for the last thirty years. It was now eleven in the morning and she had been on the beach for an hour. Nobody was around, not even fishermen drying their nets in the sun.

She cherished this hour in the morning, between breakfast and preparing lunch. Stavros left for work s at 7.45. She would then tidy up the breakfast things and leave Kyriakou to wash up and sweep and wash the floor, do the beds and dust up. Olga would join her again at 11 and help with the preparation for lunch. So this hour between ten and eleven was hers and hers alone. Walking on the beach for an hour had become a necessity, the only way she knew of bridging the gap between 7.45 when Stavros left and 1.10 when he came back for lunch. She had no friends and no relatives in Paphos except for Kyriakou who was in a way part of the family, but lovely as it was that Kyriakou was there with her, she did not make up for the lack of friends, cousins and her family.

Stavros was busy making friends with his English colleagues, especially with his boss, the district engineer, a Scotchman with a friendly, loud voice and a chuckle, a very amiable man who invited them often for Sunday lunch, invariably roast beef and Yorkshire pudding. Olga loved these Sundays with Neil and Doreen and their two lovely children, Eleanor seven and Michael five.

'I would like our children to be like them,' she once said to Stavros after a visit to Neil and Doreen's house. 'Of course they won't have blonde hair and blue eyes but they could be as well behaved and helpful and loveable as these children.'

And now her first child was only a couple of months away—a boy or a girl? She didn't mind as long as it was a healthy child, that's how she always answered people's question of what she preferred. 'I don't mind as long as it's healthy,' but she knew very well without being told, that Stavros would be disappointed if it was not a boy.

But she was sincere in saying that she did not mind. The fear of having a child like Anna was kept in the background and very rarely surfaced. She took solace in what the doctor told her many times that what Anna suffered from was not hereditary. So, Stavros and Olga never talked about this possibility and it was left to Olga to wake up sometimes in the middle of the night and imagine different scenarios, all grim and scary.

As time drew closer, Stavros who had lost his mother in childbirth when he was eighteen months, was getting nervous but his feelings were hidden, even from himself, under his congenial, eternal optimism. All the feelings of worry or anxiety, so natural in most people, were carefully hidden and suppressed under a façade of easy-going confidence. It was as if he were absolutely convinced that if he ordered the mountain to move it would move, only he wouldn't be so stupid as to try it!

Olga, who was getting to know this part of Stavros' and was intelligent enough never to challenge it, knew that their relationship began and developed with this, absolutely necessary, silent agreement never to challenge Stavros' illusion that he could do anything, anything he decided to do. It was true that the things he decided to do were mostly within his power so this illusion was by definition never put to the test. That was due to Stavros' intelligence.

It might not be an exaggeration to say that Stavros' choice of wife was based on her silent, absolute trust and submission to him in a quiet and gentle way. He found it very moving, but he nevertheless knew that this was absolutely necessary, the sine qua non of their relationship.

She was to be the mother he never knew, a mother absolutely and endlessly admiring her male son, this demi-god, this powerful scion, the hero who would protect her and defend her always, absolutely. Stavros found in Olga a mother who looked after him, admired him, never asked questions, never interfered with his decisions, never nagged. She was quietly content and happy. And now she was coming into bloom, bursting into flower and it was he, who had brought these changes in her. And this made him very happy.

Olga had a long and painful training into submission at home. Aristos could tolerate no dissent. Later when Nellie began her systematic, self-destructive rebellion against him and his world, she was the first woman who ever challenged him and eventually broke him. And Nellie, despite her very feminine appearance, was somebody Stavros was afraid of. Secretly and silently he feared her. He feared her determination, her defiance, her ability to hate and to act and to dig her heels in the sand and never budge. But Olga was different. Olga, sweet Olga, was not going to test either Aristos' or Stavros' assertion of superiority and this was the silent contract with both her father and Stavros. And one could say, this was her guarantee of security and happiness.

She knew that her mother had undergone a painful adjustment when she married Aristos. Being the youngest of five children, the baby of the family, and having been born within a liberal and artistic family, she found it very difficult and painful to adjust to the eldest son of the Judge—the stern Aristos with his absolute conviction of what was right and what was wrong, from which he never wavered. Olga's long apprenticeship into submission, at least external submission, stood her in good stead in her marriage. And external submission it was. For Olga maintained, just like her mother, the ability to see clearly. Her perception and judgement remained intact. They were both sharp and relentless. But so was her ability to recognise not only the necessity but also her husband's, and father's, absolute need to be trusted, admired, believed and obeyed. Their desperate need to be in control.

Olga's mind remained as sharp and observant as ever but her gentle nature and her ability to recognise and go along with her husband's need to be in control was what made this marriage a successful one. Olga could see no contradiction between these two sides of hers. They could co-exist, each acknowledging the other's existence and the other's claim.

Nellie arrived at 6pm as the sun dipped bleeding into the sea and the breeze began to cool the air. Olga and Stavros were already at the coach station waiting. A very elegant Nellie dressed in an expensive summer suit and hat and carrying a heavy suitcase and two shoulder bags and a handbag got out of the coach helped by a very attentive older gentleman.

'Olga, Olga,' she shouted running towards her, 'My God you are big.'

'Yes she is getting ready,' Stavros said proudly looking at Olga's belly with affection.

They embraced.

Nellie looked extremely well. This is a new Nellie, Olga thought, out of a movie. How wonderful! Elegant, sophisticated, confident. What a miracle.

They drove in Stavros' new Austen. Stavros was silent whistling his tunes, something he habitually did as he drove, and the sisters chatted endlessly. As Nellie filled Olga in with all the details of everyday life in Limassol Olga wondered more and more what has happened to Nellie to affect this kind of change—a new man in her life? A new proposal? A new "romantic" love? Was there a big "secret" to all this?

In the evening, after a light dinner of avgolemono soup and croutons and some halloumi and grapes and figs, served with abundant love by Kyriakou, they sat on the veranda, Stavros drinking his evening brandy on the rocks and Olga and Nellie sipping lemonade and listening to the distant roar of the sea. Then Nellie revealed her "secret".

'I have written an article,' she suddenly said breaking the silence. She said this in a low voice and a somewhat conspiratorial manner, as if Aristos were in the next room listening to every word she was saying.

'I want your opinion before I give to Sotiris the final version of it. He has seen it already and he wants to publish it in "The Observer",' she said.

'An article?'

Both Olga and Stavros looked intrigued as they asked the same question at the same time.

'Yes an article,' Nellie said sounding annoyed 'what's so strange about this?'

Olga and Stavros looked at each other. Except for the fact that Nellie had been depressed for months, except for the fact that she had taken no interest in the outside world for some time now, well nothing so strange at all. After all, Nellie had always been interested in writing and dreamt of becoming a novelist. But an article?

'What's it about?' Olga asked after a moment of silence.

'Ah,' Nellie said, 'this is the main thing. The subject is revolutionary.'

'Communist?' Stavros sounded incredulous. Nellie had been such a staunch Nationalist and had such a strong aversion to Communism which had its first organised form on the island a few years ago.

'Of course not!' Nellie sounded offended. 'How can you think such a thing Stavro? For God's sake!'

Olga and Stavros remained silent waiting for Nellie to enlighten them.

A few moments passed.

'It's about women.' Nellie said finally and there was triumph in her voice. 'It's about women's emancipation. There you have it.'

'How brave of you Nellie,' Olga said.

'Brave?' Nellie said provocatively, 'what do you mean by brave? It's obvious that's what we need on this island.'

'Sure,' Stavros said, 'sure. But what about your father?'

'He doesn't need to know.' Nellie had a confidence in her voice that Olga had never heard before.

'Listen,' Nellie said, 'just listen. I have worked it all out. I have a plan.'

They sat quietly for a while waiting for Nellie to say more and Nellie as if to torment them remained silent. The sea roared in the distance and an owl hooted. Olga and Stavros remained silent.

'I have worked it all out,' Nellie said again after a while. 'The postman comes every Thursday morning to deliver the newspaper and my mother collects it and puts it on the table next to him at dinner table for him to read it when he is back from work. You know the routine very well. But the week of the publication I will intercept the paper and hide it and we shall tell my dad that the postman never came that day, he must have made a mistake, mistakes do happen you know. And father will grumble and complain about the services getting worse and worse, and how unreliable the mail is these days, and blame the general decadence that has gripped the island and the world in general, and maybe he will give us a speech about the good old days when the world was in order etc. By the next day, he will have forgotten about it and that would be it.'

Nellie sounded very sure of herself. She spent hours working out every detail.

'It will work,' she added.

'But what if somebody tells him about it?' Olga asked immediately. 'What then Nellie? What then?'

'Like who?' Nellie asked in return 'Like who? You forget that our father has no friends, he doesn't belong to a club, he doesn't go to the caffeneion. Sotiris is the only person he can call a friend and Sotiris would hardly say anything to him would he?'

'Has Sotiris approved the article?' Stavros asked.

'He is very enthusiastic,' Nellie said. He said, 'This is going to be a bombshell. We must publish it,' he said.

'Oh my God Nellie!' Olga could not contain herself. 'And you think you can keep this secret? You think our father will not find out?'

'You have always been a coward Olga spoiling everything with your fears. You are now trying to spoil this, which is so important, so important for me. Always playing safe. But I won't let you, I won't let you this time.'

Nellie's voice rose to a dangerous pitch and almost became shrill.

'I am thinking of you,' Olga said. 'Your reputation, your future. It's your life Nellie.'

'What are you talking about Olga?'

She was now screaming.

'Have you not noticed that I have had no life for the last two years. I am coming back to life Olga, whether you like it or not I am coming back to life, through this article.'

A deep silence followed. The moon had risen unnoticed forming a silver shimmering path on the sea. The invisible crickets buzzed. The waves roared. They sat in silence for a while enveloped by the evening.

'For the last nine months I have been visiting Sotiris,' library every single day,' Nellie said suddenly.

Olga remained silent.

'This was a new lease of life for me, new ideas, other countries, different cultures. It's been wonderful this awakening. Learning about the suffragettes, learning about women's struggle abroad, away from this suffocating island.'

Another silence followed but shorter than the first. Nellie wanted to talk about her favourite subject.

'The struggle to get the vote, to free themselves and other women from male aggression and domination. What a heroic struggle! Women went to prison, women tried to starve themselves to death, women chained themselves to the railings outside the parliament. Amazing! Absolutely amazing.'

Olga and Stavros did not dare interrupt her.

'But what about woman's rights in love? This is a subject the suffragettes have not tackled. Women's right to have the same rights in love as men, to have their sexuality acknowledged. Women should be equally free to have sexual relationships as men.'

Nellie stopped and looked at Stavros and Olga provocatively.

A deep silence followed which now felt oppressive. The subject felt truly explosive. Sotiris was right to say "this is a bombshell", but he had no right to want to publish it, Olga thought. But said nothing for a while.

'Nellie you will burn your fingers,' Stavros said. 'This is bigger than you, Nellie.'

'Nonsense,' Nellie said, 'absolute nonsense. I didn't expect this from you Stavro, you who lived in England.'

'It will be more than burning her fingers,' Olga intervened, 'She will be destroyed.'

'Nonsense,' Nellie said again, 'You haven't even read the article.'

She stopped for a moment taking in a deep breath. She seemed to be fighting to find the right words.

'You are such cowards,' she said with vehemence. 'Such cowards. You are trying to scare me, but I am absolutely sure about this. I have never been so sure in my whole life.'

She stopped and as nobody said anything she added again.

'Sotiris was enthusiastic about the article.'

She was now shouting and her voice became shrill and sharp as razor. 'Sotiris was excited, almost ecstatic. Not like you two.'

'Sotiris wants to sell his newspaper,' Stavros persevered, trying hard to sound cool and logical. 'He is not thinking of you, he is thinking of his sales. But we are thinking of you.'

'Sotiris can recognise good writing when he sees it,' Nellie was shouting, gesticulating, her face a mask of anger and defiance 'You are philistines, small, insignificant, narrow-minded people. Oh, how I hate this island and all of you!'

She left the veranda in a fury and went to her bedroom which was carefully and lovingly prepared and equipped by Olga.

'What was that?' Olga said still under the shock of Nellie's hate and rage.

'Sotiris is not very wise,' Stavros said. 'He wants a buzz. He wants to sell his newspaper. He might even want a scandal. A scandal always helps with the sales.'

'Sotiris is not like this,' Olga said.

'I am not so sure,' Stavros said, 'he is not unkind but he is a bit naïve and over enthusiastic and he would do anything for his newspaper. And he thinks a bit like Nellie, that the islanders need a fair dose of shock to be shaken out of their narrow-minded insularity. But this is going too far. This is going to backfire.'

'We have to try and persuade her not to publish it,' Olga said.

'No you are not! No! No! No!'

Nellie was standing at the doorstep, her blonde hair glowing in the light from inside the bungalow, her face in darkness, her figure framed by the doorframe.

'What are you plotting?' She screamed, 'like conspirators plotting my downfall. You are worse than my father.'

Olga and Stavros were silent, not wanting to add more fuel to this rage.

'Here,' Nellie shouted, here is the article, the offensive weapon. 'Here! I typed it on Anna's typewriter. It took me ages to get everything right, so please look after it. But read it. You will see that it's a good article and a very serious one.'

She slapped the envelope on the garden table in front of them and stormed inside.

'I shall read it,' Stavros said quietly but Nellie had already gone.

Nellie's wrath was hanging in the air as Stavros and Olga retired to their room.

'Your sister can look and sound like a real fury.' Stavros was whispering as if Nellie would be listening behind the closed door. It was obvious that he was trying to get his humour back, which was his bulwark against the power that women had to upset him.

'She feels very strongly about these things,' Olga said evasively. 'It's my father to blame,' she added. 'He tried to keep us locked up as if we were living in the 19ᵗʰ century.'

They were lying in their twin beds with the light switched off, listening between the sentences to the roar of the sea coming through the open window.

Nellie's visit left a bitter taste in Olga's mouth and mind. Not only had Nellie not changed her mind about the article during her visit, despite Olga's and Stavros' attempts to reason with her but she accused both of them of being small-minded and "bourgeois" and "philistines", who could not understand big ideas or anything beyond their narrow, domestic bliss which, let's face it, she told them, was based on women's oppression.

Stavros had laughed it all off, although Olga knew that it hurt him being called an oppressor of women, he who had such progressive ideas. Olga herself was divided—quite able to understand Nellie's ideas of inequality and double standards and secretly supporting them and at the same time seeing that Nellie was going to destroy her life and her reputation and whatever chances she still had of getting married and having children. Did she want war? And how could she fight alone against the whole world?

Olga began to wonder about her own life. Should she be as happy and content as she was? Was it all a lie, a mirage based on giving her consent to her own oppression? Giving up her own freedom, her own mind? Was she as happy as she thought she was? Did she have a right to be happy?

She was walking, as always around this time in the morning, on the beach, the spray from the waves on her face, the sun burning her skin, cradling her big belly with both hands.

'You, my darling,' she whispered, 'boy, or girl, you will be part of a new world.'

She thought of Nellie, beautiful, angry, lonely, fiercely intelligent, abandoned, desperate Nellie and she felt such a protective love for her. Nellie on the floor with froth coming out of her mouth, her eyes disappearing into their sockets. Nellie who could not accept the world as it was with its meanness, its sordid smallness, its oppression, rigidity and its inability to include her in its cruel pursuit of happiness. Nellie who could not protect herself against the world.

She felt sad and unable to think of anything that would solve this problem that Nellie was bringing to her. How could she be happy when so much oppression and inequality was a fundamental part of her happiness? Her happiness, although deep seated and solid as a rock, or so she had told herself, was now mixed with sadness and pity and an unsettling feeling that she had not helped Nellie by joining her in her war against this world that gave her so much happiness—her own marriage.

She sat on a rock and got lost in the endless movement of the waves that were calm and easy today, gently kissing the shore, like a mother, she thought, like a mother and stroked once again her swollen belly. My lovely child, she whispered, my love, my darling, and the sea endlessly caressing the shore, kissing it gently, always whispering the same gentle, loving words, my sweet, sweet child. She thought of Nellie's visit and the events of the last few days and had no answer to the problems that Nellie had brought with her.

Chapter 17
Paphos October 1938

The day after Nellie threw her manuscript on the table and disappeared to her room, was Saturday—half working day. Lunch was as usually at 1.15 and was shared with Olga and Nellie. Nobody mentioned the article but Stavros knew that it was there, hanging like a dagger in the air between them, disturbing the otherwise calm atmosphere. After fruit was served, Stavros got up and said calmly 'I am going to the club and I shall read Nellie's article.' The women said that they were having a siesta. Nobody commented on Stavros' reference to Nellie's article.

It was two o'clock when Stavros arrived at the English Club and there was nobody to be seen, only the barman, his eyes glistening with midday fatigue and the influence of a beer or two.

'Hi Mr Stavro, early today.' Diogenes greeted him like an old friend.

'I have some work to do,' Stavros said. 'I have to read an article for a friend, so I need some quietness.'

'You chose the right place at the right time,' Diogenes said, 'as you know nobody comes before 4.30.'

'Yes I know.'

Stavros ordered a "metrios" coffee and a lemonade and found himself a table under a huge eucalyptus tree in one corner of the deserted café overlooking the sea. The café was built on a hill and the blueness and whiteness of the sea sparkled in the early afternoon sun. Stavros felt the drowsiness of the afternoon overcoming him and waited patiently for his coffee to arrive.

'Here we are,' Diogenes unloaded the tray with the coffee, the lemonade, a glass of water and a piece of baklava. 'I brought you some baklava to have with your coffee Mr Stavro,' he said. 'Coffee needs something sweet, and a glass of water.'

'Thank you Diogenes,' Stavros said. 'You are looking after me very well.'

'There is nobody else here, Mr Stavro. It's so good to talk to somebody otherwise I shall fall asleep.' He chuckled and went back to the bar leaving Stavros with his coffee and Nellie's manuscript.

Stavros took his time to begin reading. He drank his coffee slowly, relishing every bit, and ate his baklava and began to sip at his lemonade. He then began slowly, carefully, with delicate movements, as if he was defusing a bomb, to get the manuscript out of the big brown envelope. He could hear Nellie's shrill voice in his ears as he was performing this delicate operation. A real fury, he thought, a real fury.

Stavros was ashamed to admit to himself that he was afraid of aggressive women. He was a man who was fiercely proud of his independence and his ability to deal with everything that life would throw towards him. He was proud of having survived extremely difficult circumstances all by himself, or so he told himself. But aggressive, screaming women—that was something else. That filled him with primeval terror, at least for a split second, before his robust defences got into operation and his dry humour made him smile.

A combination of an amazon and a fury, he thought *what a woman! Even Aristos can't manage her. But somebody has to save her from herself,* he thought as he remembered lovely, delicate, loving Nellie, his wife's little sister. He took a sip of his lemonade and began to read Nellie's article.

'There is something momentous taking place in Europe,' Nellie wrote and Stavros thought it was a monumental first line. 'As if she were re-writing Karl Marx,' Stavros thought and smiled, but went on reading. 'The emancipation of women is taking place in most European countries' Stavros went on reading 'Women are shaking off their shackles and they are marching into freedom,' and a little further on, 'Women are waking up and what they see is oppression everywhere.'

The heat made him stop and wipe the sweat that was streaking down his face. The seagulls circulated above him and their cries filled the air. He rejoiced in these sea saturated sounds. Stavros never quite got used to this luxury—having the sea at his feet, able to see it, smell it, hear it. Coming from the mountains he spent his childhood years hearing from other people about this blue miracle, this ever-moving body of water, changing with the light, with the wind, with the heat. And now he was part of this miracle, as natural as his own body. He took a deep breath and looked at the sea below which was now a sheet of white and blue, dipped in the heat and the humidity of the early afternoon. The cicadas persisted in their endless, monotonous buzz.

'I am the luckiest man in the world,' Stavros thought and smiled to himself before he attempted to go back to Nellie's manuscript. But Diogenes intervened. He was suddenly there smiling.

'Another coffee Kyrie Stavro?' he asked.

'That would be lovely Diogenes. You guessed, I think, that I was ready to fall asleep.'

'This heat is asking for siesta Kyrie Stavro,' Diogenes commented 'and I can see that you need another coffee to keep awake.'

Stavros guessed that Diogenes wanted some small talk as well, that he was so bored that offering Stavros another coffee was another way of approaching him and starting a conversation. And he was not wrong. As Diogenes came back with another "metrio" he asked Stavros how Mrs Olga was.

'Is she nearly there?'

'Well, another two months to go,' Stavros said, 'but it will be easier when the heat gets milder.'

'I remember my first one,' Diogenes offered, 'It came in the middle of August. It just missed the 15th so we could not name her Maria,' he joked. But anyway my mother would have been very angry if we didn't give my daughter her name which is Calliope. It's a lovely name, the muse of music and song I was told. But my daughter hated it, it was too old fashioned, he told us when she was ten years old and blamed us ever since, so she now calls herself "Callia". The world is changing Kyrie Stavro, people are not proud anymore to have classical names, they want to be "modern" whatever this means.'

'Oh well the name is the last of our worries,' Stavros said, and could see that Diogenes wanted a long, heart to heart talk as two men sharing the worries about this momentous event. But Stavros wanted to get on with Nellie's manuscript so he discreetly picked it up and rearranged it on the table as if he was ready to start reading.

'I'll let you to it then,' Diogenes said taking the hint. 'I can see you have work to do, but give Mrs Olga my best wishes.'

'Thank you Diogenes, I shall do,' Stavros said and picked up one page of the manuscript just in case Diogenes was going to start another sentence.

Diogenes throwing the tea towel over his shoulder, proceeded to get back to the bar.

The sea breeze began to rustle the eucalyptus leaves and Stavros breathed a deep breath of contentment. The afternoon breeze, when it finally came made the world feel friendlier, more welcoming.

By 4.30, Stavros was reading the last page as Neil approached the eucalyptus tree with a wide smile in his lips.

'Well, well,' he said. 'I didn't expect to find you here so early. I desperately need a pint, but I see you are drinking coffee and lemonade.'

'I could do with a pint now,' Stavros said and as Neil went to the bar to order the beer Stavros reflected on what he had read. Tough stuff, he thought, not for the faint hearted. But well written and passionate and truthful. And above all brave. But was it too brave? What on earth did Nellie expect from this article? It will be a disaster, he decided in the end, if she insists on publishing it, it will be a disaster. Publish and be damned! In this case it will be a reality.

'Are you talking to yourself Stavro? Are things so bad?' Neil was saying as he approached Stavros.

'Sorry I was trying to solve a problem, an intractable problem,' Stavros smiled, 'just ignore me.'

Diogenes arrived with the two ice cold lagers and a bowl of freshly roasted peanuts.

'Here we are Mr Neil, the beer is as cold as it can be.'

'Great Diogenes, we shall now enjoy.'

They settled down sipping their ice-cold lager and nibbling at the freshly roasted peanuts and Neil asked about Olga and Stavros gave him the latest news including that her sister was over from Limassol for the first time since Olga came to Paphos. Not a word, of course, about Nellie's article and what a headache it was causing them. After Neil filled him in about his kids and wife they had a long, serious conversation about the German threat and whether there was going to be a war and whether the Munich treaty had appeased Herr Hitler.

More people had arrived in the meantime greeting Stavros and Neil and making some reference to the chess circle that was going to re start in a couple of weeks after the summer break was over. Stavros said he was looking forward to that and, out of fear that he was going to get involved with more discussions and greetings and small talk, he got up to go. It was now six and felt that Olga would be expecting him home.

'It's a good article,' he told Nellie who was eagerly waiting for his opinion 'but I still think that you should not publish it.'

'Thank you for your opinion, but I will.'

Nellie, strong headed as always, answered immediately.

The two women were sitting on the veranda sipping fresh lemonade. Kyriakou was preparing dinner—egg and lemon soup with bits of chicken, small meatballs and boiled potatoes floating in it.

'You asked me,' Stavros said, 'and I gave you my opinion.'

'Thank you,' said Nellie, 'And I will retain mine.'

Nellie stayed for a week, accompanying Olga every day to her walks by the sea and the two sisters reminisced a great deal about their childhood, about their school years, and shared a great deal of their thoughts about friends, about their mother, about Aristos and above all about the baby that was to arrive in two months. Not once did they mention the article and Olga felt relieved that she did not have to give once again her opinion. She felt that she had now regained her sister. They could now talk and share feelings and thoughts, anything else apart from the article. And Olga felt happy.

On Saturday, Stavros gave Nellie a lift to the coach station where she was to take the coach to Limassol. The two sisters shed some tears when they said goodbye and Olga gave Nellie a tin box full of home-made courabiethes for Thalia and Aristos and some chocolate for Anna.

In the weeks that followed, Olga felt the gap left behind by Nellie's departure and for the first time after her engagement she felt lonely and in need of a female presence, mother or sister, or friend. Her lonely walks on the seafront reminded her of Nellie's absence and she wished Nellie was there with her. Stavros was a big solace for her but lately she had noticed a change in him but she could not say what it was. He was the same Stavros as always, reliable, always knowing what the solution to any problem was—a man she could rely on. And yet…

The truth was that as the months passed by and the momentous event came closer Stavros, who lost his own mother at childbirth, got more nervous and a vague anxiety that he could not name took over him. As a consequence he became more ostensibly cheerful and optimistic about the future, but Olga knew that there was something artificial and exaggerated in this excessive cheerfulness and optimism and this made her nervous. He would get up in the morning whistling a tune, as always, and go into the bathroom singing one of the popular songs at the time, out of tune, as always, Olga thought silently and affectionately. For Olga Stavros' singing had a calming effect, a reassurance that the world was in order. And as Stavros' singing got more frequent and more cheerful, Olga drew a great deal of strength from it. Nevertheless a kind of unease took over her. She wished for a female presence but apart from Kyriakou, who was getting old now and easily tired, there was nobody there. And Olga as always hid her feelings from everybody and carried on.

The day Olga gave birth to her baby, Nellie had her third fit.

Olga had gone into labour the day before—a sunny afternoon in late November. Thalia, Nellie and Anna had all arrived a few days earlier as the time approached and preparations for the momentous event were taking place. Thalia and Anna slept in one room and Nellie shared Kyriakou's room. Kyriakou who had witnessed Olga's, Nellie's and Anna's birth was excited, anxious, worried, restless and kept talking endlessly reminding everybody of those momentous events that everybody had heard about before and Thalia had lived through. Thalia was also restless and anxious and excited but Anna kept her busy with her endless demands as the change of her routine made her more restless. As for Olga, she had to become used to being fussed about and talked about endlessly.

For a week, the women chatting and worrying and reminiscing were dominant in Stavros' household. Stavros' felt evicted from his usually quiet, predictable marital home which was suddenly transformed into a noisy, anxious and unpredictable women's domain, where he, the only male, was an unwanted or redundant presence.

Although the women were acutely aware of his presence and absence, his likes and dislikes and his unquestioned authority as the head of the household and tried endlessly to please him, Stavros felt excluded and utterly ignorant of this momentous event that was about to take place.

Stavros did not like feeling either ignorant or anxious. In fact, he had not much tolerance for either of these feelings, and he was aware that the two were connected. Having made his own way in life single-handed, as he had told everybody, he was proud of his intelligence, knowledge and ability to overcome all the adversities in life. He saw himself as a lone hero, standing alone against the whole world. He also saw himself as the loving, supportive husband whose task was to protect this weak, helpless woman. He saw himself as her rock. He wanted to be her rock—strong, loving, supporting her quietly with his weight, asking for nothing in return. That's what Stavros told himself.

He had lived alone ever since he had finished secondary school and left his village to go to Nicosia. He had since then looked after himself, managing his small income very effectively and managing his emotional needs even more effectively, mainly by denying they existed. He was the ever happy, ever successful, lone boy from Marathasa, the wonder boy.

In London, he was proud for managing on his skimpy grant whereas his friends were relying so much on their rich parents. He knew that he was much more intelligent than all the other students in his year—a mathematical genius, one of his professors had declared, as Stavros showed him, in a show down contest, that there was an alternative way, much simpler, of solving a particular mathematical problem and although it was different from the one the professor had followed, it was equally legitimate.

'I wish you wouldn't do that,' the professor had said to him at the end of this show down contest, as Stavros showed him step by step how he had solved the problem in a radically different way. 'Why can't you stick to the traditional way of doing things?' he asked and then he added in an affectionate way (or at least that was Stavros' memory of it) 'But you have the ingredients of a mathematical genius.' And Stavros repeated this with a chuckle that both covered up and exhibited the excessive pride he felt.

This was an anecdote that Stavros repeated many times to his family later on—to his children as they were growing up and could understand what a mathematical genius was, and to his wife and his wife's family. If Stavros were not such a warm, affable person he would have been an utter bore, repeating always the same things, but nobody thought of Stavros as a bore because his sparkling personality and his always smiling face overshadowed all other traits.

He was still smiling during Olga's last week of pregnancy despite his anxious anticipation, despite his feeling of being ousted from his own house by a bunch of garrulous, know-it-all women, who talked all the time on top of their voices and did not seem to agree on anything although, to Stavros' big relief and as if by miracle, all these disputes ended amicably.

Stavros' anxiety, however, was only partly due to the women's invasion of his marital refuge and claiming Olga to themselves. The biggest part of it had its roots elsewhere—to the fact that his mother had died in childbirth when he was only 18 months. The baby she brought to life died shortly after with her. It was always his complaint that he had no memory of his mother's face, and of course there were no photographs of her. Up in the mountains of Marathasa in 1907 cameras were unknown.

But it was not grief that he experienced the last week of Olga's pregnancy. It was acute anxiety which he experienced as a tightening of his chest so that he could only breathe if he took long deep breaths which had to be repeated again and again as he felt that his lungs were running out of air. When he had a respite from this sensation, it was quickly being replaced by a strong nausea accompanied by severe stomach pains. A fear of an unknown catastrophe filled his brain. He dreamt—a rare event for Stavros—that he was standing on a cliff facing the abyss in front of him. And there was no way back. The sea had risen and had engulfed the cliff.

Stavros had never learnt to swim. Born in the mountains he had not seen the sea until he was eighteen years old and then only for a few hours when he went to Kyrenia with a fellow student from the English School in Nicosia. By then he was deep into studying, learning, earning money and preparing himself for the first opportunity to go to university. No time to learn how to swim. In fact, he ignored the whole thing as he ignored things that were beyond his reach. It was not until he settled down in Limassol that he realised what a handicap this was. Most young men met their future wives at the "municipal baths", as they used to be known, where men and women were able to meet up and chat and have a swim together. Thank God for tennis, he often said to himself.

But in the dream the sea appeared menacing, as the element that would swallow up everything and everybody, like death. And the impending birth felt to him, when he woke up, like another face of this menacing sea that would swallow up his hard-won happiness.

But one day in November the baby arrived, a 7lb healthy boy, and Olga was well, and by the time he was allowed to go in to see her she was holding little Alexandros in her arms, surrounded by Thalia and Nellie and Kyriakou, with Anna behind her mother trying, as always, to articulate something. Stavros felt an instant feeling of relief and the returning of safety. Life as always, he thought with great relief, and looked relieved at Olga who was beaming with happiness. He didn't even look at little Alexandros until Thalia handed him the baby. 'Here Stavro, here is your son.' Stavros looked at the little swaddled thing in Thalia's arms and squirmed. He then took a step back and did not know what to do. Hold the baby? He, a man?

'You hold him Thalia,' he said, 'he is more comfortable in your safe hands,' he added making a joke out of his momentary panic.

'Look Stavro, he is lovely, absolutely gorgeous,' Thalia was now saying.

Stavros was not sure what the whole fuss was about. Was it not enough that Olga was fine and everything had gone well? Nobody was making a fuss of Olga now, he thought. She wasn't even his Olga anymore. She belonged to everybody and above all to this new intruder. It was all about this ugly, crinkled little thing, not yet human, he thought.

But Stavros managed to play his role well. He said that he was proud of his son being born healthy and proud of Olga who had managed so well and he delighted about everything. They all expressed their delight and the women took over with their chit chat about whom the baby looked like, mother, father or grandparents (or was it not like uncle Evagoras who was Thalia's cousin. Thalia and Kyriakou then competed in providing advice about how to look after the baby, how to kick start the breast feeding, which was not always an easy matter, while the new-born was still asleep in his mother's arms. After half hour of chit chat and competing advice, the nurse appeared and announced that the time for visits was over and mother and baby needed to be alone and quiet.

And so it was that they all said their goodbyes to Olga and the baby and went home to celebrate. As the family celebrated the birth of a lovely baby boy after returning from the hospital there was a pandemonium of screams and wishes, tears and laughter. As Stavros, Thalia, Nellie, Anna and Kyriakou returned home to a celebratory dinner which was pre-cooked by Kyriakou and heated up on the stove, and as Stavros raised his glass of commandaria, and Thalia and Nellie followed suite, and Anna tried her best to say 'to Olga and to baby' Nellie had her third fit. The glass fell off her hand and the red wine soiled her cream colour suite and what was by now a well-known sequence of events followed with Nellie on the floor shaking uncontrollably, her eyes disappearing inside the sockets and foam coming out of her mouth. Thalia rushed to get a towel which she stuck into Nellie's mouth while she held her head.

The fit passed after a few minutes and Nellie collapsed into a deep slumber. Thalia and Kyriakou carried Nellie to her bed and covered her carefully. As they knew by now the whole sequence of events they did not call the doctor but kept Nellie's door open and were very mindful of Nellie's every movement or sound which at the moment were none. Stavros who witnessed the event for the first time felt utterly useless. The women seemed to know what to do and he had no idea what was best for Nellie so after he suggested calling the doctor and the women said that it was not necessary, he let the women take over as they had done the last few days. He tried to be out of the way to facilitate the process, but he felt a deep sense of panic, which made him feel humiliated.

The celebrations about the birth of Alexandros had come to an abrupt end and, as Nellie lay asleep and motionless in the next room, they all sat down to a silent, sombre dinner.

Chapter 18
Limassol March 1939

Nellie's Article

It was a sunny morning in March. The sky was a deep blue, as only the sky in March can be, without a single cloud to be seen, clear and translucent. Thalia was busy in the kitchen working with Kyriakou who was now back to Limassol with Thalia making the elaborate moussaka that Aristos loved so much. The preparation took all morning, as each layer of vegetables, potatoes, aubergines, courgettes had to be fried first and then let to drain from excess fat, before it was laid carefully on to the other, previously fried vegetables and potatoes, in the big oven dish, layer by layer, with the fried, seasoned mince right in the middle. The two women worked side by side, the one preparing the mince and the other frying the potatoes, the aubergines and the courgettes. They would exchange information about the price of the vegetables, the availability of fish, especially the red mullet that Aristos loved and was so hard to find these days, about Mrs Evangelia's mother, next door, who came to stay with her daughter for a while to help with the new baby. This inevitably led to a conversation about Alexandros, Olga's baby who was almost four months old now. Olga and Stavros came to stay for a few days at Christmas when Alexandros was just five weeks old and the whole extended family had come to visit and to have a look at "the baby" and to bring their presents and their good wishes. The traditional Christmas lunch took place dominated by the joyously demanding presence of Alexandros and the fuss that all the women made around him and Olga. Now Thalia was counting the days to Easter when Olga and Stavros would come once again to spend a few days with them. She felt a surge of happiness and well-being as she ruminated on this and thought how lucky she was to have such a gorgeous grandson and such a good son-in-law.

For the last four months, Thalia would go to Maroulla's once a week, on Saturday, and would wait patiently for Olga to call. Maroulla and Sotiris were the only people she knew who had a telephone as Sotiris needed it for his business. Stavros and Olga did have a phone as Stavros, being a civil servant, was granted one. So every Saturday afternoon Thalia went to visit Maroulla. They would have their coffee and their home-made biscuits and Thalia would wait for Olga to phone.

'Alexandros is teething,' Thalia told Kyriakou as she began to make the béchamel sauce that would top up the moussaka. 'I think Olga finds it very difficult to breast feed now. He bites so hard!'

The two women laughed.

'Naughty boy,' Kyriakou said and they laughed more.

'It was a problem when I had Nellie,' Thalia said. 'Like Alexandros she teethed very early and she bit hard. I had to give up breastfeeding at six months. I hope this won't happen with Alexandros.'

Thalia was now pouring the milk into the sauce, slowly while she was stirring all the time.

'Maybe that's why Nellie is so different,' She said half joking. 'It's as if she comes from a different family,' she added.

Kyriakou was now laying the mince in the oven dish on top of the courgettes and the aubergines and began to put carefully the rest of the courgettes and the aubergines on top.

They were silent for a while. Anna's typewriter could be heard across the patio. It was an irregular sound as it took Anna some time to hit a key, but sometimes she could hit two or three keys in a row before more silence followed.

The bright red blossoms of the pomegranate tree exploded in the intense sunlight but everybody was too busy to notice. Nellie came out to the patio and blinked in the sunlight. She drew a chair and got immediately absorbed in her book. The two women in the kitchen hardly noticed her presence. Time lingered undisturbed by these changes. Silence was punctuated by bits of conversation and laughter, by Anna's typewriter, or by the stirring of birds on the pomegranate tree. One of Thalia's chickens ventured onto the patio for a moment but finding nothing to eat went back to join the other three chickens at the end of the garden.

Kyriakou came out of the kitchen carrying the big oven dish of moussaka.

'Going to the bakery,' she said to Nellie. 'Do you need anything?'

The bakery was a five minutes' walk away and served not only as a provider of everyday fresh bread but also as a kitchen oven where so many households took their Sunday roast or their moussaka or pistachio macaroni to be baked in the wood burning oven for six grosha.

'No, nothing,' Nellie answered, not raising her head from her book. 'I need nothing,' she whispered to herself.

Kyriakou disappeared with the moussaka which was to be left at the bakery for an hour and be collected at 12.45 when Kyriakou would fetch it and get everything ready for Aristos' arrival at 1.10 and lunch at 1.15.

The street vendor with his mobile greengrocer's stall drawn by a donkey was now announcing his presence outside the house in a loud, annunciatory voice. 'Tomatoes, potatoes, cucumbers, carrots' he called in a singing voice. 'Okra, fresh from the garden, only one oke left. Fresh okra, the first to come can have it,' he added.

Thalia came out of the kitchen. 'Oh okra,' she said quickly removing her pinafore. 'We can have it on Saturday with lamb.'

She rushed to the front door and shouted at the man who was already a few yards away. 'Dimitri, come back. I want to buy some okra.'

The man stopped abruptly and turned around. He was of an indefinite age—forty? Fifty? Sixty?—Thalia never tried to define his age. These country folk were so different, she could not decipher either their age or how they thought. But he was a kind man and she liked him. He was wearing the traditional "vraka", which men of a certain age wore in the mountains—loose trousers, supported by a piece of cloth wrapped around the waist in many folds. The trousers were gathered near the ankles and fitted inside the boots.

'Ah Kyria Thalia'—he smiled his generous smile—'you are lucky. This is my last oke, just three and half grosha.'

Thalia had now caught up with him.

'Aristos is lucky,' she said smiling openly as well. 'He loves okra.'

She took the small green vegetables and examined them with her fingers.

'They don't look that fresh,' she said.

'Are you joking kyria Thalia? Picked them myself this morning.'

'Well they don't look it,' Thalia said.

'You are joking Kyria Thalia, I sold three okes this morning and nobody complained. This is what I am left with.'

'Well,' Thalia said contemplating what to do, 'well, I shall give you three grosha for it. I don't think they are worth three and half.'

'Anything you say kyria,' the man said. 'Three grosha then. But you should know this is just for you.'

Thalia watched him in silence as he tipped the vegetables into her bag. She fished three grosha out of her small purse that was hanging around her neck and gave them to the man.

'Evharisto kyria Thalia. But you should know that I am losing money, but for you anything.'

Thalia went back in the house carrying the bag full of okra.

'I got it for three grosha,' she said to Nellie, 'pretty good.'

It was not clear whether Nellie heard this and chose not to acknowledge it or whether she was so intensely absorbed in her book that she heard nothing. In any case, she gave no indication that she heard anything and Thalia who was used to Nellie being absorbed in her own stuff did not press the issue.

Thalia put the okra in the part of the kitchen that served as a larder and came out onto the patio.

'Let's have a moment's rest,' Thalia said and she drew a chair on the patio. For a few precious moments, everything was still. Thalia shut her eyes and took a deep breath. She had been up since 6.15, feeding the chickens, washing the patio, preparing breakfast. These were the tasks Kyriakou did in the past, but now Kyriakou was pushing sixty-five and her arthritis made her slow and infirm and she found it difficult to cope with all the demands of the household. So Thalia took over these early tasks from her. She was an early riser anyway. But now at 11.30 she knew that she needed a moment's rest.

As she sat there with her eyes shut and the sun dancing shapes and colours in front of her eyes, she thought of her beautiful grandson and smiled. She felt the perfection of the moment and all worries were far away.

The knock on the door was sharp, almost brutal. As Thalia opened her eyes bringing herself back to where she was, Nellie was jumping from the chair and running towards the front door. 'It must be the newspaper,' Thalia said calmly. 'No reason to run.'

Nellie was already opening the door and exchanging a few words with the man at the door.

Thalia heard the front door shut and Nellie screaming with excitement.

'It's here! It's here!'

Thalia's peaceful five minutes were brutally interrupted by Nellie's exuberant cries of joy and triumph.

'At last! At last! It's here. Look!'

She handed Thalia the local newspaper—Sotiris' newspaper, "The Observer"—folded in such a way as to expose "The Rights of Women" by Nellie Aristophanous.

Thalia jumped. Any hope of peace she might have entertained for this morning or for the next few months or years, was suddenly and cruelly crushed.

'Look,' Nellie was saying again, 'Look!'

Thalia looked and looked in disbelief.

'What have you done Nellie?' she managed to say, 'what have you done?'

'I've done a wonderful thing mamma,' Nellie said still in a daze, 'I have broken free. Aren't you happy for me mamma?'

Nellie instinctively knew that the pursuit of happiness is not the lot of freedom fighters and that all she wanted was her share of happiness in this world and that this act of freedom and defiance was going to damage her options. Somewhere, secretly, very secretly she was worried, even scared. But she let none of this knowledge affect her elation.

'It's wonderful mamma,' she repeated, 'I am free, free.'

That everything was going to change from this moment on was clear to Thalia, with the clarity of nightmares, unequivocally, monstrously clear. But the immediate problem was Aristos.

'What about your father?' she managed to say, 'have you even thought of this?'

'Don't worry mum,' she heard Nellie saying. 'I shall handle this. I have thought of everything, just don't contradict me please.'

In the meantime Anna, hearing Nellie's cries emerged from her room and walked to the patio in her uncertain, spasmodic walk.

'Wwwwhat's up?' she asked.

'Oh my God, Panayia mou, what have you done Nellie? What shall we do?' Thalia was saying in a dramatic way that spelled a catastrophe ahead.

'Can ssssomebody ttttell me wwwhat's gggoing on?' Anna's question took a few seconds to form itself. Nellie and Thalia waited. Thalia's tongue was tight. Nellie jumped in.

'It's my article,' she said triumphantly, 'it's here in the Observer.'

'Aaaaah,' said Anna.

Silence followed. Everybody in the family, except for Aristos that is, knew about Nellie's article, but only Stavros had read it and Olga had told Thalia that it was quite provocative and that she should not publish it. But Thalia knew about Nellie's insistence on publishing it despite the whole world. Nevertheless she was hoping against hope that this was not going to happen. She was hoping that Sotiris would come to his senses and decide the last minute against publishing it. But now, now all hope was gone.

Some sparrows were fighting over a piece of bread in the garden and for a while that was the only sound on the patio. When the sparrows flew away, there was only silence.

'Wwwwwhat abbbbout ffffather?'

Anna broke the silence and her question hang in the air and expressed everybody's thoughts.

Nobody said anything. They could hear the grandfather clock ticking away in the hall.

A kind of dread seized Thalia. Their carefree days were over, she thought. This damn article, this Nellie madness, had invaded the morning sunshine and the domestic peaceful ordinariness of their life and all her quiet happiness and turned it into a dark threat without words and without content. A dark menacing cloud of unknown dangers silenced all of them.

When Kyriakou came back from the bakery she came to a cold, silent house. It felt to her as if somebody had died and the people who were left behind had no words to describe their feelings. Thalia told her what had happened in a dramatic, fearful voice and Kyriakou felt immediately the implications that this would have for the whole family and her utterances of 'oh my God' and 'Panayia mou' added to the atmosphere of doom that was already there.

Yet Nellie was delirious with joy and triumph but she chose to go to her room away from the grief- and dread-stricken Thalia who could see only disaster coming out of this. She looked at the printed page and was mesmerised by her name printed there for everybody to see. She felt proud and big like a statue, like an old, ageless sage who had dared to utter some truths and become immortal.

Kyriakou left for the bakery at 12.40 and came back at 12.45 with the freshly baked moussaka. Aristos arrived at 1.10pm as always and as always his first words were 'is lunch ready Thalia?'

'Yes Aristo, coming,' shouted Thalia from the kitchen.

He took his place at the table and slowly unfolded his well pressed linen napkin and waited patiently. Everybody else was rushing around to get everything to the table. Kyriakou brought the salad and went back to fetch the pourghouri (bulgur) cooked in tomato sauce. Thalia brought the moussaka and went back to get the olives and the pickled capers. Nellie brought the bread and the jug of water. Anna, with her slow, spasmodic walk, brought herself.

It all looked as usual which meant that everybody, except Aristos, was rushing around. But for the women this was not an ordinary day. Something so extraordinary had happened and could not be undone. They could all see in front of their eyes Nellie's printed name in the newspaper, there for all to see, declaring war against the good citizens of the island. It filled Thalia with dread and Nellie with a frightened euphoria, a mixture of triumph and fear. Maybe that's how all rebels feel, she thought, every freedom fighter who tried to break free from the gilded cage smothered with love and oppression and the protection of centuries old rules.

Her mother's frightened voice 'what have you done Nellie?' echoed in her ears as well as her own answer 'I've done a wonderful thing mother, I've broken free.'

Thalia began to serve Aristos the moussaka, the bulgur and the salad. He helped himself to bread and olives. Anna was making various noises trying to say something and getting very frustrated but in the end she gave up and waited for her mother to serve her. There was no prayer as Aristos was a self-declared atheist, so everybody dug into their food in silence. Thalia helped Anna to begin eating. Anna could eat by herself as long as the food was not liquid and as long as it did not require the use of a knife. She could use the spoon instead of fork and her mother would be there to help if needed. So now Anna put all her effort into managing to bring the spoon to her mouth and not to spill anything. Silence prevailed.

Kyriakou came in to ask whether everything was all right.

'Yes, thank you Kyriakou,' Thalia said.

And Kyriakou went to sit on the patio and rest for a while.

The sound of knives and forks and human chewing and swallowing followed. Nobody said anything for a while. If Aristos were sensitive enough, he would have noticed that the atmosphere was tense and full of uneasy expectation. But Aristos was too wrapped up in his work worries and his own thoughts to notice anything unusual in the silence.

Kyriakou was back after a while to collect the empty plates and the leftovers and to bring some tangerines and coffee. Aristos was now wiping his mouth with such care and attentiveness that one would be forgiven to think that it was as if he was taking care of a baby—wiping, rubbing, stroking—all in a soft, gentle way.

And then the dreaded question followed.

'Where is the Observer Thalia?' he asked.

This was the time, after lunch, that every Thursday Aristos would have a look at the Observer. He would skim the paper and make a mental note of what he might want to read more thoroughly in the evening. Usually Thalia would place the Observer on a little table next to Aristos' place at the big dinner table and Aristos would skim it while having his coffee, or would carry it to his study to read it there. Unusually the Observer was not there.

Thalia looked at Nellie.

'Do you know where the Observer is Nellie?'

'I am not sure,' Nellie said, 'I think it has not been delivered today.'

'Not been delivered? How is this possible?'

Aristos voice expressed incredulity, impatience and indignation all in one.

Nellie made a gesture with her hands.

'I don't know. The post office is not what it used to be,' Nellie said.

'Not delivered?' Aristos said again. The incredulity expressed in his voice increased. It was as if somebody had told him that the earth had stopped revolving around the sun.

A silence followed and Thalia felt as if she was complicit to a big crime and she was going to be found out at any moment.

'What is this world coming to!'

It was a kind of question but without a question mark and nobody attempted to offer an answer.

'One cannot rely on anybody or anything anymore.'

'Yes it's getting bad,' Thalia said vaguely.

'It might just be late,' Nellie dared to say, 'maybe it will be delivered in the afternoon.'

'Unheard of,' Aristos said, but after a moment he added 'but of course better late than not at all,' he added. 'Let's see.'

And with this the whole subject was dropped, at least for the moment.

Aristos folded his napkin carefully and caressed it with his long, aristocratic fingers—like a pianist's fingers—Marina thought years later as she was examining an old photograph of him—and got up from his chair.

'I shall have my coffee in the study,' he said and Kyriakou ran behind him carrying the coffee.

Kyriakou followed him to the study and placed the coffee on the small carved table next to Aristos big, carved chair with its leather seat. Usually he would retire to his study with coffee and the Observer and for the next twenty minutes he would skim the paper and then it would be time for him to go back to work. But today, how was this possible? Aristos could not understand how his routine could ever be interrupted and who was responsible for this unheard-of occurrence.

'You can't rely on anybody anymore,' he repeated to himself. 'What's the world coming to? I can't recognise this world.'

He settled down with the daily paper that Kyriakou had already placed on the coffee table and proceeded to read about fighting in Spain between communists and fascists, about the controversy that Herr Hitler was causing in Europe and the danger of a new war breaking out. He also read about local news such as deaths, births, weddings and baptisms and one scandalous divorce case.

'What's the world coming to?' he repeated under his breath. A husband divorcing his wife because he caught her with her lover—caught her with her lover? What was the world coming to?

He soon became completely absorbed in this legal case in which the wife argued that she nevertheless loved her husband and did not want a divorce. She wanted her children to grow up within a family, and the husband apparently interrupted her shouting 'you should have thought about this before you jumped into bed with this rascal Casanova?'

'What's the world coming to?' Aristos repeated 'women having lovers and couples exhibiting their dirty linen in public for the whole world to see and be appalled by.'

It was soon 1.50 pm and Aristos folded carefully the paper and made his exit back to work. Nellie and Thalia took one deep breath of relief when they heard the front door shutting behind Aristos.

'Well that was not too bad, was it?' Nellie said to Thalia. 'He will forget it by tomorrow.'

'I am not so sure,' said Thalia, 'not so sure at all.'

Thalia busied herself by helping Kyriakou wash up and clean the kitchen before she helped Anna to the toilet and to washing her hands. It was by now around 2.30pm and the women retired to their room for siesta.

That evening Aristos raised once again the question of the paper. They were all sitting around the dinner table. It was 7pm and the beef and potato soup was served with croutons and salad. Anna had never been able to manage soup by herself so Thalia had to spoon feed her and at the same time try to eat herself.

For a while, only the sound of spoons on the porcelain plates was heard and occasionally Thalia's impatient cry 'keep still Anna'. 'Try to keep still'—an impossible request as Anna could not control her movements.

Suddenly Aristos broke the silence.

'Any news about the Observer?'

'No, nothing,' Nellie said rather too quickly.

'This is most peculiar,' Aristos said.

'The Post office is becoming very unreliable,' Nellie said.

'The whole world is becoming very unreliable,' Aristos said angrily. 'I don't understand anything anymore.'

Another silence followed.

Normally Nellie would have taken her lead from her father and would have said something about Germany and Italy and the rise of fascism and how no country should have sent their athletes to Berlin for the Olympics and that that gave Herr Hitler the wrong signal. But she was too scared to open any subject that might lead in a roundabout way back to the Observer. Despite her apparent defiance of authority Nellie, like everybody in the family, was scared of Aristos. So she remained silent and the meal continued in silence.

A couple of tense days followed when conversation was strained and anxiety high in the Aristos' household. It was not certain whether Aristos noticed anything, but Thalia and Nellie were constantly on their guard. Very little was said during meals and Nellie would disappear into her room immediately after. Kyriakou shared the anxiety and said very little. Anna was her usual self, more interested in the convent life than in the family life, although the feeling of uneasiness rubbed off on her as well.

Two days later Nellie went out to meet her cousins—Maroulla's sisters—for tea and cakes at Limassol's most fashionable patisserie the "Continental". As they settled down on the plush chairs of the Continental her cousins could hardly contain themselves. They had "big news" they said, big exciting news about

Nellie's article. A great deal of giggling followed. 'My God Nellie, you are famous! You have no idea what's happening,' Deana began and Fotini interrupted. 'It's amazing Nellie, you have no idea what's happening at the Gymnasium.'

'Your article,' Deana resumed, 'your article has been explosive.' More giggling followed. Nellie looked from the one to the other and made no sense whatsoever.

The waiter came with a big pot of tea and small porcelain cups and saucers followed by an elegant cake stand full of different cakes and biscuits exquisitely arranged on it. The girls fell silent while this was going on.

Nellie poured the tea and the girls helped themselves to tea and cakes. Among noises of appreciation for the delicious cakes and biscuits the story unfolded. Deana's cousin on her father's side who was still at school, at the Gymnasium for Girls, came yesterday to visit her cousins bringing some "very explosive news".

'You are famous Nellie,' Fotini interrupted 'you are a heroine for these girls.'

Apparently one of the girls at the Gymnasium got hold of a copy of the Observer and the girls were queuing at the toilets to read Nellie's article in secret. The sensation it caused among these adolescent girls was hard to overestimate. The girls were in delirium as if a revolution was happening and they wanted to join it. They formed groups to discuss it and they wanted to send congratulations to Nellie. 'It sounds absolutely amazing,' Fotini said again, 'it's a social phenomenon, a revolution.'

Nellie listened carefully becoming more and more excited and more and more scared. She was so pleased that her article had been read by these girls, who were being educated to the highest classical standards only to disappear eventually as wives and mothers under their husbands' control. Maybe her article will raise questions which will lead to change. On the other hand, she was afraid that things were getting out of control. Apparently the headmistress, Mrs Arsinoe, took notice of these queues and having discovered the cause of this adolescent "hysteria" she confiscated the "dirty" article and forbade the girls to read it. The first "burning of books" was happening here, on this island, Nellie was thinking.

For the first time, Nellie felt a real pang of fear in her stomach as she thought that she might not be able to keep the article secret from her father and her father might discover the existence of it, or even read her article.

'It's fantastic Nellie,' Fotini was now saying, 'you are a heroine for these girls, you are a model, a new type of woman.'

'Sotiris is very excited,' Fotini added, 'he thinks it was the right decision to publish it.'

Nellie's mind was a site of confusion. Thoughts fought with thoughts, excitement with fear, pride with visions of exposure and humiliation. Being a heroine was not so easy after all. The Inquisition was out to get you. She could see Aristos' angry eyes mixed with fear and hurt looking at her. 'What have you done Nellie? Why? Why? Do you want to drag us all down?'

The feeling of having betrayed him was fighting with her excitement of having done it, having done this wonderful thing, having found her voice, having broken free. And Nellie was discovering that being free was not easy and was not necessarily going to make her happy. And she was not sure whether she was up to it after all. Not that all these thoughts were clearly formulated in her mind. She felt confused, anxious and happy all in one.

The rest of the week had a strange calm to it with both Thalia and Nellie avoiding the subject and falling over backwards to be helpful to each other and to please Aristos. Anna continued her laborious typing, making a copy of her "Poems for Jesus" to give to Mother Madeleine for her birthday in a couple of weeks. But Anna also watched silently and experienced to her bones the strange "peace" that reigned over the household. The calm before the storm, she thought as she was trying to coordinate her movements and strike the right key.

Thursday came round again. Aristos had not mentioned the missing newspaper or the article for the whole week. It seemed that nobody mentioned it to him so Nellie and Thalia felt optimistic. Maybe the whole thing would pass without a major crisis and maybe Aristos would not notice anything unusual.

At 11 am on Thursday morning, the postman came as usual and Nellie picked up the paper. Thalia who was in the kitchen preparing the stuffed vine leaves and peeling potatoes heard the knock on the door and asked Nellie whether the Observer had arrived.

'Yes,' said Nellie who was standing on the patio hurriedly and avidly going through the pages. Thalia appeared on the patio wiping her hands on her apron.

'Oh no!' screamed Nellie all of a sudden and buried herself in the paper. Thalia too impatient to wait for Nellie to tell her what was going on she went and stood next to Nellie and read with her the article that she was reading. The title of the article was "We Do Not Want Our Women to Become Messalinas"—

Answer to Nellie Aristophanous' Article, "The Freedom of Women in Love", by Arsinoe Nikiforou, Headmistress of the Gymnasium for Girls, Limassol.

The article began in a crusading spirit. 'Nellie Aristophanous' article published in the Limassol Observer on the…of March constitutes an assault on all decency and morality and is an attempt to corrupt the young generation and the future wives and mothers of our country. The shamelessness with which Miss Aristophanous argues her case of the so called "liberated woman" is astonishing. She advocates freedom for women equal to that of men—that is, freedom for women to dispose of their honour as they like, freedom (or so-called freedom) for young, decent women to throw away any decency and behave like common prostitutes. And more than that—to be proud of it. That shamelessness itself would be elevated into "freedom" and be advocated as something desirable, is shameful in itself. To advocate such abomination is truly astounding. But equally astounding is the decision of a decent paper to publish such muck.'

And a little further down, as if any doubt was left as to the identity of the author of the article, Arsinoe Nikiforou continued: 'That such a shameful article has been written by the granddaughter of the eminent judge who some of us still remember as a wise man, is still more astounding. Miss Aristophanous brings shame on herself and on her family. I call on all decent people of this city to condemn this article with all their heart and mind and the purity of their intelligence. We do not want our women—wives, mothers, daughters—to become Messalinas.'

Nellie and Thalia stood there frozen, unable to speak. Fear went through their bodies as gripped by a huge iron hand. 'Oh Jesus and Mary,' Thalia said. 'What are we going to do?'

'We shall hide it again,' Nellie said. 'Leave it to me.'

'Do you think your father is a complete idiot?' Thalia couldn't help but scream.

'Leave it to me,' Nellie said again.

The next two hours passed with Thalia helping Kyriakou in the kitchen, Anna striking the typewriter and Nellie going through different scenarios of a conversation with her father. But apart from her acute anxiety towards her father Nellie was now incandescent with rage towards Mrs Arsinoe. She was already sketching an Answer to this "narrow minded", "insular", "backward", "Middle Ages mentality", of this woman 'whose mind had shrunk so much through the confines of a repressing society that she could not distinguish black from white, right from wrong, forward from backward.'

As she was sketching the answer in her mind Nellie stopped being scared. Through her anger she had overcome her fear. She was now a fearless Amazon galloping in the midst of narrow-minded people, dominating the scene, fighting real and imaginary foes, fighting for the freedom of women.

Aristos came back at 1.10 as usual and the scene of the previous Thursday was repeated almost verbatim. After the consumption of the stuffed vine leaves and the fried potatoes and the salad and the fruit Aristos asked the dreaded question.

'Where is the Observer?'

'We didn't get it today, papa, God only knows why.'

Nellie tried to be casual with an undertone of impatience towards the unreliable Post office.

'What? Again?'

Aristos sounded incredulous. There was an attempt to control his rage in his voice.

'What are you talking about Nellie? Where is the paper?'

The threat in his voice took Nellie aback. 'Does he know?' she wondered. She tried to sound factual.

'I told you papa. It hasn't been delivered.'

'This is impossible.' Aristos was shouting now. 'This has never happened before.'

Nellie decided not to say anything, implicitly agreeing with him.

'What's going on?' Aristos shouted 'has the world gone mad?'

Nobody said anything.

Thalia got up and collected the plates and Kyriakou brought Aristos' coffee which he took to his study uttering not another word. A feeling of menace spread over the house and when Aristos went to work at 1.50 silence prevailed. Nellie kept in her room and Thalia retired for a siesta but in both their minds was this new situation that had arisen with Mrs Arsinoe's "Answer". Nellie had not bargained for this complication. In her naïve mind, she would publish the article, withhold that particular issue from her father and problem solved. But now this crazy woman, whose mind was as closed to life as a dead person inside a coffin, went to publish an "Answer" (and what a defamatory answer was that). If Nellie answered the whole thing would go on to the third week and how can they explain to Aristos the absence of the Observer?

But things took a turn before the third week. When Aristos arrived that evening his first question was 'has the Observer been delivered?'

'No Aristo,' Thalia said. She felt a pang of guilt and fear as she was forced to lie to cover up for Nellie.

Aristos said nothing. He went straight to his room, changed into more comfortable clothes, took his hat and left the house.

'I am going to see Sotiris' he said as he was closing the door behind him.

Nellie had chosen to be out with friends that afternoon and Anna was at the Convent and had not returned yet. Thalia turned to Kyriakou who was sitting on the patio mending some old socks.

'I am scared Kyriakou,' she said, 'really scared as if some disaster is about to happen.'

'It's not that you haven't tried,' Kyriakou said, 'but Nellie doesn't listen to anybody. She has her own mind and that is that.'

'Yes,' Thalia said, 'she doesn't listen to anybody. She is more stubborn than her dad. But now what? What will happen Kyriakou? What's going to happen?'

Dark thoughts came over Thalia, disasters that the family had never seen before. Shame, excommunications, ostracism, isolation.

Kyriakou who had brought up Thalia and her sisters and brothers and then Olga, Nellie and Anna sighed and crossed herself and could not stop crossing herself 'panayia mou, panayia mou, mother of God, have mercy on us.'

It was obvious that Kyriakou had no solution to the problem and could offer no consolation but that of Mary mother of God. Only God or Mary could avert a disaster now. Thalia knew that this was the truth but hoped against hope that Aristos would not find out and the whole furore would die down.

Thalia spent an hour in the sitting room doing her embroidery silent, alone. Kyriakou was preparing the evening soup in the kitchen. Nellie was out with friends and Anna was at the convent. There was an eerie silence in the house.

The last rays of sun came through the window and lingered on Thalia's greying hair very neatly gathered into a bun. Her beautiful chestnut eyes looked tired, resigned, just waiting for the storm. With Nellie and Anna out she had no distraction, no outlet for her fury, sadness, fear and bewilderment.

She wished Olga was there—her sweet, wise daughter who never put a foot wrong, who never caused trouble, who read the minds of people and talked appropriately, always measuredly, never hurt anybody, never provoked anybody. She wished for Olga's quiet presence, her loving silence.

And Stavros? She wished Stavros was there to weather the storm, to calm down Aristos, to make a joke or two about Mrs Arsinoe, her righteousness, her archaic morality, her absolute values, her narrow mindedness. And then things would be put into perspective perhaps and life would resume again. If only Stavros were there.

But Olga and Stavros were miles away. Olga had rung last week and she discussed the article with Thalia. Olga and Stavros had received the Observer by Post the next day after the Limassol distribution and Olga wanted to know what happened, whether Aristos had found out or whether somebody had told him about it. When Thalia had said 'no, everything had gone according to Nellie's plan' Olga was very relieved. But now this was a new situation, a real crisis as far as Thalia was concerned and she knew that she was right. Thalia could not see how a disaster would be avoided now. Aristos went to see Sotiris and Sotiris was bound to show him the article. Total catastrophe.

She continued with her embroidery—a big table cloth with colourful birds and flowers on the four corners, painstakingly embroidered over many months and many evenings.

At 6.30, everything happened almost simultaneously. Anna came back from the convent in her rocking, spasmodic walk accompanied by two nuns and Thalia rushed to open the door exchanging some niceties with the nuns who then left. Almost Simultaneously Nellie entered excited, full of news from her friends who thought the article "fantastic" and Mrs Arsinoe a narrow minded "witch" and her answer "utter trash". While Nellie and Anna were talking at the same time and Thalia hardly understood a word Aristos came in, red in the face, out of breath, with his eyes full of rage and waving the Observer like a weapon.

'What's this?' he screeched. 'What is this?'

Silence was restored at once. A frozen silence saturated with cold fear spread like a blanket over everybody.

'Will somebody tell me what is happening?'

Nobody volunteered. To be fair Anna tried but failed to go beyond some incomprehensible sounds and some exaggerated spasmodic movements.

'Don't shout,' Thalia said to Aristos, 'you are scaring Anna.'

'I will shout as much as I want.'

Aristos was really shouting now. His voice was thunderous with a hint of hysteria.

'This is my house. This is my family, but I don't seem to have any control over it.'

He was thumping his fist in the air as if he was hitting an imaginary table.

Another icy silence followed. It was now becoming obvious that despite his violent temper Aristos was feeling helpless. He was simply out of his depth. What can a father do when he is ignored, disrespected, disobeyed? Some fathers in the villages, in the mountains (was it true anyway, he didn't know) would have murdered their daughters for such a thing—a daughter who brings shame on her family. But that was in the past, and in the villages in the mountains and who knows whether such stories were true. Others would imprison their daughters or beat them to submission. But Aristos was a civilised man, an educated man who didn't believe in violence of any kind. What can such a man do faced with his daughter's disobedience?

For one awful moment, Thalia thought that he would start crying as he hesitated not knowing what to do. Then he began shouting again.

'You have nothing to say Nellie? Thalia? Nothing? Have you lost your voices?'

They said nothing.

'And you Thalia, knowing about this and saying nothing! You are an accomplice. In a court of law, you would be equally guilty.'

'I told her,' Thalia tried to say, 'I tried to stop her.'

'But you didn't tell me,' Aristos shouted. 'Nobody told me. I was the idiot who knew nothing. Neither you, nor Sotiris, nor Olga, nor Stavros told me anything. You all betrayed me.'

Nellie all of a sudden found her voice.

'How can anybody tell you anything? You terrorise everybody.'

She was now screaming hysterically, out of control.

'You are a tyrant, an old-fashioned tyrant. You don't listen to anybody. You want to silence everybody. I found my voice, papa, I found my voice. I found myself. Nobody will stop me, nobody will silence me neither you, nor Mrs Arsinoe and her ridiculous old-fashioned ideas tied to the Church and the priests and to the power of men.'

Nellie was out of breath—her face red, her eyes burning, her hair loosened on the shoulders she looked like a fury from the underworld. Thalia felt scared that Nellie was going to have another fit, but there was no sign of that. Nellie was robust and sure of herself and she looked, despite everything, very beautiful.

'My child, my child,' Aristos was now saying, 'I want to protect you. The world out there is a jungle. You know nothing about this. People can be horrible to each other, they can be so horrible to you. What will you do with your life? Who will marry you now? And I know I won't be able to protect you.'

Aristos' voice was breaking now. Thalia got worried now.

'Calm down Aristo, your blood pressure will go up. The doctor said you mustn't get excited.'

'Nobody thought about me or my blood pressure, or my health, or my dignity. Nobody thought of me. You all conspired to ruin me. All of you! So stop telling me about my health and that trash. Nobody in this family thought of me. Shame on you all.'

'It's all about you isn't it?' Nellie was shouting again 'All about you. You! Nothing about me and my life and my dignity and what I want to do.'

'This is not fair,' Aristos began his voice breaking again. 'It's unfair Nellie, very unfair. I *am* thinking of you. I want to protect you. I don't agree with your article or your ideas. I think they are despicable, but nevertheless I want to protect you. But you think you know everything. You read a couple of books and you think you know better than anybody else. Your mother has spoiled you with her liberal ideas. Nobody listens to me. You have your own little conspiracies, you women. You think you know everything, but you know nothing. You know nothing of the world.'

'Enough,' Nellie screeched, 'I don't want to hear anything else. I had enough. Enough! Enough!' She raised her hands and covered her ears, the way little children do when they don't want to listen to something. 'I don't want to hear anything anymore.' She was screaming and Aristos and Thalia thought she was going to have a fit. But instead she ran away to her room and slammed the door behind her.

Aristos and Thalia remained motionless, silent, frozen not knowing what else to say. Anna tried in vain to formulate a few words.

***

----Next day was Friday. The day went smoothly enough but an eerie silence reigned over Aristos' household. Everybody seemed to be preoccupied with themselves. Kyriakou who had heard the whole family fight the evening before kept her mouth shut knowing that if Thalia wanted to talk about it she would say something. But Thalia said nothing. Nellie spent the whole morning in her room and feigned a migraine so that she did not have to come to the table at lunchtime. Aristos and Thalia had an almost totally silent lunch interrupted only by Anna's almost incoherent sounds and Kyriakou's comings and goings with food and fruit.

Next day in the afternoon Thalia went to Maroulla's as she had every Saturday afternoon for the last few months to speak to Olga on the phone. She always treasured these calls from Olga keeping her informed of Alexandros' development and Olga's and Stavros' everyday life. She missed her a great deal—her calm, sometimes too quiet but always supportive, always measured presence hovering over the household like a blessing. But now the pain of separation felt acute. Thalia felt terribly alone in a strange, mad and unsupportive world—a world she did not recognise. In one day, everything seemed to have changed—her orderly, predictable world was not there anymore. Everything seemed to have collapsed and she felt that now anything was possible, all kinds of terrors and abominations were possible. It was like an earthquake—the tectonic plates had moved and the tremor was felt in the depths of her being. An uncanny feeling of a terror she had always known but kept at bay had invaded her since the moment when Aristos entered the house on Thursday evening, waving the newspaper like a lethal weapon. And this terror she found impossible to shift. It was not that she knew what she was afraid of. It went beyond 'being afraid of something.' It was sheer dread, without words, without images, a silent, deafening dread.

There were of course words like shame, being ostracised from civilised society, ridiculed, exposed as immoral and Nellie being branded a "loose woman" who brought shame on herself and the family. But thoughts like these were there before Aristos' violent entry into the house on Thursday evening. Now these thoughts were distant. Instead the dread she was experiencing went beyond particular fears. She realised, as she was walking towards Maroulla's house, that this dread had more to do with seeing Aristo's collapse in front of her eyes and realising that Aristos was not the powerful man who had all the answers to all problems, that Aristos had no power over these events, no power to avert this catastrophe, that in fact he was as helpless as she was. Nellie's mad energy— a wild maenad in a small, ordinary bourgeois household—was too much for him.

Her uncontrolled Dionysian madness was unbearable. Aristos was defeated and he blamed Thalia for the defeat and Thalia was terrified and felt she had no defence against this terror.

Arriving at Maroulla's was like a lifeline being thrown at her at the exact moment when she began to feel she was drowning under the weight of her thoughts. Maroulla embraced her and guessed at once the cause of Thalia's distraught expression.

'I shall make us some coffee,' she said immediately walking towards the kitchen. 'I baked a walnut cake today and some biscuits and will have them with coffee. Everything will feel different after some coffee and cake.'

Thalia sat on the sofa and breathed in the aroma of the Turkish coffee as it was prepared and felt for the first time in 48 hours that a weight was lifted off her chest. She could breathe more easily now as she felt embraced by Maroulla's loving voice telling her that everything will be all right. It was like the effect of a mother's voice on a distressed baby and she felt for the first time safe.

'Here we are,' Maroulla said unloading the coffee cups and the cake on the coffee table. 'Zoe and Alexis are out with grandma, so we can talk as much as you like without being interrupted.' The aroma of coffee filled the room and Maroulla busied herself with cutting a big piece of walnut cake and transferring it to a small porcelain plate adorned with flowers and birds and handed it to Thalia.

'Oh Maroulla thank you so much. I feel so wretched.' Thalia was close to tears.

'I know, I know,' Maroulla said. 'This idiotic woman, Mrs Arsinoe. She is well known, you know, for her archaic views and her traditional religious attitude. You need to ignore her Maroulla.'

'How can we? How can we, Maroulla?'

'All progressive people will agree with Nellie,' Maroulla said, 'I have no doubt about this.'

Thalia sipped her coffee and shook her head in disbelief.

'I don't know anything anymore,' she said, 'I don't understand anything.'

'I know, I know,' Maroulla said again. 'It's very hard on you.'

'It's awful,' Thalia said and she was now in tears. 'I haven't known such fear since I was a small child.' The tears ran down her face now and she made no attempt to hide them.

'It will be all right in the end,' Maroulla said. 'It will blow over in a few days. Everybody will forget about it in a couple of months.'

'I doubt it,' Thalia said.

'You must think positively,' Maroulla said. 'Sotiris and I are not the only people who agree with Nellie. All educated and progressive people do. I am sure Olga and Stavros do.'

'Olga was already very worried last week before Mrs Arsinoe unleashed her invective on Nellie,' Thalia said. 'I don't know what to think anymore.'

At that moment, the telephone rang and Maroulla got up to answer it. 'It must be Olga,' she said.

'Yah sou Olga mou,' Thalia heard Maroulla saying, 'how are you and Stavros and the gorgeous Alexandros? You must kiss him from me.'

Olga apparently informed Maroulla that they were all very well and Maroulla passed the receiver to Thalia.

'Mamma is that you?' said Olga and Thalia thought that her voice sounded anxious. 'Mamma how are you?'

'Terrible Olga, terrible.'

'I know mamma but you must not worry, you must not worry mamma.'

'How can I not worry?' Thalia for the first time sounded hysterical, half shouting and half crying. 'How can I not worry? Have you read Mrs Arsinoe's answer to Nellie's article?'

'Yes mamma, yes, we have.'

'And you are telling me not to worry! Don't worry, don't worry. What's going to happen Olga, what's going to happen? What will your father do?'

'He doesn't need to know,' Olga said.

'Olga he does know. He read it on Thursday evening. We tried to hide the paper but he went and found Sotiris.'

'Ah panayia mou!' (Oh blessed Mary!) Olga said and was silent for a moment and then she repeated 'ah panayia mou!'

'I told you it's awful here,' Thalia said. 'You are far away Olga and protected from all this.'

Thalia sounded bitter that her daughter was not there to help her.

'But perhaps this is better,' she said after a while, 'you have the baby to think about and your husband.'

A few seconds of silence followed.

'Shall we talk tomorrow mamma?' Olga said finally 'I think that Stavros has a plan. I need to talk to him and we can talk again tomorrow.'

'A plan? What plan?'

'I am not sure mamma, I shall ring tomorrow. Can you be at Maroulla's again tomorrow at this time?'

'I'll ask Maroulla,' Thalia said.

Of course Maroulla was very welcoming. 'Of course Thalia, of course. I am always happy to see you and I shall see you twice this week, how lovely.'

And so it was arranged that Olga would ring next day at 5pm and Thalia would be there to talk to her.

The evening and the next day, which was Sunday, passed more or less in the same way—silent, cold and menacing. Nellie chose to stay in her room, emerging only when Aristos was not there and retreating back to her room as soon as possible. Aristos went for his usual Sunday walk on the promenade, the only walk of the week, and came back for lunch. Thalia took care of Anna and helped Kyriakou with the daily chores. At lunch, sitting around the lamb roast and the freshly cut salad, nobody referred to the article but Aristos looked like a broken man. He looked almost frail, about 10 years older and as if he was going through bereavement. The deafening silence was truly frightening.

Thalia arrived at Maroulla's at 4.30 and Maroulla offered the compulsory coffee and cakes and the children went in and out disturbing their morose conversation with shrills of delight and excitement.

Olga rang at 5pm exactly and Maroulla picked up the receiver immediately. 'Olga mou here is your mum,' she said and handed the receiver over to Thalia.

Olga came straight to the subject. Stavros did have a plan, she said. He had thought about the whole thing carefully and came to the conclusion that somebody needed to write an "Answer" to Mrs Arsinoe's "Answer" to Nellie's article—an "Answer" in defence of Nellie's ideas. He had said to Olga that somebody needed to take up Nellie's defence and that he was going to publish his article in defence of Nellie under a pseudonym so that it won't look as if only her family defended her.

Thalia had doubts about this plan.

'But people will find out,' she said, 'it will then be worse.'

'Nobody will find out,' Olga said, 'unless you, or Nellie or me or Stavros declared it to the world. And of course we won't.'

And so it was.

The days that followed brought some hope to Thalia which moderated a little the dark, threatening atmosphere of the house. Almost no words were exchanged in the house on Aristotelous Street, except the most necessary ones. Only Anna tried to express herself as always, demanding that nobody would forget her and her needs. Nevertheless both Nellie and Thalia had their own source of hope.

For Nellie, hope lay more in the news that came from the "Gymnasium for Girls" that her cousins transmitted to her. Now that Mrs Arsinoe had entered the battle the girls became difficult to manage. They were so keen to discuss Nellie's article and to defend her ideas that Mrs Arsinoe had to impose special measures that approximated Herr Hitler's burning of the books, as the girls told each other in conspiratorial talks giggling and joking and planning how to get the newspaper without being caught. The Observer became a banned newspaper and girls caught reading it would be expelled at once, Mrs Arsinoe had decreed. This of course made the girls more determined than ever to get hold of it. Bits of Mrs Arsinoe's article were whispered around and made fun of, for instance her phase "corrupting the young", which had echoes of Socrates' trial, the girls thought, as they studied their classics at Mrs Arsinoe's Gymnasium. Nellie's article was now compared to Socrates' teaching, and Socrates' trial, and talked about in conspiratorial exchanges between the girls.

This was also Stavros' argument. In his article, he argued that Nellie's ideas were maliciously and narrowly mis-interpreted and twisted as in Socrates' famous trial in 399 B.C. He added that with this "logic" Mrs Arsinoe 'could prove Plato an idiot and Aristotle an imbecile.' Nellie's ideas were common in enlightened Europe, he continued, which was "light years ahead" of Mrs Arsinoe's archaic and narrow-minded arguments.

Stavros dictated the whole article to Sotiris over the phone. His pseudonym was to be Nestor Kamaratos. The name Nestor evoked the Homeric wise old man of the Iliad. The second name Kamaratos had some sort of Athenian sound to it reminding the people of the island of their roots in Greek culture and of their brothers and sisters in the more enlightened Metropolis.

Only a few years ago the island had rebelled against the British Administration demanding Enosis (union with Greece). The 1931 insurrection was easily put down by the British and the leaders were exiled to Greece. The Democratic Assembly was dissolved and the islanders found themselves worse off than before. The Greek prime minister had called the leaders of the insurrection "political infants". It was obvious that the whole thing had not been thought through and that a power like the British Empire could not be defeated by a few naive idealists from this small island.

The whole thing was ill thought and left the island more isolated than before. Nevertheless it had awakened deep nationalistic feelings lying hidden in the islanders' traumatised psyche going back hundreds, or even thousands of violent history characterised by invasion and subjugation. "Enosis" (union) with "mother Greece" was felt to be a restoration of dignity, a dignity that had been trampled upon for centuries.

Restoration of dignity was also what Stavros' article had achieved for Nellie. Friends began to admit that they had read it and wanted to talk about it. Instead of the awkward silence of the week before, friends were now eager to approach her and speak openly against Mrs Arsinoe, or ridicule her "archaic views" that attempted to prove Plato "an idiot" etc. On the other hand, Nellie encountered a handful of incidents on the street with people she hardly knew who shouted at her "you should be ashamed of yourself" or "you brought shame on your family".

Aristos read Stavros' article and had some hope. He could see how cleverly constructed it was to support ideas that he could not believe that his son-in-law entertained, but he was immensely grateful to him for defending, as Aristos saw it, the "family honour".

And then came the next Thursday and the next issue of the Observer. By now, Thalia was acutely tuned to the arrival of the postman who delivered the Observer around 11 am. When she heard the knock on the door, she rushed and grabbed the paper before Nellie had the chance to lay her hands on it. She quickly skipped the first few pages and came upon two new articles—one by Mrs Arsinoe herself attacking Nestor Kamaratos' despicable article that "defended the indefensible". The second article was by a woman called Melisanthe Aretaiou who was the head of a charity for "fallen" women and who was even more scathing about Nellie's "extremely dangerous" ideas "that strip women of their dignity". Mrs Aretaiou continued by making a comparison between these unfortunate "fallen women" and Nellie's declaration of "freedom in love" for women.

Thalia went white as she was reading this, and had to sit down as she thought she was going to faint. Kyriakou who realised what was going on came with a glass of water.

'Look! Look!' Thalia was hysterical pointing to the page in the paper where the offending article was. Nellie, who appeared out of nowhere, took the paper out of Thalia's hands and ran with it to her room. Thalia collapsed in tears hiding her head in her two hands. Kyriakou had never seen Thalia in this state all these years she had been with her.

'We are ruined,' Thalia was crying, 'ruined. God help us.'

Kyriakou crossed herself.

'Panayia mou kyria Thalia, what are you saying?' she cried. 'God is big.'

'I don't know Kyriakou. I think Nellie has gone too far and God will punish us all.'

When Aristos came and asked for the Observer, she handed the paper, which she had retrieved from Nellie, to him without hesitation. She felt broken.

'What shall we do Aristo, what shall we do?' she repeated 'what shall we do?'

Aristos had his lunch without speaking. Nobody else spoke. After lunch, he retreated to his study and read the two articles by the two women as well as Stavros' article. When he reappeared, his face was a mask of pain, anger and despair. He left for work without a word and the house on Aristotelous Street was steeped in ominous silence. Not even Anna uttered or attempted to utter a word. As for Nellie she left the house at 4.30 taking refuge in her cousins' house.

When Aristos came back that evening, he was a changed man. His face was resolute—angry but resolute.

'I shall defend her,' he told Thalia. 'I don't agree with her views, I detest her views, but I shall defend her. I shall write an answer to these two women and their badly written articles. They are despicable.'

So it was that Aristos began writing under the pseudonym of Socrates X defending his daughter against 'the vicious attacks of the likes of Mrs Arsinoe and Mrs Aretaiou,' that even Aristos felt that they were steeped in a kind of Medieval ideas of good and evil and virtue and sin and above all a vicious hatred against any free thinking.

Aristos evoked Socrates' famous trial once again where the great man with new ideas was condemned to death by an Athenian court led by the masses— "ochlocratia" the Greeks called it meaning the "rule of the mob"—Aristos reminded his readers. The most creative and refined mind of his generation, some say of many future generations, or of all time, was put to death under false accusations and for the sole reason that he had the courage to question ordinary views and think new thoughts. For some people today as always—Aristos did not want to mention any names—thinking was an alien activity and free speech was dangerous. These people preferred to speak (and write) before they think, he added. Society needs thinkers, he wrote, and needs new ideas to be debated not condemned.

Aristos was certainly not one for "new ideas". The words that came out of his pen surprised him as much as everybody who knew the identity of the writer behind Socrates X.

'Socrates, the hero of all thinking people, had the courage,' Aristos continued, 'to question everything. For some people'—again Aristos did not want to mention any names—"questioning is alien and dangerous". 'The blossoming of classical Greek culture was based on this freedom to question,' he added. 'Our hallowed ancestors bestowed on us this gift of free thinking and questioning and we must not trample on it.'

And thus the "war of civilisations" began in the small city of Limassol. Mrs Arsinoe, Mrs Aretaiou and their followers invoked Christian virtues of feminine decorum, the incontestable virtue of virginity, obedience (didn't St Paul say that the woman must obey the man? And wasn't Jesus born of a virgin? etc.). The other side, Stavros, Aristos and others who joined the war of ideas and values, invoked classical Greece, freedom of thought, and freedom to question, and wrote a lot about the vicious and blinkered citizens who condemned Socrates to death for his new, enlightened ideas.

The two roots of modern Greek culture were split apart with an intensity that raged for months and allowed the "Observer" to expand its readership. The girls at the Gymnasium defied all prohibitions and read the articles voraciously. There were rumours, never corroborated, that one of the authors in defence of Nellie's article, somebody writing under the pseudonym "Sappho" was one of the sixth formers at the Gymnasium.

Thalia, Maroulla and Olga got together either on the phone or whenever Olga visited Limassol, like at Easter when she and Stavros and Alexandros came to stay for a few days. They talked about the new articles, and the new situation and what this meant for Nellie's future, as her name was paraded through the paper either as a free spirit or whore, as a courageous innovator or as an advocate of "loose women". Nellie herself relished the new situation. School girls adored her and often stopped her on the promenade to ask her for her autograph or just to congratulate her and say how much it meant for them that she existed and thought and wrote for them. A few people from the local "intelligentsia", a young author called Dimitris Scouros, and some musicians, actors and artists were among her admirers. Others did not greet her, or worse than that hurled rude comments at her as they passed her by on the street, which she usually ignored with dignity or sometimes gave an answer worthy of her father.

As June was slowly drawing towards its close news from Europe made Nellie's article, and the whole furore it caused, look like a little local shower as compared with the heavy clouds that threatened to unleash a storm of immense proportions over Europe. As the world was slowly waking up to the huge arsenal that Herr Hitler had amassed, the question of war, some 20 years after the end of the Great War, loomed menacingly again. Was Herr Hitler planning a war? What would that mean for the island with its British administration? Was the island safe from German invasion?

By June, the newspapers were full of reports and rumours of war being now unavoidable and that nobody could trust Herr Hitler to observe the treaty he signed less than a year ago in Munich to safeguard peace. This referred to Britain's and France's attempts last year to extract a reassurance from Herr Hitler that he did not really mean war, he only played with words (and toy panzers and toy guns and toy soldiers). The islanders were reminded of the talks between Germany, France, Britain and Italy that culminated in the Munich agreement that allowed Herr Hitler to annex the Sudeten region of Czechoslovakia. The islanders had then read with trepidation how the Allies were prepared to sacrifice the sovereignty of another country—Czechoslovakia—to secure peace for themselves. And now? Almost a year later the world was holding its breath as Herr Hitler was mobilising his troops.

Endless discussions followed in Cafes and in private homes, on the street and at the office about the Munich Agreement, what it meant, was war to be avoided, could one believe Herr Hitler etc. So, slowly and without anybody noticing, except for Nellie's family, the furore about Nellie's article died down. No threatened lynching, no witch hunting or burning, no excommunications, or ostracisms. Nellie's article was slowly forgotten, being relegated to insignificance, as the threat of a much bigger catastrophe loomed at the background.

Nevertheless some echoes from the article were left behind. The young "Sappho", who was obviously deeply affected by Nellie's article, as Nellie found out a few years later, proceeded to study English Literature in London, eventually becoming a professor and a well-known feminist at a British university a few decades later.

Aristos was deeply affected by the experience. The shock of having a rebellious daughter, the shock of having a "sexual" daughter, as well as the shock of having a daughter who spoke her mind stayed with him. Then it was the shock of defending her and more than that, the shock of actually taking pleasure in doing so, in discovering the side of himself that took pride in having a daughter who had a mind of her own and who was feisty enough to declare it to everybody who cared to listen or read. Whenever he caught himself taking pride in his daughter, he quickly retreated into an angry silence, as if Nellie had caused more than a family crisis, but a deeply personal one.

Thalia, surprisingly for her, was more angry and more depressed than Aristos. Lacking Aristos' outlet of being able to defend Nellie, Thalia felt completely helpless. She found an outlet in discussing the matter with Maroulla and Olga but this did not alleviate her feelings of depression and doom. She felt that Nellie had jettisoned her chances of ever getting married and having children. Even people who were sympathetic to her and her ideas would not dare to go against public opinion or the opinion of their extended family. Nellie was doomed, Thalia thought, and the worst thing was that she did not know it. She basked in her ephemeral glory and enjoyed the furore. But Thalia could see beyond it and she could see the lonely years that extended indefinitely for Nellie long after she and Aristos were gone, and Anna was taken in by the nuns to be looked after, as the plan had always been.

As for Olga she was absorbed in her newly found happiness and her daily routine of taking care of Alexandros and keeping house for Stavros and herself. Her own happiness felt complete. Only in the evenings when she and Stavros sat on the veranda and he drank his usual brandy sour which he insisted on preparing himself, and she did her embroidery as little Alexandros lay asleep like an angel in the room next to them, only then with the distant sound of the sea and the silence that surrounded them, only then the thoughts came, her worry about Nellie and what the future held for her. But she quickly dispersed her thoughts as Stavros began to tell her about his day at work, what this or that engineer said to him, or what he said to them, and which bridge or road needed to be repaired or upgraded and what the Government's plans were for the development of the regional roads, and who invited them for lunch or dinner or when and in whose house the next chess club party was going to take place. Olga immersed herself in Stavros' "news" and her personal worries dispersed and their bright future together shone in front of her.

So despite the black clouds that were spreading over Europe the Aristos' family became more relaxed as if the threat of war gave this family a bit of breathing space. And maybe even more importantly the Observer began to be dominated by more important local news, first about the local elections and then the newly elected mayor's inaugural speech where he promised to improve the promenade and the surrounding area so that Limassol's seafront 'would be comparable to any modern Mediterranean city, like Monte Carlo.' The new cinema that was to be erected in the heart of Limassol was attracting a great deal of interest and enthusiasm. The Observer was full of comments of how much pleasure it was going to give to the good citizens of this very "adventurous" city. The improved quality of the local wine, was also given a great deal of attention and the Observer commented that 'it could be favourably compared to any French or Italian red wine.' The new weddings and funerals, engagements and christenings took central place as usual, and so was the building of a new big hotel in the heart of Limassol. Thalia was immensely relieved by the waning interest in Nellie's article and she and Kyriakou devoted a great deal of their time to the preparations for Olga's and Stavros' and little Alexandros' pending arrival late in August.

Chapter 19
Platres August–September 1939

It was the end of August of 1939 and the storm that had been threatening to be unleashed over Europe for months had reached a critical phase. The whole world held its breath as the great powers talked and talked and achieved nothing of substance. The question in everybody's lips and in everybody's mind was whether another war was now unavoidable. All the attempts of Britain and France to appease Herr Hitler came to no more than a piece of paper which the British Prime Minister Neville Chamberlain waved at his own people like a trophy upon arriving back to London after the Munich Conference. This was a year ago and more and more people were saying that the Munich treaty was not worth the paper it was written on. One could have written one's shopping list at the back of it and after the shopping was done one could have thrown it to the dustbin of history.

Nellie's article had been long forgotten except for a couple of vindictive women who would refer to it within other articles and other contexts. And of course there were the few men and women who agreed with it and made it the bible of their lives. But now bigger issues and bigger catastrophes were threatening the world as the biggest army Europe had ever seen was about to invade another country. The preparations of the German army to invade Poland were under way and Britain and France had sent an ultimatum to Herr Hitler: invade Poland and you are at war with Britain and France. A deafening silence followed and Europe held its breath.

The island was a long way from Western Europe where the big drama was unfolding. Although a British colony and theoretically under threat were a war to be declared, the peaceful and peace-loving islanders went on in their usual way ignoring external events and going on living their narrow lives full of family events, of loving and hating and gossiping and talking, especially talking. The alarming news from Western Europe was a topic for endless conversations and discussions and debates, but nobody lost any sleep about it. People went about their lives as they always did, in a slow somnambulant way more concerned with the heat and how much longer would it last, and how much worse it was than last year, than about Herr Hitler and his plans.

It was at this time that Stavros had decided to take his family to visit his dear friend Yiorgos at Platres. He planned the trip for months and he had asked for annual leave three months in advance, the first leave since he began working for the civil service. He had been very excited with the idea and now he was not going to allow Herr Hitler to spoil it. He wanted to give his friend a surprise, but as he had had no communication with him since that day five years ago when they said goodbye, Stavros wanted to find out whether Stavros was still alive and whether the hotel still existed. So he rang the hotel and when Yiorgos answered the phone Stavros made a booking in the name of one Mr and Mrs Theodorou and their baby, and another single room for their nanny, giving no clue to Yiorgos as to the real identity of the visitors.

It was characteristic of Stavros that he could cut off from his loved ones so totally that he would forget about them for long periods of time. Since he left Platres he had written to Yiorgos only once to thank him for his help and generosity and to let him know that things were going well for him and that he got the job as an engineer in charge of the completion of the Church of the Holy Trinity and that other jobs were forthcoming. After that, it had never occurred to him to contact Yiorgos or to invite him to his wedding, or even to let him know that he was now married with a beautiful baby. But now settled and happy with his wife and child, he wanted to visit his friend and thank him for those weeks five years ago. He remembered those weeks with Yiorgos and their evenings on the veranda talking about ancient Greek history and philosophy with great affection. They were lifesaving for him, he often thought, but never found it important to contact Yiorgos. Until now, that is.

The more he thought about this trip, the more enthusiastic he got. He bought a new, state of the art, radio for Yiorgos so that he could listen to the BBC World Service and tried to imagine Yiorgos' surprise when he recognised Stavros. So, full of enthusiasm for this re-union, and full of a sense of adventure in testing his new Austen on the mountains of Troodos, Stavros and Olga with Alexandros and Kyriakou left Paphos for Limassol.

The Aristos family was reunited once again with screams of delight and hugs and kisses. They spent a few days telling endless stories and cooking delicious meals, and in the evening they all sat on the veranda, the two men with the addition of Sotiris and sometimes Dimitris who came to see Stavros, exchanged their views about the world situation and the very real possibility of war, while the women entertained each other with endless stories from the life in Limassol and Paphos while participating every now and then to the war discussions, as if they did not trust their men to solve the world problems alone. Thalia would come and go, bringing refreshments, cakes, fruit and drinks.

A few days later, on the 31st August, Stavros and Olga, with Alexandros and Kyriakou at the back of the Austen, set off for their trip to Platres. Aristos was very sceptical of this "long and hazardous" trip by car to Platres. 'And what will you do if the car breaks down?' he asked Stavros provocatively. 'In the middle of nowhere with two women and a baby, what will you do?'

Thalia had different anxious thoughts about the cliffs and carapaces and the gaping ravines and the narrow, dangerous road. 'Panayia mou, Panayia mou,' she crossed herself appealing to the Virgin Mary to protect her daughter and her family. 'What is this crazy idea,' she kept saying, 'to travel on this dangerous road with a small baby. God help,' she added. Kyriakou followed soon by crossing herself and appealing to the Virgin Mary to protect them.

But Stavros was not to be dissuaded, and Olga became very adventurous once she joined up with Stavros. 'It will be all right,' she reassured her mother. 'You have to trust Stavros, he knows what he is doing.' Olga's trust of her husband was absolute and the timid and unadventurous Olga would change into the woman who would follow her husband to the end of the world. 'It will be very exciting,' she added. 'So many people are doing it now, mamma, it's a common thing now, it's not a big dangerous thing' as it used to be.

Despite Stavros' and Olga's reassurance the trip to the Troodos' mountains was not an easy one for the Austen which, as they ascended higher on the winding, narrow roads, began to puff and moan and kick and, as they approached the 600 metres height, it began to overheat. To make things worse Alexandros woke up and began to whine, slowly increasing the volume until the whining became howling and, despite Olga's and Katinou's attempts to calm him down by offering him biscuits and toys and of course his dummy, he continued howling at the top of his voice.

'We need to stop Stavro,' Olga said, 'we all need a rest.'

They had been travelling for more than two hours on a steep, winding road that was now revealing a big ravine on the left where vines and olive trees were growing. The view was breath-taking but the passengers of the Austen were too tired and too dizzy by the constant twists and turns of the road to appreciate it. The midday heat began to build up. And Alexandros continued to howl.

'We must all have a rest,' Olga repeated 'you as well,' she told Stavros.

'We must find a suitable spot to stop, a café perhaps.' Stavros was wiping the sweat off his forehead. All of a sudden the heat felt unbearable despite the 600 metres height they had reached. 'We all need a drink,' he added 'but also I must put some water in the car but first the engine will need to cool down.'

So accompanied by Alexandros' distressed howling and Olga's and Kyriakou's endless attempts to calm him down they travelled for another few miles on the steep winding road. Finally the car slowed down and they turned into the dusty courtyard of a country café.

'We shall stop here for a couple of hours' Stavros announced. 'This is the famous "Oak of Lania" or otherwise "the royal oak",' Stavros announced.

He stopped the car and everybody got out, Kyriakou holding Alexandros. Stavros opened the bonnet and left it open for the engine to cool down. The three, with Alexandros in Kyriakou's arms, walked towards the tables which were laid out in the courtyard. A huge oak tree, that spread its branches and foliage over the whole courtyard, welcomed them "with open arms", Olga thought. Alexandros, as if by magic, had stopped howling and was looking around with great interest. A cool breeze from the surrounding mountains made the temperature bearable, almost pleasant.

'This is the famous Royal Oak,' Stavros said again pointing at the immense proportions of the tree. 'They say it's four hundred years old. Some say one thousand years, but who knows!'

Everybody looked at the trunk that three people with outstretched arms could just about embrace. A narrow, wooden staircase led to a platform that was supported by the strong, heavy branches.

'It's part of the Café,' Stavros said pointing to the tables and chairs on the platform, high up on the tree. 'Some people choose to drink their coffee up there.'

Alexandros' eyes followed his father's index finger and made a sound that one could construe as an attempt to say "there".

'When you are bigger Alexi we shall climb together up there,' Stavros said.

Alexandros made some gooey sounds of pleasure and excitement kicking his legs and waving his arms.

'But for now the tables down here are perfectly OK,' Olga said and pointed to the tables on the ground.

Again Alexandros made an excited sound that with a bit of creative imagination could be understood as "here".

They sat under the rich shade of the oak tree and the café owner, smiling and gesticulating, with a tea towel over his shoulder, appeared to welcome them.

'Welcome, welcome,' he said in a self-important tone, 'welcome to this historic spot, welcome to our ancient oak tree. Some say it's one thousand years old but maybe this is an exaggeration. Others say it's five hundred years old. But who knows!'

'It's a phenomenon,' Stavros said. 'It's extraordinary.'

'It's a beauty,' Olga said.

'Yes it's all this and more,' the café owner said. 'It's our pride.'

Kyriakou said nothing being busy with Alexandros who wanted to leave her lap and crawl on the floor. A battle between her and Alexandros ensued, and he protested loud and clear. She looked into her bag for Alexandros' bottle of juice, while the café owner took his time with enquiries, where they were coming from, and where they were going, completely ignoring the drama that was unfolding between the women and Alexandros, as Olga joined Kyriakou trying to calm her son down.

'It's a good machine you have there,' the café owner said pointing to the Austen. 'Are you coming a long way?'

'We are coming from Limassol today as my in-laws live there,' Stavros said, 'but we live in Paphos.'

'Ah Limassol,' the café owner sounded almost dreamy. 'A lovely, beautiful city. My nephew lives there, a very lovely city, full of clever people.'

'Yes, lovely and lively,' Stavros said. 'But it's a long journey to Platres and the machine is tired,' he added pointing to the Austen that was standing in the shade with the bonnet open, exposed to the cool breeze. 'It needs some rest.'

'Yes, clever machines aren't they? I still remember horse drawn coaches making it to Platres, or just donkeys. Often people just walked. They all used to stop here to eat and drink and rest and feed their animals and admire the oak. But this was another world,' he added. 'We now have cars and buses.'

'Yes, another world,' Stavros said and a vision of his small village crouched in the valley between the mountains flashed through his mind.

'It's a lovely place you have here,' Stavros said, 'and this tree, what a treasure!'

'Yes,' the man said, 'it's a beauty and a treasure. They come from all over the island to see it.'

'But now we are hungry, famished actually.' Stavros remembered suddenly, 'time to eat. What did you cook today?'

'Louvi (black eyed beans) with white marrow,' he said, 'delicious fresh louvi, picked this morning from my cousin's vegetable plot. But if you don't like it I can make some eggs and chips or grill a pork chop.'

'No, louvi is excellent,' Stavros decided for everybody and then on a second thought he turned to the women 'or would you like anything else?'

'No, that's fine,' they both answered almost in unison.

'Louvi then,' said the café owner. 'Shall I open a can of tuna to go with it?'

'No thank you,' Olga intervened. 'We have brought with us some meatballs and a potato salad, is it OK if we have it with the louvi'

'Of course kyria, whatever you like,' the café owner replied with genuine warmth.

'But can you make a salad for us' Stavros asked 'and also bring some olives and a big onion?'

'Of course, of course, no problem.'

'Can you make a soft-boiled egg for the baby, a beer for my husband and some cold water for us,' Olga intervened.

'Of course, of course.'

The café owner disappeared inside his hutch of a café. Alexandros began to whimper and Olga took a biscuit from her bag and gave it to him. 'Your egg will be ready soon,' she said. Katinou began to unpack the food they had brought with them. She began to unpack the mashed potatoes she had packed for Alexandros and the meatballs and the potato salad they had brought for the adults.

The huge tree was rustling and whispering and the cool breeze was a welcome contrast to the hot, stifling air of Paphos and Limassol. Olga took Alexandros from Kyriakou's lap onto her own and gave him his bottle of fruit juice. He settled down in his mother's lap and instantly became engrossed in this new activity. The man came out carrying a beer and a jug of water and glasses and he then disappeared inside his hutch. Refreshed by the cool fluid inside their bodies Stavros and Olga and Kyriakou looked around. Red and yellow and orange zinnias splashed their colours against the deep green of the reeds on the one side and the proud, aristocratic dahlias emerged with softer pastel colours on the other. The sound of gurgling water could be heard behind the reeds. Behind them the mountains rose high and haughty. It was a half way station between the green, imposing mountains and the scorched plains of Limassol.

Olga felt a deep relaxation spreading through her body, a feeling she had not felt since her years at Aristotelous Street, when she would, at times, sit quietly with her mother on the veranda, on summer evenings as dusk was falling and the street would fall silent for a few minutes and Aristos shut in his study was deep into his reading of Plato. A precious time as Nellie and Anna and Kyriakou would happen to be out all at the same time and she and mother would share the deep silence of the evening. It could be a few minutes or an hour but Olga treasured these moments and kept them intact in her mind.

Stavros was also silent sipping contentedly at his beer. Katinou had shut her eyes and seemed to be resting, if not sleeping. Alexandros nibbled at his biscuit and sucked at his bottle with eyes half shut. He was the only one who made some noise, babbling gently to himself.

After some ten silent minutes, the café owner who had previously introduced himself as Vasilis entered with Alexandros' soft-boiled egg and the big village salad that they had ordered. Stavros ordered another beer and Olga looked at him with disbelief. 'Another beer?' she asked obviously disapproving of this indulgence. Stavros made a joke that women always wanted to interfere into men's affairs and the man laughed agreeing with him. Olga took the hint and said no more. There was nothing that Stavros hated more than to be told what to do or not to do, especially by a woman.

She began unpacking Kyriakou's packed lunch of meatballs, stuffed vine leaves and potato salad, while the man came back with a pot of fresh louvi and white marrow. Stavros began immediately to gulp down large quantities of food while at the same time expressing his appreciation for the food. Alexandros sitting on Olga's lap made noises of impatience as she began to prepare his lunch of mashed potatoes mixed with the soft-boiled egg and some bits of meatballs. She began to feed them into his mouth while at the same time she tried to eat herself. This was the moment when Stavros chose to exercise his paternal function by clicking the button of the newly acquired camera that was the pride of the family. They no longer needed a photographer to capture the precious moments and keep them for ever for children and grandchildren to see and wonder, he told them. He, with his magic box, could perform the same trick.

Marina who was sitting on Nellie's bed with the photographs spread out all around her, picked up this picture of her mother and her brother deeply involved with each other on the foothills of the Troodos mountains that were vaguely visible at the background, and the branches of the four hundred years old oak tree that she still remembered from her childhood, and Vasilis visible at the back, with a kitchen towel over his left shoulder and the dahlias and rushes and reeds. For a few moments, her eyes were captivated by this fading image, her mother, her brother, Kyriakou. Her mind transfixed in time, a time before her existence. Time stood still. Now. Then. Her mind perplexed. Mind and time and absence and images. Present and past and future. She then went on reading her mother's diaries.

Olga had now finished feeding Alexandros and had managed to have some food herself and Kyriakou picked him up and went inside to wash him and change him. Stavros who had finished his lunch as well, asked for a coffee for himself and for the two women. One metrio and two sweet, he shouted at Vasilis who was at the other end of the courtyard. Vasilis waved and disappeared inside the café once again.

They drank their coffee and read the newspapers lying on the deck chairs that the café had provided for an ad hog siesta. They felt tired and content. Kyriakou was the first to fall asleep. Alexandros firmly established in his mother's arms was drowsy and very quiet, his eyes getting smaller and smaller until he eventually fell into a deep, soundless sleep. Olga's eyes shut as well and she sank into a dreamless, deep sleep.

Stavros watched the whole scene fascinated but also disturbed. His state of mind was a complex one. On the one hand, he loved watching Olga and his son deeply involved with each other while he was ignored and side-lined. A mother-son love affair that made him redundant. That was how it was meant to be, he thought. He tried to remember his mother tried to feel what Alexandros was feeling being perched in his mother's lap, but he couldn't. Alexandros was now 10 months old and Stavros had lost his mother when he was 18 months—a mother he had no memory of whatsoever, let alone a photograph of her. She was a figure who appeared in his dreams as a goddess of love, Mary the mother of God, a warm presence in his whole body that made him feel safe and loved. Eight more months to go, Stavros thought, and then we are in uncharted waters. His thoughts surprised him. He was not sure what he meant but one thing he knew was how deeply disturbed he felt by the whole thing of mothers and sons.

His love and warmth for both was battling with his anger and envy. It was as if he had been forgotten, relegated to the status of a bystander, an irrelevant observer. He who had been central to Olga's life and mind and love he was now second. First and foremost was this little, inarticulate thing, this baby Prince that commanded attention, love, warmth, cuddles, changing and feeding, talking to, singing to. Everything was regulated according to his needs. His Majesty the Baby, Stavros thought, and he tried to remember where he had heard this phrase, but it was so true, so true Stavros lamented to himself even if he could not remember who said it. This endless attention got on his nerves, this endless love affair between mother and baby. It was like witnessing adultery in front of his eyes, except that the culprits did not try to hide what they were doing. On the contrary, they exposed themselves for everybody to see and admire and envy. This perfect couple.

Not that Alexandros did not try to approach his father. In fact, he had begun to show an intense interest in him, trying to talk to him making some incoherent babbling sounds, but one word or sound predominated—da-da. And Alexandros' big, open smile welcomed Stavros when he came back from work, and Olga with Alexandros in her arms would be there to open the door and Alexandros' arms and legs would push and kick in excitement. But Stavros felt this deficiency in himself, a kind of father deficiency. He had no idea how to interact with his son. He would smile and laugh and say something like "here is the big man" but after this he would hand Alexandros over to his mother and would retire to his study or ask whether dinner was ready, or go and change into his informal clothes. This father deficiency he experienced much more acutely than the zero memory of his mother, and that made him sad.

Stavros put the newspaper down and shut his eyes. For the last five minutes, he had not read a single line. The letters became little people who taunted him, forcing these abominable thoughts into his mind. Hating his own child, the child he adored—what an abomination.

He folded his newspaper and drew his deck chair closer to Olga and Alexandros so that he could feel more included in their exclusive dyad. The heat was now intense, only moderated by the light breeze that stirred the ancient oak tree and rustled the walnut and apple trees in the surrounding orchards. The gurgling of the water from the invisible brook continued unabated. He closed his eyes and fell immediately asleep.

Both Stavros and Olga woke up abruptly by men's loud voices—a lively conversation between men, arguing, agreeing, disagreeing, agreeing again, shouting, laughing. Kyriakou was still fast asleep snoring quite loudly. And Alexandros was also fast asleep, not seeming to hear or mind the loud, laddish voices. Stavros looked around.

Around the table, at the end of the courtyard, sat four men drinking coffee and shouting at each other. One of them was much older than the other three, and was dressed in the traditional "vraka". The other three were dressed in a more ordinary way wearing trousers and shirts. Stavros could make out that they were deeply and excitedly involved in a discussion about the possibility of war. Disagreements followed. Did Herr Hitler really mean it? Were the Germans bluffing? Were the English the real warmongers? Mr Churchill for instance? It was obvious that the anti-English sentiment was as high as the anti-German, or at least opinion was divided and a heated discussion followed. Vasilis came to join them and the disagreements rose and ebbed again and again. On another table, two men played gammon in contrasting silence. The throw of the dice and the click of the pieces on the board as they were moved around were the only sounds coming from this table as the two men concentrated on the game with a seriousness that was worthy of two generals moving their armies on an imaginary plain.

It was now 4.30 in the afternoon and the breeze got stronger and the shadows on the mountains longer. Stavros ordered a metrio for himself and a sweet coffee accompanied with a traditional almond sweet for Olga. Kyriakou was still asleep and Alexandros was just waking up. He opened his eyes and the first person he saw was Stavros and he gave him a big smile.

'You little rascal,' Stavros said affectionately and smiled back. Alexandros began to babble da-da and giggle and Stavros' love for his son overwhelmed him. Father and son became engaged in a giggling and babbling game for a while until the coffee and the almond sweet arrived. Kyriakou woke up and joined them and Stavros ordered another coffee and almond sweet. The men at the distant table were now laughing at some joke one of them had told.

They got going around 5 o'clock after they had one more coffee and after Stavros put water in the engine and made sure that the temperature was back to normal.

'We shall be there in about an hour,' Stavros said as they were leaving behind the vineyards and the orchards and the pine forest extended in front of them in all directions. The air was becoming cooler and a strong smell of resin entered their nostrils. The Austen puffed and groaned as the road became steeper with each turn. The mountain peaks appeared closer and closer as the sun disappeared behind them.

'We are not far off now,' Stavros said.

'Shall we stop and buy something for Mr Yiorgo?' Olga suggested as they were driving through a village square where the villagers sold fruit and vegetables, and local produce.

'If you think so,' Stavros said, 'but have in mind that he will have everything he needs,' he added.

'That's not the point Stavro,' she said, 'a little present is always welcome. Of course I have my mother's walnut cake but I want to give him something local.'

They got out of the car, Stavros whispering under his breath 'women(!) We'll never get there if we go on like this,' but he said nothing to Olga. Katinou took Alexandros in her arms and he got immediately excited with all that was going on. The place was teaming with activity—people looking, people haggling, people talking, laughing, quarrelling, discussing, fingering the goods, trying to decide on their quality. There were fruit and veg and almonds and walnuts and raisins and olives and homemade jams and crystallised fruit in jars and the traditional grape juice and flour sweets hanging like sausages from the top of the stalls. All this side by side with tablecloths with elaborate embroidery, leather goods and children's wooden toys. Olga bought a jar of crystallised green walnuts in syrup, and some baklava.

They got into the car again and the arduous uphill journey towards Platres began again. In the last few miles to Platres, the road became much steeper and the bends more dangerous. Olga remembered her parents' premonition and became nervous as the Austen began to groan and kick and threatened to put an abrupt end to the whole adventure. As the gradient increased the noise from the engine became more threatening and Stavros suggested they took a short break. They stopped at a roadside clearing and got out of the car to wait for the car to cool down. It was now 6 o'clock and the forest that surrounded them was getting dark, as the shadow from the mountain opposite fell on it. The tops of the trees were still basking in the sun adding a strange contrast to the growing darkness below. Suddenly out of the silence a flock of sparrows began to chatter and flutter restlessly. It sounded as if a big quarrel had broken out among these small feathered creatures that went on and on. Then as suddenly as they had begun, they became silent again. In the distance, the sound of water went on undisturbed.

It was 6.30 in the evening when they finally arrived at Yiorgos' hotel, thirty minutes out of schedule, not a mean feat, Stavros reminded himself and Olga. Alexandros was restless and grizzling and Olga thought that he was on the brink of a major outburst of howling, but as the car stopped so did Alexandros who, sensing a change of scene, looked around with big, curious eyes.

In the meantime Yiorgos, having heard the car stopping outside the hotel and expecting Mr and Mrs Theodorou and their son and their nanny, came out to welcome these unknown visitors. What followed was what the visitors, but not the hosts, expected to happen. Exclamations, embraces, kisses, Katina rushing down the steps with alarming haste to embrace Stavros. Introductions, 'my wife, my son Alexandros and this is Kyriakou who is a real treasure, our guarding angel!' Kyriakou laughed and embraced everybody. Tears and blessings were abundant. God and Virgin Mary were evoked by both Katina and Kyriakou, and phrases like 'I thought I'd never see you again Kyrie Stavro' came to Katina's lips many times over. 'And married with child and with a car. I always said you will go a long way.'

'Stavro,' said Yiorgos, 'you and your family are the most welcome guests here, much more welcome that Mr and Mrs Theodorou!'

They laughed heartily and Katina showed them to their rooms, and Kyriakou picked up Alexandros and went to the bathroom where she could wash and change him. Olga lay down on the bed to have a short rest, and Stavros had a quick wash himself and went to find Yiorgos on the veranda. Dusk was falling as they sat down with a glass of brandy sour that Katina had made for them accompanied by some home roasted almonds. The forest was slowly getting dark, breathing quietly. The birds were falling silent and out of the growing darkness the hotel looked like a little light oasis, a refuge from the deep, black otherness of the forest.

Katina came and went several times bringing small plates full of meze—two types of olives, pickled artichoke hearts, some feta, some fried chicken liver, some fois gras. The two men drank and ate heartily.

'I am more pleased to see you than to see my sister or my daughter,' Yiorgos said, 'you are like a son to me Stavro.'

'You have been like a father to me,' Stavros said, 'I don't know where I would be now, had I not met you five years ago.'

'You would be where you are now,' Yiorgos said. 'You are an exceptional man Stavro. You would succeed whatever you undertake.'

'You are very kind Yiorgo,' Stavros said.

Katina approached with some grilled halloumi and with a bowl of freshly roasted peanuts and put them on the table next to the other delicacies.

'Trahanas will be ready soon,' she said. 'I hope you like trahanas Stavro. And after that there is steak and chips. I hope you like our menu.'

'Please don't make anything extra for us,' Stavros said. 'Trahanas is fine Katina, we all love it even Alexandros, and steak is not necessary.'

'You must be hungry Mr Stavro after the long journey from Limassol,' Kyriakou said, 'you need a good dinner.' And she added 'I am waiting to meet your wife properly, and your little boy. He looks gorgeous.' Katina took some of the empty dishes and left.

'I have been intending to visit you for years' Stavros said and he deeply believed that this was true. 'It's been on my mind ever since I left in a hurry to do that dome job. This is like a pilgrimage for me.'

'God bless you,' Yiorgos said, 'and this from an atheist,' he added.

They laughed and were quiet sipping their brandy.

The silence of the mountains enveloped them. A lonely owl cried out from somewhere in the forest.

'To us' Stavros raised his glass.

'To us' Yiorgos repeated. 'And to your beautiful family,' he added.

As if responding to the toast Olga appeared refreshed and rested carrying Alexandros in her arms.

'Let's have a good look at this little rascal,' Yiorgos said looking closely at Alexandros. 'He is going to be very clever,' he announced. 'Look at these eyes! So inquisitive, so inviting.'

Alexandros giggled as Yiorgos came closer and began to tickle his tummy.

'You are a genuine son of your father,' Yiorgos said. 'Clever, full of life and so friendly.'

Alexandros giggled again.

'Have you heard that Alexandre,' Olga said, 'we are all so proud of you.'

Olga in her quiet way had noticed Yiorgos' comments and how they excluded her contribution to the creation of her son. He was his father's son, it was so obvious. But then, she thought, that's how it is, men need reassurance and anyway they know it of course that this was her son as well. And really this is a conversation between men. They have to brag and congratulate themselves.

Olga said nothing more and the two men exchanged some more comments about Alexandros. Katina appeared to announce that trahanas was ready and they all got up and went to the dining room which was empty of any guests. They sat around the table that Katina had set and she served the soup with freshly baked bread, butter and olives and disappeared into the kitchen. Kyriakou who was in the kitchen helping Katina also came to help Olga with Alexandros. The three of them began to eat ravenously and Kyriakou fed Alexandros. She herself was to eat later with Katina.

For a while, you could hear only the spoons hitting the porcelain dishes and the noises they all made in appreciation of the soup, the sparse words— "delicious", "excellent"—congratulating Katina as she came in to bring the steak and the chips and fresh salad and bread. After the steak and the chips disappeared from their plates Katina brought some more bread, halloumi, melon, figs and grapes.

As the two men retired back to the veranda Kyriakou provided more brandy and more roasted almonds. Olga went to wash Alexandros and put him to bed and Katina and Kyriakou were finally able to eat whatever remained of the trahanas in the kitchen. They quickly formed an alliance, asking each other where they came from, and how long they knew the families they served.

The two men established themselves comfortably on the veranda surrounded by the darkness of the forest. Stavros lit his pipe and sipped at his brandy feeling deeply content. But Yiorgos wanted to know more, in fact to know everything about Stavros' life, his current job in the civil service, how he met Olga, who her parents were, when did they get married.

Stavros reminded himself, as he was answering the torrent of questions that kept coming at him, that he had never written to Yiorgos and had not invited him to his wedding. He did not even think of it, he reminded himself, how inconsiderate. Yiorgos had just slipped out of his mind the moment he said goodbye to him to go for his first job in Limassol, just like his village and its dear, dear people had disappeared from his mind only to be resurrected in dreams and in moments between sleep and falling asleep, falling out and away from reality into the twilight world of his early mind. This trait of his, Marina knew well, as she experienced it all her life with him. He could just put you out of his mind, she thought, just like this, whoever you were—his father, his daughter, his wife or his son, let alone Yiorgos, she thought, and he would get on with whatever was there. Maybe, she thought, maybe that's how he had experienced his mother's death, when he was not much older than eighteen months. One moment his mother was there, loving, all embracing, fully attending to him, and next moment there was a deafening silence, nothing, nobody there.

But later, when he settled down with Olga, and Alexandros was born and began to thrive, and no catastrophe was taking place, Stavros began to think about Yiorgos, his kindness and generosity, their evenings together on the veranda with the forest sounds and the forest silence all around them and inside them, with dear old Katina shuffling around, looking after every need of theirs, quiet, discrete and loving, it was then that this "pilgrimage" began to take form in his mind. One day he would take Olga and Alexandros and visit Yiorgos and Katina up in Platres, where evenings were gentle and mellow and the silence of the dusk permeated the mind despite the sound of flowing water that never stopped day or night. One day, one day, he thought, I shall go back. And this day was today and it felt so easy and so natural and the conversation and the warm loving feelings flowed between him and Yiorgos embracing Olga and Alexandros as well. Soon Olga joined them and Stavros asked whether Alexandros was asleep. 'Like an angel,' Olga said and the three settled down to talk about their families and their loves and hates and grievances.

But soon the discussion turned to the menacing situation that existed in Europe, Was there going to be another war, probably bigger, longer, crueller than the world had ever seen? Nobody had the answer to this, just terrible thoughts of a menacing world they had no control over.

Suddenly Katina was calling from the lounge 'come, come there is going to be an announcement on the radio.' They all gathered around the radio in the lounge and waited to hear from the BBC. And waited. In silence. Their blood frozen in their bodies expecting the worst and still hoping that it would not come. But there was no announcement just the usual bulletin about the position of the German troops at the border of Poland and the repeat of the threats by Britain and France were Herr Hitler to invade Poland.

Back on the veranda the two men drank more brandy and ate grapes and Olga ate grapes and listened as the conversation drifted back to the understanding that Britain and France would not tolerate a German invasion of Poland and how they felt it was all hopeless, Herr Hitler didn't listen to anybody why should he listen to the British and the French?

'We are there once again,' Yiorgos said, 'war is going to show its ugly face once again and there is nothing, not one thing, that you or me can do about it. The only good thing is that this time neither you nor me has any children of a recruitable age. My remaining son is too old and my grandchildren too young and your son a baby thank God. It's the only blessing at the moment,' he added.

'I know,' Stavros said, 'this moment reminds you of the totally needless death of your son, so prematurely taken away from you.'

'And for what?' Yiorgos intervened with passion in his voice. 'For what? For Helen? For this phantom of all phantoms that ignite men's passions and their elusive concept of honour. It goes as far back as the Trojan War. But this will be different. The tragic thing about this war is that it is necessary, even I believe this. The British and the French have to fight back. And therefore there is no consolation.'

The resident owl chose that moment to give a long, funereal cry as if to lament the fate of humankind, so fragile, so unpredictable. Yiorgos' statement about the necessity of war and the loss of consolation took an almost epic quality and the three of them sat there silent and listened to the lamentation of the owl.

'The only consolation is in friendship and human warmth and communication,' Yiorgos said and raised his glass. 'To our friendship,' he said.

'To our friendship,' Stavros repeated.

They sat silent for a while. The breeze was getting cooler and Katina who could feel and foresee everything came with three wool jackets, one for each.

'The nights are getting cooler,' she said, 'soon we will light the log fire.'

'Not yet, not yet,' Yiorgos protested. 'It's still summer.'

'Tomorrow is the first of September,' Katina said, 'it's the beginning of autumn.'

'Yes,' Yiorgos said, 'and maybe the beginning of the war.'

They fell into a deep, depressing silence each one buried in his own dark thoughts and their own private premonitions. Yiorgos got up and went inside for a while. Stavros, Olga, as well as Kyriakou and Katinou, who had in the meantime joined them and were sitting silently on two deck chairs, were silent. Some time passed and the owl gave a few more lamenting cries. The moon had risen unnoticed above the mountains and spread a dappled silver light on the veranda through the pines.

Yiorgos returned with a book.

'I had to look for it,' he said pointing to the book he was carrying. 'I have not read it for a long time. It's Evripides' play "Helen".'

Nobody said anything. Nobody knew this play by Evripides, and why Yiorgos thought it was necessary to look for it now.

'It's all here,' Yiorgos said, 'it's all here in this book, the whole madness of war, the mad illusions and passions. The most bloody war fought for nothing, for a phantom.'

They all looked at him as if he had gone slightly mad. 'What war are you referring to Yiorgo?' asked Stavros finally.

'The Trojan war, of course, the most bloody and savage war of its time. Troy destroyed, burnt to the ground, its civilised citizens slaughtered, or taken as slaves or concubines, and the Greeks gloating and bragging for this annihilation.'

Yiorgos stopped for a moment looking at everybody in turn trying to decipher their responses to what he was saying. They all looked at him amazed. They knew nothing of this play by Evripides.

'Here, here,' Yiorgos pointed to the book. 'Let me read to you.'

He went silently through the pages in a hurry and stopped suddenly.

'Here, here,' he said, 'here is where Menelaus, Helen's husband meets his real wife, the real Helen in Egypt. The Trojan War had ended with the Greek victory and he now returns home with Helen, his recaptured wife, the faithless Helen for whose sake the war was waged for ten bloody years. He is now married to her once again—or so he thinks. For Evripides has a twist here using an old legend that Helen had never been to Troy and was never seduced by Paris. It was all a trick played by the Gods. The real Helen was taken by Zeus to Egypt where she had spent the ten years of the war. In her place, Zeus put a phantom, a phantom who went to Troy, a phantom who slept with Paris and a phantom who became Menelaus's wife once again. Menelaus is now in Egypt and the real Helen tells him the truth. Helen says to him that she was never in Troy, the gods had taken her away and brought her to Egypt, where she had been for all the ten years of war. And that the whole war was for nothing, for a phantom. Paris lived with a phantom and Menelaus, her husband had brought a phantom back as his wife Helen. All for nothing, the whole bloody war for a phantom.'

In the silence of the night, Yiorgos began to read.

Helen: I did not go to Troy. That was a phantom.

Menelaus: And who can make a phantom that lives and breathes?

Helen: Air! It was the gods' work. That wife of yours was made—of air.

Menelaus: What? Then you were here and in Troy at the same time?

Helen: A name can be in any number of places: a person can only be in one place.

Yiorgos stopped and looked at his friends who were listening intensely. He then continued.

'A little later,' he told them 'the messenger approaches Menelaus and seeing that he looked very happy he says':

Messenger: Menelaus, I realise that something has made you happy, though I have not yet fully grasped what it is. Will you let me share your good news?

Menelaus: 'This lady was never in Troy. We were tricked by the gods. The Helen we captured was a phantom to make fools of us.'

Messenger: What? All our sweat and blood—spent for a ghost?

Yiorgos stopped again. 'All for nothing,' he said, 'all that slaughter for nothing, for a phantom.'

For a while, nobody spoke. Then out of the silence Katina began to weep, softly, silently her shoulders convulsed. A lament that was hardly to be heard. In a dark corner of the veranda, she had sat and listened and was now crying quietly, without any drama, an old woman crying for all of them, for everybody, for the whole world, for the loss of so many. And maybe for the impossibility of changing anything through poetry, or through anything else. From somewhere in the dark forest, the owl began its own lament. The forest sighed and whispered and moaned.

***

The morning of the 1st September was warm and pleasant, like all other 1st September days had been for years. For Olga, it began at 6 in the morning, before the sun had shown its face over the mountains. Little Alexandros had been awake for a while blabbing in his crib a kind of abstract poetry, full of many syllables and no words that anybody could understand, but the deep pleasure in the sound, the music in the syllables and in the tone was unmistakable. This music and this poetry woke up Olga every morning and for a few precious moments, she felt like the happiest being on earth.

She lay in bed, relishing these few moments between sleep and springing into action, taking in the silence of the mountains and Alexandros' strange garble of sounds and imaginary words. The early light coming through the half open shutters was diffused and hazy. The world was slowly and leisurely waking up.

The conversation from last night, Yiorgos reciting Evripides' play, Katina's quiet, private weeping, the owl's cry in the dark, the talk about war, Germany's military manoeuvres, all swirled up in her consciousness. But here in Platres there was peace as the forest was slowly coming alive and a chorus of birds, and the rays of the rising sun, reminded the world that this was another day in God's creation. It was difficult to believe that something so enormous as the declaration of war would disturb this glorious day that had begun so peacefully in Platres. Alexandros' blabbing was now becoming louder, more insistent and more urgent and bordered on crying. He was slowly getting to the end of his self-soothing ability and demanded attention. The sound maaa, maaa, increasing in volume every time he repeated it, told Olga that she should now get up and pick him up. Stavros continued to sleep peacefully through all this. His regular breathing made Olga feel that the world was in order, the world was a safe place. But was it, today of all days?

She got up and put on a light bathrobe and picked Alexandros up who smiled and laughed and kicked and babbled and grabbed his mother's hair. Olga kissed his face and neck and belly and laughed. Kyriakou hearing that Alexandros was awake came in and took him off Olga's arms to wash him.

Katina was up already brushing the pine needles from the veranda and Yiorgos was sitting quietly at the edge of the forest deeply involved in the book he was reading. Olga brought the clean and changed Alexandros to the veranda and sat at the table to feed him. The forest was now full of activity. Little creatures were scurrying through the undergrowth, birds, lizards, geckoes, mice, testifying to life going on in the forest independently of anything that was happening in the human world. The sun rose slowly above the mountain and came to rest on Alexandros' forehead. He laughed out loud and Olga was not sure whether he laughed because he was happy that the sun had chosen him to rest on, or whether he wanted to involve her in some kind of game. She responded with laughing aloud and making funny faces so unlike herself,

Kyriakou thought, as she watched the scene from the lounge and smiled. Olga was becoming playful, what a change!

Slowly life began to be audible inside. Katina was preparing breakfast and Yiorgos was talking to her, giving instructions. Kyriakou was also making herself useful in the kitchen. And finally Stavros' out of tune voice was heard from the bathroom singing the same tune from Rigoletto as every day and Olga guessed that he was shaving.

'Breakfast will be served in half hour,' Yiorgos announced ceremoniously and loud enough to be heard by everybody. Olga hurried to the kitchen to put Alexandros' breakfast bowl and spoon in the sink, and gave Alexandros to Kyriakou to change him once again. She then began to get ready herself. In half hour on the dot, a deep ceremonial gong reverberated through the building and spilt into endless harmonics outside in the teeming world of the forest. The birds went silent for a few moments and then resumed their song once again.

'Breakfast is being served,' Yiorgos' deep voice announced.

They all hurried to the big terrace outside the dining room where breakfast was being served in the dappled shade of the pine trees. The sun was now well above the mountains and formed shifting irregular shapes on the white tablecloth. In the middle of the table, Katina had placed a big vase of wild flowers and herbs and pine twigs, all extravagantly entwined with each other. 'Katina is an artist,' Olga thought looking at it. 'What a beauty.' Yogurt, honey and various homemade jams, almonds and walnuts, grapes, figs and plums were lavishly placed around the big flower arrangement. *Wow*, Olga thought again as she was taking all this in. 'This is breakfast for kings'—and after a moment's thought she added, 'and for queens.'

They began with fresh orange juice and a toast "to our friendship" and a second one from Yiorgos "to peace". After the second toast, they all fell silent and Yiorgos spoke for all of them when he said, 'we shall listen to the news at nine, but now let's eat!' They settled down to fried eggs and fried halloumi, tomatoes, olives and freshly toasted bread and butter and a big pot of tea accompanied by sounds of appreciation and praising for Katina's wonderful breakfast and even more wonderful presentation. And Katina came and went with fresh tea and fresh toasts.

It was now close to nine o'clock and everybody was on their third cup of tea and tasting the yogurt and the honey and the walnuts and the ripe, succulent figs. Yiorgos turned on the big radio, the new big radio that Stavros' had brought, and which was now standing proudly, taking a big chunk of the corner opposite them. Out of the silence a sombre voice announced 'It is nine o'clock. Here is the news.'

A few seconds of silence followed and then the sombre voice continued. 'As from 4.45 this morning, German troops advanced deep into Polish soil while the German Luftwaffe bombed Warsaw and other Polish cities. At Gdansk, the German fleet blocked the port. Britain and France have not yet responded to this blatant breach of the peace treaty that Germany has signed in Munich.' Some more comments followed but everybody had already stopped listening. Then some sombre Beethoven music followed.

Yiorgos turned the radio down. A wave of helplessness and despair was palpable in the air. The five people on the terrace, who a few minutes before were chatting and laughing and enjoying each other's company were now frozen as if they were touched by an evil sorcerer and turned into marble statues.

'It's war,' Yiorgos finally said, 'all over again. War!'

Alexandros, who seemed to have sensed the change of atmosphere from friendly and warm to frozen and fearful, began to cry inconsolably as if he was abandoned in a strange, unfriendly world without anybody on sight. Olga got up and took him from Kyriakou's arms and tried to console him. Suddenly, everybody was talking at the same time, expressing anger, despair, apprehension and the impossibility of it all. In these peaceful surroundings, made for gods and the world of poetry and philosophy, the news from central Europe sounded like an impossibility. Discussions about what Britain and France were likely to do followed in an attempt to give some reality to it all. Katina got on with the cleaning of the table and went to the kitchen to begin the washing up. Stavros and Yiorgos retired to the veranda at the front of the hotel, Stavros lighting his pipe and Yiorgos playing with his worry beads.

Time passed slowly. Olga made herself useful in the kitchen while Alexandros had his morning sleep. In everybody's mind was the looming war and the imminent decision by France and Britain.

The next couple of days passed in a mixture of silent apprehension, or quiet philosophising, with Yiorgos and Stavros reading to each other passages from Homer, or Aeschylus, or Xenophon about war and human arrogance and human frailty. Olga sometimes helped in the kitchen and at other times took Alexandros for a walk to the park, in a pram provided by Katina. Or sat with the men on the veranda drinking lemonade and giving her opinion about the imminent war, which the men listened to carefully, and then went on with their own conversation quoting the ancient wise men. And the forest whispered and rustled and birds came and went and the sun peeped through the pine trees and the roosters in Yiorgos' chicken coop marked time. Time passed slowly in Platres during these two September days.

On the 3rd of September, a restlessness seized the small group at the Forest Hotel, a restlessness that was palpable, certainly Alexandros could feel it who became very grizzly and nobody could console him. After breakfast the two men retired to the veranda as this was now becoming a routine, but they were aware that there was going to be an announcement by the British prime minister at 11.15 am in London, which meant 1.15 pm in local time. Neither of them was in a mood to talk and they both buried themselves in the newspaper from the day before. The women were equally silent cleaning and making themselves busy in taking it in turns to try and console Alexandros. Time passed slowly. At 1 o'clock, they all gathered in the lounge and Yiorgos turned on the radio. The usual deep voice announced that the British Prime Minister would make an announcement at 1.15pm.

'That's it,' Yiorgos said, 'it's war.'

Nobody spoke. Yiorgos' words reverberated in everybody's ears and silence prevailed. At 1.15 local time, the British Prime Minister Neville Chamberlain took the microphone somewhere in a distant room, at Downing Street, London, and spoke to the nation and to all the peoples of the British Empire. His voice was undramatic and factual.

'This morning, the British Ambassador in Berlin handed the German Government a final Note stating that unless we heard from them by 11 0'clock that they were prepared at once to withdraw their troops from Poland, a state of war would exist between us. I have to tell you that no such undertaking has been received, and that consequently, this country is at war with Germany.'

The whole announcement lasted one minute and twelve seconds and Europe was once again at war. The small group in Platres joined many millions of little groups all over Europe and all over the world in their shock and speechlessness.

The nightingales fell silent that night, but the inhabitants of the hotel could find no sleep. Somehow, everybody felt that this was the end of an era.

END

Milton Keynes UK
Ingram Content Group UK Ltd.
UKHW022026081223
434043UK00007B/380